DARK TERRITORY
The Dominion Falls Series 3

Sarah Cass

Historical Western Romance
Erotic Romance

Sarah Cass
www.authorsarahcass.com

Divine Roses Ink Publishing
www.divinerosesink.com

A Divine Roses Ink Book
http://divinerosesink.com

Historical Western Erotic Romance
First E-book Publication: July 2013 with Secret Cravings Publishing
Second E-book Publication: September 2015
Third E-book Publication: April 2018

Other Books in
The Dominion Falls Series

Independent Brake
Changing Tracks
Derailed
Green Eye
Runaway Train
Home Signal
Red Zone

Upcoming Books in
The Dominion Falls Series

Dust Raiser
Blizzard Lights
Dead Man's Switch
Birdcage
A Highball Arrangement
Ball of Fire

Books by Sarah Cass

The Tribe Series
The Tribe
The Wolf
The Chief
The Raven
The Lake Point Series
Santa, Maybe
Deep-Fried Sweethearts
Stalled Independence
Witch Way
A Thorough Thanksgiving
Eve's New Year
Heartstrings & Hockey Pucks
Luck of the Cowgirl
Stars, Stripes & Motorbikes
Free Falling
Love for Hire
Haunted Hearts
Stand Alone Novels
Masked Hearts
Leap

Dedication

Life takes you on some crazy rides,
it turns you upside down and inside out.
You learn in those times who are your friends,
who is there no matter what,
who is always going to text,
who is always going to call
for no reason,
just to say hi,
just because.

I have few of those, or rather one.
For always being there,
Jess…thank you.

Table of Contents

The death of a beautiful woman, is unquestionably the most poetical topic in the world.
-Edgar Allan Poe

Daisy stared at the telegram without seeing the words before her. She knew it was from Mike, Norman had told her as much, but she couldn't bring herself to read whatever it was.

The very afternoon the sentencing was handed down, Mike got on the very next train out of town to visit his family in Buffalo and tell them the rest of Clara's story. Daisy couldn't blame him for not being able to watch his sister swing, she'd barely been able to stand it, and she wasn't even sure she could count Jane a friend. Perhaps with more time she'd have felt more confident calling it such.

Still, Mike had only left town a few days ago, so he couldn't be back with his family yet. She wished there was more she could have done for him, or for Jane.

To be honest, Daisy still felt guilty over not believing Jane for all those months. Now she was gone. Daisy wondered how many people in town felt the same guilt she did. The whole town's tone had changed when Jane had received her sentence, and more so when she'd been hanged.

Not helping the matter was the absence of Mike and Kat both, two people that might have had a chance of getting through to Cole. Graham sure couldn't, if he'd even cared to. Who knew anymore, though she thought he might care about his friends turmoil, he hadn't liked Jane one lick, and never trusted her.

With Cole in whatever state he was in, a hush had fallen over the usually boisterous saloon. Plenty of regular patrons still went in, but there was a silence in there that was almost eerie. Daisy had worked there as a whore for three years and couldn't remember such a somber state to the patrons.

Daisy turned over the telegram in her hand, exhaling a slow breath to retain her calm. Mike had sent it for a reason, so she might as well see what it was about. The origin was St. Louis, which meant he was making good time on his way back home. Perhaps he would be back sooner than she'd imagined.

Disembarked long enough to send this. Check on Cole, if you can. I promised. I promised. Send word to Buffalo. I would like to hear from you.

"Sure. Check on Cole. It's that easy," she muttered in a droll tone.

"What's that, Daisy?" Ike set a mug on her desk. Construction on the old hotel was going very slow. Only two rooms had been walled in to give Daisy an exam and surgery room respectively, and two rooms where she could lock away the drugs. That left her desk in the wide open space left where the gambling tables had been.

Ike was one of the former hotel employees still waiting on what would happen with the new hotel. Mike had promised him a job and to continue paying him while he waited, which meant he'd stuck around when most of the whores had left.

Daisy accepted the mug of tea he handed her gratefully. The chill in the air outside had seeped into the open room without a bevy of bodies moving about to keep it warm. "Thank you, Ike. I didn't say much of anything. Mike asked me to check on Cole, as if it were such an easy thing to do."

"Rumor is he yells at anyone that dares laugh without Janey there. People are only going to be accommodating so long."

"I know."

The front door burst open, slamming into the wall so hard a pane shattered. The large form of Graham stood there wide eyed and panting, his features pale as she'd ever seen. "Daisy!"

She rose slowly, eying him carefully. "Graham? What is it? You look as though you've seen a ghost."

Graham snorted, but then shuddered and looked almost green for a moment.

"Are you ill?" Daisy moved toward him, careful to avoid the glass on the floor.

"No, but you gotta come with me."

"I don't *gotta* do anything."

"Please, you gotta—" Graham's plea cut off when Ike reappeared with a broom to sweep up the glass. The man never asked nicely, certainly never with a please.

"Will you tell me what's going on?" Daisy narrowed her eyes.

Graham cast a glance down toward Ike and shook his head firmly. "Nope. Can't. Get your bag and follow me. Now."

"You're not the boss—"

"Just do it, woman." Graham darted out the door without another word.

Ike looked up from his position, his brows knit together in the same sort of confusion Daisy felt. "Did I overhear him say 'please'?"

"It would appear so." Daisy pursed her lips. "Well, I do have to at least try to check on Cole anyway, and while I'm there I should check the girls."

"So as long as you're out, you'll stop by and see what has Graham in a tizzy?"

"Yes. Care to place a wager what it could be?" Daisy returned to her desk to grab the bag she kept close at all times.

"Think he got one of the girls pregnant?"

"That's a fair bet. I can't come up with a better idea." Daisy laughed and shook her head. "Nothing that would make him look that nauseous."

"Let me know."

"Will do. If I spot Hammy, I'll ask him to come by and fix this door. I'm sure Mike has an account with him." Daisy slipped into her coat and left the building. The lesser of the two evils seemed to be Graham right then, so she headed toward the undertakers office.

She'd barely lifted her hand to knock when the door flew open and Graham gripped her wrist to whip her inside. "Damn it, Graham!" She stumbled a few feet, and then spun when she heard the lock click.

"Scared the living hell out of me, it did. She said she'd haunt me, you know. This has never happened, not ever." Graham still appeared as though he might throw up. "I can't help her; you gotta. I don't know what to do."

"What are you talking about?"

He pointed toward the back where she knew his sleeping quarters were. The biggest shock of all was the way his hand shook hard. "Sh-sh-she's in there."

"What has gotten into you?"

"Jane. She's alive."

"What? She can't be."

"Beating on the coffin. Like…oh, devil." Graham bent over, heaving. "Go. She's in trouble; can't breathe right. Keeps dying, or…something."

Daisy rushed toward the back, only believing Graham at all because of the state he was in. She'd never seen the man so upset. Soon as Daisy crossed the threshold, she froze.

Jane lay on the bed, eyes fixed on the ceiling, her lips blue. She certainly looked dead, but on closer inspection, Daisy realized her chest was moving in increments.

"Oh, heavens. Jane?"

At Daisy's voice, Jane's body arched, and she gasped for air. Panic, fear, and pain twisted her features into a gruesome mask.

The initial shock flew away under Jane's distress, and Daisy went right into doctor mode. First, she'd tend to her patient, and then she'd figure out how any of this was possible.

A man that all the world hates,
there must be something about him.
—Johann Wolfgang von Goethe

"Get the hell *away* from that trunk." Cole's shout rang through the saloon.

All action stopped. Drinks sat gripped in mid-air, halfway to the patron's mouths. Cards lay half folded. Cigar smoke wafted from suspended drags. Every eye turned toward the balcony railing in wide-eyed caution as two whores scrambled away from the trunk outside Cole's room.

How the bastard had heard the pair was beyond Graham, but it didn't really matter. If they ever got the trunk away from him, it wouldn't go far, Graham would make sure of it.

"He's the one that put the trunk out there." Cuddy wiped down another glass, setting it between himself and Graham. He kept his voice low. "What's he expect us to do?"

"Just leave it alone." Graham ran his hand over his bare scalp. The hanging had been days ago. No one in the saloon knew that the woman had risen from the dead that morning, especially not Cole. No one but he, Daisy, the sheriff, and the Reverend had any inkling. Mostly because the woman could still die as none other than Daisy herself had declared.

Cole had spent the first two days after the hanging in the storeroom drinking them out of whiskey. After he'd made the trek upstairs and pushed out the trunk, he'd not left his room, and refused to let anyone near the trunk.

Graham had never seen his friend like this. Cole had always been cold, distant. Violent enough when the call came for it. A sick sense of humor. This current state was unlike anything he'd seen out of Cole in all their years as friends.

Daisy burst into the saloon and rushed up to the bar. Her eyes were wide, her breasts half bursting from her corset as she leaned far over the bar. The brown hair she'd hastily pinned up was askew, and she had a white-knuckled grip on the edge of the bar. "Graham. We gotta talk."

"Mind the place." With an off-hand gesture to Cuddy, Graham moved out from behind the bar. He grabbed Daisy's elbow to propel her into the storeroom. "Well?"

"It doesn't look good." She pried her elbow free. She rubbed her hands together then over her arms to brush snow off the wool shawl she'd thrown on. He imagined she was chilled to the bone. "I'm doing everything I can."

"We need to tell him." The odd sensation of guilt made Graham uncomfortable. He was more used to not caring. "He isn't doing good at all. He should know."

"I don't think that's a smart idea. What if we tell him and it's pointless?" Daisy hauled her shawl over her shoulders. "What if she still dies? Or rather, dies again? He'd be even worse off."

Graham punched his fist into the wall. It had been the most disturbing thing in his life to walk into the room and hear pounding from a coffin. Jane had threatened to haunt him once. He'd laughed it off as a complete joke. To have it coming true was too much.

When he'd ripped open the coffin and found Jane alive he'd been in pure white shock. So had she apparently, the way she'd been in a complete state of panic, clawing and grabbing at him. Her eyes wide open, and her mouth, but no sound came out and he'd thought she couldn't see him.

He shuddered against the memory and stared Daisy down. "You figure out what happened yet? How's she alive at all? I was there when you said she was dead."

"Luck, I think." Daisy leaned against the shelves. "The tea the sheriff gave her relaxed her. I think he set the rope wrong. We didn't catch the pulse, but it was so cold that day I'm sure it was just real slow, it does happen. I just don't—"

A loud crash and thump echoed through the saloon. A pained yell and another crash followed close behind. Graham rushed from the storeroom with Daisy right behind. Everyone was again looking up toward the balcony. Graham sighed. "Cole."

Daisy gathered her skirts and ran up the stairs, her medical bag bouncing against her leg with every step. "Cole."

After a loud curse, Graham followed behind. He knew no matter what was going on, Cole wasn't up for company. "Daisy, wait. He won't let us in. He's never let anyone in but Jane. You know that. It won't do no good."

"If he's hurt, he's got no choice." Daisy pounded on the door. "Cole, open up."

"Go away." Cole's strained voice edged through the door. "I'm just fine and dandy. Get out of here."

"Open the damn door." Daisy pounded the door with her fist. "Cole."

"Cole, open up." Graham didn't bother to shout as Daisy had. He put all the power he needed into a low tone. "Or I'll open it for you."

"Bastard."

Graham smirked. Cole couldn't be hurt too bad. He wasn't so far gone that he couldn't be a brute about it. Graham rumbled low. "Now, Cole. Daisy won't stop pestering, you know it."

Fumbling grunts, a low curse, and the shuffle and clatter of things being moved around echoed from within. The door flung open to reveal Cole glaring down at them both. His right hand remained tucked firmly under his left arm. "It's open. Now get the hell away."

"What did you do?" Daisy reached for the hand, missing what Graham didn't. When Graham tugged her out of the way, she yelped. "Graham."

"Put the damn gun down, Cole." Graham's eyes narrowed. Cole looked like hell. He wondered just how many bottles of whiskey Cole had gone through, and how much, or rather how little sleep he'd gotten. "Let Daisy have a look."

"It ain't nothing. I fell." With a frown, Cole set the gun back in its holster. "It ain't nothing."

"Then it doesn't matter if I look at it now, does it?" Daisy set her hand on her hip. "Let's get you downstairs. There I can get some good light and see what you did to yourself here. You're bleeding like a stuck pig."

Graham moved just as fast as Cole did. They both drew their weapons at the same time. Graham leveled his at his friend. Cole's was aimed at Daisy. Cole switched, aiming his Colt back at Graham. "I said to leave me the hell alone."

"Jane'll never forgive us if we do." Graham's nose wrinkled when Cole flinched at the mere mention of her name. "She'd call you a damn fool."

"You ain't got a clue what she'd do." Cole's frown faltered. "Don't matter no how. She ain't here to yell at me."

"Then I'll get Kat to do it." Graham didn't falter for a second. If he waited long enough, Cole's aim would falter just enough, weaken for a minute. Cole was just tired enough that Graham might be able to surprise him.

"She ain't in town. Went to get the last of her things. Came by yesterday to tell me, remember?" Cole didn't budge an inch. The bastard had a hell of a stubborn streak in him when he wanted to. "Now leave."

"You're bleeding all over your shirt. You're not going to get rid of Daisy that easy now. Just put the gun down and let her look. Stop being such a bastard."

"It's what I do best."

"You know. Jane has a big mouth. Always happy to let everyone know that ain't all you do best." That did it. Cole cracked a smile and relaxed enough that Graham had his chance. He took it, moving fast to push Cole's arm aside. "Now let Daisy look."

"Just one thing, Graham." The arm with his gun dropped. Cole put the weapon back in its holster before straightening his slumped shoulders. "Jane *had* a big mouth. Not no more."

Damn. Stupid mistake. One like he'd not expect Cole to catch. "Well, she said she'd haunt me. Guess I'm still expecting her to show up."

Cole scoffed, but said nothing else of his disbelief. He pulled the door shut before they could see whatever damage he'd caused in the room. "Five minutes, Daisy. That's all you get."

"We'll see." Daisy turned on her heel to head downstairs ahead of them.

Graham didn't holster his weapon, but he did lower it. Despite Cole's apparent compliance, Graham wasn't about to take any chances. At the moment his friend was unstable, to say the least. They should tell him about Jane. They needed to.

"Why ain't you done the services?" Cole's silence was broken by a question Graham wasn't expecting. "Ain't nobody come got me for the services."

"Didn't figure you needed to go to Clara's." Bless Daisy for taking the reins on this one. She seemed more capable of lying to Cole about the situation. "And we haven't done one for Jane yet. You are far from ready. Mike is out of town, as is Kat. Plus the ground froze solid before we could dig. Jane'll keep until we can do a proper burial."

"You don't know I ain't ready."

"You haven't been out of your room in days." Daisy threw open the door to a room downstairs. "Your customers are afraid to laugh too loud because you'll yell at them for enjoying themselves when she'd dead."

"She's got a point." Graham leaned on the doorframe. "It's not like you."

"You've got a splinter. A huge one. What were you doing?" Daisy turned his hand in the light. She grabbed her bag and pulled supplies out of it. "This is going to take a bit, and probably a couple of stitches."

"You gonna behave?" Graham stared hard at Cole. For the moment it seemed the fight had gone out of the man. "I got things to do and don't need to worry about you banging up the only doc in town."

"What difference would it make? There ain't no more Indian attacks. No epidemics. She ain't that necessary right now."

Daisy pursed her lips, but saved her glare for the chunk of wood in Cole's hand. "I was never necessary for anything but your position in town. So it's no different now—except you have no power over me. So shut up and let me work."

Graham snorted, holstering his weapon when Cole sagged in his chair with a grumble. "Do us all a favor when she's done and eat something besides whiskey. Sleep. Down here if you got to, but sleep. You're annoying us all."

He turned his back on Cole's obscene gesture and left the room. After ordering Cuddy to man the bar for a while longer, he hightailed it out of the saloon. There was a good chance he'd lost his mind doing what he was.

Sure, the town sheriff knew, but David Schaffer had been married to Jane years before when she'd been Clara—hell the man probably still loved her. The reverend knew, but he'd always had a bleeding heart.

What were they going to do if she lived? Just trot a dead woman through the streets and not expect it to be a problem?

"Reverend." He nodded to the man sitting next to the bed. His bed. Yeah, he'd lost his mind. He didn't even like her. Did he?

"She's been asleep since Daisy left. Not a very restful sleep, though." Reverend Greene closed the bible in his hands.

"What do we do with her? Call the marshal again?" Graham leaned against the wall, staring at her. She twitched and thrashed a moment before growing still. Her mouth never once closed, like she searched for the air that was all around her. "I mean, she was hanged."

"I think it's safe to say her sentence was carried out. We almost buried her alive." The reverend leaned back in his chair. "I can't see putting her through that again. Perhaps we should see about getting her out of town. Maybe even out of the territory."

"Don't sound legal."

"Clara Young-Schaffer *is* dead."

"I'm starting to believe it."

"Starting to?"

"I thought she was lying all along." He'd taunted her with it. Threatened her. Certain she would use her wiles to betray his friend, he'd been cruel. Despite that, she'd helped him. Even gone so far to be friendly. Either he'd fallen for whatever game she was playing, or she was honest. Which was it?

"Do you now?"

"Do you?"

"I never thought she was lying." When she thrashed again, the reverend set his hands on hers. Soft words of reassurance filled the room before silence fell and Jane stilled. The reverend patted her hand gently; lines of concern creased his brow. "She carried much guilt for what Clara did. Worried often about her soul."

"Doesn't make her honest."

"Did she ever lie to you, Graham?"

Had she? When he really thought about it, he supposed not. Even when she was annoying the hell out of him. Even when she helped him, she told him how against it all she was. "Not that I know of."

"Even when it was to her detriment, she tended to not lie to anyone but herself." The reverend patted Jane's hand. She stilled and he sat back again. "Not once did she fight what she saw as her fate."

"Before we do anything, we gotta tell Cole. He's acting like a man possessed."

"He's acting like a man grieving the loss of the woman he loves."

"Cole? Sure we're talking about the same man? He don't love."

"How would you act if it was Becky that had been hanged?"

Graham pursed his lips and diverted his eyes. Wouldn't affect much. They both knew it was convenience. How many times had Jane called him a fool for that?

"All right." The reverend's voice was soft. "What if it was that young Chinese girl? What is her name? Oh yes, Linh."

Every muscle in his body tensed. He couldn't even think about it. If he'd been any closer to the reverend, he might have hit him for daring to cross that line. "Who?"

"You can play dumb with me all you want. The good Lord knows the truth of your heart. He also knows the truth of Cole's. He's your friend. Do you really think that being with Jane hasn't changed a thing?"

"He's been different." It was distasteful to think about. For as long as Graham had known him, Cole had been cold. A good laugh, a good friend, always had your back, but he was detached. That was the Cole he liked, that he was used to anyway. "Not so sure I like it."

"He probably doesn't like you getting sweet on a China-woman. Hasn't stopped you. Why should it stop him? Above all, love each other deeply, for love covers a multitude of sins."

"Don't you got a sermon to prepare or something?"

"Of course. Once Katherine returns, we will figure out the best way to approach this with Cole. When is she due back?"

"Friday. Maybe by then, Jane'll be out of the woods."

"I'll be praying." Reverend Greene rose, squeezing Jane's hand one last time. He leaned over to speak quietly to the sleeping woman before nodding to Graham and leaving.

Graham rubbed his hand over his face and moved to the chair the reverend had vacated. "Taking up my bed. You got a lot of nerve cheating death like this. Things would've been just fine. Cole would've been back to normal."

Her hand twitched, and he covered it with his own. Once she stilled, he got up again and paced the length of the room. "This is beyond stupid. That marshal comes back and finds me hiding you, it'll be my neck instead of yours."

Would it? The reverend had a point. Her sentence had been carried out. If she hadn't been pounding on that coffin, first thing in the morning, she'd have been buried under ground. No one would've been the wiser.

Too late now. Much as he hated to admit it, he was relieved. Problem was, how could she just walk around alive after everyone had seen her swing? It wouldn't be easy. She'd have to go away, wouldn't she?

Rustling, then thrashing. She slept, but in her sleep, she fought against an imaginary foe. She grabbed at her throat. Daisy said if she got panicked, she could easily suffocate. Graham frowned and rushed over.

He set his hands on her shoulders to still her. "Jane, wake up."

Blue eyes flashed open, and her mouth opened to scream. No sound emerged, and the scream crumbled into pained tears.

"Easy. Daisy said you gotta stay calm."

Her hands curled around his forearms. With a quick shove, she removed his hands from her shoulders. Each breath she took was shallow, ragged, labored. Pain radiated through her features, like every breath was more than a struggle, like it she was fighting death itself.

"You're also supposed to try to eat."

She grabbed his hand, pulling back fast. After a moment of closing her eyes, her hand settling on her throat, she mimed writing.

"I can't tell you how nice it is that you can't talk. Why would I help you talk in a different way? I like it better this way." He grunted when she poked him in the eye. For someone that was still in dangerous territory, she had a lot of gumption. "You do know that Daisy says you could still die. If you don't stay calm and get food in you."

Her eyes rolled back in her head before she turned them on him in a dark glare. Another more obscene gesture preceded the next writing motion.

"Only if you promise to not curse at me." He laughed when she shook her head in the negative. "Hey, it was worth a shot."

A tear slipped down her cheek, and she mimed again. Before he could move to get it, she pushed up on her arms. Her attempt to sit didn't get her far, and she lay back with a grunt.

"Let me help." Graham sighed heavily to show his annoyance. She didn't even smirk at him. He'd expected something. Once she was settled, he got the paper and pencil in her hands and then took the time to study her.

Every move of the pencil was slow, unsteady. Anger flickered after every pained wince, her brows drawn into a deep V. Each breath was a shaky, weak effort. Her skin was pale, marked by dark circles under her eyes. She looked like death.

"Maybe you should stay lying down. Don't want Daisy getting mad."

Cole.

"He's fine. Grumpy." No need to make her panic again by telling her about his fool injury. The man had lost his mind. Maybe his heart, like the rev had said.

The paper turned toward him again. *Why are you helping me?*

"Damned if I know."

*I became insane,
with long intervals of horrible sanity.
-Edgar Allan Poe*

Damn her.

For that matter, damn all women to hell.

Nothing but grief, that's all they were. That's all Cole had ever gotten from the lot of them. Years and years of grief.

Right then it was Daisy that stuck in his craw. She'd refused to see if it was safe to remove his stitches at the saloon. Instead, she'd made him go all the way to the Silver Saddle. When he got there, she'd acted like she had somewhere else to be and rushed through the whole thing.

Now he was stuck with stitches still in his hand he was pretty sure could have been removed, and an ache from the rushed, dismissive exam. After she'd rushed off, he remained standing on the boardwalk in front of the former hotel with a choice. Did he really want to go to Turner's for food?

Graham, bastard that he was, had ordered the girls to not bring him food anymore. It was a damn conspiracy to get him out of his room.

To top it all off, Kathy had returned to town the day before. She'd wasted an hour outside his door. In turns she yelled, cajoled, and quietly pleaded with him to come out. Through it all she'd let him ignore her.

He'd promised he'd live.

He'd not bothered to say when.

It was too soon. It had only been one week. One week since she'd been senselessly taken. They blamed her for Clara's crimes. She blamed herself for Clara's crimes. She wasn't to blame. Clara wasn't. The crimes she'd committed hadn't been by choice. The minute she'd left David all her choices had been taken from her.

A wrinkled visage came into view, smiling brightly as Hammy often did. Normally it was a welcome sight, not right then. Hammy just reminded Cole of Jane, and the way the man had been so sweet on her. "Cole, how you doing?"

There was no point in answering Hammy, so he didn't. The goofy grin faded, and Hammy quickly walked away. Cole turned his gaze toward Turner's again. The appeal of a hot meal was too great. He'd have to be seen, but that didn't mean he had to speak to anyone.

That is, he wouldn't talk to anyone if he could avoid Kathy. She'd never let him alone now. All because Jane made her promise.

Jane.

Couldn't keep out of his business, even now. Not even dead.

Jane.

No.

He wouldn't think of her. Not now. He'd just get riled up again. For now he needed food. Surviving on alcohol wasn't that tough, but you needed solid food once in a while. So food it would be. Then he'd go back to drinking.

Or maybe he was already drunk.

Or seeing things.

Daisy, who had just insisted she had a patient, ran toward Graham's building. No patients would be in an undertaker's office, just dead bodies. What in blazes was that daft woman doing?

He had the odd sensation of spying, and the way she snuck glances around to be sure she wasn't being watched didn't help the feeling. The cart of furs in front of him protected him from her quick peeks, and she disappeared inside Graham's.

Cole's brows pinched together, and his seemingly permanent frown deepened when a minute later Reverend Greene emerged, with Graham right behind. A hushed conversation between the men lasted a minute before they parted company.

Odd.

Graham only cared for the reverend or religion when Becky was around harping on him. Becky was nowhere in sight. Not that that was surprising. He hardly spent time around his future wife if he could help it. Made a soul wonder what the man would do after they married.

He shook off the thoughts to find Graham in the crowd again. He narrowed his eyes as he watched Graham's path down the street toward the saloon. Something strange was going on. He'd make sure to find out soon as he saw Graham again.

"Afternoon, Cole. Looking for something?" Hank grinned over the stack of furs piled on his cart. "Got a bear in the other day. Ain't here yet, but I'll hold it for you."

"No. Ain't interested." Cole stepped back from the cart. There wasn't any need for more talk. Chattering people up wasn't ever something he did. That was Jane's thing. Drove him crazy, too. Always stopping to talk to everyone.

Even when he had ideas.

Even when she had ideas.

Damn it, he had to stop thinking about her.

It was impossible to stop thinking about her.

She was everywhere.

Still in his room.

In the saloon.

In his head.

In his heart.

Damn her.

At least Mike hadn't been around. His departure had been timely, letting Cole adjust to Jane being gone without having to put up with the annoyance of her brother. Her brother making sure he was all right. Employing the logic she was so insistent on using.

She'd made him make promises he wasn't sure he could keep.

Pleading.

Crying.

He hated her tears.

He'd agreed to have as much time with her, without the tears, as he could. They'd wasted so much time in silence. So many words left unsaid. He hated words, but they should have used more. More than the comfort of each other.

Words that they both needed to say, though he was loathed to say them even now.

Then she'd waited.

Until the rope swayed behind her.

Until the rustle of burlap filled his ears over the complete hush of the crowd.

Until there wasn't anything he could do no matter what he'd tried. No matter what he'd wanted to do.

It was then, in that moment that she'd said it. What neither of them had been strong enough to say before. Not out loud. Not awake.

I love you.

He could still picture her mouth forming the words; hear his own shouts, the shouts of Graham and the five other men it took to hold him back.

They'd stopped him, but not her face from disappearing behind the mask, or the rope from going over her head. Her knees had buckled, her skirt pooling on the warped boards of the gallows. The creak of the lever haunted his dreams; the sharp slam of the trap door woke him every time.

Falling.

Before he could stop himself, he punched the nearest post, earning a few stares for his frustrated effort. This wasn't *not thinking* about her. This was wallowing. Wallowing wasn't allowed.

The smell of fried chicken hit him, and he couldn't have been more relieved to realize that the post he'd punched was attached to Turner's. His own wandering mind had distracted him for the rest of the walk.

"David, wait," Katherine's voice rang out from inside.

At the first hint of David's heavily coated form, Cole darted to the edge of the porch. He sank down to the ground below the elevated porch, frowning. It was foolish to hide, but he didn't really want to deal with either of them. He peered up over the edge of the porch. With them above him, they wouldn't see him unless they looked down.

Kat circled David to block his path to the steps. "Are you going now?"

"Yeah. Want to see what the latest is." David's fingers ran through his hair before he set his hat on his head. Dropping his voice a few notches, he pulled Katherine closer. "Best be getting back to your day."

"I'm going with you. I haven't yet, and I need to." Katherine's hands shook before she folded them under her arms. "I have to see myself."

"No, you don't. It isn't—"

"Mama." A small singsong voice trilled across the porch. Running behind the words came a giggle, then quick footsteps.

"Cindy, darling. I told you to wait inside." Katherine picked up the child.

"But Mama, I wanna see lec…lectri…" A tiny little mouth pursed in frustration, accompanied by a little finger to a chin.

Cole stared at the child, unable to move or breathe. Strawberry-blond hair, ten times lighter and fairer than her mother's. Her mother's? How old was she?

"Electricity?" Katherine's laugh rang out. "Is that what you're trying to say?"

The girl's eyes grew wide with her smile and nod. Blue eyes. Ice-blue.

No.

She was too young. Yes, too young for what his mind was thinking. She had to be. There was no way that child was his. None.

I just knew the minute I saw him. Everything in me told me. Jane's words rang through his head. His eyes opened again, seeing the girl peeking over her mother's shoulder at him.

And he knew.

This child was his.

And he'd never known before. In all those years, he'd never known. Kat had come and gone. She'd been nice to him, playful still. Never once had she been angry.

Never once had she told him.

Cindy was put down, and Norman took her hand and led her down the street. They disappeared into the crowd, but Cole still knew.

Kat had a lot of explaining to do.

"It isn't something we can keep silent. Someone will tell the marshal." David's voice cut through Cole's anger. The marshal? Tell him what?

"So what are we supposed to do? Pack her up and send her out of the territory? She won't agree to it. It's not honest." Kat's hushed whisper wasn't quiet enough. It also didn't make sense.

What were they talking about?

"You should go with Cindy and Norman. She can't even talk yet. She's still in shock. Nervous." David sighed. "Scared. Out of the territory might be the best thing. A new home. A new life. No one would ever know."

Kat's red curls bounced above him. He didn't dare move, didn't dare to breathe. If they saw him there, they'd stop talking.

Then again, maybe that's what he needed.

It was too much.

It sounded like Jane.

"She'd never agree. Changing who she is again? After what Clara—good afternoon, Mrs. Fries. Yes. Thank you." Kat gripped David's elbow. "Just take me. We need to stop talking about it without her. That'll make her madder."

"What about Cole? When do we tell him?" David's voice faded into the murmur of daily activity.

Cole didn't move. He stared after the two, still huddled close together.

Heading right for Graham's.

Right where Daisy had gone.

Right where the reverend had been.

Nobody had died since Jane.

So why go there?

He knew what he'd heard. He wasn't stupid. But it wasn't possible.

That didn't stop him from rising to his feet.

It wasn't possible.

That didn't stop him from putting one foot in front of the other.

It wasn't possible.

Toward Graham's.

Toward the impossible.

The heart forgets its sorrow and ache.
—James Russell Lowell

"Easy." Daisy's quiet reassurance did nothing to ease the harsh sting of chloroform.

The pain in her throat and lungs eased, though. Her breathing slowed, and she fought against the urge to sleep. She'd been sleeping far too much. Or too little.

Every time she closed her eyes the nightmares hit. The terror would last long enough to send her into another panic and leave her unable to breathe again.

So she stared at the ceiling, trying to force sleep aside. She wanted no more chloroform, no more sleep, and no more nightmares. She wanted to know what had happened, how she'd been spared, why.

The only improvement of note was that her throat felt the tiniest bit better.

It didn't help.

Not her soul. Not her heart. She wasn't supposed to be here.

Cole. They hadn't let her see him, though she'd written plenty of shaky notes asking for him. Did he even know she was alive?

Daisy said she was still too on the edge, whatever that meant. Death? No, she'd been there all too recently. She remembered. She remembered every moment of that horrible day. She remembered waking in the coffin.

Her heart pounded faster, racing up into her barely open throat. Her breath welled in her chest, begging for much needed release. The bitter stench of chloroform filled her again and she could no longer fight sleep.

"How could we? It's impossible." David's harsh whisper burst through the dreary haze. The worry in his tone was mirrored in everyone in the room in every conversation of her every day. "Someone would say something."

"Who on earth would do such a thing? She has far too many friends in this town, and you know it." Kat sounded more like she was scolding a child. A refreshing change from the worry and confusion everywhere else. Jane would have smiled if she had the energy, but her illness and the chloroform combined to rob her of such things. Kat sighed. "I think it would be safe. She wouldn't want to run."

"Jackson might try to do something," Daisy interjected. "There's no way of telling, Kat. He has his own telegraph, his own means, and a Pinkerton at his beck and call. I think David's right. It's safer for her to leave."

"She won't ever agree. I bet anything if you took her away she'd turn right around and come back soon as she was well enough." Kat knew her well enough to know as much. She was right. Dominion Falls was Jane's home, and she wasn't about to go anywhere if she could help it.

Jane would fight tooth and nail if they dared try.

"Maybe we could bribe Jackson." Kat actually laughed, and Jane heard someone gasp in surprise at the sound. No one had laughed near Jane since she'd been awake. "Or even better, threaten him. For all his money, he's got no spine, and plenty of skeletons in his closet."

If only she could laugh. Kat knew exactly what to say, and what was on Jane's own mind. She's missed her friend. She wondered how Kat's trip to St. Louis had gone. What her friend, Patrick had had to say about what Kat was doing; if Kat's daughter Cindy was adjusting to her new home.

When would Michael return? He'd only been gone a week, barely enough time to get to Buffalo, much less return. Would they tell him she was alive before his return? Would they tell anyone at all or force her out of town against her will?

The most important question of all remained.

When would they tell Cole?

Cole had to know. The man had lived through enough pain. He needed the truth. He should have been told first, or rather second after Daisy.

She needed him. As much as she'd missed everyone, she missed him most of all. The torture on his features when they'd slipped the burlap over her head haunted her nightmares almost as much as the hanging itself and waking in a coffin.

A shudder coursed through her at the trifecta of memory. A warm hand rested on her shoulder briefly, and Daisy's concerned green eyes studied her hard. Jane shook her head and turned away, tears burning for escape.

A loud masculine gasp echoed through the room. Daisy yelped, a chair scraped across the floor and there was a bustle of activity. Daisy's voice squeaked. "What are you doing here?"

"Jane?"

Cole.

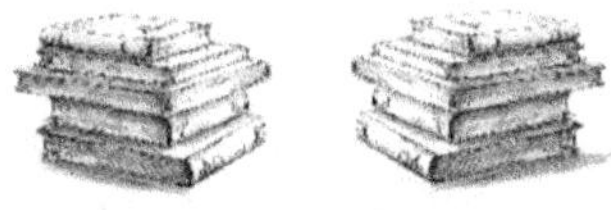

Nothing is impossible.
-François de la Rouchefoucauld

Frozen.

Time itself stopped moving.

All he could see was Jane.

Not in the ground. Not in a pine box.

Eyes open. The rise and fall of her chest. The sparkle of a tear on her cheek.

Alive.

Jane was alive.

The numbness, the pain of the previous week flew away. She lived.

His heart swelled as a joy unlike anything he'd ever felt coursed through him.

He needed to touch her. Hold her. To feel it was real. That she was real.

He needed her.

Chaos.

The moment passed in a lifetime and a flash. Bedlam took over. Shouts, denials, hands pushed him back toward the door. Jane's body arched, pain etched through her features. Her hand reached for him.

Daisy grabbed a bottle, chloroform.

No, Jane couldn't go to sleep. He had to see her eyes. Touch her. Hold her. The cloth with the drug moved closer to her.

No.

Blindly he swung, and his fist connected with David's jaw. The rag fell to the bed with Daisy's startled cry. He rushed forward, ignoring everyone but Jane. Her back still arched, her hand still reached toward him.

He clasped it, pulling it close against his heart. She stilled, but the pain didn't leave her features. Her breath was ragged, weak and forced, undoubtedly she was struggling for air. An ugly bruise still lined her neck. With great care he stretched out beside her on the bed.

His finger trailed along the soft flesh of her cheek, the gentle swell of her lips, the rolling curve of her chin. It was all the same. It was all there. She was there. "Jane."

Her eyes turned toward him. Tears shimmered before they trailed down her cheek and dropped to the muslin below. She was alive. The touch of her fingers to his cheek was like a hot brand that seared the depth of life itself back through him.

"Jane." He had no words. Nothing he could say could ever express what he wanted to. How he'd died without her. The world had lost all meaning and color. How he'd kept her books to keep her close. No words had the power to truly tell her what he felt.

She understood. Somehow, she did. Maybe she felt the same, or more so. A weak nod was her response before she turned toward him. Her head rested against his shoulder and he wrapped his arms around her in response. She didn't even flinch when he pulled her tight against him.

Where she belonged.

He wouldn't lose her again. Nothing would take her from him. No one.

"Cole, be careful." Daisy reached toward them. "She's still very weak."

Jane's nails dug into his arm, not a hint of weakness there. The lies were getting old. He wouldn't stand for them. He needed the truth. "Kathy."

"Just a minute." Kathy's voice was clear exasperation. He couldn't see her, but he could hear some shuffling around and a grunt from David. "You didn't have to punch him, you know. If you had waited just a second…"

"I think I waited long enough."

"Cole."

"How?"

Kathy's hand folded around his arm, covering Jane's fingers with her own. "A miracle."

"Miracles ain't real. How?"

"Luck."

"How?"

"Best we can figure it was the tea."

"What tea?"

"The tea I gave her." David's voice was garbled. Good, he'd done some damage. For trying to keep this secret, he deserved it. David hadn't planned on ever telling Cole, most likely. Bastard that he was. David cleared his throat. "It had herbs meant to relax her, so she wouldn't have to go up there terrified."

"Relaxing with drugs don't mean you ain't terrified." Cole winced when Jane's nails dug in his arm again. She had been terrified, and still was. "But what's that got to do with it?"

"I think she passed out." Daisy kept back from the bed now. Smart. For once. "So the short drop was even shorter and didn't snap her neck, only damaged her larynx. She ended up only being choked into unconsciousness. Close to death, but not quite."

Jane tensed in his arms, and a shudder ran through her. He pulled her closer. "You said she was dead. The marshal agreed."

"I thought she was. We all did. She was already still. We cut her down early. I couldn't find a pulse." Daisy's hands wrung together. "She was nailed into a coffin."

Now Jane sagged against him, dampening his shirt with her tears. Cole closed his eyes, trying to imagine what could have happened. She could have been buried, still alive. As he imagined waking up in a coffin, his hold on her tightened.

"Graham found her. Heard her, really. Banging on the coffin. It was so weak, he almost didn't. Said it was the scariest thing he ever heard." Daisy took a shaky breath. "Got me and David right away. Once we managed to get her over the worst, I got the reverend. Katherine just found out when she got back. Michael still doesn't know."

"You weren't gonna tell me."

"No." David had managed to stop gripping his jaw. Pursing his lips into a snarl, he leaned forward. "She needs to make a life somewhere else. We won't be able to protect her here."

"You don't got much brains, do you?" Cole's hold on her loosened. He felt her shift beside him so he could sit up.

Her grip on his holster kept him from standing to beat the man again.

"Got plenty. She stays here, someone will tell the marshal. She won't make it through the spring. I can't watch her die again." David's fists clenched, and his jaw set in a rigid line. "It's best that she goes and you don't stop her."

"Get out."

"Cole," Daisy frowned, "she needs—"

"She don't need to be told that she needs to go back into a life of lies. Get out."

"No." David folded his arms across his chest. "I'm not leaving you alone with her. You'll try to take her out of here, and it isn't safe."

"I'm not the idiot you are. Get out."

Katherine cleared her throat. "Go on, David. Daisy. I'll stay."

Cole started to object, but her hand on his shoulder stopped him. That and the fact that he was far from done with her. It would wait, but he'd let her know they had plenty to talk about.

"Cole."

"Get out, Davie, before I hit you again." Cole sat up more, every muscle tense. Jane's hand slipped from his holster, and he knew she agreed—or maybe she'd passed out. Didn't matter, he was ready to back it up.

"Please, David. Give them time. He just found out she was still alive. You've had a week to get used to it. He needs time. They both do." Kat pushed him toward the door. "You too, Daisy. I'll keep an eye on things."

Daisy gathered her medical bag, but left the chloroform and rag on the table. "If she has trouble breathing again, you have to use this. It relaxes her enough to keep the air flowing. There's a lot of damage to her larynx."

"Get out." Cole glared at her. "Not now. Get out."

She leaned in to meet his glare. "Her throat is almost swollen shut. You have to keep her calm. I'll bring more medicine for the swelling later. Her eyesight is not fully restored. Be careful, or you could lose her again."

"I ain't gonna lose her. Get the *hell* out."

In a huff, Daisy stormed out the door. Once Katherine had pushed them both through, she turned back. She moved over to the bed and sat beside Jane, taking her hand. "I can't tell you how happy I am that you're alive. I prayed that God would spare you. I couldn't imagine life without you."

Jane managed a smile, just not a very happy one.

"Spend whatever time you need to with Cole. We have all the time in the world."

Cole frowned. "Kathy."

"Yes, Cole?"

"We're gonna need to talk."

Katherine's smile faded. "I didn't know, Cole."

"That ain't what I mean. I saw the kid." He smirked when she jumped back away from the bed. A poke by Jane wiped the smirk from his face. "We're gonna need to talk."

"I suppose we are. Not now. Now you need Jane. There's time."

Cole nodded and stretched out beside Jane again. Once the door shut, she wrapped around him like a vise. He let her hold on, running his hands along her back. He'd be lying to say he wanted to talk more than he just wanted to feel her there.

Heaven.

It couldn't be better than this. Having her in his arms, living, breathing, and clinging to him so tight. Every moment they'd been apart had been too much, too long. Nothing else mattered now.

Hell.

What she'd been through. He couldn't begin to imagine. That she was still here was amazing. But she wasn't unscathed, unscarred. Her silent tears were enough to prove that. The haunted look in her eyes when she drew them up to meet his cut him to the core.

He ran his fingers along her cheek. "I meant it. I ain't gonna let nothing happen to you. Not again."

Her lips formed his name in a silent plea, and he sat up. With a gentle tug, he got her to her feet. A slight waver prompted him to place his arm was around her waist. He pulled her to the window and opened the curtains, letting in the blinding white light of winter.

"I know you don't want to leave."

Her head shook its vehement agreement before resting in the crook of his shoulder again. A soft sigh escaped, and she leaned willingly against him.

"We'll find a way. But if it ain't possible, if we can't keep you safe here, will you go?" He felt her tense and kissed the top of her head. "I'd go with you."

With a small pull, she slipped from his arms and crossed over to the bed on shaky legs. Instead of climbing into it, she stopped at the dresser. When she walked back, she had a piece of paper and a pencil.

"Jane?"

I wouldn't be free. Slow and shaky, the words formed. *I want to be free.*

"We'd find a way."

This is my home. Jesse. Kat. Michael. You.

"You're not going to leave. Ever. Are you?"

No.

He sighed and brushed her hair over her shoulder. Spotting the tear on her cheek, he wiped it away. "If you want a life, you need a real name. Jane is good. It suits you—but Jane Doe ain't gonna work."

Clara changed who she was. I won't.

"Not changing who you are. Making you real. A real person. You ain't ever thought Jane Doe was real. She didn't have enough memories." He tucked his finger under her chin. "You told me before…before this that you had enough memories now for a lifetime. First, you need a life."

When did you get so smart?

"Must be your bad influence." He smirked. "So, how about it? A real name."

I think you might be right.

"So what'll it be? Longfellow? Whitman? What are some of them other writers you like so much?" He frowned, trying to remember. It made the most sense, as her books meant so damn much to her.

No. None of them.

"Then what?"

Spencer.

"Really?" Did she really say that? She wanted to use Spencer. Only they would know the meaning of it. That it was his real name. Is that was she wanted? What he wanted? For her to have his name?

If you don't mind.

"I want you to use it."

Are you sure?
"Don't question me."
Yes, sir.

Cole tapped his thumb on the nearest coffin, unable to stop staring into the back room of Graham's building. A week ago Jane had been hanged on the gallows. He'd watched them declare her dead and stood by as Graham nailed her into a coffin. Yet there she lay—alive. Death hadn't killed her spirit. The evidence lay in crescent shapes on his forearm

Every muscle twitched. He could barely restrain himself from going back in to reassure himself again that none of this was a dream. Reverend Greene sat her with her now, holding her hand as she slept. When she thrashed in a nightmare, it was the reverend soothing her, not Cole, as it should be.

In the week he'd mourned her death, the whole lot of them kept the truth hidden. Graham, David, Daisy, and the reverend had kept her locked away in the back room of Graham's undertaker business. Cole didn't want to waste any more time in discussion.

Kathy's voice intruded on his thoughts. Even though Jane slept, Kathy kept her tone low. "What do you mean you set the rope wrong? Did you do it on purpose?"

"Of course not." The sheriff, David Schaffer, was also Jane's ex-husband and the man who hanged her. His hand absently rubbed his jaw where Cole had punched him in his attempts to get to Jane an hour earlier. "I'm not even sure if I did set it wrong. It's a possibility, I suppose. I did just fine on the horse thieves last month."

"Jane was a whole different matter," Daisy provided quietly. "You were nervous, worried, and guilt filled. It might have happened, or it might not have. None of it really matters now."

Cole found his voice once he stopped staring at Jane. "Where'd ya get that tea you gave her? What did it do to her?"

"It was a special blend." David's gaze returned to the back room where Jane lay currently still. When Cole glared hard at him, he stepped a few feet away. "Black Moon provided it for me. Said it would help make things right."

"You got it from an Indian? Did Jane know that?" Cole's hands clenched at his sides. He hated that they'd used Indian medicine on his woman. Yet at the same time, he was grateful.

"She knew it when she drank it." David sat on the edge of a table. "It was supposed to relax her. Black Moon said it might slow her breathing and heart."

"It helped her seem dead." Daisy, the town's only doctor, piped up from behind Graham's desk. Once upon a time, her doctoring skills had made her invaluable to Cole and sealed her place as his favorite whore. After Jane's arrival, she'd fallen out of favor and, with Jane's help, had won her freedom. "I've heard of something like that in a medical journal. Many doctors dismissed it as Indian medicine hogwash."

"Exactly. I wasn't trying to fake her death." David pinched the bridge of his nose. His eyes screwed shut and he coughed as if covering some emotion, before he cleared his throat and straightened. "Just make it seem to her like she was going to sleep. I didn't want her to suffer. I'm the sheriff. I keep the law, not break it."

"I wasn't making an accusation, David. I'm just trying to understand." Kathy touched the sheriff's arm. "We're all stunned by the turnaround. I'm sure Cole would also like to know what happened as well."

Cole didn't care to understand crap about what happened. All that mattered was Jane was still alive, and all this talk took up valuable time. He hated words, never ending words. Words were Jane's lot, not his.

"Cole?" Kathy stepped into his line of sight, her mass of unrestrained, red curls blocking his view of Jane. "Did you hear me?"

"No." Cole folded his arms across his chest. He'd gotten precious little time with Jane before she'd fallen asleep and they'd pulled him from the room for this pointless discussion. "Now ain't the time."

"We must figure out what we'll do next."

"She needs to heal, without all you idiots hovering and worrying about what's gonna happen next. Let her heal like she should. She hates it when ya hover." Cole fought the urge to shove Kathy out of his way and barge into the back room.

Kathy's smile formed bright and genuine. A hearty nod shook her curls. "You know what? You're right. Daisy, you said she's still in danger. Let's get her feeling well enough to fight proper and make her own case for what to do next."

"She's always well enough to fight." A smile formed despite Cole's concern for the woman in the next room. Experience had taught him that even in the worst pain, physical or emotional, Jane did whatever she needed to survive and live like no one else he'd met.

"Good point." Kat stepped aside. "Go on back with her, I think you both need more time. We'll discuss all of this when Jane can participate in the argument. It'll give her something to look forward to."

Cole didn't wait for arguments or agreement. He rushed toward the bed where Jane lay and stretched out next to her. Even in sleep, Jane turned toward him and he didn't deny her the comfort she reached for. As the reverend made his quiet departure, Cole pulled Jane close, relieved to have her in his arms again.

Jane's eyes fluttered open and a warm smile drew her pale features from the depths of pain they'd seemed wrapped in. When her fingers brushed along his jaw, he wished she were able to speak, to say the words he now realized he wanted to hear.

She'd said the words once before, but he'd walked away from them rather than face her. When she'd called him on it, she'd been too mad for him to offer a valid response, and then the stampede had knocked him out.

The last time, just the week before, she'd only mouthed, 'I love you', right before she'd been shrouded for her hanging. He hadn't been able to hear them, but he'd felt the impact of the words surer than anything.

Cole brushed his lips across hers. "You need to heal."

She offered a weak nod. When she reached for the pad she'd been writing on in place of using her voice, he didn't stop her. Once she'd nestled back against him, she wrote. *I know.*

"And behave."

Never. Her luscious pink lips curved into a coy smile. The simple playful gesture made all the weakness and fear fade into the background.

"Jane." He tried to put as much warning into his tone as possible, but he couldn't stop his own grin at her teasing.

She tilted her head toward him. Before he could chastise her more, she curled her hand around the back of his neck and pulled him into a kiss. Short and sweet, she let her lips dance with his for just a moment before she pulled back. "Promise."

Though a weak croak of a word, it would do. She wrote again. *I have questions.*

"Did everyone else turn you down?"

Yes. I believe they were worried I was too weak to handle the truth.

"You ain't weak." He kissed her temple. "But I think you are scared."

Horribly so.

"We'll find the maniac that did this to you."

His name is Sheriff Schaffer, and he's still in the next room. Another smile crossed her features, although it wasn't as strong as the last one. *He'll never forgive me.*

"He'll forgive ya. He can't help himself. He's a goody-goody." Cole set his hand on hers to still it when she started to write again. "You know I mean that Johnny fella."

The man with no name.

"Right." On of the only names they'd gotten from the one person who knew about the past seven years of Jane's life was Johnny. It wasn't his real name, and he'd claimed, to their disbelief, that he had none. "I'll call him Johnny until I learn otherwise."

She nodded and leaned against him. *Is there any sign of him?*

"No."

When Jane first arrived six months ago, she'd been near death thanks to Johnny. When she woke up, she had amnesia and no clue to who she was. Luck and circumstance had brought her ex-husband into her life and given her a clue into the life and years she'd lived before the last seven, including her given name, Clara Young. In short order, she'd met one of Clara's six brothers, Mike, and learned she'd been pregnant when she disappeared from their lives. Only Johnny knew where she'd been and what she'd done in the years from then until she staggered into Cole's saloon.

If Johnny had done one good thing, it was exposing Jane to her child whom he'd claimed had died at birth. After a rescue mission, her son was safely living with David. Jane still hadn't met the large family Mike said she had back in New York, but she'd been occupied trying to stay alive and almost failing that task more than once. Cole would do anything to make sure she didn't come this close to death ever again.

Jesse. A tear splashed onto the page after she wrote the name of the son who didn't even know she was his ma. *He must be distraught. David hasn't told him I'm alive.*

"No, he ain't. It's better that way. It keeps him safer. It keeps you safer."

I don't care about *my* safety. I care about him, and you, Kat, and—

Cole stopped her from writing more. "We know, but I think we've all had about enough of you trying to die on us. We want to do it right this time."

Do what right?

"Give you a life."

I've got one. A name too, remember?

He sure did. Jane had picked the last name Spencer to replace the plain Jane Doe she'd used the past six months. She was one of only two people in town who knew Cole hadn't been born Cole Mitchell, but Colton Spencer. When she'd asked permission to use his name, he'd said yes in a heartbeat. Nothing made him prouder than to know she'd chosen to tie herself to him. "I remember. Ain't never gonna forget, neither."

Good.

"We're also going to get the bastard that did this, took Clara's life from her, and then tried to do the same to you."

Bastards.

"Huh?"

She frowned and tapped the pencil on the paper before she wrote again. *Johnny is to blame for the loss of Clara, and for some of my pain, and Jesse's pain, and yours, but I think he is not the only person to blame for my hanging.*

"Jackson Krenshaw." At her nod, Cole curled his lip. The richest bastard in town had it in for Jane since she turned down his proposal when she'd first arrived in Dominion Falls. Pretty much the whole town was saying he'd paid off the judge to find her guilty to make sure she'd hang. Jackson was also the reason they still had her hidden in Graham's undertaking building instead of back with Cole in his saloon. "We definitely have to deal with him."

I know he is to blame for that wanted poster, but I don't know about the other things.

In the weeks leading up to her hanging, someone had been torturing Jane. Jackson had threatened her to her face with a wanted poster carrying a likeness of her which was the cause for her eventual hanging, but there'd been more subtle and devious torments left in locked buildings and rooms.

How could Jackson have gotten that hat or those medical files?

"He did have a Pinkerton on payroll," Cole pointed out. "The Pink could have gotten the files from the insane asylum you'd been put into when you was arrested for murder back when you were Clara. Don't know about the hat, though. I don't think Jackson's that smart. He wouldn't know about it. Davie, Archie, and Mike didn't tell nobody about that."

In order to rescue Jessie from Johnnie, she'd paid a vagrant woman to hand over a satchel full of what was supposed to be money. Johnny realized he'd been spotted by her brother and killed the vagrant. The hat she'd been wearing showed up on Jane's desk at the library several weeks later in a cruel reminder.

So we have two men to deal with. One right here and another God knows where. We don't even know if he knows I'm still alive.

"He don't. He couldn't. Don't you worry." Cole pulled her close when she shuddered and she buried her face in her hands. He took a deep breath. "He ain't gonna hurt you again. I won't let him. I promise you."

*The grave is but a covered bridge leading
from light to light through a brief darkness.
—Henry Wadsworth Longfellow*

The dark of night was when Jane felt most vulnerable. The hanging left her with lingering issues with her sight, and she worried if she'd ever be able to talk again. Daisy was hopeful, but Jane didn't have the energy for optimism.

During the day she could see well enough, despite the floating spots of black and the darkness at the edge of her vision. At least then she could see the paper she wrote on and the faces of her loved ones. Night was a challenge all its own that left her all but blind. Only with many lamps lit to chase away the darkness could she see at all.

Still, she was supposed to be dead. With no plans on how to deal with people like Jackson, who'd much prefer she remained deceased, they were transporting her to Kat's in the middle of the night, creeping down the dark and silent street like common criminals.

The subterfuge turned Janes stomach, for she'd always been opposed to the sort of lies her predecessor Clara had employed. Worse, she imagined anyone who happened upon the scene would find it suspicious, even the lot of drunks that wandered the streets at night would take notice of their antics.

She knew better than to protest, even if she could. The familiar debate of what to do with her would flare up again and leave her impotent to defend herself without her voice. She really needed full use of her voice back, even for just a moment, to tell them all to listen to her. Her one solace was in knowing that if she stumbled or did anything that might appear weak, Cole was right there at her side. Against protests, he'd left a full saloon to help her move across town.

The motley crew consisted of Kat, Cole, Daisy, Reverend Greene, and Norman. David had been with them until the past ten minutes, when he'd disappeared. Although she'd become accustomed, sort of, to the lot of them hovering and discussing her, seeing them work in sync to transport her from one side of town to the other was another story.

Walking like they had something to hide, namely her, didn't help. Rather than crossing town like a group out having a good time or even just walking normally, they were skulking. Stuck in the shadows, she was only allowed to move when Cole was given the go-ahead and would guide her to the next deep shadow.

The concern she had no voice to make, the one eating her up inside, wasn't eased by their attempts. That their movements could draw attention to the maniac from her past, if he was watching, only amplified her fears.

"This is absurd," Cole muttered. With one hand on her elbow, he frowned when Kat raced across the street to duck into the shadows by the clinic. "Look, she caught Mac's attention. This ain't moving you safe."

She nodded in fierce agreement. As Mac stumbled in what appeared to be a drunken stroll toward where Kat hid in the shadows, Jane drew the hood of her cape further over her head. Rather than make any more suspicious movements, she stepped right out into the street. Cole's hiss of protest faded as quick as it rose.

In the dark she had no idea if Mac noticed her, but she paid him no mind either way. Her destination was the former boarding house directly across from the saloon. With luck, he'd be going into the saloon and that would be that. If need be, she'd turn the corner around the boarding house out of his view until he went about his business.

The biggest obstacle with her plan to act normal was her poor vision. She could make out the buildings and the blurry outline of Mac. The lamps were beacons in the dark, aiding her attempt to not appear like a total buffoon. Still, it was easy enough to miss details like a dip in the road, a rock, or horse dung. If she shuffled, she'd appear suspicious. With any luck Mac was paying her no mind and his attention was on other things.

As she neared the boarding house, her strength waned enough to cause a wobble in her knees. She stumbled right into the railing in front of Rusty's small newspaper office. Mac only chuckled and mumbled something about a drunken whore.

While his notice raised concerns he might try to take advantage, she pushed herself back to her feet.

David's voice cut through the otherwise empty street and the cold wind that blasted through it. "What do you think you're doing?"

"Just enjoying my night." Mac laughed. "This little filly looks drunk. Don't know whose she is, but if she's Cole I bet he ain't gonna be too happy about it."

"Sure that's all you're doing? I just got a complaint from Muldoon that someone tried to break into his stables."

David wasn't usually a good liar, but she wondered how much truth was in this one. If it was a lie, it was infinitely believable. She crept down the street again, but her arm was grabbed forcefully enough to impede her miniscule progress.

"Maybe you should ask her. I ain't been stealing or sneaking." Mac shook her hard enough to jostle her head and rattle her teeth.

Jane grabbed her hood before it flew off. Her head pounded, and her stomach turned, but she didn't fight off Mac's hold. Most women in this town didn't dare, and she wasn't about to draw more attention to herself.

"Except Muldoon said he saw a big burly man outside by his stables, and there was a broken board in the side wall." David managed to extricate her from Mac's grasp. He released her elbow quick and stepped in front of her. "Nobody said anything about a woman, and this one sure seems too weak to break a board."

Jane leaned into David and let the weakness take over to aid in her drunken appearance. The more David talked, the less it sounded like a lie. Could that be why David had disappeared from the group? If Mac was the horse thief, an increasing problem in town, that would certainly be an interesting development.

"I know you ain't accusing me of being no horse thief." Mac pushed David hard enough to knock Jane back on her rump.

Jane wished she wasn't right underneath the ensuing scuffle. It would be fun to witness David giving Mac what-for. As it was, she only stood to be trampled on. Rather than have that happen, she scrambled back away from the foot that stomped on her cape.

Once free of immediate danger, she rose to her feet as quickly as she dared. Hopelessly confused, she turned in a circle to orientate herself.

Cole snatched her close. "What the hell do ya think you're doing out here?"

In her mind she could easily imagine the dark look he usually reserved for misbehaving whores, but the lamp was behind his head. She couldn't actually see his face. Still, it took all her energy to keep from smirking at the idea he'd use his angry face on her. The situation didn't call for brevity, so she managed to keep it in check.

She couldn't respond, but she leaned closer when he hovered in her face to appear she might be whispering. She hung her head when his hand left hers to grip her shoulders.

"I told ya, no more servicing outside the saloon. Don't care how much he offered." Cole held her firm. "Let's get moving. Now."

Jane let him lead her away from the scuffle still going on in the street. They didn't enter the saloon, but went around back to the entrance near the whore's rooms, standard procedure for a whore in trouble, she'd learned in her months with Cole.

"Smart of you to stop acting like we're up to no good. Would've worked, too, if Mac weren't up to no good himself. Although I kinda wish Davie hadn't had reason to stop him. Wouldn't have minded getting a few knocks in myself if he'd touched you. Coulda said it was for touching one of my whores." He grunted when she stomped on his foot. "Not that you are one. Damn, that hurt. Hold still a few more minutes, will ya?"

She sighed and let him lead her into the corral behind the saloon. If she had her druthers, she'd make him take her up to his room, and she'd stay there. It made the most sense. He wouldn't have to sneak into her room at Kat's across the street and possibly draw notice. She'd certainly see a lot more of him than she would staying in the old boarding house.

When he pulled her into the shadows, she willingly leaned on the wall of the lean-to. Lucky for her, he leaned into her, effectively blocking the wind and heating her up in ways she wouldn't be able to follow through on. He wouldn't let her until she'd healed more.

Unfortunately, her weakened state was the greatest defense for her staying at Kat's. There was no way anyone wouldn't be suspicious if Daisy made regular visits to Cole's room. Jane remained the only soul allowed to cross his threshold.

Infinitely logical and reasonable, Jane didn't dare argue the point. Didn't mean she had to like it. There was something to be said for healing better when you're content, and she was plenty content so long as Cole was around.

"Move it, Mac. Don't make me hurt you again, though I'd be happy to." David was close, and she guessed he'd managed to shackle Mac. She assumed he had no proof that Mac had stolen any horses, but she imagined he was happy to hold Mac for just breathing.

Cole waited until the jail door slammed loudly. "Ready to go?"

With a heavy sigh, she nodded. Cole didn't bother with the subterfuge on any level. As they stepped from the shadows, he wrapped his arm around her shoulders and walked out of the corral.

Like it was a lazy day in June, they strolled the whole way down the side of the saloon. The only time he stopped to check anything was when they reached the porch. He peered around to make sure no one was in the pool of light outside the saloon.

Apparently, he deemed it safe. He pulled her close and strode toward Kat's without another moment of hesitation. Inside the door, Kat swept her into a hug. "Sorry. I assumed he was drunk."

"Don't worry, Kat. None of you fools acted normal. Someone was gonna draw attention. Just lucky Mac's been up to no good." Cole rubbed Jane's arm when she leaned against him. "I think the time it took made Jane plenty cold, though."

Jane nodded and squeezed Kat's hand.

"Let's get on upstairs. I already sent the reverend home. Daisy's waiting with Norman. I told him to get your fire going." Kat started upstairs along with the faint glimmer of light from the candle she carried. "We're using candles. Since Jane's still getting her sight back, it won't matter to her none, and lamps at this time of night would draw attention."

"Daisy can't do doctoring by candlelight." Cole scooped Jane into his arms. Since she couldn't protest, she hit him in the chest. He kissed her temple and whispered, "Kat don't care, and you're tired anyhow."

Jane smacked him in the chest again. Just because she was still weak didn't mean she liked the constant reminder. Her life had become one frustration after another. She might have complained, but focusing on the frustrations let her forget the big problems looming before her. Like what to do about Jackson and the maniac from her past who'd rather kill her than tell her the truth about what she'd done before she became Jane Doe.

"I'm sure Daisy can manage by candlelight. She checked her over before we left Graham's. This is just making sure she's still fine." Kat chuckled. "You're adorable when you fret over Jane, Cole."

Cole cursed under his breath the rest of the way to the room.

"There she is," Daisy whispered. "I saw her stumble. Was that on purpose or did she have another spell?"

"She's right here," Cole snapped. He lowered her gently to the bed. "Don't talk about her like she ain't."

Jane set her hand on his arm when he sat next to her. After a gentle squeeze, she turned her head in the direction of Daisy's voice.

"Was it on purpose?" Daisy's cool hand touched her forehead.

Jane shook her head.

"Let me see how you're doing, then. After that I'll let you rest. All right?" Daisy scooted closer. She held the candle close to Jane's eyes and moved it back and forth. "Feeling dizzy or disoriented?"

Jane shook her head, but a shiver ripped through her. When she tried to speak, it emerged as more of a croak. "Cold."

"Norman's working on the fire."

"Fire's going." Norman rose from in front of the fireplace. "Shouldn't take no time to warm up. Is she good, doc? We should probably let her sleep. Don't want our racket waking Cindy."

Daisy nodded. "I don't see cause for concern beyond what we've come to expect. You haven't been walking much lately, and you're still weak. Probably that's the reason you stumbled. Unless you think it was something else?"

Jane smiled through the pain to try to help reassure them all and shook her head. It wasn't a lie. She hadn't felt dizzy or anything similar, just unsteady.

"Good. Then I recommend rest." Daisy set aside the candle. "I should return to the Silver Saddle. I'll stop by for tea tomorrow and check on you."

Before Jane could reply, Cole half lifted her off the bed and moved her to the edge. He unhooked her cape and pulled it off her shoulders. When he walked away to hang it up, Jane realized where she was, the same room she'd stayed in when she first arrived in Dominion Falls.

Jane still smiled when Daisy took her leave, followed quickly by Norman. Kat lingered nearby and sat next to her while Cole poured some water into the basin.

Kat sighed. "I told Cole and Reverend Greene not to worry about Cindy. She's a good girl and won't go blabbing all over town about the lady in the room down the hall. To be safe, she won't be having any outings to the depot until we've figured out what to do with you."

Jane grimaced. The last thing she wanted was to be the reason for a child to lie. Jesse had spent far too much time living in lies, the reason he hadn't been told she was alive.

Of course, he didn't know she was his ma. Jane had thought it the wisest thing to do. She didn't remember becoming his ma, and Jesse had lost too much in his young life. If he'd found his ma only to have her taken away and hanged, she couldn't bear it.

"Don't feel bad. It won't be long. I'm sure we'll figure out what to do about Jackson soon enough, and you'll be out walking through town again." Kat rose when Cole approached with the basin. "I'll come by early to make sure you're out of here before the town's up and about."

"No need. I ain't sleeping tonight." Cole set down the water. "I'll sleep during the day. I'll be gone 'fore the sun even thinks of being up."

"I think you're very well taken care of, Jane." Kat's footsteps headed toward the door. "I don't want you feeling isolated, so I'll be seeing plenty of you tomorrow, and I'm quite certain you'll have plenty of company."

Jane offered as brave a smile as she could until the door closed.

"Tired?" Cole pulled her to her feet and unbuttoned the simple wool dress she'd been wearing since she'd been walked up the gallows.

She shuddered when the wool left her flesh. A wave of revulsion ripped through her until she gripped his arms.

"Easy." Cole pulled her close. "I'm cleaning you up. No more death on ya."

A whimper slipped from her lips, as close as she could come to the deep wrenching well of pain in her belly without causing more pain in her throat. Only Cole's strong hands and his knowledge of her wanting to be rid of the sensation of death kept her standing. She nodded against his chest.

"We'll get ya cleaned up, and then you can sleep."

Sleep somehow didn't seem likely. Still, she knew she had to try. Life and death had yet to defeat her. A few nightmares wouldn't succeed.

*If our lives are endangered by plots,
or violence, or armed robbers,
or enemies, any and every method of
protecting ourselves is morally right.
—Marcus Tullius Cicero*

"Mike?" Jane might be under strict orders to not talk, but sometimes she had to in order to be heard when everyone talked around her. Every word she spoke burned through her throat like the flames of hell. Honestly, she didn't mind. It meant she was alive. Right then, she wanted to know when she could see her brother again. She missed him.

The curtains were drawn tightly across every window, and the balcony door was locked against intruders. The bedroom door was similarly locked. Daisy poured herself another cup of tea. "He's on his way back already. I've just received word from him."

Jane pulled her lips between her teeth to hide her grin at Daisy's rising blush. The woman was smitten, and Jane knew her brother was too; though neither of them did a lick about it. The sip of tea Jane took wiped away the rising smile on a wave of pain. She waved her hand to urge Daisy to continue on with what she was saying.

"Obviously I couldn't tell him what was going on. There simply isn't a safe way to do so right now."

Jane nodded agreement. A telegram sure wasn't safe, and letters might be intercepted as well. They didn't know where Johnny was or what he was up to. Total silence was best until they figured out what to do next.

Daisy smiled and added three generous scoops of sugar to her tea. She took a long sip before continuing. "I let him know that I'd been busy and the staff was curious when he'd return. Most of them don't have anything to do since he closed the hotel."

Jane pulled out her pencil and wrote. *But he's still paying them, yes?*

"Yes. I wouldn't blame him if he wasn't, though. Most of the staff is becoming increasingly lazy. None but Ike will lift a hand to help me clean the place between patients. A few have turned tail, though. I guess it's a good way for him to judge the loyalty of the staff while he decides who to keep on permanent."

"Contracts," Jane whispered. It almost didn't hurt.

"True. Most everyone worked out some sort of deal for their contract. I don't know what sort of terms he set with the others, though. I do know most of the whores left." Daisy's lips twisted in a sneer, a rare sign of displeasure when she discussed Mike. "He didn't offer to find them another job in the business, either. Gave them money, but who knows where they'll end up after this."

If Jane had any input in the matter, she would have suggested a different tactic. Then again, it was Mike's business not hers, and he had to make those decisions. After spending six months working with whores, she knew they were a breed all their own and, like everyone, individuals that had to be handled case by case.

Mike's decision seemed coldhearted given what she knew. Guy hadn't been a kind owner, and the whores could have used a little kindness in their handling after such a man. She frowned and wrote more. *Did you tell him how you felt about that?*

"It really isn't my place. It's his business." Daisy tapped her finger on the edge of the cup. "So, no. I didn't. I couldn't."

If it wouldn't hurt her badly, Jane might have unleashed a guffaw. Mike was sweet enough on Daisy he might have listened to her, far more than he ever would have listened to Jane. While she did her best to keep the laughter at bay, Jane patted Daisy's hand.

"What?"

Jane shook her head, but before she could respond a key slid into the lock. She rose and circled away from the door on instinct. Inwardly she cringed at the automatic defensive move that took over.

A shock of red hair appeared when the door cracked open, and Jane's nerves eased as she recognized her friend. She sank back into a chair.

Kat entered with a bright smile and a tray of sweets. "Cora had vanity cakes."

Jane gasped so loud in her excitement it triggered a harsh cough, followed by another and another until she couldn't control them. As the coughing continued and she tried to right her body's reaction, she held up her hand in an attempt to pause the conversation.

Unfortunately by the time she managed to ease her coughing, Kat was red-faced in her attempts to cover her laughter. Jane rubbed her sore throat. "Don't."

"If I'd known you liked them so much, I would have asked days ago." Kat giggled and set the tray down.

"My favorite." Jane rasped, but she was proud she'd managed two words that time. She grabbed a vanity cake and took a big bite. The cake's dusting of sugar added just the right amount of sweet. The white cake was soft and light, fairly melting in her mouth. Food like this was the reason Cora's restaurant did better than the local tavern.

"I was talking to David," Kat said without ceremony and with sugar still glittering on her upper lip. "Still none of us can figure out what to do about Jackson."

All the delicious flavor of the cake faded. Jane set it aside and rose. For two days they'd been in discussion over what to do about Jackson. She was tired of being locked away like Rapunzel. She also wasn't foolish enough to cross Jackson again without sufficient means to be sure he wouldn't find a way to see her hanged again—or worse.

"I sent my mother a wire." Kat positioned herself in front of Jane so she couldn't pace. "She did say she knew where the bodies were buried."

Before Jane had been arrested, Lillian Daugherty had been in town. She'd made threats of her own against Jackson. Although Jane had been reasonably sure the threat had disturbed him, it wasn't enough. She frowned and shook her head. When she opened her mouth, her voice failed her. She stomped her foot childishly and dropped back into her chair.

"What is it?" Daisy pushed the paper toward Jane. "It's all right. We understand."

There wasn't anyone who understood, but the thought was kind. Jane sighed and pulled the paper closer. After a moment, she wrote as quickly. *Threats will only get us so far and most likely wouldn't be enough to keep Jackson quiet. Also...*

Kat set her hand on Jane's shoulder. "Also, what?"

What of the answers we need? Were those things that showed up at my home and in the library from Jackson? Or Johnny or whatever his name is? If they were from Jackson, how did he come by that hat? Jane pulled her hand into her lap when it shook. The most pressing question was one she doubted even Jackson knew. Had Johnny stayed in town? Did he know she wasn't dead? If he did, the threat to the lives of those she loved would be immeasurable.

"One step at a time." Kat crouched next to her. "We'll do whatever it takes to get the Jackson problem handled so you can focus on Johnny and how to resolve that."

Jane offered the best smile she could manage. In the past few weeks her hope had taken a beating. Being dead did that to a person.

*I don't know what a scoundrel is like,
but I know what a respectable man is like,
and it's enough to make one's flesh creep.
-Joseph Marie de Maistre*

Kat did her best to ignore the bundle in the middle of her table. The tied canvas held the items used to taunt Jane before her hanging.

In the next room Cindy giggled, and Norman joined in, drawing Kat's attention away from the table. Cole stood in the doorway between rooms, observing the pair with a thoroughly unfamiliar expression. If Kat didn't know better, she'd have called it wistful.

When he turned her way she spun around, only to be confronted with the bundle on the table again. Two evils and she really wasn't sure which was the lesser just then.

"We still ain't talked." Cole's normally smooth voice was gruff. In one fell swoop the man had learned Jane was alive and he was a father—to Kat's daughter. Kat had kept the fact she had a daughter a secret from everyone in town. Back when she'd discovered she was pregnant, she could never have imagined Cole wanting to be a pa, and she'd been right. These days much had changed, all thanks to Jane.

She sighed and turned toward him. The man was downright exhausted. She wondered if he'd slept at all since the hanging. The stone wall she'd put up to brace for an attack softened. "It's been five days since you found out Jane was alive and learned about Cindy all at once."

"Don't mean we can't talk."

"You haven't had time to sleep, much less talk."

"True."

"Go upstairs. We've spent two hours turning over a problem we haven't been able to solve. Graham went to open the saloon. Jane is resting. Maybe you can help her sleep." She set her hand on his arm. "Once you've had sleep, maybe we can talk."

Whatever argument he had disappeared and his shoulders dropped.

"Jane hasn't been sleeping well, either, as I'm sure you know. Go upstairs. Maybe you'll both get some sleep for a change."

Cole nodded. "Yeah. She needs to sleep. It ain't right that she's not sleeping."

"None of it is, Cole." Kat patted his back when he turned away. With a sigh, she wiped her hands on her skirt and turned back to the bundle on the table.

Kat's mother, Lillian, had said she'd return to Dominion Falls to help with whatever Kat needed. Kat was sure her mother suspected the telegram she'd sent wasn't completely honest. Any attempt to stop her parents from coming had been ignored. Soon Kat would have to tell her mother, and possibly her father, about the dead woman upstairs.

That would be a fun conversation.

Unless, of course, Kat could find the answers before they needed threats. After everything Jane had been through, she needed peace without more hassle and fear. Kat gathered up the bag and went out the back door to avoid running into anyone.

She rushed into the barn and saddled her horse. Once Hurricane was ready, Kat climbed into the saddle and took off toward the foothills. She leaned forward and let Hurricane race fast as he could. The last thing she wanted was for Jackson to have time to anticipate her approach.

To further her surprise visit, she left the road behind and raced into the wooded foothills and circled around toward the back of the house. She hovered at the edge of the trees near the yard before she burst out and right up to the porch.

She managed to get all the way to the door quickly enough that no servant greeted her. She flung open the door. "Jackson. I have a present for you."

To her great surprise, no servants came stumbling over themselves to block her entrance. The house was eerily silent for a man who lived with a dozen servants and kept whores on a regular basis, although rumor had it that the latter were tied to the bed the whole time.

For several long minutes there was no answer. "Jackson?"

"Katherine." Jackson's voice echoed from near the office. "Please, come in."

Frustration made her stomp into the room and drop the bag onto his desk. "Tell me the truth, Jackson. Were you the one that did this to Jane? Were you?"

Jackson dabbed at the beads of sweat on his forehead with a handkerchief. His hand shook when he shoved it back into his breast pocket.

At the very least, Jackson had always played the part of gentleman well, but today he hadn't risen when she walked in the room. He didn't move his chair an inch, still sitting close as possible to the desk. He wiped at his forehead again. What was the man's problem? It wasn't that hot in the office despite the coal stove burning in the corner.

"Now, Katherine, the judge made his decision."

"I already know you lined his pocket. That isn't what I'm talking about." She gripped the bottom of the bag and dumped it out. The bloodstained horseshoe, the wanted poster, the lady's hat, and the file folder from the hospital all spilled across the desk.

"What's this? Is that blood?"

Kat leaned on the desk and narrowed her eyes. To her astonishment, he appeared genuinely surprised, but then again he was a liar and any number of other things. "You know it is, Jackson. Did you leave these things for Jane?"

"No. Well, I did give her that poster."

"He didn't leave them." A voice colder than any Kat had ever heard spoke directly behind her. "I did."

She was afraid to move, and Jackson's tremors of terror didn't help ease the rising panic. Her fingers flexed around the horseshoe. "Wh-who are you?"

"I have no name," the stranger replied.

With how often Jane had reiterated the mysterious Johnny had said he had no name, Kat had no doubt this was the maniac hell-bent on destroying Jane. The question was, did he know he hadn't succeeded?

"That's what I was afraid of." Kat's voice wavered, but she gripped the horseshoe tighter. After a shaky breath, she met Jackson's gaze. "Friend of yours?"

"I-I-I-thought so." Jackson stuttered, the sweat streaking down his face. He shifted just enough for her to see a length of rope around his waist that had been hidden by his coat and the desk. "B-b-business partners of sorts."

"Idiot." Kat muttered. Her best defense was to get annoyed with Jackson. If she faced her fear, she'd crack. "Didn't you hear anything Jane said?"

"I didn't believe her," Jackson whispered.

"Now, my dear, what are you doing here?" The man touched her elbow.

She reacted fast as she could and spun. The horseshoe swung toward his head, but he was faster.

The stranger caught her wrist and twisted until pain made her release the horseshoe. He yanked her close. "Quite unwise, Katherine. You don't want to cross me. I'd hate to see your little girl hurt."

Blinding fury took over, and she swung at him with her free hand. She kicked and hit him as much as she could while he twisted to grab and restrain her.

"Leave my daughter alone!"

Johnny pinned her against him, and Jackson remained where he sat, making no move to help her. For a smaller man, Johnny was surprisingly strong. He snarled in her ear. "What should I do with you?"

"Jackson." Kat stopped fighting to give herself a chance to breathe and figure a way out of this. Her wrist throbbed, and she hadn't made any move Johnny hadn't been able to counter. She didn't know what to do next.

Across the desk, Jackson still didn't move. Pale and trembling, he mopped his face again before he resumed gripping the edge. "It wasn't my intention to involve you. I wish you'd stayed away."

"That's all you have to say?" Kat took a deep breath before she fought again. She screamed and kicked until Johnny threw her against the wall. The impact jarred her body, but not enough to stop her. The gun he leveled at her, on the other hand, stopped her in her tracks.

"Don't make this more difficult than it needs to be. I don't like messy." Johnny's smile was so chilling and cold that it froze her in place.

"Yes, you do, messy and complicated. What you did to Jane…"

"Oh, you foolish child. There is no *Jane*. It's Clara. She fooled you all. I'd be impressed if it hadn't cost me." Johnny quirked a brow. "That's why Mr. Krenshaw's attitude toward Clara was fortuitous. It gave me a way to stay close and exact some revenge, as well as a way to recover some of my funds lost to that little whore."

"It's Jane. You're the fool." Kat hadn't met Jane until a few months after she'd arrived in Dominion Falls near death. Months after she'd come to terms with her amnesia. However, when Kat did arrive in town, they'd formed an instant bond. "You threw her from a train."

"I lost my temper." The maniac shrugged. "It's a rarity, but it happens."

"You taunted and tortured her from a distance like a deranged—"

He leapt forward and clamped his hand around her neck. "Do not call me that."

With her air cut off, Kat clutched at his wrist. Black spots filled her vision, and her lungs grew tight. Just when she thought she'd pass out, he released her. She dropped to the floor, coughing and gasping for air, and relieved that she'd gone without a corset. After she got a lungful of air, she rasped out the rest of her sentence. "Psychopathic stalker."

He took a step toward her, stopping a few feet away. "Watch yourself, my dear. I could lose my temper again, and nobody wants that. I do see why Clara enjoyed your company, though. You're a bit like her with your impertinence."

"Jackson, you weak-willed pompous idiot. Why would you team up with him?"

"I didn't know." Jackson turned toward her, still in his chair. "It's smart to know your enemy. He knew Jane as none other."

Kat pushed herself to sit and rubbed at her throat. She glared at Johnny.

"If you're expecting him to aide you, it won't happen. He's a bit *stuck*." Johnny crouched down in front of her. "I'm still unsure what to do with you."

Convinced he'd kill her either way, she lashed out and kicked him in the shin.

He didn't react at all. A moment later, his cold smile returned. He rose and crossed the room to Jackson's side, his gun still aimed at her. "Jackson, unfortunately, isn't as wealthy as he claimed to be. Did you know that, Katherine?"

"I suspected." Kat pressed herself against the wall. Jackson had sunk too much money into turning his house into a monstrosity, a visual representation of wealth. He lived alone, but had a staff of a dozen. Monthly, he'd brought in whores—bi-monthly, once he had access to a train instead of a stagecoach. Still, his mines weren't as productive as her parents'. They never had been, as he'd been left with her parents' leftovers and scraps.

"I do hate it when people misrepresent themselves. You can imagine my vast disappointment when I took it upon myself to see what my *benefactor's* assets were." Johnny gave a tug and the rope holding Jackson in place came free. He started to unwind it from around the man. "As much enjoyment as I got from watching Clara swing, my goal was to retrieve my lost funds. Jackson had no patience and called in the marshal and the judge before I was quite ready for them. Once he'd seen her hanged, he didn't have the funds to repay me for what I lost to that scheming little whore."

Kat's jaw twitched when he approached her with the rope. There was blood on the rope, and despite his apparent freedom, Jackson still didn't move. Her stomach turned, but she tried to keep herself focused on anything but her fears. "It wasn't just about the money."

Johnny paused, but then resumed his pace. "No, it wasn't."

"What else did you want from her?"

"That isn't your story to hear, is it?" He chuckled and waved with the rope. The gun remained aimed at her, leaving her with no choice but to rise. "Now turn."

"She was my best friend." Kat whispered through her dry mouth. As she turned, she clenched her fists to hide the trembling in her hands. "I just want someone to tell us the truth."

"Truth is a luxury." He jerked her hands behind her back, tugging extra hard on the wrist he'd twisted in their earlier struggle. "One you don't have."

"Please. You're going to kill me anyway."

He tightened the rope around her wrists. His low chuckle sent a shiver of fear down her spine. "Why would you think that?"

"You killed them all, didn't you? The servants, the whore, they're all dead."

"You are smart. Too bad I don't care to take a partner again. Of course, you aren't the right type; not weak like Clara."

"Jane was the strongest woman I've ever known." Kat tried to move against the rope, but he only bound it tighter. Her shoulders ached when he wrapped it up her arms, pinning them tighter.

He spun her back around to face him and pushed her back to the ground. The rope was wrapped almost up to her elbows, which left her the ability to bend them, albeit painfully, so she could sit. Johnny wasn't done, though. He took the tail of the rope binding her wrists and wrapped it around her ankles.

"What did you do to him?" Kat jerked her chin toward Jackson.

Jackson wasn't talking, the color almost gone from his features. He didn't pay them any attention. The spectacles on his nose were askew, and his gaze had wandered to the ceiling.

Johnny jerked the rope into a tight knot and rose. As he strode back to the desk, Kat did her best to find a halfway comfortable position. Unfortunately, she was almost positive the only way that could happen was if she were to lie down, and she wasn't about to do that.

"While we've been having our little chat, Mr. Kresnhaw has been dying a nice slow death."

Johnny displayed his surprising strength again and hauled Jackson, chair and all, out from behind the large desk. Kat wrinkled her nose against the onslaught of nausea. One knife was stuck in each of the man's legs, and his pants were soaked with blood. She bit her cheeks when Johnny unbuttoned the man's vest to reveal the blood staining the slashed shirt.

"It was my goal to get answers and depart. He failed to provide the answers I wanted, so his death has been slow. You're right; I was going to kill him anyway. You, though, I haven't decided yet." Johnny gripped Jackson's head and pulled it back to expose his neck. "I don't usually leave witnesses, nor do I usually leave bodies behind."

She swallowed down bile and sneered. "You're more elegant than that."

"Yes, quite true." Johnny leaned down and with one great yank, pulled one of the knives from Jackson's legs.

The strangled moan that poured out of Jackson made Kat feel sorry for the bastard. Even though she wanted nothing more than turn away, she forced herself to remain a witness to the horror. There was a good chance she'd not live to tell the tale, but she would be witness on the small chance she did.

"I think this little nothing town needs to learn a lesson." Johnny lifted the knife to Jackson's throat.

A line of red appeared. Jackson's body jerked, and his eyes flew wide open as trickles of red ran from the wound. He cast his wild gaze upon Kat before his eyes rolled back into his head.

Kat clenched her jaw, unwilling to sob in front of a man so insane. Taking every bit of strength she had along with some deep breaths, she kept her reaction as internal as she possibly could. She'd seen death, witnessed hangings, and sat at the deathbed of illnesses from consumption to scarlet fever. Something was different about staring into the eyes of a murder victim during the act, making her soul ache worse than her bound arms.

Johnny plucked the handkerchief from Jackson's pocket and used it to wipe down the blade. "Don't worry. You won't die."

Even though she wasn't certain, she remained still where she was. She wouldn't go willingly into whatever he had planned for her, but her options were limited. The gun lay on the desk, untouched. Apparently, he preferred the blade.

When he got within striking distance, she made one last-ditch effort. She swung as hard as she could with her legs, trying to sweep his out from under him. When he stumbled, she struggled to squirm away.

Amid curses, he flew to his feet. She couldn't crawl fast enough, and all she could see was his boot flying toward her face before the flash of light and blinding pain. Her body jerked, and she went limp.

Pain throbbed through her nose, into her eyes and head. The man was still close, cursing in what sounded like multiple languages. Hoping he'd leave it at that, she remained as still as possible. Even when he brushed hair from her face, she didn't flinch at the pain.

Just when she thought she'd escaped worse torture, her side started to sting. In short order the stinging became sharper and deeper, overtaking the pain in her face. When it finally stopped, a cool, dampness took over. Her mind finally clicked it all into place. He'd stabbed her.

Her heart raced, but that only made the pain worse. She had to calm down and fast. Nearby, she could hear his footfalls, through the room, and then up and down the hall. Over the pounding of her own head, she heard her assailant race up the stairs.

Kat kept her eyes closed and focused on her breathing. If the crazy man would leave the house she could send a telegram. God willing, he hadn't cut the wires. He was smart, but he'd said he didn't want her dead. He had, hadn't he? The whole scene was becoming fuzzy.

A door slammed. Hurricane whinnied and snorted, but then raced off.

For well over one hundred slow and steady breaths, Kat remained still. No footsteps reached her ears, and the house was silent. She hoped that meant he was gone. She had to figure out how to get to the telegraph and call for help. If that didn't work, she was in deep trouble. No one knew where she was.

She fought against the panic clawing its way back out. No, one thing at a time. First, she had to get to the telegraph. To do that she had to move, or even better, get out of the ropes.

With a burst of strength, she rolled onto her back. She landed on something and groped around as best she could to find it.

Her fingers closed around the object and joy flooded her soul. The knife. She could get free.

How does one kill fear, I wonder?
How do you shoot a specter through the
heart, slash off its spectral head,
take it by its spectral throat?
—John Conrad

The normal hum of activity outside carried on as Jane lay awake in Cole's arms. Through the rattle of wagons, the occasional bark of a dog, and the normal buzz of conversation a clatter broke out. A crowd of people shouted, a wagon tore through the streets.

Behind her Cole stirred and pulled her tight against his body. His sigh blew her hair up in a flurry before it settled back down. While she'd been unable to sleep, even in his arms, she was glad he was able to finally.

Then a series of loud shouts reached their room through the locked balcony doors.

Cole jolted awake with a snort. "Wha? What in blazes is that?"

She shrugged, unable to stir up the levels of curiosity she might have once had. The panicked activity continued outside, but it took someone pounding on the door downstairs to stir her interest. She sat up to grab her robe before she dropped down to press her ear to the floor.

David's voice was recognizable even in its quietness. Whatever he said, he kept his voice low. Jane wondered at what would cause David to be so discreet, unless it was because she could also hear Cindy's voice nearby. That also meant it wasn't good.

"*No!*" Norman's shout rang through the floorboards loud and clear.

Jane flew to her feet and raced toward the balcony doors. Panic seized her heart at what could upset Norman, who'd always been gruff and stoic. By the time she turned the lock, Cole had his arms wrapped tight around her waist holding her back.

"Jane! Jane, stop." Cole spun her toward him and gripped her shoulders. "Look at me. You can't go running out there. It might be nothing. Let me find out for ya. All right?"

No. She'd spent too long moping and letting death win. When she tried to push him aside, he gave her a strong shake.

"Think. You're good at that." Cole's forehead creased in concern, no not concern but panic. The now-familiar pained twist of his lips made her still. "I won't lose ya again, not for nothing. So just wait."

The door below them slammed hard enough to make the building shake. She wrapped her hands around his forearms and nodded. If nothing else, she had to find out what was going on. The only way to do that right, without danger, was to let Cole do what he needed to. If anyone saw her, who knew what would happen.

Cole kissed her forehead and held her close for several long seconds. "Don't go out there. Promise me."

"Promise." She hugged him tight before she stepped back to let him go. When he raced to the door, she followed him as far as the threshold. Only his quietly expressed fear kept her from going further. Once he'd disappeared downstairs, she closed the door and leaned against it.

More shouts and chaos filtered in through the curtained glass panes. Several weapons fired. She flew across the room to the window. She'd promised to remain unseen, but given the apparent chaos she was sure she could peek out the window without notice.

She pushed the curtain aside a few inches and found a posse gathered in the crossroads. David sat astride his horse in the middle of the large group of men. His sheriff's badge gleamed in the winter sun, and he held his shotgun over his head shouting orders at the men.

When he was done and the crowd around him scattered to their horses, David turned his head toward the building she was in. He lifted his hat briefly and she could tell his gaze was fixed on her room before he lowered it just as fast. Her stomach churned as the posse returned in larger numbers, increasing to almost twenty men.

If it hadn't been for her promise, she would have thrown on her cape and run outside, even if she was only in undergarments. She hadn't put her corset since before the hanging. There was much she hadn't done in a long time, and her nerves now made her eager to do them all.

As the posse dispersed, Jane moved to the balcony doors. Her fingers twitched over the lock, but she kept her word. Once again, she moved the curtain aside a few inches, and her stomach fell to the floor at the large crowd gathered two doors down outside what had been the Silver Saddle and was now being used as a clinic, with a destiny as a small hospital once her brother built his new hotel.

Something horrible had happened, and somehow she knew it had to do with her. Maybe she should leave town, go away and let these people have peace. In the six months she could remember, she'd brought nothing but pain to the people she cared about.

The amnesia that plagued her and left her without any memories except those she'd created since waking in Dominion Falls wouldn't be as much of a problem if she hadn't been a criminal in her past life.

To be fair, Clara Young, the woman she'd once been, had not been a criminal until seven years ago. Still, that was enough to have led Jane to being hanged for crimes she didn't remember committing. What she'd done to her family was almost worse.

David Schaffer, her ex-husband had had his heart broken by Clara, a woman that fell in love with him in a heartbeat, but ran scared at something that wasn't even her fault, or David's. She'd been naïve and immature. She'd left her husband wondering what he'd done and where she was, and the rest of Clara's family in Buffalo had been left in the same state of limbo.

Actually, they probably knew now since her brother Mike had returned to New York to inform the entire Young family of Clara's official death by hanging. He still didn't know she lived since he had yet to return.

Jane exhaled her rising tension and let the curtain go. Cole had to return soon and let her know what had happened before she did something stupid. The door creaked open, but it wasn't Cole on the other side.

Cindy, Kat's young daughter, stuck her head in the room. Her sweet, icy blue eyes so similar to Cole's were damp with tears.

The sight of the girl's tears brought a fresh wave of panic to Jane's soul. In an effort to push it away, Jane gripped the back of a nearby chair. With a firm grip on her emotions she waved Cindy over and knelt down to the girls' eye level.

"Mr. Norman said to wait with you." Cindy was just about five, her speech still punctuated with soft r's and a quiet tone. "Sheriff said Mama's got an owie."

Jane covered her mouth with her hand to hold back a sob. She pulled Cindy close and hugged her tightly. No amount of pain or swelling in her throat would stop her from comforting the girl. She took a deep breath to brace herself. "Your mama is strong."

Cindy threw her arms around Jane's neck. Her tears dampened Jane's shoulder through the thin cotton gown, and her little body shook with her sorrow.

When Cole opened the door moments later, he frowned. Jane rubbed Cindy's back with her hand and met Cole's gaze.

He looked down at the floor and nodded. "She said it was him. That's all she said before the doc had to take care of her."

Which meant Kat had either lost consciousness, was at death's door, or quite possibly both. Jane was grateful Cole kept Cindy in mind when he explained. The girl was frightened enough without knowing how bad it might be.

"Patrick," Jane whispered. At Cole's confused look, Jane frowned deeper in frustration. Kat's dear friend Patrick in St. Louis, who had helped her raise Cindy and with many other things in her life, ought to know. Cole didn't know about him, though. And Jane hadn't the vocal power to explain.

"I want Uncle Patty," Cindy mumbled into Jane's shoulder.

"I know." Jane would have to explain to Cole soon enough, when she was able to write. She didn't move though, and eventually Cole shrugged and moved to the bed.

"Jackson ain't a problem no more." Cole reached for Cindy as he sat, but yanked his hand back before he got close. Never in all his dealing with Jane's son, Jesse, had Cole acted like that. He most likely didn't know what to do after learning Cindy was his child. "Him and his whole staff are done."

Relief mixed with disgust at what Johnny had done twisted her stomach.

"They're going after him."

"Won't find him," She croaked.

Cole frowned when she winced. "You ain't supposed to be talking."

Jane pointed to Cindy and narrowed her eyes. She mouthed the word 'scared'.

"Cindy." He slid off the edge of the bed to crouch down beside them. "Janey don't feel too strong. Maybe we can sit in chairs. If you want, Janey'll still hold ya."

Cindy eyed Cole for almost a full minute before she nodded. The tight hold she had on Jane's neck eased.

Cole helped Jane into the most comfortable chair in the room, a rocking chair. Once she was settled, he turned to Cindy. "Ready?" When she shrugged and dragged her toe across the floor, Cole moved next to her. He tapped his back. "Wanna lift?"

Cindy's eyes lit up, and she climbed right up on Cole's back.

He winked at Jane. "Let's get Janey something to drink. She's been sleeping all day. Maybe we'll find some cookies."

"Cookies."

Jane smiled broadly. In just a few minutes Cole got over whatever was making him hesitate and distracted Cindy from what was going on with her mom. Jane's smile faded, and the only thing that kept her from dissolving into sobs was Cindy's presence.

Cole's grin weakened, but she waved him off. He had to focus on Cindy. Her own stupid head and heart had chosen that moment to make her focus on her own son. What he must be going through thinking she's dead. With Jackson dead, maybe he wouldn't have to hurt any longer.

That still wouldn't make him safe from facing that pain again. Until the maniac who had killed Jackson and done heaven-knows-what to Kat was taken care of, Jesse was at risk. She had to do whatever it took to be rid of him. First step, she had to finish healing. Then she needed a plan, and a way to carry it out.

If the tales of what a winter in Dominion Falls was like were accurate, she might have time to do both. With time to recover and plan in the depth of a snowy winter, she could be ready when spring came to act and end this once and for all.

Where there's life, there's hope.
–Terence

"She's going to make it." Daisy drew the curtains closed as Cole helped Jane into the living room. Cindy slept upstairs. Once the curtains were shut, Daisy turned up the lamp. "Her nose is broken, but she's lucky the knife didn't do any permanent damage."

Jane sat in the chair Cole guided her to, one hand grasped in his. When he tried to move away, she grabbed on tight with her other hand.

"Jane. I'm gonna bring a chair over. Can't do that if you don't let me go." Cole chuckled and pried his arm free. As promised, he grabbed a chair and sat next to her. He didn't fight when her hand immediately laced back with his. "She's gonna be all right?"

"Whatever he did, it scared her plenty." Daisy frowned and picked a chair for herself. Once settled, she slid off her coat and fixed an errant strap on her dress. The woman still dressed like a whore, though she was free of such duties. "She's had a nightmare or two, but I think she'll be fine. She said to tell you it's not your fault."

With narrowed eyes, Jane leaned forward. "It is. It's Clara's."

"You shouldn't be talking," Daisy cautioned.

"I don't care." Jane was tired of not being heard. She didn't blame them for ignoring her. She'd brought this all on herself by allowing herself to mope and live in fear after her hanging. After the past six months she should've known better. She should've fought harder. Still, death held a nasty hold over her fears. She wondered if Kat now felt the same.

Cole cut off Daisy's protest sharply. "Don't, Daisy. Jane's allowed to feel guilty. I think she's earned the right to feel however she damn well pleases about this mess.

Jane's anger dissipated into a grin at his defense of her. She patted his leg and rose. "I want to see her."

"You can't go out there." Daisy rose. "David would kill me."

"Jackson is dead?" The growing irritation led Jane to rub her throat.

"He and his staff died gruesome deaths." Daisy wrung her hands. "The man that did this killed a dozen people in that house, Jane. No one knew."

"Because no one cared." Cole had always been blunt, a quality Jane tended to admire when he wasn't being cruel about it. She elbowed him in the ribs. He rubbed the spot and shrugged. "What? Ain't everyone happier when Jackson ain't flouncing about?"

Daisy's lips pursed, and she sighed. "I agree with the point you're making, but still, it was a dozen people. I examined all the bodies, and you can ask Graham since he got them out of there. It was horrifying."

"I'm tired." Jane's voice cracked. After a deep breath, she pushed through the pain. "Of being afraid and letting that maniac hurt everyone I love."

Cole pulled her into his lap when she began to cough. He rubbed his hand along her back as the cough continued.

The sickly sweet scent of chloroform filled her nostrils, and Jane fought hard against the intrusion. Cole held her firm, and after a minute the coughing ease. Jane let herself breathe in the drug until the drowsiness threatened to overwhelm her, at which point she pushed Daisy's hand away.

"I told you, you shouldn't talk." Daisy touched Jane's shoulder before she walked away.

Jane buried her face in her hands to hide the tears of frustration.

"It's dark out. Can't we take her anyway? Nobody'll see her." Bless Cole for trying.

Too bad Jane knew Daisy's argument before she offered it. Daisy sighed. "And the staff at the Silver Saddle? They aren't working, but they're still hanging around. We don't know where that man is. If we're lucky, he thinks you're dead. Can you at least wait until David has finished his search?"

Rather than answer, Jane rose and crossed the room. She stopped at the door and turned back. The concern of another coughing fit was there, but she had to speak, she had to say it. She whispered to spare herself as much pain as possible. "What good will searching do? What good has it done? If he doesn't already know I'm alive, he will when he comes back after Jesse, Michael, anyone I've loved. He will find out. He will find me."

"Maybe by then you'll be healed and whole again." Daisy stopped when Cole set his hand on her shoulder. She took a moment to glare at him before she continued. "You need your strength if you're going to fight. You need your voice and your words. Am I wrong, Cole?"

Cole's hand dropped from Daisy's shoulder. He hung his head and sighed. "No. I don't like it, but you're right."

"I can't do it alone." Jane's voice faded into almost nothing. All the strength she'd gathered her was leaving as fast as it had arrived. She gestured toward the town outside the windows. "I need them."

"They'll know in good time." Cole crossed to her side. "How 'bout you write a note for Kathy? Daisy'll take it to her. Soon as she comes home, the two of you can cluck around like hens all day if you like."

Jane narrowed her eyes at him, but nodded. The ability to argue properly had faded, as her throat was more tender and swollen then it had been most of the day.

"Good. Write your note. Then we'll relax."

"Never," Jane whispered. "Again."

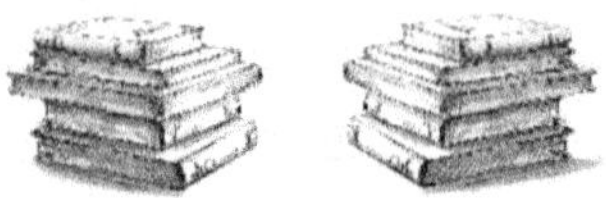

All evil is like a nightmare,
the instant you stir under it, the evil is gone.
—Thomas Carlyle

She stood on a precipice.

Far off in the distance, brilliant purple, gold, and orange streaked across the sky in a perfect sunset. Wide plains of fields below echoed with whispers of freedom. A peaceful breeze blew across her face, and she closed her eyes to take it in.

The moment her eyes closed, the wind whipped across her, shifting directions, growing hot. Suffocating, intense heat bore down on her until she was gasping for air. Her eyes flew open and the view she'd seen moments before had shifted.

The fields and sunset were much farther with barriers formed in the space between. Cyclones spun across the prairies, storms, and lightning filling the space between. The precipice grew deeper, red lava churning and bubbling beneath her.

She gasped, trying to stumble back, but there was no room, a solid stone wall pressed against her back.

The ground under her feet crumbled, falling away in chunks until only a thin lip of stone supported her. She balanced precariously on her toes, her nails digging into the rock in vain. Within moments that meager support crumbled and she was falling.

Falling...

Falling...

A hand grasped hers, stopping her descent. His dark eyes hovered before her, menacing and depraved. The hand that had caught her moments before wrapped around her throat, tightening, fingers digging into her flesh.

The pressure building, she struggled against the tight hold. Her feet tried to make purchase and push him away, but solid ground was elusive. As the airflow was choked, her fear grew, as evermore his control over her movement became complete.

Her mind screamed at her to fight, but no muscle could move—nor would it. Her fingers, immobile and impotent at her sides, flexed in a vain attempt to rip at his hands as the world grew darker and darker, pulling her down into the shadows.

Jane's eyes flew open to pitch black darkness. Pressure across her chest held her down. She opened her mouth in a silent scream, fighting. Hands closed around her shoulders, and she fought harder. Her fists beat against a solid wall, tears streamed down her cheeks, legs struggled to get free and join the fight.

"Jane." Cole's voice broke through her panic; her struggle grew weaker. "Jane. Damn it. Wake up."

Her nails dug into his arms, and she gasped for air. "Cole."

The weak squeak of a word crossed between them. A low growl from him was her only response before he disappeared. He left her alone in bed, silence lingering. A strike of a match lent little light until the lantern splashed bright arcs through the darkness.

She tugged at the blankets to pull her legs free from the tight cocoon. With a jolt, she pulled her knees up to her chest. The nightmare lingered, the feeling of hands on her throat still strong.

"You gotta stop beating on me." Cole sat on the edge of the bed. A touch of his knuckles to his eye pulled her attention to where the first hint of a bruise colored his skin. "You gotta fight him, not me."

"Thought…I…was…" Every word drew a fire of pain through her throat. She shoved away the sheets to move next to him.

"You weren't."

She huffed, exasperation pushing her to her feet. As if she didn't know that now. She stomped across the room to pour herself a drink. The nightmares had been nonstop since she woke in the coffin, and she woke up fighting off Cole every time.

His shoulders hunched, a frustrated frown on his features. He kept his fingers buried in his hair and his head down.

"Go…back…to sleep." She turned away, wincing as she took a sip of water.

"Damned if that's gonna happen. I'm awake now." A huff of annoyance snuck out. "That's three times tonight. We ain't been in bed that long."

"Four hours." She was talking way too much. Already she could hardly fight off the tears at every strain to her vocal chords. If they were going to continue this argument, she couldn't do it aloud.

"I'm good on no sleep, but I prefer to be having fun when I ain't sleeping. Getting beat by my woman ain't fun."

She wrote quickly on the paper sitting on the table. *I'm trying to stay awake. This isn't intentional.* She held out the pad for him to read. Her lips pursed when he smirked.

"Yeah? Well, tell that to my black eye."

Bastard. This time she threw the pad at his head and stormed across the room. She grabbed her clothes and started to get dressed.

"What the hell do you think you're doing?"

"Home."

"You ain't going out there. It's freezing."

Her corset could wait. There was no problem with sparing a moment to show him the most obscene gesture she knew. She turned her attention back to her corset. None of this was intentional. If her body would let her, she'd never sleep and never see the horrible nightmare again.

"Jane." With surprising gentleness he turned her toward him. His fingers brushed along her cheek. "You gotta fight him. Not me. Not no nightmare."

It was hopeless. He would never understand the endless torment of the memory claiming every spare thought.

"Jane."

"Can't." Her breath hitched, and she dropped her head to his chest. The touch of his fingers along her arms was like water in a drought. He wrapped his arms around her waist, and she let the tears fall.

"Instead of using that nimble brain of yours to keep going over the worst, why not figure out how to get rid of the bastard?"

What was he talking about? There wasn't any way that she'd seen. She didn't even know who he was.

"You got them letters, remember?"

Her shoulders relaxed, and she took a deep breath. He'd mentioned the letters before her hanging. Somehow she'd written it all down, between gaps of time, in letters extolling her crimes and her stupidity.

"Hundreds of them. They got everything. Maybe some clues."

The words soothed the last of her frustration. Clues. Maybe he was right. Maybe they could figure it out.

"Then maybe we could go to his hanging."

A smile tugged at her lips, and despite the pain she couldn't stop the words. "Too good…for him."

"Yeah, a hanging is too good for him. We'll figure something out."

Her hands moved from their resting place on his stomach, running up along his chest to circle his neck. "Sure?"

"You're plenty smart. Ain't you the one that figured out where he had Arthur?"

"Different. He told…I didn't…remember."

"Then read the damn letters." He smirked. "Or are you scared?"

He couldn't be serious. Of course she was scared. He knew that. She shoved him away and plopped herself back on the bed, folding her arms across her chest.

"Jane."

He was being antagonistic and she wasn't about to cave to his brutish behavior.

The mattress shifted, his breath teased the back of her neck. "Stop fighting me."

Her eyes closed at the soft kiss to her neck. With a quick shift of her shoulders, he was gone. She bit the inside of her cheek to keep from grinning.

"Stop fighting a nightmare."

The kiss landed on the other side of her neck, sending a shiver down her spine. She harrumphed and turned away.

"Use that amazing brain of yours."

Amazing? He was really trying to get to her. Despite her efforts to stop it, a grin took hold.

"And use your body for other things besides hitting me."

"Tomorrow."

"What? The thinking? Or the other things?"

"Yes." Her grin grew as she pulled away. She stretched out in the bed, curling her pillow up under her.

His grunt made her giggle silently, a cough starting at the discomfort. The shifting of the bed behind her, followed by the solid flop of his back against the bed brought her smile back.

She stared at the wall, listening to him toss and turn behind her. After several minutes he managed to grow still.

"What are you doing?"

Laughter bubbled up, shaking through her before she rolled over. She widened her eyes, attempting to convey innocence she didn't feel. "Sleep."

"You got me wide awake, and you're just gonna sleep."

A small shrug was her response before she touched his cheek. "You…tired. I…not let…you sleep."

"Tired, yeah. That don't mean sleepy." He chuckled when she could no longer hide her smile.

"No sleep?"

Snaking his arm around her waist, he pulled her close against him. "Thought it hurt you to talk. Ain't you tired of talking yet?"

"Never."

"Too bad. I was thinking of something with a little less talking."

"Oh?"

Nodding, he rolled with her and smirked, "Yeah."

"Like…what?"

With a low chuckle, his lips closed over hers to quiet her. His fingers danced up her leg. Within minutes they both forgot any notion of sleep or nightmares, as they happily found ways of communication without words.

One life is all we have, and we live it as we believe in living it.
—Joan of Arc

Jane sat straight in her chair, hands folded in her lap. Her gaze didn't waver from the closed door to her room. Her ears rang with the absolute silence in the home beyond.

Outside in the street, life carried on. Carriages and wagons rattled by, horses whinnied, men shouted, and children laughed. There was talk of an approaching storm, and the town came alive to gather supplies to wait it out.

Cole had gone to the saloon to make his proper appearances. A stack of books waited for her on the table, but she couldn't concentrate enough to read. Kat had been brought home two hours before. Out of respect to her friend's injuries and the time she needed with her family, Jane had remained in her room.

Never one for patience, Jane leaned toward bullying her way into Kat's room just to be certain her friend was truly all right. It was silly and childish, a fact Jane was well aware of, but that didn't stop her worried mind from pondering the idea. She was mature enough to stay put, barely.

A knock on the door brought Jane to her feet before she realized it wasn't her door that had been knocked upon, but the front door downstairs. She crept in her bare feet to her own door and opened it an inch.

Norman passed her narrow viewpoint and stomped down the steps. "I'm coming. I'm coming," he griped when the knocking resumed.

A few seconds later the latch on the door clicked. Norman spoke again, "Kat ain't up to visitors—oh, Sheriff."

Jane gripped the door and popped her head into the hall. Unfortunately, the men's conversation was held at very low levels. Try thought she might, Jane couldn't make out a word. When the front door closed, she pulled her head back inside her room.

With the door still open a crack, she remained where she stood. Footsteps creaked up the stairs, but she couldn't be sure if it was only Norman and David or if anyone else was with them.

Norman's gray hair appeared first, and as it disappeared a Stetson followed behind. When the footfalls drew close and no other people appeared on the stairs, she dared to open the door wider. Norman paused a moment at the sight of her and offered a small nod before heading into his and Kat's room.

David stopped and removed his hat. He avoided her gaze, rolling the hat around in his fingers. After a few minutes he shook his head. "I'm sorry."

The apology said it all, but Jane still sought confirmation. "You couldn't find him?"

"We've been searching for days. I even got Black Moon to help track him." The hat's brim crumpled in his grip. "We managed to track him as far as the northern break, but from there the trail went cold."

"Like when you searched for Clara and, despite the snow, there was no trail to follow." She released the tight grip she had on the doorknob and reached out to him. "You already knew it wasn't likely you'd find him. You searched anyway."

"I wanted to do right by you both, and by the law. I thought with Black Moon maybe he'd see something I couldn't." He shied away from her reaching hand, but managed to meet her gaze. "All I wanted was for this to be over for all of us."

"We all wanted that, we have for a long time."

"I'm sorry I failed you again."

"What?" Jane shook her head and stepped closer. "You didn't fail me or Clara. You need to put those thoughts from your head right this minute."

"Sorry."

"Stop apologizing for everything that isn't your fault. I'll bet anything Kat will say the same. You did the best you could, and that's all that matters." She smiled, and was relieved when he did the same. "I know this scared you, but you'd finally forgiven yourself; don't start blaming yourself all over again."

"Old habits are hard to break."

"I know." She nodded. The amount of speaking she was doing was leaving her throat raw, but she couldn't stop. She simply couldn't. He needed to hear it and she needed to say it. Thankfully the medicine Daisy gave her for swelling was becoming more effective for each use. "You tried. Just because it didn't happen this time doesn't mean hope is lost."

"We'll find him, Jane." David stepped away and set his hat back on his head. "We'll figure a way."

"I think I know the only way."

"Do you?"

She nodded. "We don't need to talk about it now. You should talk to Kat."

David hesitated, but tipped his hat and walked to Kat's room. When he disappeared into the room, Jane went back to her chair. Once again she resumed her quiet vigil, only this time she had the distraction of trying to plan what to do.

The first thing would be to read those letters. Cole had yet to figure out how to bring them over without drawing attention. Jane wanted to just go to them. Unfortunately, everyone would object to her idea, quite strongly, she was sure. She wished her voice was strong enough to be able to argue in her own defense, but she'd just have to let actions speak loudly enough.

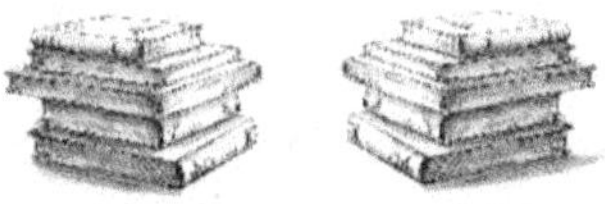

Who dares nothing, need hope for nothing.
—Friedrich von Schiller

Jane held Kat's hand in hers. Their conversation had faded a while ago. To be honest, Jane had expected more argument from Kat, but Kat had supported her decision whole-heartedly. Jane kept her back to the conversation behind her, the conversation about what to do with her.

Kat rolled her eyes and smirked. She whispered, "Don't they think they should include you in this decision?"

Jane shrugged. "Apparently not." She was happy to see her friend feeling strong enough to grouse in the same way she wanted to.

The bruise around Kat's eyes was deep and her nose was covered in gauze. By all accounts, the wound in her side was causing her a good deal of pain, but still Kat insisted on sitting. Her broken nose caused her to speak with a bit of an impediment, but she was happy to express her opinions. "They do realize we're here, don't they?"

Jane laughed and shook her head. "No, I think they've quite forgotten."

"The families at the camps are sure to support her. Perhaps she should stay there." Reverend Greene's soft voice broke through the continuing argument. "They'd be happy to protect her."

"Most of them are still living in tents. I'm treating frostbite regularly. As much as her health has improved, it's still best to keep her where we don't have to worry about other complications." Daisy frowned. "What else do we have? Someplace where only a few people will see her until we've determined we can keep it quiet?"

"I won't hide." No one paid attention to her weak voice except maybe Cole. He leaned on a chair, his gaze on the pair of them instead of the argument.

"Mike should be back tomorrow. I bet he'd take her somewhere safer." Graham leaned in. "Maybe back to her family."

Jane tried to speak louder, but couldn't break the continuing debate. "They're strangers. This is my home." She sighed when Kat squeezed her hand.

"I'm out of ideas." Daisy rubbed her hands over her face. "So far it's been safe here, but there's no trusting Cindy won't mention the lady living upstairs sometime soon."

"I could keep her at the church. It could be a sanctuary if needed." Reverend Greene nodded. "It might be the best idea."

"I will stay at my home or the saloon. I will not hide." Jane rose, still clutching Kat's hand. When they continued to ignore her, she stomped her foot.

Cole crossed the room and leaned close to her ear. "Thought the saloon was home."

Heat rose to Jane's cheeks. It must have been obvious, because Kat started chuckling next to her. Jane shrugged. "Maybe."

With a wink Cole turned back to the others. "You're all a bunch of idiots."

"Shut up, Cole." David glared at him. His hand clenched and opened, something was distressing him. Jane imagined it was more than finding all those bodies, although that would have been enough. "Despite the tendency you two have for a show, this isn't the time."

"Until we're sure it's safe, it might be best to listen this time." Daisy actually cowered under whatever look Cole cast in her direction. He'd moved close enough to the group that Jane couldn't see his expression, but Daisy could. Daisy held up her hands. "I know you hate it. I just don't know what else to do."

The argument began again, a renewed debate about what they would do with her. She dropped Kat's hand and paced the room.

She leaned her head against the cold windowpane, staring out across the snow. For two weeks she'd been recovering, first in Graham's room, and then the boarding house while the world lived around her, a world that thought her dead.

Death. She'd been there and could still sometimes feel its cold grasp.

It wouldn't do to focus on it or remain here where death clung to her. She missed fresh air. She wanted to know what the cold, crisp air of winter felt like. She had to get out.

The intense discussion kept everyone distracted from her complaints and wandering. Only Cole and Kat paid her any mind, and she knew they wouldn't stop her. She had to take a chance.

Careful to remain unnoticed, she floated across the room. She smiled when Cole shifted to block the view of the door, allowing her enough time to slip out of the room. Kat's thick wool cloak hung on the coat rack near the door. She snatched it up and wrapped herself in it.

By the time the first call of her name rang out she had the front door open. The cold air burned through her damaged throat into her lungs. Life. Invigorated, she pulled the cloak closer around her and closed the door on the shout of protest. At first, no one noticed her, and it suited her fine. Her eyesight still wasn't clear enough to make everything out, but the faded boards rang with familiarity. The carts that had dared to keep their spot through the winter were stuck in layers of mud, their wares dull in the throes of a harsh winter.

The door behind her flung open, and silence screamed out. They were afraid to draw attention. She smiled and kept her back to them. She'd told them she wouldn't hide. It was their fault for not believing her. Spinning on her heel, she glared at them, daring one of them to stop her.

"Stop." David's sharp order was a whisper. He took a step toward her and reached for her arm. Cole grabbed him and threw him back. David cursed aloud. The scuffle was drawing more attention than if David had just let her be.

If her throat felt better, she might have giggled. Taking charge again felt good. This was her choice, her life, not theirs. She'd already seen death, and while she wasn't anxious to see it again, she wasn't going to give up life.

Showing herself was a risk. As one or two people took notice of her, the risk grew. It was a dare she had to take. She had to believe these people, the ones she'd lived among for months and formed friendships with, wouldn't turn her in. She had to have that faith their silence at her hanging showed how much they hadn't wanted her to swing.

"Leave her the hell alone." Cole's voice was dark. "It ain't your choice."

"I won't watch her die again." David's voice caught. "I won't be the one to pull that lever again. I can't let it happen."

Jane stood motionless for a minute. Tears formed in her eyes as she stepped forward. Without a doubt, she understood what he was feeling, but this was something she had to do.

"No wonder she divorced you. You ain't got the slightest clue." Cole's mouth clamped shut when she put her hand on his arm. Jaw clenched, he stood stock-still.

Words would have been helpful at that point, but her voice was too weak, and she'd just used it. Instead, she walked over and pulled David into a hug.

When his arms went around her and his head buried in her shoulder she realized in the weeks since he'd been told she was alive, he'd never even held her hand. The subtle shake of his shoulders was enough to show her why. There was much to say, but not when curious murmurs built up around them. With people taking notice of the dead woman walking the streets, all she could do was hug him.

Cole's hand touched the nape of her neck, his voice a low murmur in his ear. "You should get inside. Wind's picking up. You still ain't healed all the way."

She gave a slight nod, and David's grip on her waist weakened. With a sniff against the cold she pulled back, keeping a tight grip on his hand.

"Jane?" David's voice was thick with worry and confusion.

She took a deep breath and exhaled. "I'm sorry." Often enough in her eight months of memory she'd uttered those same words. She feared they might lose their power.

"I know you are."

"Tomorrow we'll talk. I promise."

"I still don't think this is a good idea."

"It's too late." Cole moved closer. "Word's spreading faster than wildfire. Let's get you home, Jane."

With one more squeeze to David's hand, she walked up to Cole and leaned into him. His hand circled her waist, and he led her across the street toward the saloon.

She didn't balk at the fast pace he set as more exclamations rose up, and a few people actually called her name. This had been impulsive. While she was relieved to have it over, the results could get overwhelming very fast, especially with her weakened voice only lasting in short bursts. Answering questions wouldn't be possible for some time.

Cole stopped with a low growl and spun her into a tight hug. She fought against him, but he only squeezed her tighter.

"Army."

She stilled, and then fought again. The Army was no different than the town. Plus, there was Al.

"General Bryant's with your soldier boy. He won't hesitate to report you. Stop."

After a huff of annoyance, she stilled. Several long minutes later she hazarded a peek out of the edge of the hood. The General was still moving away, but Al had slowed to look their direction.

A gust of wind whipped the hood away from her face long enough for him to get a good glimpse. She gasped the little air left from her lungs. A shout of her name from the street was the last thing she heard before Cole rushed her the last few feet to the saloon door.

"Why did they have to ride through town today? Ain't been through at all the past week." Cole held onto her tightly, adjusting the hood of the cape. "You sure about this?"

Jane nodded and let him lead her inside. In the break between snowstorms, the saloon filled up. She dropped her hood, ready to stop hiding. The clamor and noise was soothing, familiar, at least for the five seconds it lasted. Primrose's scream silenced everyone before she fainted dead away. Every eye turned toward the door, and mouths hung open in shock.

A shattering glass shot shards of life back into the crowd, a low hum moved through the room. Before the first shout could arise, Cole took charge. "Shut up, the lot of you. Get Primmy off the floor and back to work. It ain't time for questions. I'll deal with you all tomorrow."

"But Cole." From somewhere in the back the protest was started. "How's it—"

"Tomorrow." Cole snarled. "She ain't—"

Jane jerked on his sleeve, looking up at him. She wanted to tell him to tell them, if only to soothe the growing frustrated mumblings. To come up with a short version, but she couldn't say anything.

"Lady Jane? That really you?" Hammy leaped off his bar stool. With an excited hop, the spry old man practically danced over to her. He whipped off his hat and performed an elaborate low bow. "I ain't sure how we been blessed to get you back, but I sure is glad to see you."

In no way on earth could she have stopped her smile. A silent laugh tested the strength of her stomach, and she heard Cole's low chuckle beside her. When Hammy stumbled back upright, she hugged him tight.

"All right. Short of it is the hanging didn't kill her. Don't know why it didn't, but it didn't." Cole wrapped a protective arm around her waist. "And it ain't Jane Doe or Clara Young no more. It's Jane Spencer."

A ripple of delight coursed through her to hear what she was almost certain was pride when he used her new name. She'd chosen his true surname, Spencer. The name he'd had before he came to Dominions Falls years ago. She set her hand on his where it lay on her waist.

"Clara Young's been buried. Ain't no one gonna tell the marshal about Miss Spencer, are they?" Cole's jaw clenched, his eyes dark as they scanned the saloon. When no protest rose he gave a short nod. "Good. Now she needs rest. Get back to it."

Curious gazes followed them all the way to the stairs, right until they got to his room door despite Cole's order. The silence lingered, but Jane ignored it, staring at the trunk outside his door.

"I said get back to it." Cole pushed open the door, and motioned her inside. Without another word, he dragged the trunk back into his room and shut the door. "Ain't been able to bring it back in. Nobody was supposed to know you weren't gone."

Her gaze fell to the shelves. The books she'd left in his room were still there. By all accounts they should have been gone with the trunk full of her things, if he'd tried to rid himself of her.

"Besides, I figured you'd want to make sure your things went back where they were supposed to."

Even if she'd had the power of her own voice, she wouldn't have been able to speak. Back in his room, the room that had become home to her, it all hit her again. A shudder ran through her body. Her knees gave out and she sank to the floor.

Every moment of her last day alive ran through her like a scalding fire—the pain of losing it all, the fear of death, the reality of it. As always his arms were there, coaxing her back from the torment with sanctuary. Once again she was safe, as safe as she could be. She never wanted to leave the security of his arms again.

"Jane." He peeled the cloak off her shoulders and pulled her close. "Do I need to get Daisy?"

"No." The word escaped in barely a squeak. No matter the pain speaking caused, she had to say it. He couldn't leave.

Everything was finally safe, even if just for the moment. She wasn't about to let it go.

"Paper? You wanna talk?"

She shook her head, pushing back enough to meet his eyes. With a slight shift she was on her knees. Her fingers danced along the scratchy stubble on his chin, tugging him closer. The gentle kiss lingered, searching and tender.

"Actions, then?"

She smiled, pulling him close, answering without any words. When the slow kiss ended, he scooped her into his arms. Within a moment she was on the bed, wrapped in his embrace.

Her small pout drew a laugh from him. "You need rest. We'll have plenty of action soon."

His arms tightened around her, and it was enough. She was right where she needed to be.

*Love and scandal are the best sweeteners
of tea.
-Henry Fielding*

"Between the dead woman walking and them murders, this town just doesn't know what to do with themselves." Graham set a glass of whiskey in front of Cole. He pulled his hand back fast and cradled his own mug full of coffee. "The near-constant snow doesn't help matters, either. Keeps 'em all close around the fire jawing off."

Cole spun his glass on the bar top. He and Jane were used to being gossip fodder, but it had always been on their terms. This turn of events, being hanged and surviving, was quite beyond their control. Jane had been as stunned by it as everyone else buzzing with the news. Of course, the recent murders added fuel to the fire, as people speculated that the murders were in some way her fault. It infuriated him whenever someone dared suggest she'd been part of that mess.

Graham shook his head. "Mostly they're all curious how she survived."

"Some wanna know about them murders." Cole tossed back the whiskey. It burned down his throat, and he glared at the empty saloon. The latest storm had caught most of them by surprise and left everyone scrambling for their homes and hunkering down. Until the men in town could get out and follow the buildings to where they wanted to go, the saloon would stay empty.

"That was a hell of a thing." The stool creaked when Graham set his weight back on two legs and rested his elbows on the bar. "Daisy tell you?"

"Been avoiding it. Jane wants to know, but she's already blaming herself. She don't need the details." Cole ran his fingers through his hair. Over the past few months, he hadn't bothered with a visit to the barbershop. Life with Jane afforded too many distractions, and now his hair hung well past his shoulders. He needed to go get it cut, but Jane had asked him to wait.

"There was blood all over that damn house. Think every room had a body in it." Graham sipped his coffee. "Only one of them was shot. They were all cut bad. Bled to death, Daisy said."

"Daisy said Jack had a whore from the city?"

"Yup. She was cut up real good. Face cut. Thing is, Daisy said she died first. She's the one that got shot. The Derringer was still on the table. Daisy thinks she was dead a while. Rest of them in the house suffered even more."

Cole poured himself another whiskey and narrowed his eyes. "Why one shot?"

Jane's voice croaked above them. "Jackson killed her."

"Damn it, Jane." Cole turned his head up. "What are you doing eavesdropping?"

"How else would I hear about it?" With each word, her voice failed more. Damn her for trying to talk when she shouldn't. She'd been doing that far too often. While she had good days, or rather hours, when she could talk quite a bit without pain, mostly she struggled. Just that morning Daisy had warned her against continuing to talk so much.

"Thought you were reading." Cole turned back to his whiskey when she disappeared from view. Her footsteps sounded down the balcony until she appeared at the top of the stairs. "Ya can't tell me you've been though all seven years already."

"Just one."

Jane was finally reading the letters Cole had found when he went on a treasure hunt thanks to clues left behind by Clara. He'd gone to Yankton in search of C. Hodgkins, the name they'd found in Jane's trunk. He hadn't found anyone by that name, but he'd been handed a bag full of letters. Those letters had been written by Clara Young to her brother, Mike, for seven years as she'd lived with the maniac now trying to kill her.

Cole himself had read a good portion of them on the long train ride. He'd proceeded to forget about them when he returned home to find Jane set to be hanged. There was one letter he'd hidden from her, but the rest he'd convinced her to start reading in hopes it would help her solve the puzzle of her past. "Then why you nosing around?"

"I needed a break from the stupidity." Jane huffed when she sat on the stool. "Clara was a naïve little fool sometimes."

"You're different how?" Graham smirked. Either the man knew the danger he was in and didn't care, or he was totally clueless. Either way, it would be an interesting show.

"Clara might have found an idiot like you charming for one." Jane swiped Cole's drink and downed it. She held up the glass and turned it with a small frown on her features. "She seemed to like all men."

"Again, how are you different?" Graham's brow rose. "I seem to remember lots and lots of men in your stable at one time. Your husband and the Major for instance."

Cole tensed at the mention of Major Webb. While he knew without a doubt that David Schaffer had moved on with his life and Jane had happily divorced him before her hanging, Major Marshall 'Al' Webb was a wild card. Jane declared it an innocent friendship, but Cole knew how the Major looked at her. He didn't trust the man for nothing. The worst part about his whole deal was Cole was certain Webb knew Jane was alive.

Jane's eyes narrowed, but her lips curved into a smile. No one but Cole knew she'd not been with any men but him, and they were both fine with the rumors. For that reason alone, Cole didn't try to stop her from playing into Graham's stupidity. "Many ways."

"Like?" Graham kept leaning on the counter. The casual stance was genuine. Idiot that he was, Graham thought he was safe.

"Clara was indiscriminate." Jane reduced her voice to a whisper, so Graham had to lean further over to hear her.

"Half the army camp, Janey. That's a good thirty men you bedded." Graham chortled.

"Did I?" She handed the glass back to Cole. When he filled it, she snatched it back and downed it. Based on her wince, her throat already hurt from the conversation.

Graham's brows furrowed. "Well, yeah, leastwise, that's what everyone said."

"Everyone? Interesting. Did I?"

Cole smirked and poured her another glass. Her dispelling a rumor shouldn't please him, but it did. First she took his name, now she owned up to being his completely. Life was improving. If they could just get rid of the maniac it might be perfect. Cole's smile faded fast as the thought came into his head.

Graham's mouth opened and closed. "But everyone…"

"The soldiers? Have any of them ever once bragged about conquering me?" Jane turned to climb onto the stool. Balanced on her knees, she leaned closer when Graham continued his gap-mouthed silence. "All you men are braggarts when you get a woman under you. What soldier has ever bragged about having me? You've heard Cole. You know how much I enjoy what we do."

"And how good she is at it." Cole couldn't help but add his thoughts on the matter. Even if Jane glared at him for it, he wasn't about to lie. She was the best he'd ever had.

Jane shook her head at him, but turned her attention back to Graham, leaning across the bar, really close to where he perched on his stool. "Has one soldier actually claimed to have had me and extolled my virtues or failures?"

Cole snorted when she mentioned failures. It earned him another glare to which he just shrugged.

"Come to think of it." Graham's forehead puckered as he tried to think. "No."

"Exactly." Jane moved fast and shoved his elbows off the edge of the bar.

Graham teetered for several seconds before the stool gave way. The legs cracked, and he dropped to the floor with a board-shaking jolt.

Cole had to move to save several glasses and tripped over Graham in the process. His forearm landed hard on a piece of the chair leg.

"Get off me." Graham shoved at him and tried to scramble to his feet.

Cole set his hand on the broken piece of stool leg, and the damn thing rolled out from under him. He cursed up a storm until he managed to plant his hands on the floor and jump to his feet.

Jane had tears streaming down her cheeks. Her face was flushed from her unrestrained glee. The only downfall to the scene was he couldn't hear her laughter, as she managed to keep it silent thanks to her throat. She pointed at him, and then Graham before bending over. With her head resting on the bar, she continued to laugh silently, her whole body quaking.

"Crazy bitch." Graham rubbed his head when he managed to haul himself to his feet. "What the hell was that for?"

She slapped the bar, still shaking from laughter.

Graham took a step toward her for retaliation, but Cole stopped him with one shake of his head. He shrugged and spoke low. "She needed the laugh…and so did we."

Graham snickered and nodded. "Guess we did."

Cole stepped toward Jane and leaned down to eye level. "You done?"

"No." She gasped for air and grabbed his hand, wiping at her tears. "So funny."

"Sure was." Cole chuckled. "Was wondering when you'd knock him on his ass."

Jane snorted and doubled over again. This time Cole didn't hold back from joining her. After weeks of hopelessness, it was the best feeling in the world.

Fear not the future, weep not for the past.
—Percy Bysshe Shelley

"Sure you want me to leave you alone with him?" Cole directed his frown at David. "Don't want him upsetting you again."

Jane tapped her pencil on the table until she had his attention. She narrowed her eyes at Cole. There were times when his jealousy of her former husband and others was amusing. Right then was not one of those times. She'd promised to speak to David the next day after her reentrance to life, but another snowstorm had prevented that and also delayed her brother's return from New York.

"Fine. I got it." He turned his back on David, tugging her gently into a deep kiss of possession. The wicked grin that crossed his lips when he pulled back was an unneeded confirmation of that fact. "I'll be at the depot, ordering my supplies."

David remained unmoving by the bar, his arms folded across his chest. His lip curled as his normally kind eyes followed Cole out the door with the fire of bitterness.

A soft sigh escaped, and Jane shook her head. She shoved out a chair for him with her foot, starting to write before he'd crossed the floor. While she'd taken to speaking as often as she could, after her laughing fit yesterday, her throat was just too sore today to be of use to her. *Bitter does not look good on you. He's being annoying and overprotective, just as you want to be. He is reveling in me being alive. I think we all are.*

"He's always annoying."

The amusement forced a smile out of her annoyance. She kicked him in the shin none-too-gently. *Be nice.*

"Don't wanna."

Child.

"Look who's talking." David's frown gave way to his own laughter. All too soon the laughter faded and he became quiet, almost distant.

Jane might not have known David for more than a few months, but she could tell something was bothering him. Something beyond the obvious issue of her death and resurrection. *What's wrong? I know what I've done is enough, but something else is bothering you.*

David's cheeks darkened red, and he looked toward the door.

"Oh," Jane whispered. Embarrassment like that only hit him when it came to one subject. Women. More specifically, one woman. "Lee?"

Lee Dynan was the woman David had been courting since shortly before Jane and David had officially divorced. Lee was a sweet woman, and Jane encouraged the match. Not only because it was fun to watch David blush every time Jane talked to him about Lee, but also because she thought the young widow was a good match for him.

David nodded. He rubbed the back of his neck with his hand. "Yeah, I guess."

Talk to me.

"I shouldn't."

Perhaps not. I can be a terrible influence.

He managed a smile, then sighed and leaned forward. "She's mad I'm sheriff, I guess. Doesn't want me doing it anymore."

She covered her mouth to hide her laughter. David truly believed that was why Lee was upset, though Jane could see more. Once she had a smidgeon of control over her laughter, she wrote fast. After she'd finished, she tapped his hand. *She isn't mad you're the sheriff. I'd bet anything she's scared of losing you. After hearing what that maniac did to those people in Jackson's house, she's realized how dangerous this is— especially now that she knows I'm alive.*

"Yeah. There's that, too." David grimaced and twisted his fingers together. "She don't like that I lied to her."

Why didn't you tell her? She frowned and shook her head. "I wouldn't have cared. If you trust her, so do I."

"I…I don't know."

"You need to figure that out." Silence fell between them—a stubborn silence, and she knew the conversation about Lee was over. She forced out the next whisper, knowing it would be her last for a few hours. "Let me have it."

He leaned his elbows on his knees. "Clara-Jane, I can't go through that again. Losing you twice was too much. I can handle you being with Cole, but I won't watch you die again."

I don't want to die again. I never wanted to die. It was a horrible feeling, death. For a moment her hand shook too hard to write. Again the darkness crept through her soul, clinging to her as desperately as she tried to cling to the light.

"Jane?" David's voice jolted through her, his hand on her shoulder. "Jane."

I'm sorry I put you through that. I would understand if what you said before still was true, if you really never could forgive me. His hand rested on her arm, and she set her free hand on it. *I want you to understand.*

"Understand what?"

Why I must stay here. Why I must risk everything.

"I want to understand. It doesn't make sense. There are safer ways."

Safe? 'There is nothing so strong or safe in an emergency of life as the simple truth'. Charles Dickens. With a shaky breath, she looked up at him. The tears she'd been forcing back spilled over before she could look back down. *I need truth.*

"At the risk of your life?" His hand ran along her back in a soothing gesture. He'd moved forward enough to embrace her, but held back.

Clara wasn't honest. She didn't live for truth. You suffered for it. She suffered for it. Jesse suffered much more than any child should. I suffered for it. The suffering needs to stop. After a quick swipe at her tears she kept writing. *The truth is all I have.*

"It isn't all you have."

It is a big part of what makes me Jane. It's not a pain-free existence, but it's a good one. I won't give it up. Hiding away, keeping the truth from these people who cared enough about me to be silent and mournful at my hanging, that wasn't honest. They deserve the truth. They deserve my faith in the friendships I've formed.

"What if someone tells?" David took a ragged breath. "I know, that's honest, and you wouldn't stop anyone. I just can't go through it again."

Clara Young hanged. She died long before the hanging. If it gets bad, I will appeal to have my sentence commuted. I will let Al speak for me if he is still willing. I will do what I can. If it does no good, I will ask to be taken elsewhere. I won't ask it of you again. Never again.

"You won't change your mind, will you? You won't go and live somewhere they don't know? I'd bring Jesse to see you."

What kind of example would that set for Jesse? That it's all right to lie and deceive, to change who you are? I'm trying to live better than Clara did, to be a good enough person to be a good... She dropped her pencil, unable to write the word.

"Ma. You could be a good Ma. You are one, worrying about him like you do."

No, she wasn't meant to be a mother. She shoved the paper away and rose. She had to accept she wasn't meant to be a mother.

"Jane, where are you going?" David placed his hand on her elbow. "You are his Ma."

Jane pried his fingers from her arm. Despite all efforts to live better she'd been unable to become a mother as Jane. A failed pregnancy and the way it had almost driven a permanent wedge between her and Cole was proof she wasn't meant to be a mother. She wasn't about to take Clara's child on as a responsibility. It wasn't right. It wouldn't be fair to Jesse.

"Will you come see him? You can't rightly decide unless you've seen him."

If she saw him, she'd crumble. David knew that as well as she did. It was too much, too soon. She couldn't handle it.

He took her hands and pulled them against his chest. Silence lingered between them until she forced up the resolve to meet his gaze.

He smiled. "Like I said, you are his Ma. Clara or Jane, it doesn't matter. You already love him. It's why you saved him. It's why you're afraid to see him."

Of course, he was right. While she'd wanted nothing more than to see Jesse since she'd been pulled out of the coffin, the moment she'd had such freedom, fear set in. The worry she'd be taken from him again and she wouldn't ever be able to be his ma. Already she felt attached, and he had yet to know the whole truth. A tear escaped, burning a hot trail down her cheek. She opened her mouth to protest, but could only nod.

A *thud* from the door echoed through the empty saloon, pulling them both from the moment.

"No." The male voice filling the quiet saloon was unmistakably Michael.

The sob that formed lodged in her throat, and her knees buckled. He'd left before she'd been hanged, unable to watch her die. She'd been grateful to be spared that pain on top of the others.

"Yes, Michael." Daisy's soft voice filled the silence. "Jane is what Cole wanted you to pick up at the saloon."

"God. Clarabelle?" Mike's voice broke, another *thud* echoing through the room. "Is it really you?"

David released her hands and grabbed her around the waist. "Easy."

She planted her hands on his chest to steady herself. Once she felt strong enough she turned. Mike was on his knees, tears visible at the edge of his reddened eyes. After a moment she stepped toward him, holding out her hand. Daisy slipped out of view, and Jane was grateful for her respect of the moment.

Mike scrambled to his feet. Racing over, he caught her around the waist and spun her before clutching her tight against him. "How? How is this possible? Clara. God, I just told them all you were gone–truly gone, but you're here."

She shook her head. It didn't matter just then. The other Young family members were strangers. Mike wasn't. No matter what, he'd needed to know the truth. She wanted to tell him Clara was dead, that she wasn't coming back.

"Are you all right? Talk to me."

"She can't." David cleared his throat. His shoulders sagged as he put his hat back on his head. "Throat's still swollen. It's going down, but we don't know how much is permanent. She still tries to talk more than she should, but I heard she talked too much earlier today."

At that Michael pulled back and cupped her face in his hands. "I can't believe this is really happening. I must be dreaming."

Jane dragged him toward the table.

"I'm going to let you have time with Mike." David shrugged. "It's important."

She shook her head and grabbed David's hand. They weren't done. Even if she wanted to, she wasn't walking away from their discussion.

"I'm not going anywhere. Apparently, neither are you." One corner of his mouth turned up in a boyish smile. "I know we aren't done. For once, I'm going to get you to admit that I'm right."

With a huff she folded her arms across her chest. Her toe tapped indignantly before she turned her face away.

David kissed her cheek with a chuckle. "I promise, Clara–sorry, Jane. This time I will get you to admit I'm right, and you'll come see Jesse tomorrow, no matter what."

She waved him off, refolding her arms across her chest. Once David left, she looked back at Mike.

"Clara?" Mike looked from her toward the door and back again. "What was that about?"

With a sigh she sat in her chair, rolling the pencil between her fingers. Once he sat, she wrote quickly. *Go ahead. Let it out.*

"How?" he asked again.

We aren't entirely sure. I remember it all, the pain, the feeling of death. I still feel it. Waking up in a coffin and thinking I was under the ground, that I would die again like that. Graham found me. Every day since then, I've worried I would fall back into hell.

His hand closed over hers when she didn't stop writing. The shudder vibrating through her led him to hug her. "I can't begin to imagine how horrible it was for you."

She shoved him away, wiping at her tears. *Is. It is still horrible. I don't know what to do. How to make it stop.*

"Make what stop?"

Reverend Greene says I was saved; that God spared me because I was never her. I don't live like Clara. I'm trying to be better.

"I know, Clara."

Clara is dead. She died years ago. She was a stranger to you. I am Jane. Jane Spencer. Please don't call me Clara any longer.

"Spencer? Not Mitchell?" Michael laughed when she refused to meet his gaze. He slapped the table. "All right, how is Spencer connected to Cole? Well?"

You assume too much. She flipped the pencil through her fingers, biting her lip to cover her smile. *We have to find him.*

"I'm already working on it." He shrugged. "You were dead. My limitations were removed. I've got Tommy doing some digging. If anyone can find out the information he can."

Why? I was hanged. What was the point?

"Answers, I needed them. Not as much as you did, but I needed them."

Cole found some answers.

"What?"

She smiled at the eager glint in his eyes. *In Yankton he found letters. I haven't read them all yet.*

"Why not?" He stood, leaning on the table. "Let's go see them now."

I'm afraid to finish. One year's worth was difficult enough to read. I'm afraid to read more.

"Of course you are."

What if they aren't what you want to hear? What if Clara really was the horrible person he said she was?

"I'll never believe it."

Jane stared at the paper in front of her, the pencil tapping on the paper uneasily.

"What is it?" Slowly he sank into the chair beside her again.

I remember everything about that day.

"You said that."

Every time I close my eyes, it happens again. The nightmares are much more than nightmares. I remember it, over and over again. Have you ever had a nightmare in which you could not scream?

I do think that families are the most beautiful thing in the world.
—Louisa May Alcott

Jane tapped on Kat's door.

Lillian Daugherty, Kat's mother, beckoned her in. Jane and Lillian's first encounter had been rocky to say the least. Jane had challenged Lillian's authority, but over the next few days the conflict had morphed into a bond of friendship.

Without hesitation, Jane pushed open the door. She smiled brightly and tipped her head to the elegantly dressed woman.

Lillian rose. "Katherine has been filling me in on the past few weeks of your adventures. I admit I would have come to enjoy my first Christmas with my grandchild anyway, but seeing you here alive adds even more joy to the holiday." Lillian smiled and extended her hand. "Come. Join us. Henry went with Norman and Cindy for some lunch at Cora's."

Jane crossed the room to accept Lillian's hug. Once they both sat, Jane took Kat's hand in her own. Kat's eyes were still deeply bruised, her nose swollen, and overall she truly appeared to be exhausted. Jane whispered, "How are you feeling?"

"Better than I look. However my doctor and my mother refuse to let me move about." Kat pouted and huffed. "I keep telling them I'm plenty strong."

"If you don't listen to Daisy she gets grumpy and annoying." Jane pointed out. "I imagine Lillian is far worse."

"She's the worst," Kat concurred.

Lillian chided Kat, but she continued to smile. "You were stabbed and kicked in the face. I think that requires more than four days' rest, thank you very much. Your father and I are here to keep an eye on Cindy while Norman works."

Jane tried to keep her chuckling quiet, but Kat stuck her tongue out at her anyway. All Jane could offer in return was a shrug. "I don't have the voice to argue."

"Good. Really, why are you speaking?" Lillian tsked. "I heard that your throat is still swollen, and you shouldn't be talking at all. Instead, here you are, speaking out loud, if only in a whisper."

"Cole says I don't know how to shut up," Jane replied.

This time it was Kat laughing. "He's got a point. You really don't know how."

Lillian joined their cheer with a bright smile. "Good. No woman should let a man shut her up. I'm pleased the two of you know that. We are smarter than them, after all."

"You couldn't tell by looking at the two of us." Jane pursed her lips. "Both beaten up and faced death recently. We should be smarter."

"Yes, you should. I still can't believe Kat went to Jackson's alone without telling anyone." Lillian sighed. "It was impulsive and foolish."

"I see that now. At the time I didn't. I was just angry and wanted answers." Kat winced and pressed her hand to her side. After a deep breath, she frowned. "I didn't realize I'd get that and more. My poor nose."

"You're worried about your nose when you almost lost your life." Lillian shook her head. "I think you are feeling better."

Jane's reply was interrupted by the front door banging open. Sounds of small feet tore up the stairs. She furrowed her brow and glanced at Kat. She'd never heard Cindy race about like that, but she hardly knew her. "Cindy?"

"I don't think so." Kat shook her head. "Cindy only runs with—"

The door flew open, and a small boy stood in the doorway. Even though he was seven, Jesse was small for his age. His curly blond hair, like Jane's, was disheveled and stuck out all over his head. He wasn't wearing a coat, only trousers and a shirt. His wide, hazel eyes stared at Jane and his mouth worked silently.

Jane's heart leapt into her throat, and she rose.

"*Jesse*," David's panicked voice echoed up the stairs.

"He's fine." Cole sounded more annoyed than anything.

Jesse tore across the room and latched onto Jane so fast she stumbled back a step.

"Easy," Jane whispered and brushed her fingers over his curls. "It's all right."

Jesse gripped tighter, his small fists clenched in her skirts.

David and Cole both strode down the hall side by side, but David stopped in the hall. Cole brushed past him and into the room. He paused at the door and looked back at David. After a shrug, he walked to the end of the bed. "Still look like hell, Kathy."

"Your concern is overwhelming." Kat snorted, then groaned. "Ow."

David turned away and pulled out his handkerchief. Once he'd wiped his face, he stepped into the room. "Mrs. Daugherty, good to see you. Sorry for the interruption. Cindy mentioned Jane to Jesse, and he took off without his coat."

"It's nothing to worry about," Lillian replied. "Kat is welcome to as much company as she can get, especially if it means she stays in bed longer."

"Mother." Kat's exasperation was clear.

Jane managed to pry Jesse's hands free and sank down in front of him. She wiped the dampness from his cheeks. "I missed you too."

Jesse threw his arms around her neck. "Don't let the bad man hurt you again."

"I'm going to do everything in my power to stop that from happening." Jane ran her hand over his head. She met Cole's gaze briefly before she sighed and hugged Jesse closer.

"What is this? A party?" A strange man joined them at the door. Jane assumed he was Kat's father by his brilliant red hair and beard. He wore a well-cut suit, but had an air of laughter about him that made her think instantly of Kat. Of course, since he came into the room with Norman and Cindy, her theory was pretty much confirmed.

"It certainly seems to be," Lillian concurred. "A reunion, at the very least."

"If it's a party we need libations," Cole offered.

"No, we don't." David glared at Cole. "We're just fine."

"Suit yourself." Cole shrugged with a chuckle. "But all you people are crying. That's not a party. Maybe we should have a party. What do you think, Jesse? Cindy?"

"Oh sure, ask the children." Jane chuckled. "You know they'll say—"

"Yes!" Jesse clapped his hands behind her head. "Party, can we?"

"I bet Miss Katherine would like that. She's been a bit bored in bed," Jane whispered. "Even with guests, it can get boring. Maybe we should get some popcorn from Cora's?"

"That is the greatest idea." Kat clapped. "I would love a party. It would certainly feel less like everyone is hovering at a deathbed."

"Then we'll have a party." Lillian rose. "Henry?"

"As you wish, my dear." Henry kissed Lillian's hand. "A party to end all parties. Anyone else you wish to have here, Katherine?"

Kat smiled. "No, I think this will do. These people are my family."

"Mine, too." Jane agreed, ruffling Jesse's hair. "Oh, wait, some of our family isn't here yet. We need Mike and Lee."

"I'll get 'em." Cole shrugged his collar up to cover his neck. She really needed to get him a muffler. "And some libations."

"I'll get Lee." David stepped toward the door to follow him. "And no libations."

"That ain't a party," Cole contradicted.

Jane sighed as they disappeared down the steps with Henry right behind them. "Will those two ever stop fighting?"

"It's not a family if someone ain't fighting," Norman muttered.

Jane met Kat's gaze, and they both giggled. She'd take all the bickering if it meant her family was close. Safe would be better, but for the time being, she'd take close.

*Put more trust in nobility of character
than in any oath.
-Solon*

Kat laughed when the two children ran past them again. "Between Cindy and David, I think his head has been completely filled with tales of Santa Claus and all of his wonders."

Santa Claus. She'd completely forgotten the date in her recovery. What day was it? "Christmas." The croak of her voice was barely heard over a squeal of laughter.

Jesse scrambled across the floor between them and ducked under the tablecloth. His feet kicked Jane's shins. Cindy rushed up. "Jesse."

Katherine grinned at his giggle, nodding to Jane. "He's really come out of his apparent mute nature while you've all but retreated into one. It still hurts?"

Jane nodded and sipped her coffee. It wasn't that she didn't want to talk. That was never the case with her. It was just very uncomfortable. Long sentences were the worst. Plus, she'd been told to take it easy. Much as she hated it, for once she was listening to her doctor's instructions. Despite this she sighed and spoke again. "Christmas. I forgot."

"You did a little preparation before…" Katherine's smile faltered. She took a sip of her own coffee. Rather than finish the sentence, she turned her attention to the children.

Jane watched as Cindy dragged Jesse out from under the table and started another game of hide and seek. After another sip of coffee she looked back at Katherine. "Talked to Cole?"

"Don't play coy. You know I haven't. There hasn't been time." Katherine folded her napkin, playing with the edges. "He's been spending time with you which is what he needs. I've been healing and dealing with my parents."

"Excuses."

"After Christmas."

"Excuses."

"Christmas is two days away. It's not an excuse. It's simple fact. After Christmas and my parents leave, I'll talk to him."

Jane's brows rose. She smirked and pulled out the paper and pencil she carried all the time. *I forgot about Christmas. Before I was arrested I made sure David could buy what Jesse needed. Other than that nothing.*

"You're alive. Cole doesn't need anything else. It's the best present any of us could have asked for."

That goes both ways. Jane squeezed Katherine's hand with a warm smile. *Promise me that you will talk to him. Soon.*

"I promise."

"Jane!" David barely knocked as he rushed into the boarding house. "You need to come with me."

Her lips pursed, Jane glared at him.

"Please. It's important." David held out his hand. "Then I'll make sure you get home safe. There's still some curiosity that might get to be too much."

"Go on. I made my promises. You can consider yourself finished with pestering me. I'll keep an eye on the little ones." Kat smiled. "If I get tired, Mother is right upstairs, eager as all get out to take care of the children. I'll see you tomorrow at evening services."

Jane sighed and folded her arms across her chest.

"Please, Jane. I promise it's nothing bad. Don't you trust me?" David flashed his teeth in what she supposed was a charming smile. The wink he added in didn't help his case at all.

"No."

"Come on, Jane. Aren't you a little curious?"

He had her there. Jane was curious. What was so important? Begrudgingly she took his hand. "Fine."

"Good. I thought it would take more of a fight." David chuckled. "And I didn't have time for that."

Jane elbowed him in the ribs. "Not funny."

"Sure it was."

She rolled her eyes, shaking her head. It was really annoying when he acted like he knew her. On the other hand, she was relieved that he didn't hate her. Things would be much worse if he did.

Rather than take her through town, he led her out of it, past the railroad tracks and through the meadow. "Here we are."

Jane stopped short with a frown. "Church?" Why on earth had he brought her here? She didn't mind going to church, but what could be so urgent on a Saturday this close to Christmas?

"Trust me."

Easy for him to say. Despite whatever trepidation she had, she followed him inside. Reverend Greene waited for them, and she took his offered hand. "Reverend."

"Know that this is a sanctuary Jane. You are safe here. Nothing that happens here will leave these walls." Reverend Greene smiled and stepped aside, revealing another individual in the pews.

Jane didn't move for a long minute, not sure she should take a step further.

Then he stood up and turned around. Al looked every bit as unsure as she felt. His hat twirled in his hands. Although he'd been shot a few months back trying to save her life, he stood tall, without the sling he'd worn when she last saw him.

He'd gotten his strength back and regained the weight. The brown eyes, that had always been kind, rose to meet her gaze. He smiled, although it was hesitant, and she dared to say, worried.

"He saw you with Cole." David set his hand on the small of her back. "I told him the truth once we were in the sanctuary of the church. He's leaving today. He wanted to see you, see for himself that this was real."

That may be true, but he had a duty. How could she ask him to keep this secret?

"I'll be done with the Army in just a few weeks." As if he'd read her mind, he answered the question. "I told you I wouldn't be staying in the Army once the year was over. Remember?"

Jane nodded, but kept her eyes lowered.

"Clara Young is dead. I've been to her grave."

"Jane?" David squeezed her arm. "I wouldn't have brought you if I thought he'd get you in trouble."

"Go." This was wrong, but she'd yell at David later. Right then, it was already too late. She'd spend some time with Al and deal with David another time.

David chuckled. "Who?"

"You." She nudged David in the ribs and nodded to the reverend before stepping further into the church. Once the door closed, she sighed and shook her head.

"Is that all I get?" Al smirked and held out his arms. "Thought we were friends."

It was much more complicated than that, and she cursed her inability to talk like she would have liked. Instead, she gave in and rushed into his arms, hugging him as tightly as she could.

"They say that it still hurts you to talk a lot, so why don't you let me do most of it?" He laughed when she pulled the pad of paper from her pocket. "All right, we'll both talk. Let me start with the promise that I won't tell anyone."

She frowned, writing fast. *I can't ask you to do that. You have a duty.*

"You aren't asking. Besides, I'll be leaving town on the train this afternoon. Far as I'm concerned, I came here for one last talk with Reverend Greene. I did prefer his sermons over the army chaplain."

He led her to a pew, and she sat beside him. *I don't know how this happened.*

"I don't need explanations. David handled that. I just want to be sure you're all right and certain you want to stay here. I can help you if you don't."

Help me?

"I told you. A few more weeks and I'm done in the Army, if you need somewhere to go where no one knows who you are."

She ducked her head. *Thank you. It's unnecessary. If I must leave, I will have company.*

"You sure about that?" Al's grin was crooked when she looked back at him. "I know. It was always Cole."

Rather than acknowledge the direction of the conversation, she chose to change subjects. *Why are you still here? Shouldn't Martha have been taken back already?*

"If I were a betting man I'd say that General Bryant planned it this way. Our train will get to Cheyenne on Christmas Eve and be tied up there until the holiday is over. He's got family in Cheyenne."

But he says different?

"Of course. Between the storms that delayed our men that took the prisoners to the northern territory and the large one after their return, he's got plenty of reasons."

Convenient.

"I'll say."

What will happen to Martha?

Kat's sister, Martha Starbird, the wife of an emancipated Indian, had committed treason in order to save her husband from the renegades.

"I don't think the charges will hold. That's another reason to delay. Once she gets to Washington, the trial should happen fast. There was only one witness, as I didn't actually see anything. I think she'll be back here before the child is born."

Her husband will not be here. That much she knew. He was ready to go to the northern territory. There weren't many people in town that were the least bit sympathetic to what he'd been through.

"Then she will probably join Starbird in the northern territory, although it wouldn't be safe to travel there alone and pregnant." He took her hand in his. "Are you sure you're going to be all right here?"

I certainly hope so.

"Now that you're Jane Spencer, will you do me one favor?"

Depends on the favor.

"Try to stay out of trouble."

She gave a weak laugh and poked him in the side. *I'll do my best. That's the all I can offer.*

"I guess I'll have to accept that."

You will write me? Let me know where you end up?

"I promise." He placed a gentle kiss on her temple. "Work on your poker. I expect you to win some of your money back when I see you again."

I'll miss you.

"And I'll miss you. I hope you know what you're getting into with Cole."

The door slammed open. Cole stormed into the church. "Get away from her. You got no right."

"Cole." Jane flew to her feet and planted her hands on his chest. "Stop."

"You shouldn't be talking. I got this." Cole grabbed her arms, grunting when she stomped on his foot. "Hey."

"Stop." With a sigh she turned back to Al. "Sorry."

"He's right about one thing. You shouldn't be talking. You sound terrible." Al shrugged and set his hand on her shoulder. His frown deepened when he cast a glance over her shoulder. "Like I was saying—are you sure?"

"Certain." Before he could argue further she pulled him into a tight hug. "Goodbye."

"Goodbye, Jane." His arms pulled her close, holding on tight. After a kiss to the top of her head he pulled back. "I've got to get back to work. Take care of yourself. I'll write once I'm settled."

"Don't bother." Cole spoke under his breath, but it wasn't missed by either of them.

Jane gave Cole a glare before taking Al's arm to walk with him to the door. After a kiss on the cheek, she closed the door behind him.

"Are you insane? He's in the army. He'll report you for sure." Cole stormed over and grabbed her shoulders. "You gotta be more careful."

"Stop." She shoved his hands away. Plopping into the nearest pew, she tapped her foot on the floor. "Idiot."

"You really don't expect him to keep quiet."

She held up her hands and waved them around. "Sanctuary."

"Bull."

"Prick."

"You shouldn't talk."

"Neither should you."

Truth is a gem that is found at a great depth; whilst on the surface of this world, all things are weighed by the false scale of custom.
—Lord Byron

"She should have told me." Cole paced incessantly, his hand fidgeting behind his back. It had been several weeks since Kat's attack, two months since Jane's hanging. For the first time, Kat and Cole were finally sitting down to discuss the matter of Cindy's existence.

Between the horrible winter storms occurring every few days, and the healing wounds of Jane and Kat, it had taken some doing to work it out. Kat was now healing well enough, and Jane was almost there. With a break in the storms, Jane had pushed the matter of getting Cole and Kat together.

Almost six years before Kat and Cole had a brief fling. Unbeknownst to Cole, the fling had produced a daughter Kat had never told him about. She'd given up her chance at a serious relationship with Norman and moved away to have the baby in secret.

A few months back, Kat had returned again for another brief visit. Norman, fed up with their sometimes-relationship, had given her an ultimatum. Kat had decided to take a chance and move back, which forced the matter of Cindy's existence into everyone's life.

The whole time Cole paced and ranted over the injustice of the matter, Jane wrote. He was upset, and rightly so, but she also knew that underneath the anger there was more. She held up the paper to him. In large, bold letters she'd crudely written over several times was her only statement on the subject. *Cindy is* not *Lydia.*

"How *dare* you." Cole glared at her like the fault was all hers. Lydia was the daughter he'd had with his wife years before he'd come to Dominion Falls back when he'd been a young man with the name Colton Spencer. Lydia had died while she was sleeping when she'd been a very young baby.

Jane slammed the pad down so hard her pencil flew across the room. She wanted nothing more than to yell at him, to tell him what an ass he was being, that he couldn't see the forest for the trees.

Not that he'd listen.

"Why don't you go ahead and get on outta here?" Cole folded his arms across his chest. Narrowed eyes conveyed anger directed right at her, but she knew different. He wasn't angry, and certainly not with her.

For a moment, she considered consenting to his request. Then, she changed her mind. If he was going to do things the hard way, he wouldn't listen to reason. Instead, she slapped him. When he opened his mouth to yell at her she slapped him again.

"Damn it, Jane!"

"Done?"

"Done with what?"

"Idiocy."

His glare lost strength. She knew him well enough by now to see the smirk hidden under his attempts at anger. He rubbed his red cheek. "Depends."

"On?"

"How bad to you wanna yell at me right now?"

"Infinite amounts."

"Good. Suffer." His smirk broke free. Her half-hearted attempt at another slap got stopped easily and he used her caught wrist to draw her close. "Thanks."

She didn't shy away; glad he'd seen what she'd been trying to do. Nothing worked fast to shock a man out of something than to catch him off-guard. She cupped his cheeks. "Be nice. Listen. Anger will not help."

"Says the woman that just slapped me twice."

She shrugged and slipped from his arms. On her way to the stove, she grabbed her pad and ripped out the sheet of paper she'd written on. Within moments it burned on the stove, the words flickering into ash. "Kat did not know about them?"

"You're the only one that does."

"But she knew you. She was not dumb or blind. I even saw your need to avoid attachment before I knew. You made no secret of it."

Cole wrapped his arms around her from behind. The weight of his chin settled on her head. "You're taking all the argument away before I even see her."

"Good."

"What do I do?"

"What do you want to do?"

Silence.

She knew he didn't have the slightest idea what he wanted to do. He felt slighted by what had happened, never knowing Cindy existed, but was unsure how he would have reacted if he had known.

Neither of them could be certain what he would have done, even if they were both fairly certain he would have reacted the same as he had when he'd first heard of Jane's pregnancy a few months back. It was a fair bet Kat had made the right choice, even if Cole wanted to be angry and act as though she hadn't to cover his nerves.

"Do you want to know her?" Jane rested her forearms on his where they settled around her waist.

"Don't matter. I ain't exactly what a pa should be."

"Do you want to know her?"

"I run a brothel."

"Do you want to know her?"

"Yeah. I do." There was no denying the shock in his tone. "Damned if I could tell ya why, though."

"There doesn't have to be a why." She squeezed his hands and turned. Her hand covered his heart, one finger tapping in rhythm with its beat. She sighed. "Not when it comes to this."

His hand closed over hers and pulled it toward his mouth. A gentle kiss brushed across her palm. "Wouldn't have mattered a year ago."

"That was a year ago."

A knock on the door ended all further discussion. Jane patted his chest before she extricated herself from his arms to get the door. Kat stood on the other side, fidgeting and frowning like she was just as uneasy as Cole. Her fingers wrung together as she nodded at Jane.

"Jane, how are you feeling?" The smile gracing her face was nowhere near the easy smile Jane was accustomed to seeing.

She clamped her hand on her friend's arm. Jane smiled and whispered, "Fine. He won't yell, so stop looking so nervous. Come in."

"Wish I could believe that." Kat's smile grew a little warmer before she stepped into the room. "Cole."

"Kathy." Cole didn't bother to turn around. He remained staring at the open stove grate where the paper had long since turned to ash. "Just tell me. She's mine?"

"No. She's mine."

"Katherine." Jane frowned.

"I'm the only parent she's had. She's mine." Kat lifted her chin. Hands on her hips, she straightened her back. "The choice was made long ago.

Jane sighed and dropped into the nearest chair. It figured that she'd spend all this time talking Cole out of his tizzy when Kat needed some talking down of her own. She didn't blame her friend. Jane had made the same choice when she had realized she was pregnant as well. It had just had a much different ending.

Cole still didn't turn around. His hands curled into fists so the tension shot through his arms to his back. In any normal circumstance seeing Cole ready for a fight was an exciting sight, but Jane wasn't ready for this situation to get out of hand. For heaven's sake, they'd only just started the discussion.

She got to her feet and crossed the room. With a touch of her hand to his back, tension raced across his muscles. After a moment, the tension eased.

Cole let out a deep breath, rolling his shoulders. "That ain't what I meant. Just tell me the truth, Kathy."

Jane remained where she stood, smiling when Cole glanced down at her. At the touch of his hand to her arm, she moved aside to let him turn and face Katherine.

He didn't let Jane get far as his fingers sought out hers. "I get why you did it. Jane did it, too."

Jane couldn't have been more surprised at his admittance. Granted, she knew far more about Cole than Kat had when she'd made her choice, but the knowledge he'd made the connection meant a lot. She smiled and squeezed his hand in encouragement. This time, using calm instead of anger, he was on the right track.

"I ain't saying I wasn't mad. I just got some sense knocked into me."

"What do you want, Cole?" Kat leaned on the back of a chair. Her stern expression didn't waver or show any sign of softening. "Really? You're not exactly overcome with paternal feelings. So what is it you want?"

Cole hesitated and sought out Jane again. At her encouraging nod, he took a shaky breath. "I want the truth. If she's mine, I wanna know her. She don't have to call me Pa or nothing. I just wanna know her."

"Why?"

"Does it matter?" Jane's whisper barely cut through the conversation, much less the tension. She knew Kat was working on the defense, and she knew why. Underneath the anger was pain. Jane knew Kat could, and would, be reasonable. "And do you really have to ask?"

"I won't let you use Cindy to replace the child Jane lost." Kat's tone didn't hold half the venom of her statement. Her stance was wavering. "You can't use her like that."

"Don't wanna. I got a lot to make up for." Cole released Jane's hand and crossed the room. "We were just having fun. You weren't wrong to do what you did, but it didn't do nothing to me like it did you."

Jane couldn't help the smile that formed wide enough it made her cheeks hurt. Maybe he was right. Maybe she was rubbing off on him.

"Did you tell him what to say, Jane?" Kat's eyes flashed the accusation at her. "That isn't fair. He's got to mean it."

"I just calmed him down." Jane shrugged. "I told you he was smarter than he looked. Scary, isn't it?"

"Took a lot of thinking. I ain't even sure half the time." Cole quirked an eyebrow. "Would you have stayed here if you weren't having a kid?"

"I don't know." Katherine sighed. "Since it wasn't how things happened, I try not to think about what would be different."

"Kathy. Is she mine?"

"Yes. It was our tryst that made me pregnant. Cindy is yours." Katherine sat in the chair she'd been leaning on. Her struggle against saying it out loud was obvious, but neither Jane nor Cole stepped in to help. Finally she sighed. "She's your daughter."

"Thank you." Cole sank into a chair and let the silence linger. The moment Jane touched his shoulder, he clamped his hand on hers.

Kat fiddled with the edge of her blouse. "You don't push yourself on her. She's got a good sense about her. If she doesn't want to talk to you, I'm not going to make her, but I won't stop you from trying."

Cole nodded, still gripping Jane's hand. He didn't mention he'd already talked to her a few times and played with her just as he had with Jesse when Kat was sick. Jane didn't push the issue, in hopes Kat would see for herself.

Once the silence dragged into an uncomfortable stretch, Katherine stood. "I should go. I have things to tend to."

"Thank you." Their hands clasped briefly before separating. "Supper tomorrow?"

Katherine nodded, slipping from the room in silence.

Jane stayed where she was. Cole hadn't released her hand, and she wasn't about to try to break free. Neither of them spoke for a long time, and she rested her free hand on his other shoulder.

"I thought I was cursed."

Her eyes closed, the pain in his words striking deep into her heart.

"Lydia, then Ella. Even you. Pa said I wasn't worth nothing. Figured he was right." Cole's grip tightened, twisting her fingers together. "There ain't nothing wrong with her. She just don't know me. Maybe that's why."

"No." Jane tugged her hand until he released it and moved to sit on his lap. She cupped his cheek. "No curse."

"You sure?"

"I'm alive."

"Yeah."

"I think your fortune is turning." Jane smiled and pressed her hand over his heart again. "Unless you think having me around is bad."

"No, that's very good."

"And knowing about Cindy?"

"Yeah, that's good."

"Then stop pouting."

"I'm a pa?" He grinned at her laugh, pulling her closer when it turned into a cough. "But she don't know it."

"She will. In time."

"Sorry."

"For what?"

"Making you think you had to hide it, when you were having my kid."

She brushed her lips across his. "It's the past."

"So I ain't cursed?"

Wicked thoughts entered her head, and she knew her renewed grin had to reveal some of it. Just in case it didn't, she shifted in his lap. Her hand slipped down to his trousers. "Do you feel cursed?"

"Not right now."

"Good."

A letter always seemed to me like immortality because it is the mind alone without corporeal friend.
-Emily Dickinson

October 27, 1865
Michael,

HE told me I could change. Be anything other than what I was. I felt weak. Foolish. Stupid for running. There was never a time before I'd felt like that, not even when I ran to Utah.

I had let David down. I had hurt him. Instead of turning to him, I ran away. Now it is too late. I cannot change what I have done— the damage, the pain. They may never be eased.

HE holds all the cards. HE alone knows everything. HE is good to me, keeps me safe. Sheltered.

Secluded.

HE says I am not yet ready. There is more to learn, more to understand. I am a quick study, but not quick enough for him. There are days, moments really, where I see another side to HIM. I worry what is hidden behind HIS kindness.

I never before thought myself a fool. Foolish, perhaps. Impetuous, always. I never thought myself a fool.

Was I a fool?

February 12, 1866

I am in the hospital. HE put me here, though the doctors were told I was in a wagon that overturned. In here I can write many letters, HE cannot keep watch over me all the time. The doctors don't suspect it was HIS hand that put me here.

The nurses are wiser, they know. They help me. Without question. Without payment. I will tell you all I can in my time here. Outside of HIS watching eyes.

July 18, 1866

We change so often. Everything. Names, location, everything. When I question HIM why, He evades me. I wonder sometimes who HE used to be. Why HE wants to leave the past far behind.

As more time passes, it becomes easier to forget. Forget what I've done. Push it behind me.

But it will never go away.

October 4, 1867

Three years have passed. Three whole years, is that possible?

I have not been the same person for more than five months, usually far less. HE made it seem like such an adventure, Michael, but the adventure is wearing thin, as is the mask HE has always worn.

HIS deception is keen. I question how much of himself HE actually shows to me. Have I been a part of the lie too?

The day he found me, I never told you about that day. The worst day. David went hunting. The first snow had fallen, and the cold seeped in through the windows. Even the fire seemed cold. Being in the house, alone again, feeling the swell where the baby had begun to make its presence known – all of a sudden I felt the terror. The terror I'd felt those two days, of how David would react.

I had to go. I had to run, and so I did. I took Longfellow and let him run as fast and as far as he could. When he stopped, I switched to walking on foot and kept going. My dress soaked through fast, but I couldn't stop walking.

Your words that were meant for comfort ran through my head over and over again. I couldn't block you out. It might have started to make sense – but then HE was there. I stumbled on HIS campsite and immediately panicked.

Once I had calmed through HIS assurances, HE offered me food and warmth for the night. HE told me little at first…but HE was charming…and immediately understanding of my distress. HE said nothing wrong…and before I knew it I was telling HIM how much I just wanted to forget…

I didn't know then that words and charm are HIS best weapons. I've seen HIM beguile so many now I wonder how I was beguiled so easily. I thought I was smarter than that.

December 19, 1868

With Massachusetts far behind us the intoxication has worn off. HE still gets such a thrill from every change, and continues to pick lives that are very disparate. Sometimes I wonder what the point of it all is.

With fortune perhaps turning toward my side HE has come to leave me alone more often. I have used every opportunity I can to learn more. More about what HE did with the child. Could it have been David's child? Why keep it from me? Why can I not remember the night the child was born? Or the days after? Did the child truly die in birth as I have been told?

I can think on it no more without tears belying my sorrow.

Money is a big part of every deception. The acquisition of wealth or materials; sometimes just knowledge. For the latest deception I was forced to learn French. I am grateful for the memory I was bestowed with because if I had failed...

January 23, 1869

I am in the hospital again. I am unsure how long this time. As much physical pain as I am in, I am always grateful when HE loses his temper so harshly and I am forced into medical care, for it gives me much more time to write. To let you know the truth. Even if by now you are sickened by all I have done, there is still so much more to tell.

There are times HE looks at me and I have to wonder who HE sees. Who is it that haunts HIM? What is it HE wants me to be? It's not any of these people. These characters. These faces. They are all wrong. They are not who HE is looking for.

I believe the truth is right around the corner. I simply keep missing it.

I've been too content in my shame. Too convinced I deserve this pain and torment. Too compliant to HIS demands. I believed myself stupid, naïve.

I am smarter than this.

I will find that truth.

October 4, 1869

Five years.

I was such a fool. With all I've learned in the past five years, with all that I have been through I can see it so clearly. It haunts me daily the sheer stupidity and fear I allowed to rule me that day.

I wish to escape, but I see no way to free myself. I keep getting pulled deeper in to the lies and deception. My own fears have let HIM manipulate and bully me into submission. I'm so far down, how can I pull myself out?

Who is the man behind the mask HE wears? The more I see hidden behind HIS deception, the more I fear. The dark and evil undertones. I fear for the people we deceive. I fear for myself. I fear for those I left behind...the ones that haunt my every dream.

HE holds my secrets like a trophy and uses them to taunt me. They are the saber HE uses to cut off my grasping fingers, the ones that cling to the truth I once knew. I thought I had forgotten but it always returns—the spirit of what I thought was dead never died...

Is there anything that haunts HIM?

February 28, 1870

I have learned the truth. I saw the boy. His father's eyes. Oh, the eyes. New eyes to haunt my dreams. What did HE do? What did I do?

It was dangerous to follow. The last time I tried the consequences were so great I was in the hospital for a week...but I had to see what HE does when HE departs my company. It was there, in the veil of deep morning fog that I saw him.

I can't explain what came over me. It was like my whole soul erupted, and the fog cleared not only from the docks, but also from my own head. I knew he was my son, David's son. It was only the fear of certain death for the young innocent that kept me from running out of my hiding place.

My heart is bursting with joy, yet being smothered by the overwhelming grief. The fear of the knowledge that to destroy the monster I must become HIM.

I will learn with a voracity HE has wanted from me all along. Everything I can. Then I will learn what haunts HIM. And I will free myself of HIM. I will rescue the child and then...and then...Michael, I will destroy myself. I must sacrifice myself to ensure HIS end.

August 3, 1870

The time is drawing near, dear one. I have learned so much. I do hope my cryptic notes are decipherable. The letters that are nonsensical. You should know that nothing is nonsensical about them. Puzzles. Search them, find them, and solve them. All the answers I may be unable to give you are there. It is the best I can do. To speak directly might curse my task. It is a chance I cannot take.

My life depends on it. My son's life depends on it. I pray I can be forgiven, Michael. For what I am doing to achieve this. HIS crimes are becoming mine as well. Each one I commit sickens my very soul. I feel myself dying off piece by piece.

I hope you have long since bid your farewell to Clara. She is no longer here. I love you, dear one. And my son. And yes, even David. Know that these sins I commit are to free you all.

God help me.

Better a broken promise than none at all.
-Mark Twain

The words on the page blurred from Jane's tears. She wiped her eyes. What she'd read couldn't be true. The letter couldn't be real, simple as that.

"Jane." Cole set his hand on her arm. The simple action brought her back to the present, and eased some of the chill in her heart.

"Why did you keep this letter out?" She'd finished all of the letters two days before, then Cole had surprised her with one more, one he'd kept hidden since he'd first read the letters months before.

"Figured you'd stop reading if you saw it. Didn't think you'd wanna stop before the end."

"It should have been first."

"Sure about that?"

"No." Jane took a ragged breath and leaned her forehead against the heel of her hand. Too much information had been departed with the one heartbroken letter, and she had no idea what to do with any of it. Her heart was overwhelmed by it all. It was now February. After so much time taken to read all of Clara's letters, some of which were true puzzles she wasn't sure how to solve. This one letter was clear as a bell, though. It needed no deciphering.

"Go see him."

"I can't. Not after this." She rose and paced the room. A combination of nerves and guilt gnawed at her frayed heart. Every time she thought her heart couldn't break further, something happened to prove her wrong. This was worst of all. "I don't know that I can ever look at him again."

"That's Clara talking. She was scared and ashamed. You ain't. You never have been. Don't you start now." He turned her to face him, holding her firm by her shoulders. "Go see him."

He was right, of course. This was something she had to face. Head on, without any sign of wavering. Of all the things she couldn't make right, this might just be something she could, if she could find the strength.

Before she could finish her thought process, her wool coat was draped over her shoulders. The letter she'd dropped on the table was placed into her hands. She felt numb through her fingertips and couldn't even put her hands through the sleeves. "I'm not so sure."

"Don't care." He guided her arms through the sleeves. "This is something you gotta do, and you know it."

"I know."

He pushed her toward the door of their room, going so far as to open it for her. "Go on. Don't make me throw you over my shoulder."

"Cole." She turned back, desperate to have someone with her as she faced the challenge ahead. "Will you come?"

"No. You gotta do this alone. I read that letter. You have to go see him."

A nod was the best response she could manage. Her throat seemed to have closed off against the words she loved so much. He turned her around and pushed her away from the door. He was right, again. Damn him. Her nerves strung up tight, causing her whole body to shake before she ever reached the cold outside.

"Jane." Michael appeared in the doorway before she made it through the saloon.

"Leave her alone, Mike. She's got something to do." Cole grinned down from the railing he leaned on when she glared at him. "Go on, Jane."

"Jane?" Michael frowned, his brows creasing together. "What's going on?"

"I'm on my way to see Jesse. Walk with me." Jane laced her arm through his, glad Cole couldn't hear her talking. Her voice was still far too raspy for it to carry far. "Cole is being mean and making me do this myself, but I wouldn't mind company along the way."

"Do what yourself?"

"Something that could very well be a mistake."

"You aren't making any sense." The moment they stepped outside he pulled his collar closer against the cold wind. "Would you just tell me before you lose your voice again?"

"I must see Jesse."

"How could that be a mistake?"

"So many reasons." She couldn't begin to list them all. The maniac was still out there. Who knew what would happen if the law learned she was still alive. Plus, she'd hurt that child so many times as Clara, and unknowingly since he'd come back into her life.

"Hey." Michael stopped her, turning her toward him. "It's not a mistake to spend time with him. Let him get to know you, just like David did. He's smart. Eventually he'll figure it out. He figured out David was his pa. He'll know you're his ma."

"You don't understand." She lowered her head, taking a shaky breath. "He already does."

"What? How?"

Her hand shook, but she held out the letter to him. The crumbled paper was all she dared see. If she looked at her brother, she'd fall to pieces again. "You read it. I can't read it again. It's too painful. I broke my promise."

Before he could read, she resumed her journey to Turner's store and restaurant where Jesse and David had been living. She left Michael behind to read, as she had no need to see the paper again. Like everything she'd ever read, the words were burned into her memory. This time they left behind a scorching pain right down to her heart.

September 15, 1870

> *Oh Michael. Today I took the biggest risk of all. I had no choice. My heart made me take it.*
>
> *I'm so close to the end of this journey. So close to finishing what I need to do. I had to see him. To hold him. To let him know that soon he would be safe.*
>
> *HE went to scout our next position somewhere over in Colorado. Manitou, I think. I knew that the last time he sold the child it was right in the next town. A mere hour by train.*
>
> *So many things could have gone wrong. If he'd returned early. If he'd taken the boy with him to sell ahead of our arrival. If he'd stopped there to check*

on the boy. I didn't know how long he'd be gone, but I prayed my estimate of four days was enough.

Fate may be turning to my advantage. None of those things happened. The boy was still there. Silent as a church mouse, obedient as any child could be.

Quiet.

Waiting.

I watched for almost two days. I had no time left, and I had to take the chance. The woman that had bought him like merchandise, a child to display, her name was Charlotte. She took him with her to the mercantile.

I followed them in, watching as she ignored him. He wandered to the candy, as all boys are wont to. Within moments Charlotte wandered off, lost in the depths of the mercantile.

My heart in my throat I approached. I knelt beside him, slipping a piece of candy easily from one of the jars. Once I'd tucked it in his pocket he smiled at me.

So like David. It near broke my heart.

One small hand reached out, touching my cheek. He didn't fear me, and he seemed much more intelligent than they gave him credit for. I looked for his owner, but she was still aisles away.

I knew the smile he was still offering was foreign; the light in his eyes was unaccustomed to being there. It would change, it will very soon, but first he had to know. I had to tell him.

Taking his tiny little hand in my own I asked if he had a name. He shook his head no. I had to remedy it. I asked if he wanted one. Amazingly his smile grew. The fierce nod he gave me left no doubt that he wanted a name.

There was no question. I gave him the name Jesse. David's middle name.

Then I asked if he knew who I was.

You could not begin to fathom my surprise when he nodded yes. How could he know? It didn't seem possible, so I asked again if he knew who I was. He stepped closer and whispered in the softest voice that he knew I'd come.

If it had not already been shattered by my actions in the past, my heart surely shattered in that moment. For I knew I would never come to know this child, the wonder that he is, but by the same token I feel as if I'd always known him.

From the moment I'd seen him, I knew he was my child and by some miracle he'd known the same when he'd seen me.

I couldn't help myself. I embraced him in the tightest hug I've felt in years. For a few brief moments I held my son, and he hugged me back. In that brief time I no longer doubted I would succeed.

Time was running short. Charlotte was drawing near. It took everything I had not to take him then. If I had, surely that woman would have screamed, and we would never have escaped.

I didn't want to leave him, but I have to be smarter than that evil creature.

I could not steal him away in broad daylight, desperate as I was to try. I had to be smart. With a broken heart I promised I would come for him. That the next time he moved I would be there to send him to his true home.

I made him promise if the bad man was nearby not to come to me. Not until I was alone and called him by his name would he be safe.

"Soon," I promised. "When you get off that train. When the bad man leaves, I will be there. Then you will be safe, Jesse. I will make sure you are safe."

I have located David. I will send Jesse to him, and then I will see that the bastard pays for the lies he told. I will face my own punishment in peace, knowing that I have made it right for Jesse.

Right at the bottom of the steps to Cora's, Michael's shout reached her. She stopped and waited for him to catch up. Every ounce of strength she had was being used to keep the tears back. She had to pull herself together before she saw Jesse or she'd be incapable of doing what needed done.

"You gave him his name?"

"I also promised I'd get him to safety, that in a very short time I would send him to safety and his true home." Her eyes closed against her eyes tears. "As if that wasn't bad enough, I don't remember any of it."

"The moment you saw him get off that stagecoach, you knew. When you spoke to him here in town, you knew. Just like you said in this letter." He shook the letter gently. "You knew in your heart. You did all you could to save him. That's what matters."

"I don't know how I knew. How he could have known."

"That part doesn't matter." Michael squeezed her arm. "As far as the promise goes, you did keep it. It just took longer than you'd hoped."

"I've kept no promise. I betrayed his trust worse than I did David's."

He pulled her into a hug. "In all of these months have you never been alone with him and called him by name? Hasn't he shown you he knows?"

"No." Her weak voice faltered, and she buried her face in his shoulder. When she thought she had control again, she stepped back. "I made sure we were never alone. I don't know why. I've just always been worried he would know I was his mother and hate me for not being there sooner."

"He doesn't hate you. Everyone can see he adores you." Mike sighed. "And you did keep your promises. You brought him to his pa. He is safe."

"Safe? We still don't know where that man is. What he's planned. If he knows I'm alive. We don't even know his real name."

"Jane."

"He isn't safe yet. I will make sure he is. Somehow." Before he could offer any further helpful advice, she swiped at her tears. "I should go do this before I lose my nerve. Then I can go back and try to solve those puzzles. They have to help. They just have to."

"All right. We'll go up and do this. Then I'll try to help you with some of those puzzles. The letters were addressed to me, after all. I haven't read one of them." Michael winked, helping her up the slippery steps into the store.

"Jane. Mike. Here for some food today?" Cora smiled as she walked up. "Got a few tables left and just pulled some corn bread out of the oven."

"Where's Jesse?" Jane's grip on Mike's hand tightened when she noticed David sitting close by.

"Upstairs reading. Can't keep that boy's nose out of a book once it's been read to him once." Cora chuckled. "Think he's like his Ma that way."

Jane cleared her throat and forced a smile. "Thank you."

Mike leaned closer. "I'll go talk to David. Cole was right. You've got to do this part alone. We'll give you some time, before we go up."

One last squeeze to his hand was all she could manage before she headed to the stairs. The short flight looked a mile long with her worry over how Jesse would react now that she was alone.

Despite the fact her heart had stopped beating, she grabbed her skirts and started up the steps, one at a time, until she stood just outside his room.

Nerves rattled through her into the weak knock she managed. The small voice that responded barely made it through the door.

After a moment's hesitation she pushed open the door, her gaze immediately falling on Jesse. Curled up on a small bed, leaning toward the light from the window, his attention remained fixed on the page in front of him.

"Jesse?" She wasn't certain he'd even heard her soft whisper.

The book dropped, and he stared at her. He set the book on the bed and climbed off of it. "Safe?"

Lip trembling, she nodded. The moment he took a step toward her, she dropped to her knees. "Yes, you are safe here, and I will do whatever I have to so you will always be safe here with your pa."

"And you, ma?"

Her heart swelled up until the tears poured down her cheeks, "Yes. God willing…and me…"

She wrapped her arms around him tightly, and everything fell into place as his little arms did the same.

Every gift which is given, even though
it be small, is in reality great,
if it is given with affection.
—Mark Twain

The whole world had been silent moments ago. Now the wind howled and snow raced past the windows of the former boarding house.

Jane sipped her coffee in an attempt to get rid of the chill that had cropped up with the sudden storm. Cole's laughter drew her gaze back to the checkerboard. In one swift movement he lifted his piece, jumping three of Norman's to land in the king's square.

She chuckled as Norman grumbled under his breath. As Cole swept Norman's pieces off the board, Jane leaned in toward Kat. "If Cole keeps this up, Norman's going to start accusing him of cheating."

"He wouldn't dare with Cindy keeping such close watch over everything they do." Kat laughed. "Then again, she doesn't really know how to play."

Jane smiled and took another sip of coffee. "She doesn't seem to mind Cole."

"It's almost disturbing how comfortable he is around her." Kat's brow furrowed. "Did you think he'd be good with a child?"

"Haven't you seen him with Isaac or Jesse?" Jane knew that despite his protests, Cole was actually very good around kids. Of course, Cindy being his own child was another matter entirely. "He doesn't hate kids as much as might have claimed."

Kat grunted in half-hearted agreement.

"They seem to enjoy the way he teases them. I've never seen him talk down to a child unless they were trying to peek in the girls' windows."

"I guess."

"And Cindy is different." A wave of grief hit Jane hard enough to turn her gaze away from the small group gathered around the table. Most days she was able to ignore the what-ifs that filled her life. There were so many that if she dared dwell on them for too long, she'd never get out of bed.

Every once in a while though, they still hit her heart. Talking of how Cole would handle Cindy was a gut-punch of a reminder of her own lost child. Jane took a ragged breath and another sip of coffee. It was easier to change the subject and push it all away again. "Have you heard from Martha?"

"Mother received a telegram yesterday and contacted me right after. Martha is in Washington." Kat sighed. "She still won't let Mother's lawyer help her. In normal circumstances I'd agree, but this is treason."

"Treason is difficult to prove. Either she's confident or simply does not care."

"Or both." Kat's frown deepened and she stared out the window at the swirling snow. "It seems like this winter we've had far too many storms. We get a break of a day or two and then another hits. I hope this one doesn't last long."

Jane wasn't surprised by the subject change. She'd expected it, much as she imagined Kat had expected her own subject change when they talked about Cindy. The swirling snow swept by the window, but it didn't disquiet her as it did Kat. Rather it gave her a sense of relief. "I hope it lasts forever."

"What? Why?"

"If it's storming like this, there is nothing else out there. No one else. I know he is not out there watching." Jane rose and left the room in the guise of getting more coffee. Her hands shook as she poured.

Kat's entrance to the kitchen was silent. She set her mug down next to Jane's. Once the coffee had been poured into both she pulled Jane into a chair. "I guess you haven't had any luck with the letters then?"

"Even if I do, what will I do with the information?" All of Jane's plans were mere theories. Even her craziest thoughts of what to do were weak and lacked solid form. Johnny was crafty, cunning, and evil beyond belief. How on earth could she compete with such a skilled criminal? One with years of experience when all she had were letters with details of lessons in evil?

"I'm sure you'll think of something."

"Sure I will."

The concern in Kat's features disappeared into another wicked smile. Jane sensed another subject change, and one she wasn't sure she'd enjoy. Kat leaned forward. "I have a question for you. With all of these storms and your lack of a solid voice, I haven't been able to really pin you down and ask."

Jane knew this question wouldn't sit well, but couldn't imagine what it was. The gleam in Kat's eye was all the proof she needed that her friend was up to no good. Escape seemed like the best idea, but she wanted to give some more time for Cole and Cindy to spend together. With a great deal of hesitation, she finally allowed the question. "What?"

"Have you told him again?"

Jane had no idea what Kat could possibly mean. She was outright baffled by the question, as it had nothing to do with any of the lead-in conversation. Kat sat grinning at her without any assistance in the matter. For the life of her she couldn't figure out where this was going. "What in heavens are you talking about?"

"You can be amazingly dense when you want to be, Jane. You know exactly what I'm talking about. Cole. Have you told him how you feel?"

Heat flooded Jane's cheeks so fast she broke out in a cold sweat. She slipped her thumb along the rim of the mug that suddenly became the most interesting thing in the world. "I have no idea what you're talking about."

"Of course you don't." Kat snorted. "Give me some credit. The whole town saw you say it before David put that mask over your head."

"You know that we aren't...that we don't...oh, Katherine." Jane pushed to her feet, smoothing her hands over her hair and then her bodice as she walked away. "No, I have done no such thing. I'm perfectly happy the way things are now. We have enough chaos, I see no need to further complicate it."

"Sure you are. Perfectly happy. Thrilled, even. What's so difficult about saying it? It's not like everyone on earth doesn't know what you two feel for each other."

"'When one is truly in love, one not only says it, but shows it'." Jane kept her back to Katherine. She forced herself to stand where she was rather than flee for admitting as much as she was. "Longfellow."

"Ah, but you still should say it. Why are you afraid to say it?"

The last time she had, even in a dream state, he'd walked away and disappeared into the night. He'd left, and she couldn't bear it if it happened again. Besides, she didn't need to say it. Did she?

"You can't tell me he doesn't feel the same."

To be honest, Jane wasn't certain. She liked to imagine he did. It wasn't that she wanted to have flowery declarations. For now his commitment to her and her alone was enough. It would be for a long time. "I wouldn't know."

"Jane."

"What about you? You and Norman seem rather content together. Are you getting married anytime soon?"

Katherine flushed red and shook her head, "Changing the subject?"

"Same subject. Fear." Jane smirked and looked toward the other room where the checkers game kept going strong. "Well, no matter what you say, you seem content to have him staying here. Or was I mistaken when I saw Norman bring the rest of his things over from the depot right before Christmas?"

"You know you weren't mistaken." Katherine nudged her with a small laugh. "It has been nice. I'd be lying if I said

I hadn't thought about it. I'm certain he is still. In fact I thought…"

Jane pulled her gaze from the game to focus on Katherine. "You thought what?"

"Well, it's silly really."

"Now you have to tell me."

"He kept hinting that he had gotten me something special for Christmas. I wondered if he wasn't going to risk asking again."

"He didn't?"

"It was a new bed warmer."

Jane covered her mouth to try to contain her laughter. "A…A…new bed…warmer?"

"Shhhh." Katherine pursed her lips. "It's not that funny."

"Of course not."

"Jane…"

"A bed warmer?" Laughter burst from its seams, and Jane covered her mouth to try to stem the volume.

"He wanted to make sure my feet were warm." Katherine's lips twitched. "Although that may have been more for his comfort than mine, protection from my cold feet."

A fresh round burst out until they were both laughing hard enough that tears formed.

"What are you two hens cackling about?" Norman's shout echoed in from the next room. His face appeared when he craned back in his chair with a frown. "Thought you was just getting coffee."

Rubbing her throat as it grew raw, Jane's laughter slowed, and she held up her hands. "Nothing." Coughing and shaking her head when Norman turned back with a grumble about women, Jane tried to settle down.

Katherine wiped a few tears from her cheeks. "Oh, dear. What about you?"

"Hmm?"

"Did you and Cole exchange gifts?"

"Why would we?"

Katherine gasped. "You did. What did he get you?"

"It's not important," Jane muttered.

"Tell me. If I can tell you about a warming pan…"

Jane's hand went to her neck, and she pulled out a chain from beneath her collar. Dangling from the chain was a simple pendant, a swirl of gold like the symbol for infinity with a garnet at either end.

Katherine stepped closer and reached for the pendant. "Goodness."

"Shh." Jane hushed her this time. Even though the flames of embarrassment still lit her cheeks, she couldn't help the bright smile. "It's just a simple pendant."

Katherine chuckled when Jane slipped the chain back under the collar of her dress. "Norman gets me a bed warmer, and that is simple?"

Jane giggled and shook her head. "A warming pan…"

Both women laughed again, wrapping their arms around each other's waist before heading back toward the checkers game.

"I still say they're up to something," Norman muttered.

"They're always up to something," Cole agreed. "They're women, and that something is always no good."

"Not always," Jane contradicted. "I do believe I've had a good idea from time to time. Like the one I'm having now."

Cole raised a brow. "That so?"

Jane nodded. "Yes. I'm thinking it's time to go back out into the storm."

"It's cold out there." Norman shook his head, studying the checkers board intently. "Besides, our game ain't over."

Jane shrugged with a sigh. "All right."

Once Norman had made his move, Cole took two more of his pieces. He chuckled. "Norman's got a point. Still got another few more moves 'til I win. Besides, wind's blowing something fierce. Should wait 'til it slows."

"Suit yourself." Jane walked over behind him and set her hand on his shoulder. Leaning down she whispered, "Sooner we get cold, sooner we can warm each other up."

Cole was on his feet so fast that Jane had to jump back to avoid spilling her coffee. "I got you beat anyhow. We're gonna head out."

Norman grumbled. "Fine. I know you were cheating anyway. Go on."

Jane let Cole help her into her coat. With a wicked grin, she leaned down and kissed Norman's cheek. "We'll see you once the storm blows over."

Norman flushed and brushed her off grumbling about annoying women.

Still chuckling, she turned to Katherine and whispered, "Keep your feet warm."

Katherine hugged her tight. Her whisper was just as quiet. "Tell him."

*Plots, true or false, are necessary things,
to raise up commonwealths and ruin kings.
—John Dryden*

Cole frowned as Jane ran a brush through his hair. After months of neglecting the barber, first because of the distraction of Jane, then at her request, his hair had become unruly and annoying. He wanted nothing more than to have it chopped off. "Mind telling me why ya still won't let me go to the barber?"

In the reflection he could see a half smile on her features. Even as she worked, focused on his hair. Jane shrugged. "I don't know."

"Bull."

"Maybe I just like it."

"I call bull." He tilted his head back to meet her gaze. "Tell me?"

"I cannot say for certain yet." She leaned down to brush her lips across his forehead. "I have been mulling over some ideas."

"About?"

She met his gaze briefly before she pulled away. With her back to him she set the brush on the dresser. Rather than speak she rearranged every item on top of the dresser until her hand came to rest on the dog-eared Poe book.

The book had been the first thing they'd found with a tie to her past. In the months since she'd deciphered the notes in the margin as a confessional, but there was still a page's meaning that eluded both her and her brother.

He knew it bothered her to not have all the puzzles solved. Beyond the one page in her Poe book, the letters she'd been reading from Clara contained more riddles that left her baffled. Everything tied back to that maniac out for her blood, Johnny.

"Why do I need my hair like this for them ideas?"

One elegant finger tapped on the book, while she continued moving things around on the dresser with her other hand. Finally she sighed. "You won't let me say I'm not entirely sure yet and leave it at that?"

"Nope. Wanna know what you're thinking."

"I'm thinking Clara had a point, that to catch the monster she needed to become him. I'm thinking we need to draw him out. Once this winter finally breaks, we need him to know I'm here and alive. We have to know that he knows, and we need to use his own deceptions and single-minded focus against him."

"I don't like the part about him knowing you're alive." He hated it, to be fully honest. Already Jane had been close to death too many times for his liking.

"How else will we get him to act?" She turned toward him, her features stoic. No fear as he'd expected. Her lips were set in a determined line. "And act strong enough that we might know where he is."

"What if he calls the marshal again?"

She waved her hand in dismissal. "He's already done that. It was beneath him, but I'd bet he was aiming to make me admit the amnesia was false. I think he hoped I'd kowtow and offer him all the information to save my own neck. I truly believe he thought I'd have done anything to get out of being hanged."

He didn't like how much surety she put in her words. It seemed like too much of a trap to be so certain about the crazy man. "You don't really think ya know him."

"No, I don't. This is all speculation, but I've had many hours to think and consider the motives behind all that's happened. I've also had plenty of time to ponder how we'd be best to counter-attack this time. I refuse to sit by and let him win. I can't wait and fear my own fate any longer. I have to act."

Cole got to his feet and pulled her close. "I don't like sitting by neither."

"For all intents and purposes, he killed Clara. He took a scared young woman and manipulated her into giving up everything, including her life and hope."

When she trembled, Cole ran his hand along her back. He hated when her strength wavered at the mention of her former self.

"When she realized her mistake, he kept her from returning to the man she loved and he coerced her with shame and fear. He stole her son, my son, from her when she gave birth. He stole Jesse and used him to keep her in shame. He sold my son to complete strangers and then stole him back to repeat the cycle over and again. He almost killed Kat. He almost killed me. He did kill me."

While her words were strong, her body trembled in his arms. He shook his head. "If he knows you're alive, he'll try again."

"Exactly."

"What?"

"If we draw him out and he acts, we can react. I've been studying the letters, the ones where she details the things he taught her. I'm more equipped to act." She tilted her head back to meet his gaze. A steady strength beat behind them. Despite her fear, her will to fight was growing strong again. "I will act to protect you all, but there's something else that needs to be done."

"There is?" Cole let her lead him to the table. While she rifled through the letters she'd organized in a box, he spun a chair around and straddled it. "What else is there?"

"The money she stole from him. I don't know why it bothers him as much as it does. It might be the value or that she bested him in some way."

"Or both."

"Exactly. I'm guessing it's a significant amount. Probably upwards of five thousand dollars." Her delicate fingers flipped through paper after paper, distracting him from her words as they always did until they snapped in front of his nose. "Cole."

"What?"

She set her hand on her hip and waited for him to meet her gaze. Her brows were set in a stern expression that didn't match the amused quirk of her lips. "Can you behave just a little longer and listen to me? Or have you forgotten you're the one that wanted to know what I was thinking. Perhaps I should continue to scheme on my own."

"Don't ya dare." Cole half-rose out of his seat. "You're not doing nothing on your own again, understood?"

A sexy flush spread across her cheeks and down her neck where it was cut off by the high collar and lace. He looked forward to opening that collar later. "You're doing it again."

"Sorry," He grumped and sat back in his chair. "What are you plotting?"

"I'm thinking you need to go after the money." She pushed a letter in front of him, and then resumed rifling. "I think that letter and this one both refer to it."

He took the second letter she'd handed him and looked between them with a frown. There were ridiculous nonsense poems at the top of each, followed by Clara's letters to Mike. On one letter it was just the poem. If that's what she thought, he believed her, he just didn't understand why. He was pretty sure she wasn't asking him to understand, though. "All right."

"Using these you need to go after the money."

"Continue."

"We have to use his own game against him. You can't look like you. I also think you should adjust your speech."

"Ain't nothing wrong with my talking."

"There's nothing wrong with how I speak." Jane sat next to him as she corrected him. The only thing that saved her from his volatile reaction was that she lacked the patronizing tone she used on others when she corrected them. "And use the name Charles Hodgkins."

"Why Charles?"

"Every instance of the name we've seen has been C. Hodgkins. All the letters you went after are addressed to C. I don't know if she ever used a full name, but in one of these poems she mentions a brother. Clara's six brothers were, in age order—James, George, Thomas, Charles, Nick, and Michael. There is only one brother with a C, and that's Dr. Charles Young."

It made sense. "So?"

"Once we've drawn him out, you'll go after the money. I'll go after him."

"Now wait just a blasted minute." He stood so fast she jumped back with a yelp. "What do you mean, you'll go after him? All by yourself? You insane?"

"I can't go with anyone. He'll kill them."

"He'll kill you."

"If I admit I know where the money is, that's less likely to happen." Her hand shook, but she set it on his. "I can draw him to where you are. He'll keep me alive until I've told him where and how to get his money. Once we get there, I'll no longer be alone. You'll be there."

"I don't like it." Not even a little bit. He didn't think they could trust that maniac to be predictable in any way. "It ain't a good enough plan."

"Then help me make it better."

"I don't know about this."

Her lip trembled, but otherwise she remained strong. His fingers twisted in the grip she had on his hand. "I won't sit and wait any longer. I don't want to be the prey. I want to be the predator. I haven't been able to figure out where he'd go, so drawing him out is the best way. Soon as the weather clears, I bet he'll be around again. There's still the matter of Jesse."

"You want to attack a man and trust Clara's ideas about him? She's the one that said she was safe with him."

"Those were her earlier letters. In the last two years she changed and let herself see him for what he was. Those are the insights I'm trusting."

"We should ask Mike, too."

"He'll try to get the rest of the Young brothers involved."

"Still not seeing how that's a problem." Cole knelt in front of her. "If they can help, then we should let them."

"You're afraid this plan will kill me, and Mike will fear the same. Why should I tell the family who finally believes Clara is dead that I'm alive and breathing if I'm only facing possible death again. Isn't that cruel?"

"At least tell me you'll think about it."

"I'll think about it."

It may well be doubted that human ingenuity can construct an enigma...which human ingenuity may not, by proper action, resolve.
-Edgar Allan Poe

Shortly after Cole opened the doors, a familiar scruffy figure darkened the doorway. Cole immediately set to pouring a beer for the man, but when he sat Hammy muttered, "Coffee, please."

"Coffee?" Cole snorted and turned. "Hammy, you can get coffee at Cora's. I'll get you a whisky if ya want something different than beer."

"Nah. Coffee. Still got some work to do." Hammy shrugged. "If I'm not drinkin', I wanna at least be in the saloon. 'Sides, I like the coffee better here than at Cora's."

"Hammy. You sober?" Cole leaned on the bar, eyeing the old man closer. He frowned and his nose wrinkled. "And you bathed. What's going on?"

"Lady Jane asked me to do something for her. Figured I'd better do a good job." Hammy kept his eyes on the bar, his ruddy cheeks growing darker the longer Cole stared at him. He cleared his throat and shrugged. "It's just that I ain't done yet."

"What did she get ya into?"

"Making sure them families got some place to stay what with all them storms we been having. She got the wood somehow, not sure where. I got my men working on a roof."

"Wait, in the northern settlement? I thought back in November you built that shelter for the families that lost their homes in the attacks."

"We did. The storms destroyed a few more houses. Paxton's roof clean fell in, near killed them too. So we're making a shelter for them and a couple other families."

"You're building houses in the middle of winter? You insane?"

"Nah. She ain't that dumb. We're just building another long cabin. It's gonna be tight, but it's a roof, and walls, and a fireplace." Hammy shrugged. "Only got enough for one layer, but she says it's better than the tents."

"She did all that?"

"Yeah. Got donations for the families too."

"Huh." All without telling him. Cole wondered when she'd set it up and how long she'd gotten Hammy to stop drinking. It didn't seem possible for Gilbert Hamm to live any length of time sober.

"So, uh, could I get that coffee? Need to get back to work. We probably don't got long before the next storm."

"Sure." Cole got the coffee, still pondering what he'd just learned. He leaned on the bar. "Jane got any other surprises in store I don't know about, Hammy? Any other good deeds?"

"You mean like getting Hank to give them half his furs for blankets? Don't know how she did it, neither. He got a good price outta Denver." Hammy took a sip, his lips pursed. "Wills said he got some extra cattle and game this year, but he didn't. Don't know how much he gave her in the end, but ain't no one out there cold or hungry."

"Anything else?"

"Uh, no."

"You don't sound so sure." Cole chuckled. "What else?"

"Why you asking me? Can't you ask her?"

"Don't worry, I will." When Graham got back, he would. He didn't mind Jane doing stuff like that. It was part of why he liked her, the way she did that stuff without looking for acknowledgment. For that matter, she could do whatever the hell she wanted. He just preferred to not hear about it from everyone else.

He'd rather it came from her, her voice, growing stronger every day, the husky whisper lingering in his ear, her soft lips brushing along his skin, the curve of her—damn it. Where was that lazy bastard Graham?

Maybe it was better he calmed down first. After all, this train of thought was probably what kept Jane from telling him things. Then again, who was he to complain? He had a sweet deal going, he wasn't about to muck it up.

Yeah, soon as Graham got in, he'd take an hour to see her, or two, maybe even three. Hell, the rest of the night would suit him fine. The saloon would be covered anyway. Somehow he doubted Jane would complain.

"I don't have to ask where your brain is." Graham's timing couldn't have been better. "Stop staring at the stairs. It won't make her come out looking for you."

"Actually, I was just gonna go on up."

"Aw, no conversating today? Here I was looking forward to your top-notch brilliance and wit." Graham laid the newspaper he'd carried in out on the bar with a snort. "No, wait. That's Jane. She's the brain. You're the…what is it you are, anyway?"

"Guess we need to start keepin' the door open again to remind you." Cole sneered. He didn't care for the insinuation none, though it was what everyone thought. "Least so far as anyone cares, that's all I'm good for anyway. Right?"

"Easy. Didn't mean nothing by it. What's got you wound so tight?"

"Nothing."

Graham gave Cole a sideways glance. Doubt furrowed his brows.

"Before I go up, what's the latest? Any problems?" Since Jane's return from the dead two months before, they'd been working the town in between storms to figure out who was likely to get her in trouble.

Once they had the information, they took steps to make sure nothing happened. Cole knew Jane would protest, so they'd done it secretly, with her bother Mike's help, to make sure she didn't have any other problems.

After a sigh, Graham turned back to the newspaper. "Nothing major. A few grumbling complaints. Mostly talk, no one's taking action. I think she's safe as she can be with that maniac still out there."

"Don't remind me." Before Graham could jump on that comment, Cole forged ahead. "Who was complaining? I thought we took care of most of them."

"A few old biddies that aren't good for anything but gossip anyhow. Chuck said if she's all for honesty, he'd just go ahead and wire the marshal."

"What stopped him?"

"The threat of losing out on some whores."

Cole nodded. Graham was a good one for threats when they were required. He knew what would make certain people stop, from threat of violence to other means. For that matter, they both agreed there were some things Jane didn't need to know.

Eventually he'd tell her what they'd had to do, once everything died down and it wasn't so new. When people got used to her being around. When the threat of her being taken away wasn't immediate.

Graham burst into laughter. The shock of the noise pulled Cole from his thoughts. "What the devil?"

"I told him to come up with something. This is too much." Graham slapped the bar, his face turning near purple in his laughter. "You wouldn't think it to look at the runt, but Rusty's got some spunk for sure."

"What in blazes are you talking about?" Cole snatched the newspaper from Graham. At first glance, he saw nothing of note. He frowned as he skimmed the page again. Then a headline near the bottom of the page caught his eye.

Town has new librarian. Library to reopen in one week.

"I told him not to report about Jane's non-demise. Didn't expect that." Graham's laughter boomed through the near-empty saloon again. Even Hammy turned his attention from his coffee in curiosity.

The paper said they had a new librarian instead of just saying it would be re-opened. With Jane returned to almost full health, she was eager to return to work. Reverend Greene had happily restored her job at the library. How was that funny?

The Town Council has named Jane Spencer to the position.

Graham's continued laughter grated on Cole's nerves. The article was cut and dry from what he could tell. Her credentials were listed, and Rusty said she'd been a librarian out east.

Mail-order bride, brought out West by Cole Mitchell.

"What?"

That was all it took to send Graham reeling again. The man was literally purple when he fell back on his ass, pointing at Cole.

"That little son of a bi—"

"*Ha.*" Graham slapped the floor before hopping back on his feet. "You're the one that wanted an alternate story. That's what you get for leaving it up to Rusty. You know he's still mad at you."

"I didn't do nothing to him."

"You sent him a whore at church."

"Well, he said I watered down my whiskey."

"You do." Graham snickered. "Wonder what Jane's going to say."

"I don't. She ain't gonna be happy." Least he didn't figure she would be. Marriage sure wasn't something they talked about. He couldn't tell her since she'd want to know why there was a lie being printed anyway. Who was he kidding? She'd find out soon enough. Not a day went by that she didn't read the paper.

"It's a small article. Sure no one will notice." Graham made a very poor showing of trying to stifle his laughter.

No time like the present, he supposed. After giving Graham a smack to the back of the head, he snatched the paper from the counter. "She will. She notices everything. Why does that ninny have to publish every damn story? This one wasn't worth nothing."

"Blame Rusty. Sure. Next time, don't upset the guy that makes the news."

"Shut up, Graham." Cole stormed upstairs to his room. For a minute he leaned on the doorframe, gathering up courage to show her. Of course, that was ridiculous. This wasn't his fault, and if it were, she'd see it had been necessary.

Right?

There was no other option, and stalling wouldn't help. With a sigh he pushed open the door, stopping just inside.

Jane stood in front of the dresser, a pencil in her hand. A book lay in front of her wide open, several sheets of paper spread out beside it. It was all rather normal, except it wasn't. It was the exact same place he'd left her three hours ago. She hadn't moved an inch.

"Jane?"

Nothing. That wouldn't do. He knew this was important to her, but it was just plum crazy to stand there staring at those papers all this time. After two steps he stopped behind her, the newspaper tossed aside. It could wait.

He slipped his arms around her waist and placed a kiss on her neck. "You ain't moved in three hours. You're making me doubt your sanity."

An absent wave of her hand in his face was her only response.

"Jane."

"I don't doubt it. I'm totally insane." No humor or a quirk of a smile showed.

"Know what you need?" He grinned when her head tilted to the side, giving him perfect access to her neck. He nibbled up along it, chuckling when she hummed with a bit of interest. "Distraction."

There wasn't a chance in hell he would let her object. The previous months had made him aware of every prime spot to make her respond, each sensitive crevice, and tiny dip of flesh. A brush of his lips here, a nibble there, one little suck here, and it would be over.

The pencil clattered to the desk, rolling across to the floor. He chuckled. He had her now. In one swift movement he pulled open the ties of her robe, grinning at the sigh that escaped her lips.

"Cole." Pleading. Perfect.

He spun her around and slid the light fabric from her shoulders. With one tug, his lips crushed hers and she came back with fire that blazed right through him. As always, even though she'd been in only a robe, there were too many layers of clothes between them. Before he could start pulling off her corset, she ripped at his shirt.

Every plan he'd had to talk ran off. The heat of her touch burned every thought away. All that was left were the two of them.

Clothing was torn and tossed aside. The bed was too far. She pushed him to the floor, overpowering him as only she could. He tugged her close, eager to feel her skin against his.

A moment later she jerked against his embrace. Now wasn't the time to back away, not with what had been started. He grunted and pulled her closer.

She gasped and hit his chest, scrambling out of his arms. "That's it."

Cole stared at the ceiling. Every nerve screamed, and his mind was a blurry haze of unfinished passion. Confusion sank in. With the exception of when she was really mad, she'd never left him unsatisfied. Yet here he was, untouched, and for the moment, completely ignored. What the hell?

"Jane." It was little more than a growl, and all he could manage.

"It wasn't the words. It was the letters. I can't believe I didn't see it before." The pencil scratched against paper. "It's so clear."

"What the hell are you talking about?" She couldn't be serious. She'd pushed him away for that? He knew it was important, but it couldn't have waited?

"Just a few minutes."

"You're kidding." The lack of response spoke volumes. Frustration blinded him as much as the desire had a few minutes before. "I was right. You're a crazy bitch."

There was still no sound but her writing. He got to his feet and grabbed a fresh shirt, fixing his half-opened pants.

With one last look at her he stormed from the room.

She pushed him away? Really? He put up with a lot from her because she was amazing, but when she stopped being that way he'd have to move on. Or would he?

Damn her. She had him trapped, even if he'd never admit it to anyone. He wasn't just trapped—he was trapped willingly. This frustration would pass. They all did. Then things would be even better than they would have been this time.

"Problem?" Graham snickered before he got behind the bar. "Girl leave you high and dry?"

"I don't got a problem." Cole wasn't about to admit it to Graham or anyone for that matter. "Just getting a drink."

"You got whiskey in your room. What's the matter? She don't like you making sure no one reports her?" Graham shrugged. "Crazy lady. She should just let it go already. There's no other way she's going to live."

"Ya don't know nothing." Cole took a swig of whiskey. He'd had enough of being the brunt of Graham's digs. "Besides, you're one to talk. Your future bride don't want you touching her for even a kiss. Your Chinawoman's gonna have to move soon since Becky's got most everyone going elsewhere for their wash."

"That's not right."

"So whatever my problem is, it's a damn sight better than yours." Cole grabbed another bottle of whiskey and some clean glasses. Graham's frustrated frown was enough to brighten his day. Next he had to get through to Jane, again.

When he entered the room, Jane spun to meet him. A smile lit up her face brighter than he'd seen in a long time. He forgot his frustrations. "What?"

"Alan Bingham. March 24th 1834. Atlanta."

"This better be a damn good thing. Otherwise, what you just did—"

"It's his name, birthdate, and birthplace. It's *him.*"

Before he could react, she'd launched herself at him with enough force to knock him into the door. The bottle of whiskey and glasses crashed to the floor. As her mouth assaulted his, he buried her fingers in her hair. Gripping it tight, he yanked her back and met her eyes. "I still say it coulda waited."

"Let me make it up to you." She grinned, her hands slipped down his chest and stomach. Within seconds his eyes rolled back from her enthusiastic touch. Her lips brushed along his neck before she grabbed his shirt and pulled him back to the bed. "By the time I'm through, you'll be as happy as I am."

He grunted when she shoved him down onto the bed, his arms going around her the moment she stretched out on top of him. "I damn well better be."

"Oh…you will…"

* * * *

December 18, 1870

Young love, so true and deep;
A fount of pride and jealousy.
Can rip a soul, split right in two;
Fundamental duplicity
Betrayal hath to light that spark
A temperamental flame
Burns with searing heat a soul
It now seals its claim
War builds on such wounds
Scars deepen, never heal
What little feeling left is lost

None that are so real
Cruelties felt are learned and turned
Returning to the source
The cycle moves, turning on another
No regret, no remorse
The burning fire, the searing pain
Singe deeper with every turn
The pain is passed driven deep within
To a soul that cannot learn.
Help. God give me strength. I never knew.

All persons are puzzles until at last we find in some word or act the key to the man, to the woman; straightaway their past words and actions lie in light before us.
-Ralph Waldo Emerson

July 10, 1870

Michael,
Dearest Michael.
Remember the day,
A simple one of play,
Beneath the stormy sky,
Rather uninviting,
A streak of burning lightning,
Massacred the neighbor's dog,
Simple really, but yet so true.
The most Central of facts is that it really is not true. I must State emphatically that this is so. I am not a Lunatic; I assert that I just play. For only an Idiot would believe that lightning massacred a dog—it was merely Epileptic. The dog sought Asylum in a barn and the lightning never touched him.

"Like I said, I couldn't make sense of some of them." Cole kept a possessive arm across the back of Jane's chair. Despite the appearance of looking over her shoulder at the puzzle of a letter, he glared across the table.

Annoyed, Jane gave him a sharp jab to the ribs with her elbow. She offered a subtle shake of her head in annoyance before turning away from him. Instead, she turned her attention to the man he glared at. "Did I always enjoy puzzles?"

"You sent me all over the countryside one Saturday with a treasure map. It took me near four hours to get it all figured and find you. My reward was a picnic." David chuckled. "So yes, I'd say you did."

"Well right now puzzles annoy me. Clara ruined what could have been good fun." Jane rubbed at her tender throat. Even though she had healed well over the course of the months, and sounded almost human again, the pain lingered. Daisy had made the carefully delicate suggestion that it was likely mostly in her head, but who could blame her for that?

"All that looks like gibberish anyhow." Cole frowned and tapped the paper with the knuckle of his forefinger. "You wouldn't think nothing of it if you hadn't seen that letter saying there were puzzles in some of them."

"But I did see that letter, and I know without a doubt that this is a puzzle." Jane bit her lip as she studied the paper in front of her again. Memorized or not, she just knew she was missing something right in front of her. "It's right there, just like it was in the Poe book."

Cole grumbled, "You're thinking too much. Spend day in and day out with them damn letters anymore."

"Jealous?" David leaned back and took a long sip of his coffee. A wicked grin crossed his lips. Even though he was, by all accounts, happy and well moved on from his marriage to Jane so he might court the young widow Lee Dynan, David spent a fair amount of time needling Cole. Jane was certain it was all in good fun, but Cole was far more temperamental about it since Major Webb had left town.

"David," Jane warned gently.

Instead, David grinned broader. "When Jane's spending time with Clara, she isn't spending it with you."

"Least she makes time with me. Ain't done much but put you down since you got to town. So much for *true love*." The derision in Cole's voice could have sliced leather like a hot knife through butter.

Jane smacked his leg, unwilling to let things get any worse. Cole had no reason to be jealous of David, and he knew it. She made that point clear on a regular basis. "Stop it. Both of you. I swear you would think I was at the table with Jesse and Isaac the way you two are bickering. Children. All of you."

Before they could reply, they were interrupted by the familiar voice of Michael. "I think it's a prime location. It's part of what the town wants to use to draw visitors. The view is perfect. I couldn't be more pleased." Michael was all smiles as he leaned down to kiss Jane on the cheek. He nodded to both the men as he straightened.

Rusty walked close behind him, so engrossed in writing on his pad he bumped into Michael at the sudden stop. "Oh. Sorry. I was trying to get all of that down."

"Why are you talking up the press?" Jane eyed Michael's too-cheerful visage for a moment. "And what is this about a perfect view? Are you bragging about your future hotel again? People will grow tired of your bluster if you keep it up."

"My plans, Jane. It is ridiculous to expect people to visit this town once the mines go dry. There has to be something else for them to come see. Something else to do besides make fool attempts to pan for gold scraps." Michael leaned forward; a wicked smirk and a wink crossed his features. "There has to be more than two dingy little hotels."

"Who you calling dingy?" Cole grinned and leaned back. "I think it's comfy."

"Of course *you* do." Michael tapped Rusty's pad. "I have plans already drawn up for the hotel and resort, and expect to start construction as soon as the snow is gone. All will be built with as little damage to the natural beauty of the land as possible. I want it to be true in nature."

"With a real Indian guide on staff to help show people why Colorado's so great." David sat straighter and nodded with a smile. "Black Moon already agreed."

"Indian guide?" Jane leaned away, her nose wrinkling with a shudder. Cole's arm around her shoulder eased some of the nerves that rattled. "You don't honestly think that will be appealing?"

"Actually, it will. To be honest, I'm surprise Black Moon agreed. He knows that they'll all look at him like one of those *tamed savages*." Michael sighed and shook his head. "You know how those unfamiliar with the territories talk. It's quite a draw to see a real *savage* in its natural setting."

"That's vile." Even though she didn't care much for Indians, seeing them as little more than a freak show turned her stomach.

"Sure is." Michael chuckled. When he was brought a cup of tea, he accepted it gratefully before taking a big sip. "Unfortunately, it's also the way things are. I think we are all well aware that society is not all it's touted to be."

"How true." Jane couldn't stop herself. The swell of conversation was losing its interest and she found her gaze drawn back to the letter in her hands. The last thing she wanted to be doing was talking about how an Indian could possibly be beneficial. She had for worse things in her life to worry about.

"Stop looking at it. It's not helping." Cole tried to slip the paper away.

Panic coursed through her like a jolt of lightning. "No! Wait."

"What is it?" Michael turned his attention to the letter.

"Nothing." Jane tried to redirect his attention. He'd been excited enough over the hotel when he'd arrived it could be a good diversion. "So you're starting your new hotel in the spring? You make it sound far off, but March is in a week?"

Mike ignored her and reached for the paper. "What is that?"

"This is nothing." Jane pulled it close. She slipped her hands over the words so he couldn't see them. "You've decided to go through with a new place instead of keeping the Silver Saddle as a hotel?"

"There are only two hotels in town. One that barely calls itself one."

A low snort came from Cole. "Watch it."

"Along with the Silver Saddle, which has been closed since Guy's death." Michael's eyes never left the sheet of paper Jane guarded.

"You mean murder," Jane corrected under her breath.

"Right," Michael agreed. He leaned on the table, grinning broadly. "I'm building something more suited for me, and for the sort of clientele this town needs to draw. There'll be no whores, no gambling."

"You gamble." Cole's brow popped up. "So why not have it?"

"Variety. You can keep the whores." Michael laughed when Jane cleared her throat and glared at him. "For his customers, of course. And, you can keep the gambling as well. My new hotel is going to be more of a resort, a health resort. A good place for people to come for escape and recuperation."

"I think it is utterly pretentious." Jane knit her brows together. The plans didn't make any sense from her point of view. Michael was many things, but pretentious wasn't one of them. Touting this new hotel to Rusty, he'd sounded the height of pretention. "And annoying. You are not high-brow."

"Pretentious ploys bring societal money. This town could use some. Might as well give the wealthy a place to spend their money in this fine town." Michael shrugged. "I don't have any hot springs, but I do have a doctor on staff to assist in such matters. Daisy has agreed to stay on part time at the new hotel."

"Part time?" Cole sat straighter. "Why only part time?"

"The Silver Saddle will continue its transformation into an actual clinic, or rather a small hospital suitable for the needs of this town. Perhaps once the transformation is complete we'll bring in another doctor."

"It's going to take a lot of work to pull the gild off of that place to turn it into something worth recuperating in." Jane laughed and relaxed against Cole. "After months of work it's still obscene. I would think you would have to tear the whole inside out to make it come together into something decent."

"You're probably right." Michael chuckled. Before she could react, he snatched the paper out from under her relaxed hands. "So what exactly is this?"

"Michael, give that back."

"It's addressed to me." Mike frowned, studying the paper intently. "Jane, what is this?"

"It's just one of Clara's letters. Give it back." Jane tried to grab it away, but he pulled it out of her reach. She groaned at the loss, a sick urge to see the words again welling. Her exacting memory meant nothing when she could see the words before her. "Please."

Mike's brow furrowed. "This is one of the letters? No wonder she ended up in an asylum."

Cole tried to cover his laughter, but his body shook behind Jane's. "I tried to tell her that. There ain't no reasoning with her. She's convinced Clara meant it when she said there were puzzles in them letters."

"A puzzle?" Michael sat slowly, intent on the letter before him. He rested his chin in his free hand. "Such a thing is certainly possible. Clarabelle excelled at such things. She truly enjoyed a good mind teasing puzzle."

"Just give it back." Jane slapped the table. This was ridiculous. She hated to be ignored, and now that she had her voice back she'd be damned if she allowed it. "I can figure it out just fine, thank you."

"Did it ever occur to you to ask me? After all, this letter is addressed to me, as all of them are according to Cole. Did you ever think that Clara wrote it with the idea that I would be able to solve such puzzles?" Mike slammed the paper on the table. Fury like she'd never seen in him lit his eyes. "It wouldn't kill you to ask for help."

"I can figure this out." Jane rose, leaning toward him. "All on my own. I do have brains, you know. I'm the one that needs to make sure—"

"I. I. I. That's all you can say. Did you forget that Clara did the same damn thing to the point of her own destruction? She didn't trust David or me or *anyone* to help. Look where it got her. Where it got you. Swinging at the end of a rope." Michael threw the sheet of paper back at her so quick she flinched.

She couldn't have caught it if she'd tried. Her limbs wouldn't respond to commands. Michael's words echoed through her head until it was numb, and her whole body followed suit. A cold chill raced through her limbs and she sank back into her chair.

Damn him for making such a valid point. Sometimes it didn't help having so many people pointing out her faults. Asking for honesty didn't mean it was always fun.

"Jane?" Cole's hand ran along her back, sending warmth back into her soul. "You still alive?"

"I'm sorry." Jane sighed. "I just thought I'd gotten you into enough trouble and caused enough pain. I thought if I could handle it and make it right, then perhaps…"

"The way to make it right is to take the help this time instead of pushing everyone away." Michael took her hand in his. A crooked smile erased any hint of anger. "Don't make the same mistakes Clara did. Besides, you've already got that letter, all of the letters, memorized. Why not let me have a look?"

"Go ahead, Mike. Think I'm gonna take Jane home." Cole stood, tugging on her arm. "We'll get you the other letters later."

"Good. I'd like to read them. All of them." Michael gave Jane's hand another squeeze before he bent over to pick up the paper.

Jane attempted a smile, nodding toward David. "Tell Jesse I'll see him tomorrow. Weather permitting, as usual."

"Will do. Careful getting back. The snow's starting to get thick again." David smiled, rising with his coffee.

Cole's hand tightened around her waist, and he propelled her toward the door. "We'll get the letters together tomorrow. Ain't no need to rush. Mike's right, you got them all in that head of yours anyhow. Not even being in an asylum stopped you from rememberin' everything you ever read."

"Remembering and understanding are apparently two very different things." Jane couldn't stop the sinking of her voice. Perhaps she was just tired. It was a constant with her brain trying to get answers that would help them find Alan before he tried to take away everything again.

"You're just tired. Ain't gonna get stopped by nothing when time comes you figure it out. We'll get him. He'll pay."

"How can you be sure?"

"If you can come back from the dead twice, nothing's gonna stop you from getting back at the bastard that put you there twice." Cole stopped and stood nose to nose with her.

Ignoring the flow of people around them with curious looks, and the snowflakes fluttering down on them, his lips closed over hers. A tender caress unlike their usual public displays warmed them both against the lingering chill of March.

By the time Michael's call reached their ears Cole was just releasing her from the embrace. Winded and a bit lightheaded, Jane leaned against Cole. She paid no heed the increasing loud shout from Michael. "You might just have me convinced."

"Might?"

"I think I need a little more convincing."

"Right here?"

"Ja-ane." A finger tapped her shoulder to force her attention to Michael. His brow furrowed in clear frustration, which conflicted with the scary bright smile he wore. "I thought you wanted the answer to this particular riddle."

"Oh, it'll come to me." She waved him off, content to keep her focus on Cole.

"Clara Louise Young."

"Go jump off a cliff, Mike. We're busy."

"If I wait until you're *un*busy, we'll never have this discussion." His arm broached the narrow space between her and Cole, hard enough to push her back. "It's an asylum, Jane, a different one than the one Clara was in."

"A what?" The physical separation cleared her head a little, but she still didn't unlock her gaze from Cole's. "That's not surprising, Michael."

"And a doctor's name."

An asylum. The tingle of Cole's kiss started to fade. A doctor's name? Jane blinked away the last whispers of passion, replaying the words in her head. "Doctor's name? Asylum?"

"Refocus on the poem. The first letter of every line." Just to prove the point, Mike held the paper right in front of her face.

"M-D-R-A-B…" Jane snatched the paper from his hands. Cole's reappearing touch relaxed her enough so she didn't start trembling. A quiver of her knees succeeded in making her lean against him. "MD? Doctor? Doctor R. Abrams."

"That's all it was? First letters?" Cole snorted. "How 'bout that."

"I couldn't see the forest for the trees." Jane's hand lifted to her lips. "Oh. Michael. The rest of the letter!"

"You see it too?" Michael looked as though his face might split in two. His eyes gleamed with humor. "Years of solving Clara's riddles. It took me a few minutes, but I got it."

"Got what?" Cole's chin rested on her shoulder. "What are the two of you all excited about?"

"There are a handful of words capitalized in the middle of a sentence. They have no reason to be. Central. State. Lunatic."

"Idiot." Cole nodded. "I see them."

"Dr. R. Abrams of the Central State Lunatic, Idiot, and Epileptic Asylum." Jane smacked the paper with the back of her hand. "Right there. How could I have missed it?"

"I'm going to let Tommy know. He can find out more information." Michael slipped the paper from her fingers. "Won't take any time."

"No." Jane grabbed his hand before he could start yelling. "Please. You told them I was dead. You already have him looking without any of the information we've learned. I know you want this done. We all do."

"Tommy can get us the information we're lacking. Trust me." Michael stepped closer. "It's the best way."

"But it's not the only way. I don't want to reopen that wound if we don't have to." Jane took a deep breath. "I learned my lesson. I don't want to hide from them forever. I just don't think this is the way. I could still end up dead in the end and never have remembered them."

"Jane."

"Please. Let's have Daisy, who is a doctor and knows what to ask contact Doctor Abrams. See if we can't get the information that way."

Michael's lips pursed, his gaze focused on the task of folding the paper in his hands with intense precision. Almost as if avoiding her, he glared at the letter. "You have to tell them sometime, Jane."

"If this does not work, you have my permission to call in the cavalry."

"Don't think I won't."

"I wouldn't expect any less." Jane smiled, "We will take care of Alan. In the end, he'll get what's coming to him. Once it is settled, and I am really free, you can tell whomever you want. I promise."

"I'm holding you to that."

*Woman's influence is powerful,
especially when she wants something.
—Josh Billings*

The saloon sat near lifeless.

Thunder rumbled all around, and the constant patter of rain drowned what little conversation tried to spring to life in the saloon. Unlike the previous year's drought, for weeks it had rained. The constant wet, muddy state drove away business and much of the sense of life the town carried.

Whores lounged by the door, ready to leap to life and entice any man that might pass, but none did. The ceaseless downpour kept them away. Inside the saloon a handful of men nursed their liquor while they draped lazily on the tables.

Laughter didn't breach the endless miserable gray skies and rain that had besieged the town for ten days straight. Some mines were flooded and closed, and the streets were pure water and suctioning mud. Familiar faces that had always been friendly and playful moped into their mugs.

In the back of the room sat one man less familiar to her. His arrival in town weeks ago had concerned her, especially when he started visiting the bar often. She'd surreptitiously studied his features many times over, but no sign of the three scars that lined the cheek of her nemesis, Alan, existed on this stranger. Plus, the man's eyes were blue, unlike Alan's brown eyes. She doubted that, evil though he might be, Alan had figured out how to change the color of his eyes.

Still, this new man's presence unsettled her. An instinct in her gut urged her to recognize him much in the same way she'd first sensed she should recognize Alan. The main difference being that this time the stranger didn't frighten her. He kept mostly to himself, but always seemed to be observing. Still, he'd get bawdy and jovial with miners and proper folk alike. Rumor had it that he was looking to establish a new bank in town.

"Slow day." David walked into the near-empty saloon and right up to the bar.

Jane finished wiping down the glass in her hand. She set it down with care in an effort to keep her annoyance well covered. "The rain is part of the problem."

"Part?" David hitched his leg over the stool and took a seat. "What else is there?"

"If you're sitting, you're drinking. What'll it be?"

"If I have to drink, I'll take coffee, but you're the one who asked me to come and specifically said to not bring Lee, even though she doesn't like to come in the saloon. What's going on?"

Jane took her time pouring his coffee and pouring a second cup for herself. She sighed and rested her cheek on her hand, staring across the bar. "Absolutely nothing."

"You were just bored?" His low chuckle grated on her nerves. "Usually you don't got a problem with that. Where's Cole?"

"Pouting."

"Oh?"

This wouldn't do. She couldn't give David any ammunition against Cole. Her attempt to make the two of them get along had stalled, and she couldn't add fuel to their bickering fire. Then again, her annoyance with Cole's decision to choose their current point of argument as place to be stubborn was winning out. "Business has been down, quite a bit."

"Not surprising. Winter. The rains."

"I suggested that we get some entertainment in here. It would draw in people."

David's lips pursed together, his eyes darted to the girls lounging near the doors. "I thought entertainment was already provided."

"Of course, you would. You're a man." Jane rolled her eyes, grabbing her mug and holding it closer. "I meant real entertainment, like a piano."

"And Cole said?"

"To put it mildly, I was told it would never happen."

"Interesting. Won't budge, eh?"

"I haven't been able to change his mind, even with my best argument." Boy had she tried every means at her disposal. Cole just wouldn't budge. David's laughter broke through her angry thoughts, and she straightened. He was having too much fun. Time to change the subject. "Has Mike heard anything?"

Once again a chuckle reached her ears, but before she glared, he spoke through his own laughter. "Not since the last telegram about a week ago. Tommy says getting the records is tougher than he thought it would be."

After Daisy hadn't been able to get anything due to the gentleman refusing to believe a woman doctor dared contact him, Jane allowed Mike to tell Tommy to try. She'd still refused to let Mike tell any of the Youngs she was alive.

"I don't think it will help much even if we find any information. Once again, those records are the past. We need to find Alan now."

"We will."

"Pffft." She dropped her head to the counter. Despite all the success they'd had deciphering her letters, they were still no closer to figuring out how to find the man. Until they did, she wasn't sure she'd ever feel safe or free. Daily she woke to the feel of the shackles on her wrist, the noose on her neck.

"Tell me the truth."

The words were soft and kind. If she were pressed, she'd say they sounded sad. For that reason alone, she didn't dare lift her head. "I always do."

"How often do you go to see him?"

Further detail wasn't needed. She knew exactly what he meant, Jesse. Despite her protests, she felt drawn to him. From the minute she'd embraced him as her child, she hadn't been able to stay away. "I don't know."

"Jane." The warmth of his hand surrounded hers. "Nothing to be ashamed of."

"There's plenty to be ashamed of." His hand hadn't moved, so she studied it where it lay on hers. Rough, callused, and strong, soft, caring, and warm, the contradiction of David wrapped into one appendage. "Jesse is one thing I'd never be ashamed of. I really don't know. Once, twice a week when weather permits."

"You've been teaching him?"

"Of course not." The warmth of his hand became scorching heat, and she jerked away. She turned to the mirror behind the bar to smooth out her hair, but found him staring back at her in it. "That's just silly."

"Jane, you're no good at lying."

"All right. I have been teaching him. Just a little. He's really quite smart." She returned to the counter to refill his coffee cup. "I just want to be sure that when he actually starts school he's not behind. He's been behind more than enough already."

"You know what you're doing, don't you?" His grin annoyed her. For once he was right and wasn't worried about throwing it in her face.

She pursed her lips together and moved the coffee pot closer to him. "Pouring hot coffee in your lap if you continue."

"All right, all right." He lifted his hands in surrender and scooted the stool back a few inches. "I get it. I won't say anything."

"Good."

"But if I did."

"You know he's quick. I dare say he learned to read faster than you."

"Clever." Despite the down turned lips, his eyes twinkled with laughter he couldn't hide long. "You're very funny."

"'One never needs their humor as much as when they argue with a fool'." She pursed her lips to hold back the laughter.

David sputtered, trying to come back with something. After she released a giggle, all hope was lost. "You're terrible."

"I know." She patted his hand before wiping at a tear. "Oh, goodness. I've been waiting to use that one for weeks. Linh said it once, and I thought it was rather perfect."

David shook his head, trying to push back laughter when Cole stormed into the saloon. The smile disappeared from David's face when Cole moved behind the counter. "Cole."

Cole only grunted, grabbing a bottle of whiskey. After a swig he directed his glare at Jane.

"Don't look at me. I've been having the girls go outside when the rain slows a bit. No one is biting. If I leave them out too long, they'll get sick and be no good to you." Jane, for her part, didn't even flinch when he threw a shot glass in frustration. "Good. Let's make more loss of income while we're slow."

"Don't, Janey." Cole grabbed another glass and a towel, wiping his soaked hair while crossing the floor. "Figure something out."

"Yes, sir." Jane mock saluted him, sticking her tongue out when he turned his back. She chose to ignore David's curious stare, until the door slammed behind Cole. "I've told him what he should do. He won't listen."

"He's not happy."

"Business is down. We're still out money from Graham's fit last year. Grumpy is a state of being for him these days."

"Fun for you."

"Actually it is. I get to cheer him up." At his groan, she flashed her teeth with a wink. "I speak the truth."

"Don't mean I always want to hear it." He rubbed his hand over his face. "I hate to change the subject."

"No, that's what you want to do."

"Why did you want to see me?"

"Oh. Right." To delay a moment longer, she took a long drink of coffee. She set the cup down, pulling her lip between her teeth. "I know it's crowded at Cora's."

"We're managing. Getting tougher with all the books you keep stuffin' into Jesse and Isaac's room."

"That's the thing. There shouldn't be a problem with that. You shouldn't have to sleep in the jail while he's crowded into a room with Isaac." Gathering up her courage to take the step she was about to, she exhaled some of the nervous energy. "I told you before my hanging I wanted you to have the homestead."

"You didn't die, so it doesn't matter."

"Yes, it does. I want you to take it."

"What? No."

"Yes. I have no need for it." That was it, she'd just committed to living at the saloon with Cole. She'd been debating for weeks over whether or not to make it official. If she did she'd have no out. It scared and exhilarated her. "It will give you both room and keep you close to town. It's silly for it to sit empty. I don't live there any longer, neither does Mike. Please. I want you to have it."

"I can't take it."

"There's no mortgage. Jesse deserves a home. A real home. Please. Let me do this for him. For you."

"I don't know."

"Just think about it." Jane grabbed his hand, squeezing tight. "Please."

"I'll think about it."

"Good. Now go away. I have some cheering up to do." She grinned at his groan, taking off her apron with a wink. "Or you could stay."

"No, no, I'm good."

Jane waggled her fingers at him in a form of goodbye before heading toward the stairs. She directed Iris to head behind the bar and gathered her skirts to rush up the steps.

Truth was, Cole had a lot to be grumpy about, including the thought they might need to be separated again for a few days. Or the fact her plan to try to get Alan caught involved using live bait.

Jane pushed open the door and slipped into the room quietly as she could. He lay on his stomach, whiskey bottle on the floor near his hand. One boot was off and his shirt was unbuttoned and untucked from his trousers. She figured he hadn't cared to finish either job in his snit of anger. He didn't move or make a sound when she approached.

Once she'd moved the bottle to the nightstand, she straddled him. The moment she started to remove his shirt, he came to life. Jane bit her lip to hide the smile when he helped her remove his shirt, only to remain face down.

Her fingers moved along his back, gently kneading his muscles. She remained silent until he relaxed. "Focusing on the saloon won't—"

Grumbling something into the pillow, Cole tensed again.

"Look at me when you yell at me." She laughed when he shook his head, and his shoulders wiggled under her hands.

"Not yelling. Work," he grunted when he turned his head to the side.

"Fine. Then don't yell at me." She kneaded his shoulders again, fighting the nerves keeping her silent. The breath she'd been holding blew out in release. "I offered David the homestead."

"Thought ya didn't wanna do that."

"I changed my mind."

"So there's no place to run?"

"If David accepts my offer, no. This is my home."

"You really giving up your house?"

Her hands grew still when he shifted beneath her again before turning over to face her. She shrugged. "No reason for it to sit empty."

"Guess not."

"Unless you're bored with me."

"Definitely not."

She fell forward when he pressed his hands into her back, her hands landing on either side of his head. She shifted against him. "You're not?"

A low groan was her only response.

"Well, when you do get bored with me, I can move back there into the second bedroom or stay with Kat for a while. Until then, or he and Lee get close enough to consider marriage, he'll have to be alone as far as adult company goes…"

"He's gonna be alone a long time."

A man that studieth revenge keeps his own wounds green.
—Francis Bacon, Sr

April 1868

You must be thoroughly ashamed of me by now. I think back on what I should have done and am ashamed myself. I look forward and to the present. The opportunities are there, why do I not take them? Why don't I make my escape and right my wrongs?

Because unlike my own unfortunate state—he knows from whence I come and where I would return. The harm to those I love beyond the harm I've already caused could be immeasurable. He knows that though I play the part, I long for the home of my heart, the heart he can no longer touch. Every time my eyes wander, the ones I love are at risk. If I could just forget the ties as I had hoped all along, perhaps you would all be safe.

The latest installment of the novel she'd been reading since she awoke held Jane's attention so fiercely that she closed the library door one-handed. Once the lock clicked into place she tucked the key into her reticule and stepped back.

The solid wall that stopped her startled her so much she shrieked and her book toppled to the ground. Her hands shook as they flew to cover her racing heart. She spun around. "Michael Jacob Young! What in blazes are you doing? You about scared me back into the grave."

Michael didn't move a muscle, didn't react.

In a moment, Jane's racing heart stilled. In the months she'd known him, she'd never seen her brother look like this. Ever. His features were pale, his normally bright eyes dull and hollow. It shook her to the core. "Michael? What's wrong?"

"If you remember anything. Anything at *all*, tell me. Tell me now. I need to know. I need Clara. I need my sister."

Jane fought against her sudden dry mouth, only able to shake her head at first. "I'm sorry, Mike. I don't. There's nothing."

"I need Clara." Just a whisper escaped, but the tension seeped out of every line in his face. His shoulders sagged and a wad of paper fell from his fist as he sank to his knees on the boards of the porch.

"What has happened?"

"George."

"George?"

"Our brother…George…killed."

Silence.

Neither of them spoke. She found herself at a loss for words for the first time in her conscious memory. Mike didn't seem able to say anything else.

Part of her was pulled to comfort him, but the other felt too guilty to move. What if this was her fault, too? The wad of paper he'd dropped seemed safer so she grabbed it. The penmanship on the crumpled letter might have been written in her own hand the script held such similarity.

Scanning the letter, she found the important paragraph quickly.

The constable is unsure as to how or why. No horses were stolen. He had little of value besides those. It was senseless and cruel. By the time you have received this we will have already had the burial. You have a business to run, and it is a very long trip.

The lump in her throat was unmovable, but her body wasn't. After just two steps closer to him, Mike leaned back against her. Just as she lowered the letter to speak, another paragraph caught her eye.

James is still very ill. Every time he falls ill, he returns again to the hospital. Charlie is constantly searching for the cause, but never finds it. He is able to get him well only to fall ill again. We have replaced all food and grain, and even checked the well. The source is a mystery.

"Mike." Barely a croak of a voice managed to edge out over the lump in her throat. Her gut told her it was Alan. She couldn't bring herself to say it aloud. "Oh, Mike."

She dropped down to her knees beside him and was surprised by the tight hold he had on her within moments. Her eyes closed as she responded in kind, letting him cling to the memory of who she'd been. Hoping against hope that it would give him the comfort she didn't know how to deliver.

"I'm so sorry," was all she could manage, her hand running along his back in a vain attempt at comfort. Her heart broke with his loss, wishing more than ever that she could share in it with him.

When his hold grew lax, she pulled back. She brushed aside a stray hair, pretending she hadn't seen the tear she'd also wiped away. "Will you ever forgive me?"

"He did this, not you. I forgave you a long time ago. I just wish that for one day you could be Clara and tell me how to handle this and what to tell Ma."

She picked up his hat and set it back on his head. "We should tell her the truth."

"What?" Michael looked up at her in surprise, "Are you serious?"

"It's not fair for you to be the one to handle it."

"Before…or after?" Their plan to capture Alan was in place, and since she knew where he was, it was time to put it into action.

"I don't know. There isn't much time. Even less now that we know where he is." This wasn't how she'd wanted to figure it out, with more death, more pain, and loss that wasn't hers. "What do you think?"

"After, so we aren't pressed for time, and we have more reason for it to work."

Jane hugged him tightly. "There's reason enough, but if you think that's what we should do, we will."

He nodded. "I think so. Besides, looking at it logically, there's also no reason to let them know the truth only to face the possibility of another loss."

"Logic seems to be our foe as well as our constant companion." She grabbed her book. Once the letter was safely inside it, she rose.

He took hold of her hand when he stood. "I think you're right. Logic is what made Ma send a letter instead of a telegram which would get me on the first train out of here."

She wrapped her arm around his waist and started down the street. "Let's get some food in you, and you should rest. Then we'll figure out what to write in your return letter. All right?"

Mike's nod was dazed, his eyes still vacant and distant. Somehow, she got him all the way to Cora's. There the distraction of Isaac, Jesse, and Cindy pulled him out of the darkness for a while.

Jane kept a concerned eye on him, for even as he smiled he remained pale-faced with shock. When Daisy arrived, Jane pulled her aside. "I have a favor to ask."

"A favor? Of me?" Daisy's brow furrowed. "Are you still ill?"

"No."

"Do you need the whore's tea?"

"What? No." Jane gasped at the suggestion that not only was she pregnant, but that she wanted to be rid of it. "How could you even ask?"

"Just wanted to be sure. I know last time things went poorly." Daisy shrugged. "Besides, what else would you want me for?"

"It's about Mike."

Daisy cleared her throat and looked at the floor. She fiddled with a lock of hair. "What does that have to do with me?"

"He's hurting." Jane set her hand on Daisy's arm. "I know you care for him, and I want to make sure he's being taken care of when I go to tell Cole what's happened."

"What's happened?" Daisy's concern apparently overran her embarrassment, as she met Jane's gaze dead on.

"He received a letter from his mother. One of the Young brothers, George, was murdered, and they don't know who's done it or why."

"Alan is going after your family?"

"Yes, much as Clara suspected he would, as he often threatened her with." Jane bit her lip and turned her gaze back to her brother. "He's distraught. I told him I'd help him compose a letter to his mother, but first I need to talk to Cole."

"I'll take care of Mike. I'll get him back to the clinic and resting. We'll wait for you there."

"Thank you, Daisy."

"It's no trouble. I want to help how I can."

After one more long embrace with Mike, she rushed back through town.

By the time she got to the bar, she was breathless. Cole's lips twitched in amusement, "Told ya. Stop lacing so tight."

"Then you," Jane took as deep a breath as she could, "would miss the fun of undoing the tight laces."

"Maybe."

"He's in Buffalo."

Cole froze. The moment of relaxation fled, the harsh lines returned to his forehead. "How d'you know?"

"He's killing Clara's family. He's killed George, and I think he's poisoning James."

"Could be a ploy. Maybe he ain't there."

"I don't think so." Jane took a deep breath, picking at the edge of the bar. "The poison is too frequent. He's trying to draw me out, just like I was hoping to do for him."

"You got what you wanted. Now it's time to give him what he wants."

"No, what he deserves."

*Every tomorrow has two handles.
We can take hold of it with the handle of
anxiety or the handle of faith.
-Henry Ward Beecher*

"Cole." Katherine stopped short in the middle of the hall. "What are you doing here? I was just about to have tea."

"With Jane?" Cole gripped the doorknob, every angle of the crystal knob dug into his flesh at her nod. "She told me to pick her up here."

"Pick her up? She hasn't been here." Color flooded her cheeks. "She did this on purpose. What was she thinking?"

"I'm gonna kill her."

"No, you won't."

"No, I won't. I'll make her suffer."

A small face peeked out from behind Kat's skirt before disappearing again. Kat cleared her throat. "Well then, I guess you should go find her."

"If I do, I'll be the one suffering. I know why she did this."

"You don't have to. You've never had to. Don't make her force you." The rose of her cheeks almost matched her hair. "You can go. That would be just fine."

"It ain't that I don't want to. Just don't know how."

Katherine exhaled slowly. "There is no *how*, Cole. Jane didn't know *how* either. In fact, she was rather opposed. It didn't stop her."

"Seems silly. I'm leaving in a few days."

The face poked out from the other side of Kat's skirt and the wide, blue eyes wouldn't let him shirk away. "Where you going? Is it far? Is it 'nudder country?"

"No." Cole chuckled. "She's spent lots of time around Isaac, ain't she?"

"I'm five."

"Just," Katherine said with a warm smile. Her hand brushed along the little girl's hair. "She just had her birthday."

Cole's mind went blank, focusing only on the rush of blood through his veins. This wasn't working. He'd said he could handle it. How could he have been so wrong? Kathy's lips moved, and she pointed back to the kitchen. All Cole could manage to force out was a nod.

By the time he made his feet move, Cindy peeked out at him. Tucked behind a hall table, her fingers gripping the edge. The moment he noticed her, a quiet giggle escaped, and she was gone from sight.

In that brief moment the emotions that had kept him frozen dissipated into the air with his chuckle. "This place haunted?"

Another giggle.

"Keep hearing something."

"What?" Kathy's head poked out, "Oh. Cindy. Come here, darling. You're going to knock over Aunt Martha's vase."

From his toes to his shoulders, every muscle tensed. What was his problem?

"Sorry I'm late." Jane's voice was like a cool rush of air and hot brand in the same moment. Much to his chagrin she used his moment of hesitation to grab his ass as she passed. "Cindy, my dearest little thing, you'll never guess what I saw."

Cole still didn't move. They were gone from sight. Almost out of earshot, all he could hear were mumbles, punctuated by a screeching giggle. Despite himself, another smile emerged.

"Cole. Stop dawdling this minute or you will be a very unhappy man this evening. I'll stay at the homestead with Jesse."

That got him moving.

There is nothing more dreadful than the habit of doubt. Doubt separates people. It is a poison that disintegrates friendships and breaks up pleasant relations. It is a thorn that irritates and hurts; it is a sword that kills.
—Buddha

"I told you he was good with kids."

"Could've fooled me the way he acted when he first got here." Tiny lines pinched up around Katherine's lips, her remaining displeasure all too clear. "Acted like it was the end of the world you leaving him here with us."

"I'm sure you were just as thrilled to see him instead of me at the door." Jane huffed, hitting Katherine's hand lightly. In the next room Cole wrote on a slate. Whatever he wrote brought endless amusement to Cindy. "Now just look at them."

Kat's shoulders didn't lift. Instead she dragged her chin onto her hand, her tense lips relaxed into a pout. "I don't know, Jane."

"He's still not asking to be her pa."

"He better not be. Until now he hasn't talked to her."

"Yes, he has." Jane fought back a smile when Kat almost knocked her teacup to the floor. "She plays all the time with Isaac and Jesse. Cole is often with me when I'm with Jesse giving him lessons. Who do you think distracts Isaac and Cindy while that's going on?"

"I thought it was Cora or Arthur." Kat's pale features were almost white, her fingers covering her lips. "He doesn't like kids. Wants nothing to do with them. Never has."

"I'm pretty sure that was always a façade. Even Cora knew it. Cole wasn't ever mean to Isaac or Arthur." Jane squeezed Katherine's hand. "Keeping up appearances can pertain to the bad ones, too."

"But he said—when he first walked in, he said he didn't know how to do this."

"I'm sure he doesn't. No matter whether you love or hate children, things are very different when they are your own. Of course, there is the other matter."

"What other matter?"

Jane didn't bother to hide her laugh. Katherine's eyes were a mile away. "The fact that you are sitting here judging his every move. Trying to make sure he does absolutely nothing wrong. It isn't easy to live with someone tracking your every move."

"Still…"

"Katherine, stop. I did this for you."

"What in heavens for? I was fine."

"No, you weren't. You needed to know that she knew him, even if it wasn't as her pa. You had to know he was capable of this."

"I told you. I was fine." Balling her hands into fists, Kat tucked them under her arms. "I didn't need to know anything."

"Fine, I needed you to see it, just in case the worst happens to either of us." Before Kat could protest, Jane barreled on. "This way if I don't come back, you might relax a little. If he doesn't, you'll have this to remember if she ever asks."

Katherine twitched her shoulders, blinking a few times. "Yes, well, how are you holding up? When are you planning this again?"

If she'd felt up for an actual fight, Jane might have protested the subject change. Instead she shifted her focus into her cup, trying to brace herself against the conversation. "I'm fine for the moment. We'll test a disguise in the next day or two. He'll leave on Thursday's train."

"Thursday? Jane, that's just three days away."

"I'm quite aware. I'll leave on Saturday."

"Are you sure about this?"

Jane had to blink back the tears when Kat's hand clamped on hers. "We have to stop him. I know where he is. It's the only plan we have. I have to be all right with it."

"It's suicide."

"God willing, it won't be."

Kat finally released her hand. "Michael doesn't seem too thrilled about it."

"He wants to call in every last one of the Young brothers."

"Would that be so bad?"

"I agreed to tell them, just not like this. Once this is settled, once we have him, then he can tell them." Jane gripped her lip between her teeth, "The problem is in outsmarting a man that is quite insane."

"From what little information Tommy was able to get out of his records at the asylum, I do believe that insane doesn't begin to cover it."

"Thank you. You do know how to ease my mind."

"I'm not here to ease your mind. I'm here to try to talk my best friend out of putting herself in the line of danger again." Kat set her hand on Jane's, far more gently this time. "Promise me you'll get through this."

"I promise I will fight with everything I have. I have to do this."

"I know."

"I can't live the rest of my life in fear of what he will do. For as long as I live, I would have that fear. This has to end."

"Just be sure it doesn't end you."

We are only falsehood, duplicity,
contradiction; we both conceal
and disguise ourselves from ourselves.
—Blaise Pascal

"Sit still." Jane nudged Cole in the back with her knee. Though it had only been a few minutes over an hour, the man hadn't sat still for any of it. "You are worse than a child. So impatient."

"No I ain't."

"I'm not. We don't use the word 'ain't'."

"I do."

"Cole." Her attempt to be stern was interrupted by a heaving, dramatic sigh on his part. The fierce scowl she tried to keep faltered under his grumbling pout. "The whole point of this exercise is to not be you, remember?"

"Ain't. Ain't. Ain't."

"Child."

"You've had me in this chair for over an hour. Ya been pullin' on my hair, not touchin' me nice at all. Worse, you put these dang clothes on me." Cole's nose wrinkled and he tugged the collar of his shirt.

"The minute you put this fine suit on, you ceased to look anything like yourself. Unless you want me touching another man, you best hush." To assert her point she gave another firm tug on his hair. She'd have lied if she said the smile that formed at his pained protest wasn't borne out of satisfaction.

"I'm tellin' you. It ain't."

"*Isn't*, Cole. Really. You spend endless hours around me and listen to my so-called annoying words. Is it that difficult to take a moment and think before you speak to form real words for a change?"

Slow as cold molasses, the words dripped from his lips. "You are crazy as Archie's old coon dog if you think this is going to work."

"That is far better, I knew you were capable." Jane moved in front of him and knelt on the floor. With a few last tugs on his shirt to straighten imaginary wrinkles, she could no longer delay the inevitable.

His hands closed over hers. His silky voice pitched higher than usual. Not so much to sound false, but just enough that he no longer sounded like the Cole she'd come to cherish. Each syllable poured out in deliberate measure without coming off slow. "With all this touching and fussing, you make it hard to concentrate."

Contentment that the lessons of the previous weeks hadn't been in vain clashed headlong into the sickening flop of her stomach at the loss of comfort in his voice. She tugged her hands free and rose. When he reached for her she took a step back, hands clasped firmly behind her back. "Take a look."

"Jane?"

This whole plan, the ruse itself, had been her idea. They'd worked on it for weeks. Planning something drastic was one thing. Seeing the man who meant everything to her disappear under clothes, spectacles and mannerisms that weren't his, turning him into the deceit she hated, and watching it come to fruition before her was far more difficult.

"This don't make me no different."

With her eyes closed, and him giving up the proper speech for the briefest moment he was the same. His touch was the same, only his scent was different this way. She opened her eyes to face what she'd done to him. "You look handsome. Rather attractive, actually. I just prefer Cole."

"Well." His lanky frame took a step back and his arms spread wide. Before he spoke again, he bowed low to the ground to pick up the hat she'd left on the floor. He slipped on the bowler and gave her a nod. "I apologize, ma'am. My name is Charles Hodgkins. I'm afraid I don't know anyone by the name of Cole."

"Now you look and sound the part." She turned him toward the mirror so he could see the change. She stepped back as Cole appeared at a loss for words, his jaw working soundlessly as he stared at his reflection. "Mr. Hodgkins."

Every bit of stubble was cleared from his face. She would have preferred a moustache, but they couldn't do anything too noticeable so close to departure. Instead, she'd darkened his eyebrows, and then done the same to his hair. Rather than cutting off the long locks he'd grown in the past year, she'd slicked it back with pomade.

Though he'd tried to cut it after her hanging, she had convinced him to keep it long, and let it continue to grow. After so many months, everyone in town, or anyone spying, would be used to his hair being long. So any change in appearance would be drastic enough that he'd be tougher to recognize.

For the moment she'd tied it back secure at the nape of his neck, then tucked the length into his shirt. After that the added touches of spectacles, a bowler, and some incredibly gorgeous clothes Michael had purchased on his last trip to Pueblo made the change complete.

The appearance of the man before her was so far from Cole, even she felt as though she was looking at a stranger. A solid lump of disgust lodged in her throat, blocking her ability to speak. She coughed against the lump, until she managed to find a squeak of a voice. "What do you think?"

"Don't look like me at all."

She was grateful he used his own voice. It eased some of the discomfort. "Could probably fool Graham."

"Ready to try?"

To fool Graham would mean the transformation was enough. Truthfully, it might not be in the least bit necessary for his task, but she was not about to take any chances. "The sooner we try, the sooner this look is gone."

"Don't like it?"

"I don't like the deceit."

He brushed one finger along her cheek. "The lie isn't against any you love."

"The only thing keeping me going. Stay here. The train should be here any minute. Wait five minutes and head on over." Jane pulled free of his reaching hand and left the room.

They'd used the old boarding house for the transformation, going through the extremes of slipping out of the bedroom through the window. Graham had never seen them leave. Jane had made sure he'd been distracted.

She took the back door of the boarding house, walking several buildings down before crossing the street and heading back to the saloon. Before she'd even arrived, the train whistle sounded.

Jane didn't pick up her pace, taking her time getting back. She set the ladder they'd left leaning against the side of the saloon against the porch roof and climbed back to their room.

Cole should have made it to the saloon and have a drink in his hand. If he were smart, he would have forgone his usual whiskey. After one last bracing breath, Jane slipped from the room.

She leaned on the railing, taking in every soul in the bustling bar. It didn't take long to spot Cole despite the fact that he'd removed the hat. Rose draped on him whispering something in his ear.

The hot fire of anger couldn't be stopped and grew worse when Graham spotted her.

"Janey. Tell that no good lie-abed we got business."

At least so far, he hadn't recognized Cole. Step one complete. They'd have to take it further by getting Graham to actually talk to Cole. "I will not. He's exhausted. We've had a rather busy afternoon."

The chorus of hoots and hollers covered her grin when Cole turned away Rose's advances. If he'd taken it that far, she might have had to kill him.

Luckily the train had brought several new faces. Some that were dressed as he was had stopped at the first saloon they'd seen. Still, Cole managed to shift in his chair, drinking his beer quickly enough to appear that he wanted to get out.

"Lots of new faces," Jane called to Graham, slapping away a pinching hand. After a glare at the offender, she managed to make her way behind the bar. "Any of them staying?"

"Half of them look more like your brother's type of visitor."

"Does that mean you don't even try? Really, Graham. Get out there. Sell rooms and women. There's still plenty of money you need to pay back."

Jane didn't bother to hide her laugher when he stormed off under a stream of curses that would have made a more proper woman faint dead away. With one eye on Graham's progress through the newcomers, Jane tended to business.

Drink orders came along fast enough, a call for a game of poker meant she needed to set up. By the time that was done, Graham was walking away from Cole's table, and Jane had missed the show.

The wink Cole gave her was the first hint the encounter had been a success thus far. The way Graham kept pausing to study the back of Cole's head wasn't a good sign. At the very least, Cole had given him pause. Even if he didn't know for certain.

It was time to squelch the doubts and see what he thought. "Well, Graham? Any takers for rooms, or women, or both?"

"Both rooms are taken. We got two more wanting company." Graham leaned on the bar. "Where's Cole, Janey?"

"I told you, in our room. He's exhausted. We were up all night and most of the morning. I promised him I'd work in his place tonight."

"Staying up all night hasn't stopped him from working before."

"I don't think he's ever done what we did last night before."

The distraction proved enough to yank Graham's attention right back to her. "That so? Care to elaborate?"

Despite the eyes that turned her way, hoping for the answer, Jane only shrugged. "Why should I tell your perverted mind any more details? It has far more fun coming up with scenarios all on its own."

"Details help."

"All I'll say is that we weren't in our room, and there may have been a horse involved." Another round of cheers came up from those closest to them. Jane stepped closer to Graham, leaning right up against him and pushing his mouth shut. "Nothing like a naked moonlight ride to get the blood flowing."

Graham didn't move a muscle for almost a full minute. "Jane."

"Sucker."

"What?"

Jane laughed outright, pushing him back a bit. "I didn't think Graham Cooke was gullible enough to get played."

"I'm not gullible."

"Of course, you aren't." She lined up several drinks, handing them out to everyone at the bar. Clearing away the dirty glasses as she moved, she winked at Wills. "Do you think I was being serious?"

"No tellin' with you, Janey." Wills held up the glass. "For another round I might be willin' to say you were just teasing."

Jane set another drink in front of him. "I suppose only Cole and I will ever know the truth."

Graham shook it off. "I, uh. I should get the girls working on those men that want 'em. No sense wasting more time."

"Who wanted women?" She followed his pointing finger. "I'd go with Dahlia and Fern for the two higher class. Use Lily and Ivy for the others. What about him?" She intentionally brought Graham's attention to Cole.

He grunted. "Said he might like a woman, but Rose wasn't to his taste."

"Then find out who is." Jane shook her head when he wandered around the bar, but failed to take a drink even though Cole's beer was empty. A grin tightened across her cheeks, she was beyond ready to end the game. She grabbed a full mug of beer and walked up behind Graham.

"Isn't there one of them that light your fancy?"

"She does." Unlike the usual lounging stance Cole adopted, he hunched forward. His legs drew up under the chair, fingers fidgeted with a coin. "How much?"

Graham snorted. "She's not for sale. Pick another."

"Everything has its price, Mr.—what was your name again?"

Excitement bubbled in Jane's belly. Once into it, Cole was perfectly in character. Only his choice of her seemed to re-spark the doubt in Graham. "His name is Graham. Don't bother with the Mister. He's not quite honorable enough for propriety."

"Jane." Graham gripped her elbow, his eyes narrowed.

"What?"

"Your name is Jane. Good to know." He pushed his glasses up his nose. "Like I said. Everyone has a price. How much?"

"You couldn't afford me." Jane set down the beer. One by one she removed Graham's grasping fingers from her elbow. "I can handle myself, Graham. Go on."

The minute he walked away, Cole leaned closer. Once she'd bent down to meet him he spoke low in her ear. "What sort of price couldn't I afford?"

"Hmmmmm." She pressed her hand into the table, leaning in close enough she almost tipped herself and the table over. "Every inch of you, body, soul, forever."

"I can handle the body."

Jane straightened and picked up the beer from the table to take a drink. With a shrug, she lifted her skirts and straddled him, grinning at the way the activity in the saloon slowed.

The minute a protest rose from Graham's lips, she crushed hers to Coles. Ignoring the questions aimed toward their table, she slipped her hands along his shoulders. Her hips ground against him, eliciting a deep moan.

She felt the beefy hand of Graham grab her arm and moved quick, hitting him right where it counted. When he doubled over, she winked at Cole and pulled off his glasses before pulling his hair from his shirt.

"It's Cole?"

"Can't be."

"His hair's black."

Cole gripped Jane's rear and stood, wrapping her legs around his waist. He strode toward the back of the saloon. "Want me back now?"

"Heavens, yes." She tugged at the ascot, since it was most accessible.

"Jane." Graham shouted. "Cole?"

"Thank you for proving my point, Graham. Just a few changes and Cole is almost unrecognizable." Jane looked back toward Graham. "Leave us the hell alone. You're working tonight."

"But-wait!"

The door to the bathhouse slammed shut.

"Cole."

"We got one day."

"Let's make it count."

In the confusion we stay with each other, happy to be together, speaking without uttering a single word.
—Walt Whitman

Foreheads pressed together, Jane and Cole remained frozen, until Graham's cursing faded into mutters, the buzz of activity in the saloon dissolved into a meaningless hum. He pressed his palms into the wood of the door, despite their twitching desire to run along her body. This wasn't the time for rushing. It was the time to take it slow. Just as he leaned in closer in an attempt to capture her lips, she pushed her hands against his shoulders.

His weak protest was covered with her hand. The simple shake of her head told him everything he needed to know. He still wasn't Cole. She needed him, not the stranger they'd created. He backed off, moving in silence to the stove where there were four hot pails of water.

They worked together, pouring the hot water in before refilling the buckets. They placed the fresh, cool pails on the stove to heat while they got ready.

As he undressed, he watched her undo the long row of buttons that ran up to her elbows and roll up the sleeves like she was doing the wash. Standing still, he studied her every movement, taking it in, memorizing every action.

Seemingly oblivious to his stare, she lifted a foot onto the stool and quickly removed her boot and then slid her stocking down her leg before moving to the next. Only then did her eyes dart in his direction before looking pointedly at the tub.

He still didn't move, wondering just what she was doing when she removed only her drawers before walking over to the tub.

Gathering her skirts, she stepped into the tub and sat on the edge. Her skirts and petticoats floated over the sides like cotton waterfalls. She looked up at him with a soft smile, chuckling when he moved quickly and finished stripping down before getting in the water.

Her hands went to his hair when he turned his back toward her and leaned his shoulders against her legs. She released the restraining strip of leather before running her fingers through the length. The scrape of her nails against his scalp rushed the last bit of tension from him, and he sank back against her.

Closing his eyes, he let her take control as she tilted his head back. When she shifted behind him, he opened his eyes and found her leaning over toward the stool. Despite the flash of thought to take advantage of her position, he didn't move a muscle.

When she pulled back with the cup in her hand, she leaned down and gently kissed his forehead before getting back to her task. Cupful by cupful she poured the steaming water over his hair before leaning over again to get the soap.

The way her eyes radiated their intense focus on the simple task made him content to watch every furrow of her brow and flicker of an eyelash. As her fingers worked the soap through his hair, his eyes closed. Intentional or not, each pass of her fingers along his scalp sent shivers down his spine, relaxing him all the way to his toes.

He didn't bother to stop his moan and relaxed completely against her. She took her time, her fingers continued to massage his scalp with each pass. The relaxation set in so deep he lost count of how many times she washed his hair.

The power of the serene moment lingered as her hands slowed, and Cole remained still to keep it in tact. Even the muffled laughter that filtered in from the saloon didn't break their quiet connection. Slowly, Cole opened his eyes to look at her, and as her hands continued their tender journey, he nearly choked on a sudden surge of emotion he didn't want to acknowledge.

She skimmed his forehead with her fingertips. Her sharp gaze followed their slow trail as they moved back through his hair. While he studied her, she avoided his gaze. The way her jaw worked, he could tell she was holding back her emotions. She took a shaky breath and leaned over to get something. He touched his fingers to her hand to stop her, and she finally looked at him.

Examining every curve of her features with an intense gaze, he reached up toward her and let his fingers trail along her cheekbone. She cupped his cheeks in her hands before her thumb ran across his lips. Her own lip quivered slightly, and he slipped away just far enough to turn toward her.

Keeping her eyes lowered as he moved closer, she reached toward the hand he had wrapped around the edge of the tub. Her fingers slipped along the damp skin, tracing every curve and line up his arm to his shoulder. She pulled a trembling lip between her teeth.

He used his thumb to pull her lip from the tight grip of her teeth before he slipped his arm around her waist and pulled her into the water. Ignoring the volume of fabric between them, he pulled her tight against him. She trembled in his arms, and his breath grew shaky. He knew she was holding back.

She leaned into him, her eyes focused on his shoulder where her thumb traced along the curves of muscle. The powerful, emotional silence lingered until her skirts had become as heavy as his heart and sank into the water. He trailed his thumb along her lower lip before letting his fingers bury in her hair to pull her forehead against his.

"Cole." She whispered so quietly it barely broke through the wall of silence. Her hand slipped up his shoulder and around his neck. "If things go wrong we might never…"

He pulled back when her voice faded and studied her face intently. Slipping his thumb under her jaw line he used a gentle pressure to tilt her head back, forcing her gaze to his. Words he didn't trust himself to speak thickened in his throat as her eyes closed again. The glimmer of a tear caught his eye, the evidence of all she was holding back, clung precariously to the apple of her cheek.

The moment his lips touched her cheek to kiss away the tear, she collapsed against him. Her nails dug into the back of his neck. Before she could cry or sob, he crushed his lips to hers with a force of longing that nearly consumed them both.

He clung to her like a lifeline as he let her lead him down an unfamiliar path, feeling every emotion he kept in check coming at him like a stampede from her soul, the soft caress of her lips against his, their tongues lost in a gentle, searching dance, the tender touch of her fingers to the nape of his neck. There was no rush, nothing but a depth of feeling that would have terrified him if he hadn't been completely ensconced in it right along with her.

Long before they felt finished, the water cooled around them, soaking through the heat of their bodies until they reluctantly pulled apart. Her fingers laced with his as their eyes locked in a hooded, intense gaze. In silent agreement they moved, and despite her heavy, wet clothes, she stood gracefully. He stepped out behind her and moved to get the hot water from the stove

While he worked, she peeled off layers of clothes, the intense heat of her stare never once leaving him. When she struggled with the wet corset ties he set his hands over hers.

He popped open the busk and let corset fall to the floor when she inhaled deeply. With the restriction gone, he moved behind her and reached for the bottom of the chemise. A soft sigh slipped from her lips as he let his fingers dance up along her thighs until he caught the bottom of the muslin. Bit by bit, he lifted the damp fabric.

When he got as far as her hips, her hands settled on his, and she leaned back against him. He nipped at her neck and his hot breath brushed her ear. The deep moan that escaped flamed the growing fire inside. He was determined to contain the fire in order to make this moment last as long as possible.

Working the chemise up along her body, he took care to let his fingers skim her skin. When her arms lifted, he pulled the chemise over her head and let it fall to the floor. Turning her to face him, he pulled her shivering body close.

His fingers danced up along her spine, slipping into her hair to remove the pins holding it in place. When the last pin was pulled free, the golden locks shifted to float down her back. Goose flesh raised on his arms as the soft tendrils brushed along them.

At his shiver, her lips brushed across his chest and she pressed into him. Her fingers slipped along the muscles of his back, each one trembling in response. When he pulled back she whimpered slightly as a weak protest before they moved together and sank into the water.

The soft caress of her hands and lips pulled him deeper into her, and he fell freely into the abyss. His fingers found a rhythm of their own as they swept along every inch of flesh. Each movement they made became enhanced as the water responded, caressing behind the touch, building the fire inside.

Searching and memorizing with every lingering touch, every slow caress, there wasn't a part of each other they neglected. The water cooled around them again, but still they explored each other until she was shivering.

Reluctantly he backed up and pulled himself from the water. Grabbing a towel he walked over and wrapped it around her, wordlessly lifting her from the tub. Intent to keep the quiet of the night, he moved behind her to run the towel along her back.

He rubbed fast as he could to keep her warm while he dried her off. Focused on her back, he was relieved she didn't move a muscle. It might have made him act too fast on the burning desire they hadn't yet sated.

Kneeling before her, he ran the towel up her legs drying them quickly and thoroughly. As he got to her stomach he was unable to stop himself from following behind the towel with his lips. When her fingers buried in his hair, he nipped gently at the delicate flesh. Her soft gasp pulled him up to capture her lips again as he quickly dried off her arms.

While he kept her trapped in the kiss, he skimmed his body with the towel to create some semblance of dryness. Her arms circled his neck, and when he pulled back she was breathless, her eyes filled with passion.

He gripped her arms tightly, taking a few steadying breaths before pulling back. Immediately missing her presence, he grabbed two blankets and wrapped one around his waist before wrapping the other around her.

Scooping her up in his arms, he carried her past the empty saloon and up the stairs to their room. He set her on the bed, pulling aside the blanket to let his eyes caress her body. When she trembled, he stretched out beside her, his palm skimming along her stomach as he nibbled at the sensitive pocket of skin just below her ear. A soft sigh burst from her as his lips traveled her flesh, searching every inch his hands had just a short while before. Her body arched into the heat of his.

He kissed along her soft curves, her flesh pebbled beneath his touch. Her soft moans filled his ears and fueled the flame of his own passion. Working his way back up along her, he found her mouth again open and eager. Their souls locked together, drawing them closer until they finally joined, completing a connection stronger than he'd ever felt.

Every slow, deliberate movement focused on expressing what words never could. Savoring every feeling, they made every touch count, lingering as if it was the last chance they would have to be together, while knowing every moment it very well could be.

Moving together in harmony, the slow burn grew into an intense flame threatening to consume them. With a last desperate pull into each other, they reached the inevitable peak, still moving together slowly as their bodies shuddered with release.

They clung to each other until the last tremor subsided. Breathless, their lips parted, but their bodies remained entwined and their foreheads pressed together.

Her hand rested on his chest, her eyes were wide when she met his gaze. Deep passion remained there, one that matched his own. With a soft smile, she ran her thumb across his lips before pulling him into another slow kiss.

Reaching behind him, Cole turned down the lamp slowly. In the dark, they searched each other again, making every moment memorable, and getting lost in each other until the harsh light of day would split them apart.

27

*There is no disguise that can for long
conceal love where it exists.
—François de la Rochefoucauld*

Driving rain pelted the train platform. The sheer force drove people toward shelter quick as possible. No one rushing to and from the train paused to take notice of the couple in the midst of it. Huddled close together, they ignored the water pelting them. Their whispered words barely crossed the short distance between them.

"Remember what I told you." For the tenth time, Jane straightened the sopping lapels of his jacket. She ran her trembling fingers through his hair. The truth of the distance they were about to face weakened her resolve in its rightness. "It will be easy to do what I did with your hair, your appearance. Just remember…"

Cole grabbed her wrists to stop her fussing. He pulled her hands against his chest. "Ya taught me well. I ain't gonna forget for nothing. You told me twenty times a day the past two weeks."

"I know. I do. I know you can." She fought against the tears that threatened to mingle with the rain streaking along her cheeks. No one would know if she dared set them free. No one but Cole, he always knew. Right then she couldn't allow such weakness to show. She had to be strong. "I'm just worried."

"I noticed." His thumbs ran along the back of her hands. The simple gesture soothed her roiling stomach, her taut nerves. "What do your words say 'bout worrying?"

"'Concern should drive us into action and not into a depression. No man is free who cannot control himself'. Pythagoras." The words spilled out automatically by his simple question. She felt nothing when she said them. They had no impact, for she was numb from her heart outward. The danger of the coming weeks was too prevalent. The knowledge she could lose him; could lose everything. "That is what I have been doing. However now, in this moment…"

"It ain't so easy."

Jane could only nod. To speak would make her lose what strength she'd gathered. Silence settled between them like the heavy clouds above. A loud hiss of the train's brakes finally pulled her back to the present. Their time was growing too short. There was too much to be said, but they'd said it already, and repeating it would only delay the inevitable. "Be careful."

"You're the one that needs to be careful."

"Please, Cole."

"Jesse already gone?"

"Yes." Grateful for the change of subject, she sniffed against the threatening surge of tears. She blinked against the rain and nodded weakly. "David took him to Black Moon last night. On the off chance Alan does come here, he won't be able to find Jesse."

"Go see him. It'll make you feel better." He released her wrists to squeeze her arms. When she didn't respond, he slipped his hands down her back to her waist. "I'm sure if ya asked, the sheriff would take you."

"It's best I don't. I shouldn't know where he is, I would remember the details." Jane cleared her throat as a call to board cut through the pounding rain. "You should go."

Her voice broke, and he tugged her closer when it did. For a brief moment his hand left her waist. He placed it under her chin and lifted it with a tug. "I should."

Every thought she had felt insignificant. Thousands of words in her mind were worthless. The only words worth saying got lodged in her throat behind a thick wall of fear. She pressed her lips together, pulling them between her teeth.

With another gentle pull, both his arms were around her waist again. Not a breath of space existed between them. His forehead pressed against hers. "Say it."

She knew what he meant, what he all but dared her to say. There was no way she would say those three all-powerful words like this.

"I ain't gonna run."

Her laugh barked out, and she clutched his sopping lapels. "You're boarding a train in a few minutes. No. Go tend to your business in Denver. Then after…after…" Her voice caught again. After was when the trouble would begin.

"I'll be careful."

"Good. Now go. I—just go."

"You can say it."

"No. I can't. Not like this." As deep as her love ran, she couldn't bring herself to say it aloud when she might lose it all anyway. She'd already lost too much, and so had he.

"You promised. No more hiding." His words were gentle, the touch of his lips to her cheek even more so.

"I know. I promise that is not what I am doing. I just can't say such things when you're walking away, when we don't know what will happen." She could no longer see. The tears were too thick, slipping out to mix with the trails of raindrops on her cheeks.

He didn't respond aloud, but his hold on her grew impossibly tighter.

"After it's all over. When I'm free, I mean truly free. What I'm using to get me through all of this is that hope, the simple idea of what can happen once I am free."

The final boarding call jolted through them both, and Cole reacted by pulling her into a brutal kiss. Every bit of fear and anger at their parting seeped in, leaving them both breathless when she pushed him back.

"Go. Send me a telegram when you arrive in Denver. Be careful."

He moved as instructed, but let her cling to his hand until it had to be released. With a final wave, he disappeared into the train.

Jane didn't move a muscle, standing in silence as the train prepared to depart. If she'd had any strength left she would have looked for him, but there was none.

Kat appeared at her side. "I heard what you did to Graham." Her arm laced with Jane's, providing support just when Jane thought she might crumble. "He's still ranting about it to anyone that will listen."

"We had to be certain it was effective. You know that."

"Of course, I do. I just need to keep you talking. Last thing Cole needs to see is you passing out when the train pulls away."

"I know. Thank you."

At the final whistle before the train pulled away, Katherine squeezed her arm. "I don't like this plan of yours one bit. I just hate the thought of you and Cole out there without any support whatsoever."

It wasn't until the train was some distance off that Jane could snap herself back to the present. "We have to do something, Kat. I can't live the rest of my life wondering when he's going to show up again or who he's going to kill next."

"I know. Doesn't mean I have to like it."

"I wish I had made David wait to take Jesse away. I just don't think it's right to go out and see him, especially in this weather."

"Especially when he's being watched by an Indian you'd rather shoot than talk to?" Katherine's laughter was warm, just a little forced at the moment. "You are soaking wet. Let's go to Cora's and get you some nice warm tea."

"I don't much feel like going to Cora's."

"You're not going anywhere by yourself, and that's final. You're just going to have to manage to handle having company today to distract you. We are going to Cora's." Kat left no room for argument and dragged Jane from the platform with her umbrella centered between them.

Despite already being soaked through, Jane moved quickly through the streets. They rushed under each porch shelter until they were both laughing at the silliness of trying to stay dry.

Under the safety of Cora's porch, Jane paused. "We really should have stopped to get me a change of clothes."

"I'm sure you're not the only person soaked to the bone. Let's get tea. If nothing else, this will give you an excuse to buy that dress you've been eying inside."

Jane allowed a brief smile and let Katherine push her into the store. The moment she was inside, she froze at the sight in front of her. "Jesse."

"Ma." Jesse launched himself at her, throwing his arms around her neck.

"Oh, Jesse. I'm so happy to see you." She fell to her knees and clung to him. Kissing the top of his head, she ran her fingers over his hair. "I thought you were with Black Moon."

His gentle voice whispered in her ear. "Pa said I could see you today."

Jane sought out David. She found him across the store. "Thank you," she mouthed. Cole had been right. She needed to see Jesse today. She was terrified enough. Seeing Jesse safe gave her such comfort.

Katherine's warm laughter filtered through her relief. "We thought you might need some sunshine today. What better way to do that than with a happy little boy?"

Jane finally pulled back and cupped Jesse's cheek. "I can't think of any better way."

"Candy?"

Amusement filtered through the room, and Jane nodded. "Yes. Get whatever you want. Pick your favorite." She rose to her feet. On the way up, she ruffled his hair. Once he'd gone on to the candy jars, she raced across the room into David's comforting arms.

"Whoa, easy." David stumbled back a step. He held her close, running a soothing hand along her back

"I needed to see him today. Thank you."

"You sound like a ma."

She laughed weakly. "That's your fault."

"Good. Nothing better to be blamed for." He squeezed her hand. "You going to be all right?"

"I will be." She took a shaky breath and forced a smile. "I have to be. In two days I've got to leave town."

David sat down and pulled her onto the bench beside him. Once she moved closer, he handed her his coffee. "Try to relax. Enjoy the time you got with Jesse today. I'll take him back to Black Moon tomorrow and stay with him until it's all over."

"Is Lee all right with that?"

"She's crazy about Jesse and knows his safety comes first. She's just fine. She was mad she couldn't be here today. Unfortunately, she won't be back from Denver on Mike's errand until tomorrow." David nudged her. "I think you soothed her fears by agreeing to divorce me."

"Scoundrel." Jane gasped. The divorce had been her idea, and she'd pushed for it before he took up with Lee. That he'd say it was his idea? "You lied to her?"

"No." He chuckled. "But I had you fooled."

She wrinkled her nose at him.

"She did agree to officially let me court her."

"How quaint."

"Be nice."

"I am being nice. Trust me." She smirked and polished off his coffee. "I'm glad you are happy, David. It's what I wanted for you."

"I know."

Once again the mood hinted at being far too serious and emotional. A subject change was sorely needed. "When will Mike be here?"

"I think to make up for sending Lee off to make purchases for the hotel, he's trying to make up for it in misery. He's getting some work done out at the new hotel despite the rain. Said he'd be here for dinner. He'll stay at the homestead while you're gone."

"It was kind of him to hire Lee to manage the hotel. I know she's wanted to do something more than work for her cousin." Jane smiled. When Lee's husband passed two years ago, her cousin Cora had hired her so she wouldn't have to leave town. It had been a good fit at the time, but Lee wanted to do more.

"You teaching her to read helped." David nudged her.

"That part was easy." Her gaze remained on Jesse as he happily ate his candy and played jackstones with Cindy. She took a sip of coffee. "I'm glad that you'll be with Jesse."

"Jane," David said, softly. "Maybe it isn't a good idea to be staying at the saloon tonight. Stay at the homestead."

Tears hit her eyes faster than she could blink them away when he spoke. "Thank you, but—"

"No. No argument. Kat and Mike will both argue my side if I ask them to. You need the distraction, not being in the middle of it."

"You're being too good to me."

"It's what friends do, right? No matter what we've been through, I don't like to see you hurting. You mean too much to me."

She gave him a quick kiss on the cheek before she hugged him again. "You're too nice for your own good, David Schaffer, but thank you."

He grinned and hugged her back, "You aren't the first to tell me that."

"Probably won't be the last either." She laughed along with him.

Jesse rushed up and held up a piece of candy. Once she'd let him put it in her mouth, he grinned. "Good."

Jane nodded. "Mmmm. It's very good. Are you eating all of Cora's candy?" Jesse nodded and tugged on her hand.

Following without any argument, Jane walked over to the candy bins. From that point on, there were plenty of distractions to keep her occupied throughout the rest of the day. She was certain it had been planned that way, but no one could keep her occupied once night fell.

As she lay in bed that night, it all came crashing down on her again. Rolling onto her side she pulled a pillow tight against her chest and gave in. When she finally fell asleep, tears still shimmered on her cheek in the moonlight.

Those who live to the future must always appear selfish to those who live in the present.
-Ralph Waldo Emerson

November 1870

It would do you well to say your goodbyes, if you haven't already. I bid farewell to Clara, to the true Clara, many years ago. Well before you ever imagine I had.

While I miss her at times, at others I hate her. Naïve, immature…so very wrong. Please, Michael, do not hate her as I do. Perhaps you can remember more of her redeeming moments; perhaps you can remember a time when she was not so blind.

No matter what the outcome of the coming weeks, I loved you, dear one. I loved David. I hope he will know that when he learns of Jesse, when I have returned the child to him. Tell him the truth for me. Read him these letters. Better yet, teach him to read them.

As much as he never got around to teaching me things, I never got around to teaching him to read.

I'd thought he'd failed me so much, but it was I who failed him more.

Do not mourn Clara long. She was not worthy of the love of any of you. I only hope my efforts to repair the damage done aid in easing some of your pain.

'Art is long, and time is fleeting, and our hearts, though stout and brave. Still, like muffled drums are beating, funeral marches to the grave. In the world's broad field of battle, In the bivouac of life, Be not like dumb, driven cattle. Be a hero in the strife'. ~Longfellow

With a heavy shawl drawn tight over her head, Jane knelt in the dirt. The name carved into the cross mocked her, *Clara Louise Young-Schaffer*. No one had moved the grave or removed the cross, and for that she was glad. It was best this way. Clara was dead, after all. Barely a spark of her remained any longer.

"You were right. You were not worthy of any of their love. You were stupid. You were naïve. You were weak." Jane swiped away a tear as she spoke in low tones to the empty grave. "It's your fault I am facing this monster I know very little about and putting a man that I—a man the likes of which you could never have had—in danger."

She dug her fingers deep into the mud. "David was a good man, too. David *is* a good man. I may never love him like you did, but I can see where such a love would have existed. I cannot believe you would abandon that. Abandon him."

Silence lingered heavy in the air. For a fleeting moment Jane almost wished for a glimpse at the personification of insanity, a chance to have this invisible, yet prevalent being coalesce before her in some human form. Or for a chance to see if Clara could or would defend herself.

Jane knew deep in her soul Clara would never return. If all these months without any true, deep memories despite the family around her weren't enough to prove it, the letters were a testament to Clara's disappearance. Clara herself had been ashamed of what she'd done, too ashamed to return, and too afraid for her child and family.

"You left me with your messes and unpayable debts. I will never forgive you for any of it, Clara." She pushed herself to her feet, wiping at the mud on her hands with her handkerchief. Her feet remained affixed to the ground despite her urge to depart. "Yet, I will also be forever grateful to you."

A short laugh burst forth. "What a contradiction. I despise you, but if it was not for you, for your mistakes, I would not be who I am. I wouldn't have the life I do. I quite possibly would not have Cole, David, or Jesse. None of them would be in my life. For that, I am grateful."

With one step, she stood at the plain wooden cross. She placed her hand on top. "Thanks to you, I know what not to be, how not to act. I'm far from perfect. I will never claim to be, but I am not you. I never will be. I will do everything in my power to avoid your mistakes. For that, I am grateful."

She gave the cross one final squeeze. A sliver of wood pierced her flesh, and broke off into a sliver that remained beneath her skin. A fitting testament to the piece of Clara she would always carry with her. She turned away from the gravesite. "Goodbye, Clara. May you rot in peace."

"You do know there isn't a body to actually rot."

"Drop dead, Graham." Jane didn't bother to look at him or wonder how much of her one-sided conversation he'd overheard. None of it mattered anymore.

"Jane." Graham huffed his way into an even pace beside her. When she sped up, he kept up with her. "Just wanted to make sure you're all right. I was expecting you back at the saloon half an hour ago. You never showed. I wasn't eavesdropping."

"I don't care."

"Jane."

This time she stopped. "Graham, please. The less I discuss these matters, the better. After yesterday when I first had to say goodbye to Cole, and now today I must do the same with my child, unsure if I'll see either of them again—the last thing I need is the hassle of a very large idiot."

"Excuse me, then."

"Sorry." With as much effort and nervous energy as she could, Jane blew out a deep gust of air. She counted slow as she could to ten and inhaled again. "I apologize, it isn't your fault. My nerves are shot. If you tell Mike I said this I will shoot your prick off, but I'm wondering if we're doing this right."

"Near as I can tell there is no right way. No matter what you do you're going to have to face that maniac. Might as well make it on your terms." Graham squeezed her shoulder in a surprisingly comforting gesture. "I'd best get outta your way. When you're done, come have a drink. I think you need one…or twenty."

She managed to force out what she hoped was some semblance of a smile, and nodded her appreciation. The tug on her skirt was her answer to any question as to why he was so quick to vacate her company.

"Ma?"

Jane spun quickly. She dropped to her knees to pull Jesse close. "I am going to miss you so much, little man."

"Then don't go." Jesse's soft whimper didn't escape her notice. Her shawl slipped backward, threatening to reveal her hair when his small fists grabbed hold and refused to let go. "Stay wif us."

Eyes closed, Jane fought to steady her trembling lip. A sniffle escaped her control, but she caught it best as she could and cleared her throat against the next. "I promised you I'd make sure you were safe. Remember?"

After a tiny nod, Jesse pulled back enough to be seen. "I 'member."

"If I'm going to keep my promise, I must do this. It is the only way to make certain you and your pa will always be safe. It took every bit of her strength to not crumble as tears slipped down his cheeks. She had to be strong; much as leaving the child yet again pained her to her core. "You've got to stay with your pa and Black Moon. They will make sure you are safe, and that no one hurts you."

"No. You don't go. Bad man will hurt you." Jesse's little fists pounded against her shoulders. "He don't like you. He'll hurt you."

Jane held him close and let him continue to fight and beat his fists against her back. Looking to the heavens for help in how to answer, she found David's hazel eyes instead. Her lip trembled and she shook her head, unable to say a word.

Jesse sobbed loud against her neck. "You no go. Stay here. Safe here. If you go, I won't see you again."

She tried to find the words to soothe him, but everything seemed empty in the face of his justified fear. "The bad man won't hurt me. I promise I'll come back, Jesse. Then you'll truly be safe. All of us will be safe."

"No. Stay." His words muffled against her shoulder, but his tiny sobs were inescapable. Each heave of his chest pummeled her heart.

"Your pa is here, Jesse. It's time for you to go." Jane tried to pull away, to disentangle herself from the child's tight grip. Jesse remained stuck firm to her side. "Remember what I told you. Your pa will keep you safe."

"*No.*" Jesse shrieked louder than she'd ever heard the previously nearly-mute child be. He refused to budge, his grip on her neck almost choking. "If you go, Pa go. Uncle Mike keep me safe. Pa keep you safe."

"I already have someone going with me to help me." With what little strength she had, Jane rose to her feet. "Your pa needs to keep you safe, like I know he will. I am going to be all right."

David rubbed Jesse's back. "Your ma is right. She's got Cole. He won't let anything happen to her. I know it."

Jane turned toward David so Jesse was between them. His arms went full around them both. Jesse's tears fueled her own, and they clung to each other as thunder rumbled in the distance.

David cleared his throat. "We should head out before the storm hits."

Jane nodded, wincing when Jesse protested and clung to her more fiercely. A sob welled in her throat. How could she send him away like this? He would never forgive her if she didn't return. "It's all right, Jesse. Shhh…it's all right."

Both of the adults fought their own distress as they tried to calm the child while simultaneously trying to pry him from Jane's arms. When David finally got him free and in his own arms, the little boy that had been silent for so long screamed and fought him tooth and nail.

"David." The simple word choked her up, catching and breaking with her heart.

Clinging to Jesse, David met her eyes helpless to stop the horror they both felt at his cries. He took a shaky breath, "I don't know…"

Michael must have been close because he folded her in a tight hug. He nodded to David. "Just go. Nothing else to do."

Jane buried her face in Michael's chest, but she was unable to block Jesse's cries. She kept her face hidden until she couldn't hear anything but the usual sounds of the town and the increasing thunder in the distance.

"He's going to be all right." Michael's voice broke the sound of her sobbing. "He's a tough little guy. He's going to be just fine."

"I've already hurt him too much." Somehow Jane found the strength to straighten. "I despise hurting him again."

"You're going to come back. You'll return and finally be able to be his ma. That's not hurting him." He squeezed her hand. "You are coming back."

"I can't think about it." If she thought about it any further she'd chicken out. So much was at stake, she didn't dare to risk turning yellow. "I need to finish packing. Come with me? I would appreciate the company."

"Of course. What else do you need to do?"

"All that's left is the packing. Everything else is done."

"Everything?"

Jane afforded him a brief frown. She knew what he was referring to, and it was the precise reason she wore a shawl so secure over her hair. Rather than answer, she dragged him through the saloon. It wasn't until they'd managed to get to the room that she pulled the shawl from her head to reveal her freshly dyed and cut hair. "Yes. Everything."

"Red? You went red? It looks awful." Michael didn't bother even trying to keep his laughter at bay. He snorted and chuckled until he dropped into a chair. Before he'd managed to get control he pointed at her. "Red?"

"Quiet." She dropped the shawl on the bed and turned her attention to the pile of clothes she'd gathered in recent weeks. "The whole point was to make myself appear different. The henna was expensive, but it did its job."

"You look ridiculous."

"I hate this color. I cannot carry it off as Kat does, not that anyone could. However, I figured going with a color I despise was my best bet. I also hate how short I cut it." She patted the short, now extra curly locks. "Wearing it down may kill me before Alan does."

Michael's laughter ceased mid-guffaw. "Not funny."

"Good. I am rather sick of your laughter."

"Where did all of these clothes come from?" Michael picked through the variety of clothes and styles Jane had gathered along with several bottles of hair dye she hoped to never use, including chestnut and black. He raised a silk skirt and pursed his lips. "Did this come from Daisy?"

"It figures you would recognize it." She smirked when he dropped the skirt and glared her way. "Yes, it did. When I travel I need to look like a whore, or close to one. Anything that makes me look as far from what I am as possible. He's supposed to believe I'm leaving of my own accord, and I'm hiding from this life. Making myself look like a whore is definitely one way to do that."

Mike's attention had wandered mid-explanation. Puzzlement creased his brow. "Jane?"

"What?" She gathered some skirts and folded them carefully, trying to fit more outfits than was reasonable into two carpetbags. "I asked you here to help, Michael. If you're not going to assist me in any way, you can leave."

"Who's that?"

With her mind focused on packing and picking clothes, it took Jane a few minutes to figure out what Michael was talking about. The picture that had once hung above the bed but now rested on a shelf above the desk seemed to have caught his attention. The woman and child in the image looked exactly as they had when she'd first seen it.

Once she'd moved into Cole's room permanently, Cole had moved the picture to the shelf. He'd said they didn't need his dead wife watching over their every move. It was an allowance she'd made and let him choose where to leave it.

Jane resumed stuffing clothes into one of the satchels. Of all the things to ask her, he'd chosen one thing that it wasn't her place to tell. "I can't discuss it."

"That little girl looks just like Cole."

"Enough." She'd snapped, probably more than she'd needed to. "Leave it alone. I told you, I cannot discuss it."

"Hey." Michael clasped her hands in his. "Easy. Sorry. I wasn't thinking."

"No, you weren't." She snatched her hands back with a jerk. Arms folded across her chest, she looked over the shelves in silence. Her first day in the room they'd been empty, barren. Now the room and shelves all but overflowed with her books, pieces of Cole's life, and mementos from their brief time together.

"You'll be back, Jane. Stop looking around here like it's the last time you'll see this place. You will be back."

"Michael, listen to me. Whether you want to hear it or not, you need to hear this." A flash of lightning illuminated the room. The storm was getting closer. She'd be going out in horrible weather. Time had moved too fast once again. "If my interpretation of Clara's clues were right, if Cole finds what I think he will, I want you to know that I have set up a will."

"Jane."

"I met with Lloyd. Most everything is Cole's. The rest goes to Jesse. You are already rather well set. I wanted to make certain they had something."

"I know. I never expected anything." He folded her into his arms. "I didn't want anything."

"I do not want to die. Please understand that. I've already come far too close to death for my liking, I've shaken its hand and I didn't like it. I want to live, Michael. I want to live."

"I know."

"But the reality is—Alan is insane."

"I know. We knew that before the miniscule file we got from Dr. Abrams." Michael sighed and perched on the edge of the bed. "I don't think I like the thought of you trying to outwit an insane man, Jane. Clara couldn't."

"Clara was alone. I am not. I can only hope that counts for something."

"I think it counts for everything."

That I should after death invisibly return.
-Walt Whitman

From the moment the rail car reached the outskirts of Buffalo, Jane remained all but glued to the window. She studied every house, every field, and every tree. Nothing failed to avoid her searching gaze.

Outside the depot, she ordered the cab driver to go slowly. Right up to the expensive hotel she'd chosen, she didn't let a single building go unnoticed. She hoped and prayed for a spark of recognition. Anything.

Her distraction made it easy to ignore the hotel receptionist's disdain at her still whore-like appearance. When she got to her room, she went right to the window to gaze over the city she'd grown up near, and by all accounts visited often. Nothing happened; nothing proved even the slightest bit familiar.

A year had passed since she first woke in Dominion Falls without a memory to call her own. Much as she disputed the thought, there was a small part of her that did wish for some spark of recognition. The tiniest glimmer of hope remained that returning to where she'd been born and where a good portion of Clara's family still lived would bring something back.

After she brushed aside her tears, Jane straightened her bodice. None of this would do her any good. She had to focus on finding Alan and getting him far away from Clara's family before another life was lost.

Somehow she had to convince him that she'd left Colorado willingly and wanted it over for no other reason than to spare the family she couldn't remember. She wasn't lying about that part. She did want it over for the family she couldn't remember as well as the ragtag family she'd created back in Dominion Falls.

There was no more time to waste. Sitting in her room wishing for a memory that wouldn't come wouldn't resolve the pain or troubles. As much as she'd rather avoid it, she had to go to the one place she knew Alan had been and was likely to return. The hospital.

Without a doubt she knew he'd murdered George. Instinct told her he'd also poisoned James and done both to draw her out of hiding. The logical place for him to be was near the family where he could continue to draw out the agony to force her to resurface.

The problem was, even if her memory was fully intact she doubted she'd be ready to see them. Without it she was certain she wasn't. She hadn't the time or the inclination to explain all that had happened.

She had to be smart.

Dying and cutting her hair had been the first step. In the end she'd emptied her satchel of all but the whore's clothes and one simple dress and a nurse's apron. She had no designs on lingering, so she'd brought only necessary clothes.

Hopefully, it would be enough. Considering she had only an old grainy picture, with one brother missing from the image, to use to recognize her family, she could only pray she'd identify them before they could spot her.

Jane focused on getting dressed to distract herself from the negative thoughts. After she set a slate pencil on the stove to heat it, she slipped into the simple dress. She curled her hair even more than it already was, careful not to burn it, until it became utterly unruly. With care she manipulated the mass and placed a few pins to give the illusion of a messy tie back. Then she grabbed the nurse's apron and glanced in the mirror one final time.

"Please let my instincts be correct. I cannot bear for this to go on any longer. The sooner I find Alan, the sooner this can all be over." Jane spoke her prayer quiet, but with her whole heart. With nothing else to do, she let out a long breath. "No more wasting time. Either this will work or it won't. Worrying about it won't get me anywhere."

With that, she hurried from the hotel. She didn't dare to allow any time for thought or fear. The cab was hailed immediately and within ten minutes they pulled to a stop a block from the hospital.

The minute she alighted from the cab, her nerves kicked in. A shiver traveled up her spin until the hair on the back of her neck raised. Rather than giving into the urge to look around to figure out if there was a reason for her instant fear, she bolted for the hospital.

She threw on her apron and slipped into the hospital without stopping. Only when she found herself in a quiet hallway did she pause to breathe. The picture she'd slipped into her pocked was pulled free so she could study it again.

Even with her exacting memory, she worried about the pressure and fear of the situation interfering, and she could not be recognized or all would be lost.

Satisfied she would know the faces of her other siblings if she saw them, it was time to set about finding out where James was. Of course, she also had to keep an eye out for Alan. Without any certain idea how he would have altered his appearance this time, which seemed infinitely more difficult.

Determined to look purposeful, like she belonged, Jane straightened her shoulders and left the hallway. She crossed to the reception desk a nurse had just vacated to search for the information that would lead her to James.

"What are you doing?"

Jane froze at the sharp, feminine voice for a moment before she plastered a bright smile on her face. She rose and extended her hand to the woman before her. "I apologize. I was looking for the room number of a patient. Dr. Young told me when he sent for me, but I went and forgot. I'm his nurse in Amherst."

The nurse before her looked doubtful as she looked her over. "Is that so? There is no Dr. Young that works at this hospital."

"No, he isn't a regular doctor at this hospital, but he's received special privileges. His brother, James, is a patient."

"Oh, yes. Such a tragic case. What was your name again?"

"Louise Schaffer." It was the closest thing to a truth in her story. If Charles had revealed his real nurses name, she was done for. If this nurse didn't know the name, the name could be passed onto Charles. If he was as intelligent as Michael claimed all the Young's were he might recognize her use of Clara's middle name and married name. Considering Michael had returned home to tell them of her death, hopefully Charles would contact Michael with questions.

"Do you usually just walk into a hospital you don't work and nose through their files, Miss Schaffer?"

"Only once in a while." Jane laughed it off. If she displayed her nerves or guilt, she'd have reason to doubt. "What room would I find Mr. Young in?"

"I can take you there."

"Oh, no. That won't be necessary. I can see by your patient load you're very busy. I can find it on my own."

"Very well. Room two-sixteen. That's in Ward C on the second floor. Just take the main stairs there. You can't miss it."

"Thank you." Jane shook the woman's hand again, and waited for her to get settled back in her chair before she headed for the stairs. Halfway up, she spotted two faces from the picture in her pocket, locked deep in conversation. She turned her head to keep her face hidden until they passed her going down the steps.

If she wasn't mistaken, it was Nick and Charles, based on the picture and Michael's detailed descriptions. Since they were heading down the stairs, that meant there was a good chance James' room might be free of visitors. Perhaps it meant Alan was taking a chance at getting to the Young brother himself.

At that thought, Jane took off like a shot up the steps. If she'd thought hard about what she was doing, she might have turned tail, but she wasn't there to run away. She was there to trap the maniac in her clutches.

In record time she made it to Ward C, rushing down the hall. She scanned every face to no avail, stopping only when she got to room two-sixteen. The room sat empty, save for the tall man on the bed. His face was instantly recognizable, the tallest of the brothers in the picture she carried in her pocket.

After a cautious glance behind her, she slipped into the room. If she found Alan, it wouldn't be safe to have the picture on her. She set the picture face down on the table beside the bed. She thought about hiding it, and the note she'd written on the back during her long train ride full of second thoughts. However, he idea of catching the attention of her siblings seemed wiser.

"I wish I could remember you and mourn what is happening to you as a sister should." She set her hand on his shoulder, her voice quiet as possible. The words were barely intelligible to her own ears. "I am sorry. I'm quite certain I am the cause of your grief and pain. I hope one day you and your family can forgive me."

She backed out of the room slowly, pausing at the door to peek into the hall. At the end of the ward Charles headed her direction. A gasp eeked from her lips, and she rushed away in the opposite direction.

The shadows were sufficient enough for her to hide a few doors down. Just as Charles disappeared into James' room, a doctor emerged from the room across the hall. The crown of his head was bald, and he wore glasses. The low chuckle that carried toward her pulled her attention closer.

Hints of stubble showed in the bald circle, proving the hair loss was not natural. Within moments brown eyes lifted, seeming larger behind the lenses in his frames. A false friendly smile creased his features, three small white stripes of scars on his cheeks more pronounced by the action. "I knew I'd find you here eventually."

"Of course you did, Alan."

The smile disappeared. In one quick step he closed the distance between them and gripped her arm. "I have no name."

"'I was mortal, but am fiend. I was merciless, but am pitiful. Thou dost feel that I shudder…Is not this a spectacle of woe'?"

"Your obsession with citing Poe is no more acceptable now than it was near the end of our time together, my dear. Now be good. Be quiet. You were wise to avoid drawing attention to yourself or saying anything to your conscious brother. Keep being smart. Walk with me."

Jane didn't argue or pull free of his tight grip. She ignored the pit of fear in her stomach threatening to overtake her. Her focus had to remain on her goal. To give up now when their plan was moving along would be foolhardy.

Alan pulled her down the hall to the stairs; his grip on her arm much tighter than it appeared. "You never did forget, did you? You had an entire town fooled enough to help fake your death. I am impressed, though not enough to forgive you such a transgression. Don't worry. Before this is all over, you'll get to see much more suffering brought by your hand."

"By your hand," she hissed through her teeth. She had to fight the urge to correct him. The town hadn't helped fake her death, she nearly had died. They'd simply not reported her return from that cold fate. "I have harmed none."

"How quickly we forget." He chuckled. "Oh, excuse me."

"You lied to me for years."

"I lie to everyone, Clara. You were supposed to be highly intelligent, not just have a perfect memory. It isn't my fault you couldn't figure it out sooner. Then again, it all has worked to my advantage so I can't complain. At least until you got it into your head to try to turn the tables on me."

"You tried to kill me."

"Only after you'd forgotten just what sort of loss you'd suffer if you did what you wanted. I was protecting you. I was protecting your family."

"Protection? You call killing them protection?" Already they'd arrived at the bottom of the stairs. The doors sat only a few feet away. She knew once they were outside, perhaps a few buildings away, his calm demeanor would disappear. These few moments remaining in the hospital were her last vestige of safety.

A shout echoed from above them. Alan forced her to continue facing forward rather than find out what the commotion was. However, he glanced behind them. His features twisted into furious lines. "What did you do?"

"Nothing." The note she'd left had to have been found, or that's what she hoped. A simple note: *Ask Mike about Jane and her plans*. Alan couldn't know. If he did she'd be done for. Jane whispered, "I did nothing."

"Of course not." Alan yanked on her arm and propelled her toward the doors. "You're the one that's killing them, you know."

Jane managed to crane her head to peer behind her where she found Charles looking right at her from halfway down the stairs. With a lump in her throat, she stumbled after Alan's next yank on her arm. A sob escaped her control. "I know."

"Give me what I want, and it can be all over." He threw open the door of a cab and shoved her inside. He called out an address to the driver, and they were off. "Simple as that."

"It's never simple as that." She didn't bother to look out the window to see if Charles tried to follow, for it no longer mattered. He'd seen her, and that had to be enough. Maybe now they would know. Michael could have his peace, and she knew Cole would find a way to dispense of Alan if she failed.

"Of course it isn't. See, you do remember. Nothing is simple. First, you return what you stole from me."

"Your money?"

"For starters."

"You're going to kill me either way. Why should I tell you where I hid the money?" She peeled off the apron in an attempt to appear more casual than she felt. "After all, you've already shown your word means nothing."

"If we don't retrieve that money, my dear…well, you will be plenty alive. Alive enough to see the pain you've caused destroy the last vestiges of your lost life, long before yours is over."

"Negotiating with guilt?" It seemed, brilliant as he was; Alan was content in the same practices he'd used on Clara.

"It always works with you. Guilt has always been your biggest weakness. You never were strong enough for this life."

"I told you I wasn't like you."

"You were right."

There is no wealth but life.
—John Ruskin

The red man had no need for money,
But in this land that didn't get him far.
The Sioux, Cheyenne, the "noble" tribes.
All reduced to meager land, their history a
scar
On one such tribe I stake my claim.
The first, the next? You must choose.
None are innocent, but one young son
For him, pick wise, pick true.
For a Rattle I never gave him, a home, a life.
He was too Little, it was unfair, unjust, base.
Dear One heed me now. For his future, mine
is gone,
One last deed, some good, to save me from
pure disgrace.

"I sure hope you were right, Jane." As had become his ritual every morning, Cole stared in the mirror at the increasingly familiar new look he'd adopted. He made sure every hair smoothed back straight as Jane had done.

After four days of tending to business in Denver, he'd boarded the train as Cole. Instead of returning to Dominion Falls, he'd traveled the opposite direction.

In Sioux City, he'd disembarked as Charles Hodgkins. Jane might be impressed with the way Cole had managed to grow himself a decent moustache between Denver and Sioux City. In the days since it had grown more under some careful tending and styling he'd managed.

"The Sioux name was derived from Nadowe Su, which meant Little Rattle," she'd said upon reading the letter. When he'd questioned how she could possibly know something like that about a tribe of Indians, she'd muttered, "Know your enemy."

With Cole's extensive doubts, she'd brought Mike into the mix to decipher the letters, and the shrimp had agreed. So, despite Cole's qualms, they'd made the final plans for the deception.

Cole would go to Sioux City in hopes of finding the last part of what Clara had left behind. For the past three days, Cole had lived exclusively as Charles Hodgkins. He'd accepted telegrams that had been pre-arranged to be sent from Denver business associates.

Today was the day Jane was due to arrive in Buffalo. If she were successful, Alan would let her lead him to Sioux City. They would arrive within a week if they left right away. If she wasn't successful, Alan would probably arrive alone. Just the thought tightened up his fist until the letter in his hand crushed into a dense ball.

"Don't mess this up."

You worry too much," her whisper lingered in his head. *He wants his money. He'll keep me alive until he gets it.*

There's no way he'll learn how to acquire it until I see your face again.

Cole tugged on his lapels in an unnecessary attempt to straighten them again. Everything was riding on Jane's guess that Sioux City was the right place to be, on her ability to get Alan where they wanted him, and on her final bets that all was riding on her typical key phrase.

Annabel Lee. She is everywhere. Jane had done her best to soothe away his concerns. Her fingers ran along his back, kneading away every knot of tension that formed. *Even in this letter here. Another reference to money. Another reference to Annabel.*

> *Money can't solve problems. It can't erase the past.*
>
> *It can ensure a future, never meant to last.*
>
> *Charles will take you there. Annabel will make it free.*
>
> *From depravity to hope. No more reason to flee.*
>
> *For the first at the first. No more no less, it's true.*
>
> *My only hope to help. Not near my total due.*

He'd done all he could to deny her logic. He tried to explain it all away, saying she was trying to make sense out of nothing, but the last letter had mentioned puzzles. Mike's agreement on most of it sealed the deal. So there Cole sat, in the Cataract Hotel in Sioux City, waiting on Jane, and blending in until he could complete his own task.

He was about to take a huge risk in hopes she was right about everything, that her sharp mind hadn't failed them this time. Every step of the plan from here on out was unsure and based on the belief she had enough of Clara in her to decipher the letters and that everything she'd taken from Alan awaited in Sioux City along with whatever else Clara had managed to stash away.

Pushing aside all the doubt in a long breath, Cole grabbed the bowler from the end of his bed and set it on his head. "Time to take the risk."

Part of the plan had been for him to make himself familiar in the town. Over the course of the past few days, he'd visited a couple of saloons, gone to restaurants, and bought enough merchandise at the mercantile to catch notice.

Questions were met with a vague suggestion that he was buying land in the area. Everything Jane had suggested, he'd done.

Now, as he met with the most difficult task, nerves kicked in. On the stoop of the First Bank of Sioux City, his stomach twisted into knots. This could be a dismal failure. Everything relied on the words Jane had fed him and the hope she was right.

An over-friendly banker greeted him at the door. "Afternoon, sir. Louis Jacobs. How may I help you?"

Cole focused on his speech and manners. Jane's instructions and constant corrections beat through his skull in a cadence. He shook the man's hand less firm than he usually would. "Afternoon. I need to close my account."

"Close it, sir?"

"Yes. I've decided to consolidate my funds." Cole repeated the words verbatim as Jane had told him a plausible excuse. Now he'd see if she'd thought of everything and her assumptions were correct.

"Please, come back and let me see if I can help you." The man led Cole back toward his desk. "First I'll need your name."

"Charles Hodgkins," Cole said smoothly.

"Let me go check my records, Mr. Hodgkins." Louis went to a file cabinet and leafed through the folders.

On any normal day it would take every ounce of effort to not lean back and relax in the chair like he did back home. In this situation his nerves were too tight. His body was so tense he was naturally as nervous as they'd created Charles to be.

Hands clenched tight in front of him, he sat erect. For the first time in a while he was truly nervous. Asking him to do this was insane. Outside of one time, he hadn't changed who he was, and even then it hadn't gone beyond a name.

"To verify who you are, your date of birth?" Louis sat back down and looked at him expectantly.

A point of contention, they'd finally settled on Alan's date of birth over Michael's. Only on the belief that Clara would appreciate the irony, and the idea that if Alan had found the letters he'd assume she'd use her brothers. Too many assumptions. "March twenty-fourth, 1834."

"Very good. Now, there was one other thing before I can allow any transactions or exchange of information."

Cole let a smile form. Crazy as it seemed, Jane had been right. Everything was falling into place. Maybe the tides were finally turning to their favor. Maybe they would win after all.

"There is a pass code on the account." Louis folded the file over to cover it, even though Cole couldn't see it from where he sat.

"Of course. Annabel Lee."

"Thank you, Mr. Hodgkins." Louis flipped open the folder again, leafing through the papers in quick order, finishing with the top one. Once he'd finished, he cleared his throat. After scratching his forehead, he cleared his throat again, leaning forward a bit. "You said you wished to close the account?"

"Yes."

"Do you want me to transfer the funds to a different account?"

"No, I'd like to take the funds with me."

"Cash?"

"Is there a problem?" Cole leaned forward. Something was certainly unanticipated by Jane, something that had Louis wrapped tightly. "I believe I made myself clear."

"Well, sir. This is a substantial amount."

To hear a man behind the desk of a bank say that made Cole's mouth go dry. Jane had guessed that at most it would be several thousand dollars. Trying to sound normal, he nodded. "I am aware of this, Mr. Jacobs."

"All right, sir. Let me see what I can do to get this ready for you." Louis stood, tugging on the end of his jacket. In an attempt to appear calm, he failed at hiding the fact he was actually wiping his palms off. "I'll need you to sign for it, of course."

Cole gave a short nod, unwilling to give away his rate of tension. Once Louis stepped away from the desk, Cole leaned forward more to look in the folder. For a long minute he studied the initial signature for the account, relieved to see it was something he could easily copy.

He gave a quick glance to the number written at the bottom of the top sheet. His body went numb, and he slid back in his chair. Nerves threatened to bring back favorite habits, but he sat still. His jaw clenched tight, he stared at the desk before him. It was far easier than thinking too hard about the number he'd seen, *$15,973.89.*

That which deceives us and does us harm,
also undeceives us and does us good.
—Joseph Roux

"Mind if I join you?" Kat's voice broke through the swirling mass of thoughts racing through Mike's head.

"Of course." The polite reply came automatic, not needing any space of thought. Mike was still too focused on the newest puzzle he'd been confronted with.

"Mike?" After a moment Kat closed her hand over his. When he didn't respond immediately, she squeezed gently. "What is going on? You look just awful."

For a moment, Mike pulled free of his thoughts. He laughed. "Thank you for telling me. It's good to know my lack of sleep hasn't been for naught."

"Have you heard anything?"

"I have, actually. Only this morning. It simply is nowhere near what I was expecting." Mike sighed, unwilling and unable to explain further. He had to talk to someone about it. However, the person he had to have a discussion with was not Kat. "But how are you holding up? How is Cindy?"

"Changing the subject? We're both fine. Cindy misses Jesse. I believe Cole is too stubborn to die or screw up. Jane? Well, I'd rather not think about that. Except for—"

"As neither of us wants to think about it, let's eat." Mike forced a smile and straightened as Cora walked up. "Nothing is more pleasing a distraction. Well, almost nothing."

Katherine allowed a laugh. "I certainly hope you have other plans for distraction. For that one will only make you fat."

"I'm well on the way," Mike leaned back to pat his belly. "I can't help it when Cora serves up such delicious food. I'm spoiled rotten."

"You're rotten, all right." Cora's lips twisted into a smirk. "What do you want today, Mike? I got a good meatloaf or some vegetable soup."

"He'll take the meatloaf," Katherine piped up. "So will I. It sounds delicious, thank you. What would Jane have to say about all this gluttony?"

He pursed his lips. "'Worthless people live to eat and drink, people of worth eat and drink only to live'. Socrates."

"That sounds about right," she chuckled.

"But I hear no chiding ringing in my ears, and thus," he grinned when his plate was set before him, "I eat."

"Gluttony." She shook her head.

"It's divine. No wonder it is a deadly a sin."

"Enough stalling and distracting, Mr. Young. What has you anxious today?" When he failed to give her any answers after several bites, she poked him with her fork. "Did you hear word from Jane?"

"Sort of."

"Please elaborate. I promise I'm not as empty in the brain as I might seem."

Mike kicked her under the table. "Nobody said you were."

"Then elaborate."

"I got a telegram from Charlie. All it says is '*I was told to ask about Jane and her plans by Belle in red hair. Explain.*'"

"Belle…oh, dear. You call her Clarabelle."

"Exactly. He saw her. Somehow she told him to ask about Jane and her plans. But why? Was she already in danger?" He set his fork aside and ran his hand through his hair. On instinct, it went back to his pocket where the telegrams hid. "Then I got a telegram from Cole."

"So soon?"

"He said that Jane was right, but very, very wrong. He says I need to get to Sioux City quick, before she does."

"That means awful quick. Are you going?"

"Already got my tickets booked." Mike met the gaze of a large cowboy across the restaurant. When the man got up and left, Mike sighed. "I'm going to go make Jane one angry woman."

"How?" Katherine leaned forward, her green eyes bright. "What are you up to?"

"I don't have time to explain. I have a couple of telegrams to send before I leave on the train. I just hope I succeed before it's too late."

"Too late for what?"

"To be smarter than my sister."

She laughed. "Mike, you have totally lost me."

"Then I'll leave you the way that would make Jane proud. With a quote by Jean de la Fontaine…"

"He was a poet, yes?"

"Yes, and he once said 'It is a double pleasure to deceive the deceiver'." Michael winked with a grin and kissed the back of her hand before rushing from the restaurant.

He would reply to Charles. He would make it to Sioux City—with a new plan, one that Jane didn't need to know.

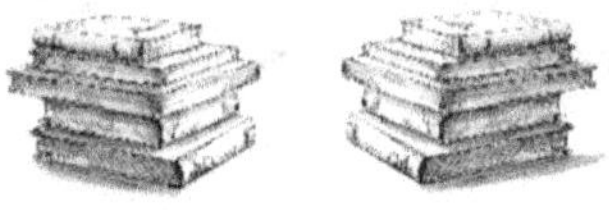

Courage is resistance to fear, mastery of fear— not absence of fear.
—Mark Twain

Perhaps if she'd been a more dignified woman, or had not long ago given up on being close to respectable, she'd be embarrassed. Maybe if she was the slightest bit ashamed of the scars the past six months had left on her flesh, she'd be horrified over her current state.

Jane wasn't embarrassed, horrified, or ashamed in any way. On the contrary, she was infuriated.

Either for some sort of sick pleasure, or to teach her a lesson, Alan made her strip down, claiming the need to check and be sure she had no weapons on her person. He then left her sitting tied to a chair for over a day. Her only respite had been bits of food and water.

Even though her position was dangerous, she took care to eat calmly and sip her water. It had been her plan to get caught, she'd known he would be there, and Alan knew she'd known. In that brief glimmer of time, there was no deception.

However, the final act had yet to start. He thought he could break her. He didn't realize how much she wasn't willing to give it all up this time. This was how she would figure out if she really was no better than Clara.

By the time he finally removed the bindings and let her stand, her mind became more set than ever. No matter what he did, she wouldn't let him get to her. Somehow, she would win this battle, even if it hurt. The knife he kept out even after her ties had been cut led her to believe it very well could hurt.

As he circled, he began another thorough examination, commenting on the scars she'd received since he'd thrown her from the train.

Instead of giving him the pleasure of seeing her disgust and fear she chose to annoy him in return. Staring straight ahead, she pulled on Whitman's words. In hushed tones she spoke under his stream of conversation and remarks. "'You degradations—you tussle with passions and appetites'."

"Your biggest mistake was admitting you understood me." His finger pressed into the scattering of white dots and lines that pebbled her flesh at her ribs, the sole reminder of the Indian attack. "Why on earth would you remember how to speak French if you'd truly lost your memory?"

She'd often wondered over the things she'd managed to remember. Rather than argue, she continued. His annoyed twitches and tics were ignored in favor of her own sanity. "'You smarts from dissatisfied friendships, Ah wounds, the sharpest of all. You toil of painful...'"

The knife poked through the flesh of her stomach as his dark eyes leveled on hers. "Answer my question."

The sharp sting of pain made her pause. She knew this was minor, and she had to be prepared for far worse. With a deep shaky breath she continued, "'...and choked articulations—you *meannesses*'."

The knife pulled across her stomach, not deep enough for serious injury, but enough to draw blood. "I told you to stop citing. It is annoying."

She stared straight ahead, determined to remain unresponsive to his intended threats. "'You broken resolutions, you *racking angers*, you smothered ennuis; Ah, *think not you finally triumph—my* real *self has yet to come forth'*."

"I know your real self. I'm the one that helped you destroy her, remember?" He moved back behind her, pulling her back toward him with the knife blade pressed into her back, and hand around her throat. "Of course, there was the boy. I had my suspicions that you'd known for some time, although how you found out is a story I'd appreciate hearing."

She gasped when the tip of the blade pierced her skin again. Exhaling against the already fading pain, she lifted her chin. "I wish it was a fascinating story. I followed you. I saw him, and he looks too much like his father for me to miss the connection."

"You followed me? Even after that incident in Galveston?" He clicked his tongue. "You really are far more trouble than you're worth. You can't be trusted."

"I guess you would know. You certainly can't be trusted for anything." Any thoughts of keeping silent fled as her temper flared. "You've killed and hurt innocent people for your revenge. You're deranged."

Her shriek when he backhanded her resounded around the room, followed by the *thump* of her body hitting the floor. He leaned down toward her. "What was that?"

"'A lunatic may be *soothed* for a time, but in the end he is very apt to become obstreperous'. Poe."

"You stupid woman." He grabbed her arm and yanked her toward him. "Do you want to try that one more time?"

"Since you are too dense to understand what I said the first time." Jane glared up at him, "I'll say it again. You're *deranged*."

One more shriek was heard through the door as a man walked past, but after that, only a few *thumps* before silence descended.

Sin goes in a disguise, and thence is welcome; like Judas, it kisses and kills; like Joab, it salutes and slays.
—George Swinnock

Consciousness tugged with faint insistence, tickling the back of her mind with thoughts of food. Slumber tried to pull stronger with dreams so vivid and real she was content to remain wrapped in their warmth. Over them both pain crept in, wrapped tightly into every breath, stretching across every muscle with increasing insistence. A soft cry escaped her lips, protesting the parting from her dreams.

Darkness greeted her open eyes, her mind trying to reconcile her last conscious memories with her current state of being. Once consciousness was more than fleeting, the pain settled in. Her cheek took the brunt of the focus, while the rest of the lit nerves settled into her ribs. Nothing more than soreness lingered elsewhere. Everything else settled deeply into a sense of plush luxury and comfort. After beating her, he'd gone to the strange extreme of tucking her into the softest bed she could ever remember being in.

A small shift of her position made her ribs smart, and she groaned aloud. It was the only sound in the silent room, but she sensed someone else there. Gooseflesh raised on her arms.

She clung to her hope, determined to always remember what she needed to do.

The only problem was that she had no idea how long she'd been unconscious. He'd held her for a day before this beating. While he might have had the luxury of time, she had very little.

At the moment he had most of the control in this situation. She grasped what little she could. After checking her cheek with a soft touch that stung but didn't blind her, she took as deep a breath as her ribs allowed. "What now?"

"Either you cooperate or we start the process a different way. I can get creative when the need is there."

She focused every effort on remaining calm. Her breath steadied. "I came of my own volition. I knew you would be there. Why would I not cooperate?"

"I hardly believe you are here for any reasons other than payback. You foolishly cling to life. Payback won't happen, so cooperation is key."

"'In taking revenge, a man is but even with his enemy, but in passing it over, he is superior'. Francis Bacon."

The cluck of his tongue echoed around the room. "You? Passing it over? You may be clever, but you're also very passionate. Releasing transgressions isn't one of your many skills."

"I think we can agree I have learned a few new skills." What was she doing? This conversation was going nowhere. If she just gave in, though, he'd never believe her. No matter what, she had to keep this up.

"Not nearly enough. As you can tell it's the middle of the night. When morning comes we get on a train. You are the one who will determine its destination."

"Oh?"

"Either to Colorado so you can watch everyone you love become utterly destroyed, or to my money."

"Is this just about your stupid money?" It was preposterous. They both knew that much. How long would they keep that up? More importantly, how long would he?

"It's a start."

"'Where wealth accumulates, men decay'." Her eyes closed as the words flew from her mouth without censor. "Oliver Goldsmith."

"I'm getting very tired of your continual tendency for verbosity. Just tell me where the money is."

"'What difference does it make how much you have? What you do not have amounts to much more'. Seneca."

"Clara."

She didn't even flinch at his tone. "You want your money? Money is a fool's gain."

"You liked it well enough to steal a good portion of mine." With a long scratch a flicker of light filled her vision. After another flicker it grew stronger, the lamp lighting her field of vision. He hovered just out of the edge of it, eyes hidden by shadow. "You also always preferred to take the life of the wealthy over the poor."

"You tried to whore me out when we were without the extensive funds. Why wouldn't I prefer the life of the wealthy?" Clara's letters to Michael proved invaluable. They probably wouldn't save her life, but they would certainly help extend it just a little longer.

"You claim such disparity. Yet you didn't mind becoming a whore for that saloon owner, a very willing whore, at that."

Despite her best efforts, her eyelids fluttered. Her stomach twisted at the comparison. "I did not become a whore."

"Even a private whore is still a whore, Clara."

Her breath caught in her throat as the words hit her hard. She closed her eyes and let them sink in. For a brief moment, her heart's grief swallowed them whole. Her mind raced as her heart sank, but then it all came back.

The chain trembled along her skin as he pulled it out from beneath her tight collar. Cole let the pendant drop into the middle of the cascade of lace at her throat. "No reason to hide it."

"Staking your claim on me?" The attempt to be light-hearted faltered in the catch of her throat. Her hand shook when she reached for the pendant. "Your prize."

"You're no prize."

"Thank you."

"No, I mean no man could own ya."

The way his voice grew thick made her body shudder. The room blurred, and she leaned back against him.

"You're stronger than that."

"I wasn't always."

"It weren't you. He got her at her weakest. Now he don't stand a chance." The squeeze of his hands on her shoulders cleared her vision for a moment. He winked at her in the mirror, "Not against you."

"Am I different enough?"

"Got more to fight for."

"I do?"

"You got Jesse."

"I had him before." With her voice catching again, she stepped away.

"That was different. You didn't know he was David's."

"Michael, David, the Young family, I had all of them. Now, they are strangers."

"You got me."

That made her pause. A smile tugged on her lips, but he wasn't as quick to hide his grin. "I suppose I do."

"I ain't easy to shake."

"No, you're really not. I've tried." She took his offered hand, letting him pull her close. "But she had David."

"You ain't her."

"So?"

"Do you want to forget? Give all of this up? Hell that it might be?"

"God, no." Her sob was unstoppable, filling the void they'd sworn they wouldn't cross. From there it went downhill, tears slipped out of their tenuous bindings. "I don't ever want to forget again. I want to remember it all, every joy, even every pain."

"Then don't forget. Don't forget all the people that are waiting for you." He tucked his finger under her chin, swiping tears from her cheek with his thumb. "Don't forget I'm waiting for you. Fight for that."

She didn't try to stop the tear that slipped down her cheek. It could help her case, make him think his words had hit their intended target and she was truly as wounded as Clara had been.

"What will it be, Clara?"

"Either way you're going to destroy everyone I left behind and kill me eventually," she said quietly. "What incentive, have I?"

His finger ran lightly along her cheekbone, erasing the tear as quick as it had fallen. "If you cooperate, I'll make it quick and painless. The longer you fight, the worse it is for all those you hold dear."

"I hold no one dear anymore. That's why I left, why I was hiding again, changing again. I didn't want them to recognize me, but I had to see James first, see what you did to him."

"If I could believe that, you would not be here in front of me. You obviously do still care a great deal."

"No, I just wanted to know how much payback you deserve."

"See? I knew you were out for revenge. What is the plan? To lead me into a trap? You don't think I'm that gullible."

"I think you're that determined, but I don't believe I'm quite so stupid."

"I used to believe you weren't. Now I believe differently, my dear."

She shivered at the endearment, looking up at him again before pushing herself to sit. Turning to face him, she was vaguely aware of the fact that he'd dressed her back into her under things. "I won't be your puppet again. My eyes are open to your manipulations. I've seen your lies, and you sicken me."

The flame of the lamp flickered bright enough to catch the maniacal look in his eye when she spoke. His body remained still except for the quick movement of his hand flipping the blade of his knife into view. "We'll come to an agreement, Clara. By the time the night is through, you'll see you have no choice."

*Absence from those we love is self from self—
a dealdy banishment.
—William Shakespeare*

"'Do then I not become wise when I trace with my eye her sweet bosom's form'." Jane's voice carried over the book, her laughter clear in her tone. "'And the line of her hips stroke with my hand'?"

"You're lying." He trailed one finger up her leg. "It don't say that."

"It does too." Her hand ran through his hair, nails scratching his scalp. The flutter of pages in his ear let him know she hadn't dispensed of the book yet. "I told you, poetry can be very stimulating. You just have to know where to look."

"Seems like an awful lot of work."

"For something this stimulating, the pleasure is worth a little effort I think."

If effort was what she wanted, he could accommodate. Turning his head, he kissed her stomach. Slipping up toward her delicious lips, he grinned. "I can think of better ways to be stimulating. Better ways to work for it, too."

She giggled when his lips continued up between her breasts, "I said effort, not work."

"That is work," he mumbled against her skin. Tugging the book from her hand, he looked at it. "All the reading, looking for words you like. I like my ideas better."

"You would."

"Don't you?"

"In most cases."

"Besides." Her body sank lower into the bed, his argument was almost won, not that it was much of one. He ran his tongue along the sensitive dip of her neck. "If you gotta look in another language, that's really too much work."

"It's not just German." Her words mere whispers, her body reacted to every touch. A soft whimper interrupted her next thought as his thumb grazed her breast.

He captured her earlobe and hummed against it. He rumbled, "Not convinced."

"Whitman... 'Hair, bosom, hips, bend of legs, negligent falling hands all diffused, mine too diffused', " she whispered breathlessly, her hands running along his back eagerly. " 'Ebb stung by the flow, and flow stung by the ebb, love-flesh swelling and deliciously aching'."

There was no way to stop the moan as she breathed the last words in his ear. Maybe she had a point. He was more than happy to prove it, rolling with her and letting the book drop to the floor, forgotten.

Cole's eyes flew open. Groaning, the dream flew from his head much faster than his body forgot. The memory of that night would have been best forgotten until he saw Jane again.

A pounding on the door broke through his discomfort, alerting him to why he'd had to wake up in the first place. "Wait just a minute."

He'd snapped out the command, but there was no stopping the irritation. Just then, he'd tear about anyone to shreds just for breathing wrong.

"Hurry up."

The muffled voice of Mike brought him back to attention, and he flew to his feet. With a quick swipe of his hand over his face to chase away the lingering dream, he threw open the door. "Get in here."

"Hello to you, too." Mike didn't even nod, walking right in when told.

"You hear from her?"

"Sort of."

Deep in his chest a rumble started. "Mike."

"The message I got wasn't directly from her. All I know for sure is she made it there. She found Alan."

"Don't you mess with me."

"It was from Charlie. Now tell me what the hell you meant in your telegram."

Cole sank into a chair. Under the bed was the trunk he'd bought to put the money in. "Under the bed. You'll need this."

Mike caught the key Cole tossed him, kneeling down next to the bed. He stopped short of bringing the box out from under the bed. "This isn't exactly what I expected."

"Ain't exactly what the bank expected. Even much as they keep on hand, took two days to get me all of it. I thought maybe they were just stalling to have me arrested."

With a grunt, Michael dragged the trunk out from under the bed. "I don't want to know."

"Yes, you do."

"Yes, I do."

"Near sixteen thousand." The *thump* of Mike dropping to the floor echoed through the room. Cole reached out and poured himself a glass of whiskey. "Yeah."

"How did she? Was it all his?"

"Open it. It's got a copy of the records too." Cole tossed back the glass, letting the fire burn down to his belly. Didn't matter, the lump stayed in his throat. At this point, the burn was weak. Everything felt numb and not in the good way. "Weren't just from him."

"You got the records?"

"My accountant will want to verify that our records match yours." The words sprang forth without a stitch of effort. It's what she'd told him to say, because she'd been curious, too. "She explained what it meant. I didn't care."

"Right." The trunk top fell back with a *thunk*. "All here?"

"I kept out some. Pay for the room, the whiskey, train tickets, emergencies." Another full glass interrupted him. "Why the hell did Charlie send you a telegram instead of Jane?"

"She told him to. I guess she was ready for them to know the truth."

"Or she's in trouble."

"Both possibilities considered."

"Mike." His hand tensed on the glass as Mike kept himself distracted, his answers short. The trunk shutting didn't ease Cole's tension. "Much as I hate words, you ain't using enough."

"Whitman?" For a moment, the tense lines of Mike's face relaxed. He picked up the book Cole had left abandoned on the bed. "That's the one you chose?"

"No, she did. Found it in my bag." Cole leaned over and snatched it away, throwing it back on the bed. "What in tarnation is going on?"

Mike sighed. "You're going to have to trust me."

"Can't do that until you start talking."

"I can't do that just yet."

"Jane could arrive at any minute."

"She left Buffalo last night." Mike flew to his feet when Cole did. Despite the height difference, his fists were clenched, and he was ready. "Her plan was foolish on its own. You know it as well as I do. I've added to it."

"You sure she just left." Cole didn't back off, but he made no further move to attack. At Mike's nod, his lips tensed. "How?"

"A favor from a friend. That's all I can say right now. Give me two hours. I need to call in another favor to make sure we get this trunk back to Colorado safe. Then we'll sit down for supper real nice and polite-like."

"I want to know what you added to the plan. All of it."

"You will. You have to know. It's the only way it will work."

"Two hours."

"I'll be right back at that door, answering every question you're going to have."

Cole fought against every urge to beat it out of Mike right that second. If Jane had just left New York like he'd said, she was still days away, if she got to Sioux City at all. Another couple hours seemed like forever.

In the end, all he could manage was one tense nod. Mike was right, after all. They all knew Jane's plan was far from perfect. He could only hope the new one was better. He didn't move out of the way, forcing Mike to move around him to leave.

"Mike."

"Yeah."

"Not a minute more."

"Not a minute."

By the time the door closed, Cole already felt the pull of the dream. Being apart from Jane got worse each minute, and not just because he ached and feared for her or even because every thought was of her. No, she was a part of him, deep inside to his very soul. She consumed him in a way no other woman had before. If he still believed in it, he'd call it love.

Cole sank onto the bed. Who was he kidding? If he didn't believe in it, why did he long to hear her say it? Or to have her in his arms, breathless and wanton, free, like she'd said she wanted to be. He needed her to not be afraid to say it like she had in the past and know he wouldn't walk away this time. For the first time, he wasn't afraid to hear it.

He dropped back onto the bed, grunting when his back hit the book. "Poetry." After grumbling about the discomfort, he fished the book out and read the inscription.

From the one so unwilling to have me leave, and me just as unwilling to go. Unwilling...to say goodbye. Whitman himself describes us best—"In the confusion we stay together, happy to be together, speaking without uttering a single word." Remember me. Look over at page 61.

Cole turned to the page of her favorite poem, the one she was always reading, Pent-up Aching Rivers. Still within the same poem, she'd marked section, her markings shakier than her usual notes.

Hark close and still what I now whisper to you,
I love you, o' you entirely possess me.

His thumb covered her markings before he closed the book and tossed it aside. "She did say it. In poetry. Damn crazy woman."

Absence from whom we love is worse than death, and frustrates hope severer than despair.
—William Cowper

With every heartbeat blood rushed through her head, roared along the veins, leaving her cringing from the noise of her own life. With the way her head hurt, there was no staying asleep. An old lady could have beaten her in a race getting out of the bed, but Jane still managed to find her feet. One long-held breath let her know she'd done it without waking Alan.

After another day—or was it two? —of forcing her into submission, they'd boarded a train. His strategy included injecting something he'd said would make her tell the truth. The drug's supposed effect was likely a lie on his part. She'd told him the same thing she would have without it. "The money is in Sioux City."

In accordance with her declaration, they were headed that way. She had no idea how many days it had been or the slightest clue of where they were. She'd told him the bank and the town, but blurred the truth on the name. A slur on the words, it might have come out more like John Hodgins than Charles Hodgkins.

Another day, maybe two, she had to make it.

On shaky feet she crossed to the dresser, looking into the mirror in the dim lamplight. Even in the dark, her appearance drew a gasp. She clamped her hands over her mouth, immediately regretting the action. Fresh pain raced across the darkened cheek, radiating into her sore head. Another few minutes passed before her vision was clear enough to see straight again. With her lower lip pinched tightly in her teeth, she let her hands drop.

Purples and greens radiated across the cheekbone up around her eye. Every day he'd added to it, until it was painful just to the touch. It was the only visible bruise he'd made. She wasn't sure if that was why he kept adding to the same one or if he just liked to backhand her.

Her hands trembled, running along the bruises she knew covered her body. She'd known this was inevitable. He had to believe he'd broken her. Had he? For the first day, it had been easier to believe he hadn't. She'd just had to act like she would have anyway. When the beatings started, things had changed to become much harder. The harsh blows disrupted her minds attempts to disappear into her memories. Each impact forced her in the present, under his control, his, not hers.

Her knees buckled, and she floated down to the floor. Cole. Soon she would see him. God willing, he would help her remember her strength and hold onto it. It felt so far away. If he was there. He had to be there. She needed him. Cole's silky timbre flooded her memory and that of his strong arms still holding her close at the depot. *"Say it. I ain't gonna run."*

Why couldn't she just say it? To get through this, that's why. It would have been much easier to let go and give up with no unfinished matters. She wouldn't give up. She couldn't.

Her mouth clamped shut, but a sharp pain rushed through her chest. Her whole soul screamed out against his absence, the injustices done to her, the blows dealt, and the words that lashed at her own beliefs.

Fibers from the carpet squeaked as her hands clenched into fists, pressing into the floor with the force of a thousand invisible blows. Her shoulders shook with silent sobs. He hadn't won. Cole was right. She was stronger than this, stronger than Alan. She was still alive. Despite his attempts, she'd still deceived him enough. He was evil and evil would not win. She would see Cole again and destroy Alan, and together they'd finish this.

Her toes curled under her, and she pushed to her feet. Against every turn of her stomach, she returned to the bed and lay back down beside Alan. There was no telling how soon he would wake her again. Until then, she would lose herself to the memories and wrap herself back in the safety of Cole's arms. The warmth of his touch and the tenderness of his caress filled her dreams and her soul. In the safety of her mind, he held her tightly and rocked her in a soothing rhythm.

"Wake up, Clara."

It wasn't Cole. A low groan pulled up from her belly, the noise adding to her headache. The rocking had been the train.

The train? When had they boarded a train? The shriek of the train's whistle ripped through her skull like a bull gored it, and she flew to sitting. The whole room swayed.

"Easy. Don't want to fall down."

"What 'av 'u." She sucked her lips between her teeth, rubbing them together. Odd. They felt numb. The room blurred for a minute.

"Don't bother trying to talk. It's opium. You probably feel a little out of sorts. It will get worse. I just gave it to you. Take it easy, my dear." He gripped her arm and helped her to her feet. "Wouldn't want to get hurt again."

"O…pium?" She could have sworn she was shrieking. Hundreds of words and curses flew by, but disappeared before she could form them. In attempt to keep it simple, she managed to blurt, "You drugged me."

"Of course. The chloroform was to get you on the train and in a sleeper. As your doctor, I required it. Now that we're in Sioux City, I'm the embarrassed and concerned husband of a hopeless, clumsy drunk."

"Not…drunk…."

"Of course, you aren't, my dear." He soothed her, patting her arm.

Vaguely, she became aware of murmurs around them. Oh, this was part of his show. She had to force her mind to work, a task that grew more difficult and slow as time passed. Wait. Did he say Sioux City?

"That's it, dear. Take a seat."

A seat? Goodness. Where were they? What was she doing? Oh dear, not good.

"Ow." Jane groaned when she leaned on her bad cheek, shifting sides. A long sigh escaped, and she tried to focus her eyes. Blurry shapes took focus. She was at a table in a restaurant, people bustling around her.

Habit pulled her eyes to the nearby bar, trying to find something familiar among the blurry shapes. Blue, ice blue, Cole, it had to be Cole. Why couldn't she focus?

I cannot let you go, I would do you good,
I am for you, and you are for me, not only
for our own sake, but for others' sakes.
—Walt Whitman

"Dammit, Jane. Wake up." Cole shook her, trying to get any response. "You gotta be sober to think. Talk to me."

He pushed away from the bed and her prone form to pace the room. She didn't move an inch, as if she wasn't even breathing. He'd seen such a thing before. Hell, she'd seen it too. When the whores had started getting opium from the Chinese, they'd ended up in the throes of such spells. There was no way Jane's current state was caused by alcohol.

From the moment she'd been dumped into the chair at the edge of the restaurant Cole had known. Every inch of him had screamed to run for her then, but he'd leaned harder on the bar. When Alan walked away to get a room, Jane had almost fallen from the chair.

She'd looked drunk, but Jane didn't get drunk. She drank, a hell of a lot for a woman, but he'd never seen her drunk. For a woman with very few limits, Jane had a good grasp on every one of hers.

No, she wasn't drunk. Then she'd moved again. Maybe she'd been trying to seem less intoxicated, he couldn't be sure. Of anything, really. Still, she'd looked right at him.

Nothing.

For a long minute there was nothing. No semblance of any recognition at all until one small sob had escaped, and her head had dropped to the table. After that he'd been a blur of anger and rage and had needed major restraint to stay put. Damn, he wished with all his might that Alan was already dead. It just wouldn't be smart. Not yet, certainly not in such a public venue.

He had to talk to Jane. Find out how much Alan knew. He didn't have much time. Alan had already been gone five minutes. The chambermaid Cole had retrieved the key from was long gone.

Cole took a deep breath and returned to the bed. Jane remained still as he pulled back the covers, not even the flicker of an eyelid. She wore nothing but a thin chemise, one that didn't hide nearly enough from the maniacal fiend. Stains of purple mottled her flesh, and strips of red rippled across its creamy perfection. One thigh bore the unmistakable evidence of a hand, bruised in colors that showed it had been there for days.

"If he violated you," the words caught in his throat. They'd discussed the possibility. She'd dismissed it as unlikely, saying it wasn't what he was after. Cole swallowed the lump in his throat. He had to stop looking for more cause to anger. There wasn't enough time for his rage, although it was doing wonders for his plans to torture the bastard within an inch of his life.

Cole forced his eyes closed to hide the sight of her injuries. With an exhale he pushed out as much anger as he could. "All right, let's get you on your feet. You need to wake up just a little bit, Jane."

He grabbed her arms and tugged her to her feet, stopping at her whimpered yelp. She slipped back a bit and sat on the edge of the bed. "No, Jane. Stand up."

A groan was his only reward when he yanked her to her feet again. She crumbled against him.

With each step he forced her to take around the room, soft mumblings of complaint escaped from her parched lips. Finally she graced him with a whispered, "Cole."

"Jane. That's it. Come on. Sober up. We need to talk."

"Free?"

"No. Not yet." Cole stopped in the middle of the room and spun her toward him. He gripped her shoulders. Nose to nose, he muttered a 'sorry' before giving her a brutal shake. The inside of his chest constricted at her pained cry. "You're still in his room. *Jane*."

Lips normally supple and delicious now dry and thin, curved into a smile. Blue orbs fluttered open, but the familiar sparkle of life was gone. Dull. Witless. "I…was wrong."

Her soft, barely intelligible sigh twisted him in knots. He cupped her cheek. "Wrong? About what?"

"Alcohol…can't make the…words stop. This?" The idiotic grin she wore grew, her head lolling to the side. "Opium is the way…no words…just pretty colors. Ice blue. Such blue. Cole blue. My favorite."

It was so unlike Jane that for a split second he grinned, but it vanished fast. That was the whole problem.

"Jane. Damn it. Snap out of it." The knowledge of what he had to do about killed him. If he wasn't desperate and pressed for time, he'd never do it. The situation was dire. He needed her far more sober than this. Tension ran through his whole body in the moment before he shook her again, harder than before. "Snap out of it."

"Ow." Jane's hands actually flexed and reached for his arms. Some tension returned to her limbs. The floppy legs took some responsibility. "Oh."

"Jane."

"Cole." A sob and her legs gave out again. Another pained cry twisted his gut when he caught her, but she gripped his coat. "Opium."

"I know."

"Can't…think…"

"You need to. It's got be fast."

"Mind slow."

"Does he know where the money is?"

"Yes."

Cole squeezed her side when her head dropped. "Stay with me. Does he know it's at the bank or with me?"

"Bank." She gripped his arm. "Safe."

The lump reappeared in his throat against his own wishes. He wanted to get her the hell out of there. "Does he know how to get it?"

"No."

"So he needs you sober."

"Hmm?"

"Jane."

She gave a soft yelp when he squeezed again. "Cole…sorry."

The minute she curled into his lap, he gave up the fight. He surrounded her with his arms and pulled her back against him. "We're gonna make him pay."

A quiet hum of agreement against his chest was all he got. It was enough.

"I want nothing more than to take you out of here right now." In his arms it felt like her whole body jumped. Against his will, he unfolded them to let her free.

"No. Can't. One day." The delicate curves of her face hardened into deep lines. She fought to appear strong, against him, and managed to appear sober for a moment though her words were unsteady. "You…were right…He needs me sober. Or close. One day."

"I know."

"If…leave now…lose control."

"You're not in control."

"I won't…Don't…Can't." She dropped her head to his chest. "He would be hunter…again. Can't…let him."

"I know. I said I want to. I know I can't–yet."

"Not safe here."

Cole pulled her tighter against him. "I know. Just one more minute. I gotta hold you one more minute."

"Damn…fool."

He broached no argument to that. He knew it was foolish. Every minute he'd been in here was dangerous. Why Alan had left the hotel and how long he'd be gone were complete unknowns, but he'd had to know she was alive, still fighting and still his.

Once the minute had elapsed, he stood with her still curled against him. If he doubted she was still fighting off the drugs, she reassured him with a squeeze to his arm. The bed welcomed her back into it, but he couldn't take his hands from her side.

"Must."

"I know, damn it." Cole brushed his fingers along her cheek. "You trust me?"

Her hand closed over his. "Always."

A key slid into the lock, clicking into place. Cole moved fast, dropping to the floor and rolling underneath the bed. Two more minutes. That was all he'd needed it. Damn it. Damn it.

One shiny black shoe appeared in the doorway. "Are you awake, my dear?"

Cole's lips twisted. How dare he address her like that?

"Mr. Hodgins? Sir, I apologize. I'm sorry, sir." The pretend chambermaid who gave Cole the key to the room stammered. With every word her voice got weaker, more timid. She was a good actress, and Cole was grateful Jane's family had access to some Pinkertons themselves.

"What is it?" Alan made no disguise of his temper. "Have you no decorum, girl?"

"I'm very sorry, sir. I have no excuse." Her feet shuffled just outside the door. "There's, um, there's a telegram for you. It just arrived at the desk, sir."

"I was just there. I doubt that."

"It came in just a moment ago, after you left the desk. I apologize." One white shoe crossed behind the other, disappearing under skirts when she curtsied. Then the white shoes were gone.

"I can see you're starting to wake up. Not quite enough yet, though." The door remained partway open, but Alan's shoes drew close. Cole held his breath when they stopped just a few feet away.

It was difficult enough to hide his tall frame under this bed, but knowing Alan had a knack for deception made it worse. Any little, tiny hint could give away his presence and ruin every plan that was in place.

"Clara? Are you with me?"

"Black." Her muffled sigh drew a chuckle from Alan.

"Then I'll go check on that telegram. When I get back, I'll wake you up. Don't you worry." There was a rustle of movement, followed by a pained cry from her. "You need to finish telling me what I need to know."

Cole stayed still as a statue, running out of oxygen with how few and far between his breaths were. Every step Alan took toward the door took what felt like an hour. When he paused partway, Cole thought he was done for, but then he was finally gone. Silence lingered, until a soft whimper reached his ear.

Cole scrambled out from under the bed, leaning over Jane. "Jane, I need you to trust me. Whatever happens next, trust me."

"Always. Go."

There was no way he was leaving without one more thing. Gentle as he could, he brushed his lips across hers, letting several small kisses dance across her parched lips before he pulled away.

"Hurry."

Cole made the impossible break away from her. She was right. There was no time, but leaving her wasn't easy. Somehow he made it out of the door and halfway down the hall before he was yanked into an empty room.

"Key." The false chambermaid held out her hand as she shut the door she'd just yanked him through. Her dark eyes stayed on the door. Her false brogue of the chambermaid fell away with the red wig she pulled off her head. "Hurry."

Cole handed the woman back the key before slumping against the wall. Already his arms felt cold, and he hoped that everything that had been planned would really ensure they'd be filled again.

Right in front of him the woman stripped off the boring gray dress of the role she'd been playing. Bright yellow skirts tumbled out from under the dark layers.

She leaned over in front of a mirror, pinching her cheeks. When she spoke again, her voice now carried a southern lilt and was soft as a breeze. "Better. I do hate boring."

Cole blinked at the transformation, stunned from his angry stupor. He'd been watching the change, but even he hardly recognized her.

"That's the signal. It's clear." The chambermaid slapped his arm at a passing brief knock to the door. "Go."

"Right." Cole came back to reality. "You'd better get out of here fast. He ain't gonna be happy that you were wrong."

"Even less happy when he sees who the telegram was for. My mistake. John Hodgins and Charles Hodgkins sound very much alike when you are a stupid servant, after all. Too bad for him I don't work at this hotel or in this town. There'll be no one to punish." With a wink, the woman rushed from the room.

Cole wasn't far behind, heading downstairs to his own room. There was still a lot to be done if Jane was going to be safe. She had to be safe.

*Men are so necessarily mad, that not to be
mad would amount to another
form of madness.
—Blaise Pascal*

Did Clara really think he was too blind to recognize her lover? She thought he was stupid. Did she really think she could outwit him? For years he'd kept her by his side. At one time it had been willingly. She'd given herself to him with abandon. So grateful he'd resolved her little problem of the parasitic child.

It had been easy to see why he'd picked her, not just for the similarity.

Oh, she was so like his Constance. It was almost enough. He'd needed more. Her intelligence. Her wit. Her willingness to be in the life. Most of all, to believe she deserved wickedness.

He'd seen it in her.

She didn't know how long he'd watched her before they met. Since the first time he'd wandered into Heber City. Just two short years after the loss of Constance. But there she'd been. A vision. A ghost. Clara.

His whole life he'd learned to wait, to learn when to strike. The kill was always easy. The waiting was what took time. It had been no different. For weeks he watched and waited. Letting it turn into months.

Normally he'd have moved on, but this was different. For her, he would wait forever for the right opportunity. To know her better than she did. So he watched. Saw her string of suitors.

Noted how many she willingly entertained, and the few that were far less welcome. Each got what they wanted. Every time. With a pleased, smiling yes from her lips, or a whispered, painful *no* that was erased with no other objection.

One by one, Clara welcomed them in. The Superintendent that forced her with power over her job. The Pinkerton she welcomed with a smile in public, but tried to escape in private. Cowboys passing through town, men of business she appeared to enjoy watching work, miners and farmers alike.

He'd seen her broken tears, hiding behind the school away from the students. So easy to swoop in. Except for the students.

He'd studied people his whole life. He knew that's why she didn't leave. She was too attached to her students. Something had to break that attachment. He had no idea what it would be. How to snip that final thread. Then everything had changed. David.

Out of nowhere the cowboy miner had arrived. Clara was slipping away to the idiot. Enamored. Obsessed. Married in weeks. She was destroying his plans.

He had to have her.

It was a matter of time. He had to be patient longer. Something would happen. One of her men would make her forget.

Only the *no*'s weren't needed. Over protests from the town, David lived with her. She fought to keep her job. Men that always ignored her refusal became powerless against her new strength. She was the one refusing to accept a no. Using their own transgressions against them.

Through it all, the moon-eyed husband-to-be was blind. Foolishly selling all the gold from his last strike in Dominion Falls to buy her a house. It wouldn't do. Somehow, there had to be something that would end this.

Alan had smiled into the rising sun. It had been easy to figure out what would break her. The same weakness she always had. A man. Not any man, though. One she was too terrified of to say no to. From there her downfall had been fun to watch. The helplessness of her weak-willed husband. That nobody was no match for a woman like Constance.

Clara. No match.

He'd known she was coming. His camp had purposely been small. Like he hadn't been there for as long as he had. Just over the ridge. Living, watching, waiting.

It was his mistake. Letting people close always got messy. He'd lived with people. It was messy. Complicated. Deception was easier.

So long he'd done it. Even when he'd been Alan. Even with Constance. Her no's still whispered in his ear. Gurgling with the delicate scent of her blood.

The one time he'd tried honesty, he'd been deceived. Going back had been easy. Destroying everything from the past. Including the foolish Alan. Oh, Alan had been successful. Murder and fraud, burglary, extortion, even embezzlement all as himself. Never caught.

Constance had been his undoing.

Trying to create a companion with her doppelganger. That was his newest and biggest mistake. At least he still had his wits. His intelligence. His gift to spot such deception a mile away.

The stupid saloon owner had been unable to hide his presence. More than hair and a few mannerisms were needed. He'd planned for such an event. Such a horribly laid plan to trap him. Even allowed the idiot to see her, although he wondered how Cole got in the locked room. All he could imagine was the stupid little chambermaid had given into his way with the fairer sex.

It didn't matter anymore. With the sun climbing higher into the sky, he guided his horse back into town. Back to the hotel. All of his things were already at the boarding house. He'd taken them there yesterday to give Cole time to see Clara.

Now it was a matter of cleaning up the mess and waiting to set the trap that would work. The one that would get the last bit of nuisance from his life. It was just too bad he'd likely not see his money again. It would have helped. But he had more.

In the room, he worked to clean up the blood left on the pillow. The broken glass ground into the carpet. Once it was presentable, he returned to the restaurant and ordered his meal. His smile was genuine. He did like winning. It was her fault for believing him stupid. She would suffer for it.

The tall figure was unmistakable as it passed. Taking a seat and ordering his breakfast, which was more like lunch he'd woken so late. Opening a paper. Nice touch.

Once Cole's food had been brought, Alan folded his napkin and rose. "Mr. Hodgkins."

Cole's fork stopped halfway off the plate. Alan was surprised with the control he showed in lowering it back to the table. "May I help you?"

Oh, she'd taught him well. He knew she'd been lying. She did remember. "I think we have something to discuss. Something of some importance to you, I believe."

"Is that so?"

He could see Cole's hand jerk to the gun at his side. No, he wasn't stupid enough to do that in public. The gun would remain where it was. "Clara Young."

A smile twitched on the idiot's face before Alan got the privilege of his full attention. Little did he know he had no room to be cocky.

"I don't know anyone by that name. Never have."

"Too bad."

"If you say so."

"I do." Alan sat down, keeping the attention to their table minimal. "It seems she's in a bit of a scrape."

"A scrape?"

"I've always been curious." He picked up a fork, poking a tine into his finger and twirling it haphazardly. It was so much fun to play with idiots.

As expected, Cole's veins stuck out on his forehead. Each movement of his jaw caused them to grow. "About what?"

"Well, Mr. Mitchell. I've always been curious how long a person can really live without food or water." He pursed his lips. "Of course, then I have to think about the weather. There's a storm brewing out there that looks like it'll be fierce. There are also the wild animals as well. So many things to affect her situation."

"What did you do?"

"Worried about your whore now? She's just one. You have a full stable."

"What did you do?"

*Suffering is permanent, obscure and dark,
and shares the nature of infinity.
-William Wordsworth*

Blackness, suffocating and damp, surrounded her when she woke. No light breeched the dark, not even a firefly. The encompassing depth of the hotel bed was long gone. Her body protested every movement as she tried to sit. When she pushed to rise, her hands pressed against damp, cool, firm earth. There was no floor beneath her, no sky hung above her.

What fresh hell could this be? How could she be in such a lightless vacuum?

There had to be walls, or a ceiling, something. There was no such thing as a wall-less pit. What had he done to her? The memories from her drugged stupor were faint and distant. The loss of more memories, no matter how unpleasant caused a familiar ache in her soul. She'd never understand the allure of drugs.

Cole had been there. For a few minutes he'd given her hope and comfort in that horrible room. Unfortunately, Alan had known. All along he'd known Cole was there. He'd forced the rest out of her with all the means at his disposal. Between the drugs and pain, she hadn't been strong enough.

Cole.

He'd said to trust him no matter what, but how could she now? She had no idea what had happened after the last beating, much less where she was. Did he know she was gone? Or where she'd gone? If she had no idea where she was, how on earth could he?

She couldn't wallow. She didn't dare. Cole would never forgive her.

On her hands and knees she crawled in search of the end of her prison. She reached out into the void until her hand made contact with a cold, damp, and very compact dirt wall. In cautious inches she moved her hand up the wall.

A loud screaming cry in the distance hit her ears and she froze. She knew the sound all too well. She'd heard it back home. A mountain lion. Heart pounding, she rose the rest of the way. Finally the dirt wall gave way to a new feeling.

Wood. Could it be a cellar? If it was, there was an exit somewhere. There had to be.

Despite the crushing wave of panic, Jane moved slowly. The cold seeped into her bones and every wound that had been inflicted. Ignoring the beating she'd endured was getting harder to do, as was the scampering of the smallest little feet nearby.

Her eyes began to adjust to the dark, letting in glimpses of smooth earthen walls, empty and broken shelves, and a short ladder with a couple of missing rungs.

"Oh, thank heavens."

Panic took firm hold when she touched the ladder. Alan wasn't so stupid as to leave her with an easy escape. He'd proven that. She was the stupid one. All along she'd been so hopeful she could outwit him, and look where she'd ended up.

She scrambled up the two lowest steps, grabbing the latch and shoving hard as she could. Nothing happened.

"No."

Grasping, she shoved again and again until the rung under her feet broke and she toppled to the floor. Pain flooded every nerve, radiating right through her. Old wounds responded to the new offense as if Alan had resumed her beating. Every inch of her shook as she crawled on her forearms to a broken board on the floor.

"No, you won't win Alan. *Do you hear me?*"

She grabbed the board and forced herself to her feet. All along the ceiling above her she moved to test the strength of every board. She beat at them, screaming with every fiber of her being.

Hours passed in an interminable night. She gave up the fight against the ceiling when her arms grew too tired to lift above her head and her voice too hoarse to use.

Over her head, animals scampered all night while in the corner she could hear the mice moving around. Dawn finally broke with a storm in the distance. The thunder trembled across the sky, though the sunlight seeped through the cracks in the floorboards to show the truth of her despair. Lines of light creased above her right up to the hatch, where a solid black mass hovered right over her escape.

The reality crashed in against her and she sank to the floor. Shivering, she pulled her knees to her chest and prayed her aching belly would cease to allow in the elusive specter of sleep.

"Whatever happens next. Trust me."

The warm sanctuary of Cole's arms and the touch of his lips felt far away now, wrapped in clouded memory. There was no way he could know. Alan would use her to get him. He'd never outsmart Alan. They were doomed.

"I'm so sorry, Cole." No tears would fall, though her body wracked with sobs. The oblivion was welcomed as the first drops of rain dripped from the floorboards that comprised of her ceiling. A tickle touched to her legs, and then another.

Jane fought off her shriek as she realized it wasn't raindrops tickling her. She flew to her feet and stomped at the ground until several mice fell from the shelter of her petticoats. A sob wrenched free as she stomped repeatedly until one mouse was long dead.

Her clothes were soaked through to her body from the rain that still dripped through the slats. The worst of the storm had passed, but now she shivered on top of hurting. What a mess she'd made again.

Only the sound of approaching hooves stopped the next sob from rising. It was just as well, that one had been pure self-pity.

The horse stopped nearby and a heavy thump hit the ground after. Unrushed, heavy, thundering footsteps echoed across the boards.

Panic seized her heart, and she couldn't seem to take a breath. What would she do now? Jane searched for anything to use in defense. In desperation she grabbed a nearby board. A grunt reached her ears, and wood slid against wood, drawing a muttered curse. It wasn't Cole.

The board in her hand shook, but she slipped into the darkest corner, watching the hatch without moving. Bit by bit, grunt by grunt, everything cleared away from the opening. She would be free if she could get past him and to the horse.

One foot dropped into the cellar, testing the strength of the ladder and then another. Just as the head got beneath the hole, she bolted. Shrieking at the top of her lungs, she hit him in the head. He lost his footing and fell back. Still shrieking, she ran into him, pushing him off to the side. With a leap, she scrambled up the ladder. A hand grabbed her foot, and she screamed, kicking against it.

She knew he was talking, she could barely hear murmurs under her screams. He was pulling her back down, grabbing her. "No!"

When his hand came into view again, she turned her head toward it and bit down hard. With a yelled curse he let go, and she was off again, scrambling up out of the cellar, slipping in her muddy shoes across the floor. The horse was close, but she had to untie it, and there wasn't time with her assailant right behind her. An unseen rock tripped her up and the ground met her with shocking intensity. He was on top of her, trying to still her fighting, scratching limbs.

"No!"

"Clara Louise!"

"No!" Jane fought against every pain; panic giving her strength her body didn't quite feel. Somehow she freed her hand long enough to hit him in the eye.

"Aw, damn it, Lou. Don't make me hurt you." Her wrists were grabbed, and her attacker spun her around. "Look at me. It's Tommy."

"I don't know you!"

"Stop fighting before you really hurt yourself, you fool. Cole will kill me if I break you more, even if you do deserve it."

What? Cole? He'd said Cole? That was all it took. The adrenaline seeped from her body. It was then that she actually noticed him. He looked familiar.

The beefy hands holding her wrists loosened their hold, and she followed the arms up to the face. A cowboy hat was pulled low over a round, bearded face.

"I can't see your face."

"Oh, right. Damn. You're not going to run. Right, Lou?"

"Why do you keep calling me Lou?"

A flash of white teeth and he lifted the hat from his head. He helped her to her feet as he spoke. "That's what I've always called you, Clara Louise. You were too much like one of us boys to be called Clara all the time."

Jane shook her head. She'd seen him all right at the saloon as the new addition to town everyone had said was opening a new bank. She'd doubted it, and also felt he was familiar somehow. "I'm confused. I saw you in Dominion Falls at the saloon. Right?"

"Yes, that's how I knew Mike was right. You done lost your mind."

"Who are you?"

"Tommy Young, your brother." His hand was under her elbow the second her knees buckled. "Easy. You're not a delicate flower. That shouldn't have sent you passing out. How much pain are you in?"

"You're one of Clara's brothers."

"Yes. That didn't answer my question."

"Prove it."

"Lou."

"*Prove* it. You're not in that picture I had."

"I know." A chuckle reached her ear. When he sat down on the broken wall next to her, the size of his grin made his eyes almost disappear. "Mike and I did that on purpose. Once we heard your fool plan, we knew we needed to start making alternates."

"Prove it."

"You are fooling around with Cole, a man very unlike your former husband. He's a great gambler and a fool for you. You go by Jane Spencer and live in that saloon. You like to drink, but hate getting drunk."

"You could have gotten that all from hanging around the saloon."

"It about killed Cole to leave you in that room yesterday. After telling you to trust him no matter what happened, he went back, tore up his room, and drank three full bottles of whiskey trying to wipe the image of you looking like this from his head. You need to trust me, Lou. I can take you to him."

"Alan knows. He knows everything. He's going to kill him. He left me here so I would know it." Her shoulders trembled, each sob blasting fresh pain through her heart until she dropped from the wall.

"Jane, there is no way he knows about me being here. If he did he would have said something this morning when he was busy threatening Cole."

She flew to her feet, "I have to go. I have to."

"Wait. Listen to me."

"He'll kill him. I can't let him kill Cole."

"*Lou*, listen to me." He spun her around. "You're soaking wet. Cold. You have injuries that need to be dealt with. Heaven knows when you ate or drank last. You need to be taken care of first. Cole is a damn sight more healthy than you right now."

She couldn't stop it. "I have to see him."

"You will. Trust me." Tommy walked over to the horse and threw open the saddlebag. One tug produced some clothes he held out to her. "They'll be better for what we're doing the next few hours at least."

Jane turned the clothes over in her hands. Pants. It was better than wet petticoats. She slipped behind the half fallen wall. "Where's Michael?"

"Back in Colorado keeping an eye on your young'un. You managed to produce a cute one there, Jane."

"You've been in Colorado for months. Why haven't you said anything?"

"We were going to until you got this damn fool plan in your head. We figured keeping our traps shut until it was time to step in was best."

Jane left the wet clothes on the floor of the broken down cabin. Thoughts and details spun in her head. There was no way to figure out what to ask first. There had to be something she could pick. "Are you sure we shouldn't be going?"

"We should be going in about half an hour. I got a good head start, and I knew where I was going. Cole's using a map and moving a bit slower. Nightfall was the assigned time."

"Assigned time?" She snatched the offered jerky from his hands and chewed on it eagerly. The canteen was even more welcome, the water dribbled down her chin in her haste.

"There isn't any ginger in there. Go slow." Tommy pulled it from her lips. "You'll give yourself a cramp and yes, assigned time. Alan was specific. Even better, once he told your boy where to take the money for the drop, he stayed and watched. Made sure he didn't send any telegrams or letters."

"He didn't know about you."

"No, Cole had a room on the first floor. I'd followed Alan out here to see what he was doing with you. I was able to get into Cole's room through the window and take a nap, then see the map Alan gave him. It just wasn't safe or smart for Cole to come for you, so I did."

"Why didn't you get me when you followed him before? I was…"

"We didn't know if Alan would come for you before he went to the drop site. We couldn't raise suspicion, and we needed a solid plan."

Jane closed her eyes, trying to digest everything. There were many more questions to ask, many unnecessary questions. Right then all that mattered was Cole.

"By the way, Lou?"

"Hmm?"

"'Absence extinguishes small passions and increases great ones'."

"Rochefoucauld?"

"'Love, like fire, cannot subsist without constant impulse; it ceases to live from the moment it ceases to hope or fear'."

She allowed her eyes to open, meeting his dark blue ones. His frame was far more stocky than her or Mike. She'd dare to call him rotund, but he was tall. The smile he flashed her seemed close to one she'd seen in her reflection. "You really are my brother."

"You couldn't tell from these roguish good looks?"

A smile tugged at the corners of her lips, drawing a wince. With a weak laugh, she nodded, "Yes, now I can."

"The guy is nuts about you. Don't ask me why."

She cleared her throat and changed the subject fast. "Let's go ahead and get ready. You're going to have to go slow anyway. I've got some bruising."

"He did a number on you."

"He has before. Hopefully, he won't ever again." She brushed her hands along her pants and started toward the horse. "This is going to hurt."

"It'll get you to Cole."

With that, he helped her up before climbing up with surprising ease. Every movement of the horse sent a jolt of pain through her. Behind her, Tommy encouraged her to give into the pain, assuring her he'd wake her up when they got there.

Within minutes Jane gave up her weak argument and gave into the blackness. The pain kept the pleasant dreams away, but it was far less pronounced.

"Lou," Tommy's voice was low and quiet.

Sharp discomfort in her ribs stirred her back into the present. Tommy, her brother, was taking her to Cole. A gasp flew from her lips and a jolt ran through her. A hand clamped over her mouth, and she bit it out of instinct.

"Damn it. Lou, stop biting me and hush up." The harsh whisper in her ear was tense. "Remember what Cole told you."

She followed the direction of his pointing finger. Cole walked along one of the hills in the distance. In that instant her heart stopped. There he was within sight. What was he doing? What were they doing?

Once again her heart started beating, then raced. He walked away from the shelter of nearby trees into a wide-open valley, into a trap.

Her mouth opened, but the hand was there again. "I said hush."

His grunt when her elbow connected with his rib brought a brief smile of satisfaction that was quickly squelched. "It's a trap."

"No? Really? I couldn't tell."

"Tommy." She fought to get down, but he held her tight. When she didn't give up he squeezed tight enough that tears formed. The injured rib sent blinding pain through her again. "Please."

"Just—"

A shot rang out through the woods, and Cole dropped.

Jane screamed and fought tooth and nail.

"Jane. Lou, stop."

Twisting against her own pain and Tommy, she grabbed the rifle from his saddle holster. The puff of smoke disappearing in the distance was her only indication of where Alan was.

"Lou. Wait."

There wasn't any time; she fired at the first sign of movement. Two gunshots rang out after hers.

Without any time to digest anything, she flew off the horse and toward Cole. "Cole!"

The crack of gunfire sounded in the distance, a whistle sounding behind her. Another shot rang out, before silence fell.

"Cole!" Running until she was out of breath, blinded with pain and not stopping even then. "Cole, please!"

Tears streamed from her eyes when she finally saw him, face up, unmoving.

"No. Cole!"

While grief is fresh, every attempt to divert only irritates. You must first wait till it be digested, and then amusement will dissipate the remains of it.
—Samuel Johnson

"Cole!" Jane slipped down the hill toward his prone body.

"Lou. Be careful, you crazy loon."

Someone else approached from the opposite direction fast, but she couldn't be careful, she had to get to Cole. Her feet gave out under her, slipping in the slick grass. The unforgiving ground vibrated through her on impact.

Tommy grabbed her arms. "What the hell were you thinking? You can't shoot worth a damn. Crazy woman."

Jane was surprised to find herself on her feet quicker than she could wink. Despite his size, Tommy was strong. When she tried to move again, he held her firmly and kept her facing him. Her hand flashed out to slap him, but he caught it before she made contact. "Let me go, you big ugly brute."

"Let Charlie tend to him first. He's the damn doctor."

Jane's struggle eased. "Charlie?"

"Yes. You know him, right?"

"I know of him. He's in Buffalo, though. I saw him. I did." She craned her neck around in an attempt to see Cole, but Tommy snapped her back to face him. "Thomas, stop. Please. I must see Cole."

"Let Charlie work without a hysterical woman getting in his way." Tommy kept her still easily enough. The small bit of energy she'd gathered on the ride was already dwindling. "You impatient fool."

"It was a trap."

"We know. We're not stupid."

"You let him walk into a clear trap. How could you?"

"The same way we could let you sit in that cellar all night. We had to. We didn't know where in these damn hills he was hiding and couldn't figure it out without giving him a target."

"You made Cole a target. How could you?"

"You made yourself a target by going to Buffalo in the first place. Who're you to judge?" Tommy smirked and offered no apology beyond a shrug. "If you'd listened to me and sat your ass still on that horse back there, you'd have seen Charlie's no shrug with a rifle. They kept trying to stop him from being a doctor to become a sniper."

"But Cole!"

"Then you had to go and try to shoot him yourself. You were always impatient. Damn it, Lou. Now we've only nicked him instead of killing him. Do you know what that means? Where's he going to go?"

Her struggled stopped completely as his words sank through her concern for Cole. Two seconds later the truth hit her as to where he'd go to hurt her most. With a shriek, she resumed her fight. "*Jesse!*"

"What are you going to do? Run all the way to Colorado? Settle down. We have things covered. Can't you ever relax?"

An unfamiliar voice interrupted her reply. "'Never be in a hurry. Do everything quietly and in a calm spirit. Do not lose your inner peace for anything whatsoever, even if your whole world seems upset'."

Tommy chuckled when she stilled. "Unlike me, Charlie loves the battle of wits with you. I know you haven't been properly introduced. Meet Charlie."

"St. Francis," Jane mumbled the origin of the quote with a pout instead of the smile perhaps Tommy expected. "He didn't know everything."

"Mike said your amnesia did no preclude your tendency to memorize every word you read." Charlie's tone held the amusement she couldn't muster. When he lifted his head to show the face hidden under the brim of his bowler, he smiled from ear to ear. "Much to my chagrin, it appears he's right."

Jane didn't bother with politeness. "Tell me how he is."

"It's a pleasure to meet you as well." Charlie turned his attention back to Cole, his focus seemingly on his shoulder. "Cole's fine. Like you said, it was a trap. We knew he wouldn't go for the kill on the first shot. Cole wasn't carrying those saddlebags because they held the desired money. More like metal."

Jane managed to finally fight off Tommy and took a step forward. Cole lay propped on his unwounded arm. A twitch of a smile crossed his lips. She sighed. "Oh, thank God, Cole."

"You never listen, do you?" Cole barely winced at the next stitch, his gaze never leaving her as she fell to her knees. "Might as well give up on you ever being patient."

"'Who can be patient in extremes?'" Jane ran her hands along the rough fabric of the pants she wore, trying to stimulate some feeling. Her whole body had gone numb.

"Shakespeare is off limits, Clara." Charlie tied off the stitch, clipping the thread in a swift motion. "He's far too easy to use. Cole is going to be fine. Like we figured, Alan didn't aim for his head."

"Nah, he wanted me to suffer." Cole still didn't move, looking right at her. He'd already loosened his hair from its ties. It was still dark, but more like his style. She needed to be closer but couldn't move. "He wanted her to suffer."

The sob wrenched out before she could stop it. She buried her face in her hands, trying to get herself back together. It still wasn't over. There wasn't time for crying.

"I'm just looking forward to returning the favor." Cole's usually silky voice was rough, hard.

Jane managed to push back the tears into the lump in her throat. Once her hands were back in her lap, she whispered, "Jesse."

"Didn't I tell you to trust me?" Tommy knelt beside her. His elbow moved toward her, but froze before he actually touched her. Maybe he'd noticed how tense she was, or maybe he was just smart enough to know better. "We're going to make camp."

"You're going to need some actual medical attention, Clara." Charlie closed his bag and stood. For a long minute he stood there, but Jane didn't move a muscle. There was no way she was going anywhere yet. "Clara."

"We'll give you two a few minutes, and then get her back to camp, Cole. Don't take too long. It's going to cool off fast with the sun going down." Tommy bounced once, and then rose with a grunt.

Jane still didn't move. All she wanted to do was go to Cole, but she couldn't make herself move.

"I'll get her there." Cole rolled his wounded shoulder, keeping his head down.

The two men finally walked away, but Tommy's voice carried back toward them. "'And like the murmur of a dream, I heard her breathe my name. Her bosom heaved, she stepped aside, conscious of my look she stepped. Then suddenly, with timorous eye, she fled to me and wept'."

Echoes of their mutual laughter drifted through the trees and bounced around the couple before fading into nothing.

"It ain't just you that's nuts." Cole leaned on his good arm. "No one in your damn family knows how to shut up."

The laugh wouldn't come, and a tightness in her throat rose without her permission. She couldn't let the despair win. He was here, safe, only a few feet away.

In that instant, she moved. As if there was a magnetic pull, he moved right with her, closing the short distance between them. They met with a brutal force, every emotion pouring into a desperate and vicious embrace.

Physical pain was abandoned in the passionate tumble of lips and tongues, their arms and hands clinging tightly to bring them closer together. Salty remnants of despair, grief, and pain brought a sobering reminder of anguish they'd suffered separately.

Slowly, she pulled back and took a ragged breath as they remained wrapped tightly in each other. Her lip trembled, and she pressed her forehead to his. "Cole."

"Tell me." His voice was gruff, eyes still closed. Fingers tensed, pressing into her back as they tried to clench into fists. "If he…"

"He didn't violate me like that." Her hands covered his cheeks. She let her thumbs trace the line of his lips, reveling in the comfort of his arms around her, no matter how furious those arms were. "He beat me. He drugged me. That's all."

Ice blue depths opened, pulling her into his anger and pain. "That's enough."

"I thought I'd never see you again."

The crack in her voice broke his tension, his hands smoothing along her back to pull her closer, into his lap. Taking his turn, his hand traced the uninjured lines of her face. "I know."

Damn it. Her lip kept trembling, and the first salty trail of a tear wove down her cheek. That was all it took for the dam to break, and she buried her face in his neck.

He didn't hush her or try to rush. The gentle comfort of his stroking hand along her back, her arm, never ceased. For what seemed forever, they sat in the silence until she'd managed to get a hold of herself again.

She wiped at her tears, sighing in exhaustion, as she settled against the comfort of his chest. The pain started to return, and it was getting cold, but she was not ready to head to the camp. If she could, she'd stay where she was forever.

The minute she felt truly relaxed, the chest she'd found comfortable started to shake. A deep rumbling laugh soon followed. Cole grinned at her when she straightened.

She pouted. "What is so funny?"

"Never thought I'd see the day a woman looked so good in men's clothes."

The attempt to stop the twitch of her lips failed. "You're incorrigible."

"Complaining?"

"No."

His laughter faded when she shivered. "Let's get you to camp. Let Charlie check you out. You need to sleep. Your brothers will make us move real soon."

Nodding weakly, she let him help her stand. She leaned against him and walked to the camp in silence. The climb up the hill brought each injury to the surface in a painful reminder of its presence. By the time they got to the camp, she sank willingly onto the bedroll.

Charlie knelt by her. "Clara—"

"Clara is dead," she whispered. "Stop calling me that. My name is Jane."

"Jane." Charlie squeezed her shoulder gently. "I promise to be quick. I just need to see how bad he hurt you."

Her eyes closed as she nodded, and she took a bracing breath. Cole's hand tightened on hers when the cuts on her stomach were revealed and the bruising on her ribs. A low growl reached her ears, but he said nothing.

"None of these cuts look deep enough to require stitches any longer. You've already started to heal over most of them." Charlie's gaze snapped up to hers when she yelped, "But this is a broken rib. I'm going to have to wrap it. The rest is superficial, but I'd like to give you something for the pain."

"No," she choked out. "The pain is tolerable. It lets me know I'm still alive."

Cole frowned. "Jane…"

"Please, I don't want to have anything."

"All right," Charlie said quietly. "I'll agree for now, but the minute the pain gets bad I'm giving you something."

Jane nodded and closed her eyes. "Fine. Just…finish up. I want to rest."

Charlie smiled and nodded. "Got it."

Cole stayed quiet as Charlie wrapped her ribs tight. Effort alone kept her face as still as it was, which wasn't enough. His frown was deep when Charlie finished. "She good?"

"You'd know better than him," Jane muttered.

Every harsh line smoothed out into Cole's laugh. "I'd say she's feeling better."

"You think so?" Charlie chuckled. "Get some rest. Behave yourself and do what I say for a change. You only have a few hours before we start moving again."

"Just go away."

Cole smirked and nodded to Charlie. "Thanks."

Charlie nodded. "All right, I'm going. Try to relax, Jane. Like Tommy said, we've got things handled. Let us do the worrying. You do the healing."

"Yes, sir," she grumbled. When he disappeared to the other side of the fire she tugged on Cole's hand. "Come here."

Without a moment of hesitation, Cole shifted and stretched out beside her. Pulling her close, he sighed when she relaxed against him, "Better?"

"I missed this," she whispered.

"Yeah?"

"I missed you."

*Love reckons hours for months,
and days for years;
And every little absence is an age.
—John Dryden*

Gentle warmth, a soft, supple lingering touch, his tender kiss to her brow eased her into consciousness. The tickling, light stroke of his fingers across her belly evoked a soft sigh. Each gentle touch lit the nerves beneath, awakening her to his presence.

The encompassing warmth of his hand closed over hers, gently lifting it from its resting place. Her eyelids fluttered as the gentle pressure of a nibble touched each fingertip. A light suckling drew a quiet moan. Lips brushing across her unbruised cheek drew her eyes open.

The flicker of firelight caught his intense, blue eyes before she met his lips with a reckless abandon. Cupping his cheek before slipping her arm around his neck, she let the rest of the world fall away.

Without hesitation, she opened up to him, letting their tongues meet in a slow dance, searching, remembering, making up for time lost. Ever so slowly, they withdrew from the depths of the kiss, staying close to each other. Tender kisses, gentle touches, a languid embrace unwilling to release—each of them were content to lie still and enjoy the nearness of the other. The murmurs of nearby conversation didn't pull a flicker of focus away from the moment.

Cole's hand never stopped running along her arm, her hip, her waist, whatever part it could touch. His nose brushed her ear, and he kissed it. "I ain't good with words."

"Don't need to be." Jane smiled, letting her fingers dance up his arm to settle on his neck. "Your actions say plenty."

"You ever do that again, I'm gonna lock you in our room and make sure you get no desire to ever use yourself as bait again."

"Why our room?" Her mouth had a mind of its own. She couldn't contain the way the smile kept growing. The pain seemed to have no effect.

"Best place to use actions. You won't be wanting to go anywhere."

"Except anywhere around town, like behind the newspaper office."

"In the back of Cora's general store?"

"Oh, that was my favorite." Her soft chuckle joined his until another flash of pain ended it. "I'm afraid it may be a few days until I feel up to that."

"No matter. You're back where you're s'posed to be."

"Sure feels like it." With a sigh, she glanced toward the two men across the fire. "How did they get you into this?"

"You did it."

"No."

"Did you leave the note for Charlie?" At her nod, he squeezed her hand. "I probably would'a anyway, but that told me you wouldn't mind."

"But how?"

"Tommy's been in town for couple months." He put his finger over her lips, "No, I didn't know it was him. Mike kept it secret."

"That's what Tommy said." Jane snuggled closer to him. "What about Charlie?"

"Well, he, Tommy, and Nick were a shock to me."

"Nick?"

"Just listen."

"Yes, sir."

"Time's up, Mike." Cole leaned on the door. "Get in here and start talking."

"First there's a few people you have to meet." Mike's kept his wide grin in place. "Don't say no. Just invite us in. You want to save Jane. It's the best way to do it."

"I don't like you."

"Too bad."

Cole frowned at the small parade that followed behind Mike, each man progressively taller than the shrimp until the fourth man, only a few inches shorter than Cole himself. "What the hell?"

"These are a few of the Young boys."

"Jane is going to kill you."

"Not necessarily." The tallest spoke up, his dark hair and moustache capped under a proper bowler. The moustache twitched, "I'm Dr. Charlie Young. This brute here is Tommy."

"Wait." Cole got in Tommy's face. "I know you. You beat me at poker couple weeks back."

"Good memory."

"No, I just hate losing." Cole smirked when Tommy laughed, turning his attention to the one that hadn't spoken. The thick, black goatee hid any expression, and a pair of piercing blue eyes studied him.

"That's Nick," Charlie finished. "The reason I say that Clara will not necessarily kill Michael is she is the one who told me to contact him."

"How?" Cole didn't turn away from Nick until, apparently satisfied, the other man finally looked away.

"A note on the picture Tommy provided her. It said simply to contact Michael and ask about Jane and her plans. He's spent the past hour filling Nick and I in on the story. Of course, being the insinuating bastard he is, Tommy already knew everything." Charlie set a bag on the table. "Let's get down to business."

Cole tried to keep his jaw from dropping. "Ain't you mad?"

"Bet your ass we are." Tommy made himself at home, lounging on the closest chair with a bottle of whiskey already in his hand.

Charlie muttered under his breath, withdrawing a folder from his medical bag. Once he'd set it on the table, he stowed the bag away before taking a seat. After a glare at Tommy he rolled his eyes. "We're family."

"Damn straight." Tommy folded his arms across his chest. "End of the day, that's all that matters. We're used to Lou getting all girly and losing her brain to emotions. She's made plenty of stupid mistakes in her time. This just happens to be the biggest, most idiotic thing she's done to date."

"Eloquent, Tommy." Charlie settled back in his chair. "You'll have to excuse Tommy. He talks prettier than he acts."

Michael ignored the ensuing exchange of playful punches to look back at Cole. "She obviously doesn't know Tommy. He can be your second pair of eyes. Charlie will have to stay hidden. Nick will go back with me to make sure Jesse is protected."

"He attacked your family," Cole frowned. "What makes ya think he won't recognize them?"

"I'm certain he would recognize me." Charlie nodded. "If he's been watching James and the family around him, he'd recognize me in a heartbeat. I've been at the hospital every time James went in. He'd recognize Nick, too. Tommy, on the other hand—"

"I haven't been around Buffalo for over a year and put on a bit of weight." Tommy patted his stomach. "I grew a beard in that time, and I didn't go back for the funeral. I've been working some distance from home for years, was out of the country for a few years before that. I'm not in any family pictures because I always found a mud puddle right before. I'm the big fat black sheep ready for slaughter."

"I'll stay in the room," Charlie interrupted. He muttered under his breath, "Mudsill."

"Nancy."

"Hey," Mike snapped at them to interrupt the insult exchange. "Focus."

"Point is, it isn't likely he's going to recognize me. I can be incognito." Tommy pulled his hat low. "And we know Lou won't either, except maybe that I was in your saloon. That gives us the upper hand here."

"She ain't gonna like it." Cole shook his head.

"She'd say it was illogical to put more lives in danger." Mike nodded. "We know that."

"And we have counter-rationale that three men against one are better odds," Charlie said, simply. "Another argument with her I'd win."

"Sure. What's that make it, two to you, five hundred to Lou?" Tommy chuckled. "Wouldn't bother trying to keep score, Chuck."

Cole rubbed his hands over his face. "They always like this?"

"Only when they get together," Michael grumbled.

"Clara knew this wouldn't work." A new voice piped in. Despite being quiet, Nick's voice was powerful enough to still all action. "Based on the information acquired by Charles, there is no doubt she was right. We have to be prepared for every contingency. Believe me, we will be."

The whole time Nick hadn't moved a muscle. Even the goatee seemed to be still. How the hell did he do that? Cole tried to blink away his stare from the odd sight. "Maybe Jane just got scared."

"Of course, she did." Mike nodded. "I'm sure of it. Either way, it's time to take charge. You can't tell me you've liked this plan at all. Ever."

"Can't say I have." Cole straightened. "Wait. What information?"

"The mudsill." Charles cleared his throat when Tommy made a threatening grunt. "May have connections, but the south is still very protective of its records, especially those of confederate soldiers and most especially when those records

are tied to some of the highest ranking officers. Those records tend to disappear."

"So?"

Tommy pursed his lips, "What he's saying is I didn't get all of the details. I got only the most basic sketch of Alan."

"Thanks to a friend I worked with during the war—"

"He went to the South," Tommy whispered loudly to Cole. "Only fight he ever won with Clara. They haven't spoken since."

"Thank you for the aside," Charlie started.

"Enough." Nick had produced a pistol from beneath his jacket and leveled it at Tommy. "Business now. Be an ass later."

"War did him in. It killed his sense of humor," Tommy muttered. He opened the bottle of whiskey when the hammer pulled back on Nick's pistol.

In a breath the pistol was away. Nick nodded to Charlie. "Keep it short. We don't have enough time for this."

"Right. Essentially, Alan is far more unstable than the original file gave him credit for, cunning and exceptionally intelligent." Charlie leaned forward. "It's good we have Nick and Tom here. If anyone can plan for every contingency, it's the two of them combined. That is precisely what we need to do."

"If what Charlie is saying is true, Clara has nothing on him. Her exacting memory and high intelligence can't compare to his kind of guile." Tommy handed Cole the bottle.

Cole took it and downed several large swigs. "So we stack our odds."

"Precisely." Charlie leaned forward, "No matter what happened to her memory, ours is fine. She is family. We are

willing to do whatever it takes to keep her from actually dying. What about you?"

"I'm willing to risk her ringing my neck for letting ya do this." Cole didn't waver an inch under Charlie's scrutiny. "'Cause that's exactly what she's gonna do."

Tommy snorted, coughing to cover his laughter.

"You all like to talk as much as Jane. I'm betting ya already got at least five plans laid out." Cole looked between them. "So what are they?"

Letting his laughter out, Tommy shook his head, "You really do know Lou well."

"Better than ya know."

"You just agreed to shut them up."

"Nah, I agreed so I could shut you up, as often as I need to." Cole interrupted her soft laugh with his lips, pulling her into another searching kiss.

Still smiling when he pulled back, she nodded. "Good reason."

"Lou." Tommy cleared his throat from a few feet away. "Time to go."

"She's gonna need something for the pain." Cole looked up at him. "We ain't gonna be riding gentle."

Tommy moved closer and crouched down. "Lou?"

"Yes," Jane sighed. "Either way I'm going to be passing out, either from pain or medication. I'd rather do it the less painful way."

"I'll get Charlie." Tommy squeezed her shoulder and stood, whistling to Charlie as he headed back toward the horses.

Cole helped her sit, looking down when she touched the wound on his shoulder. He closed his hand over hers. "Don't hurt too bad. The saddlebag took most of it."

"Which we'd filled with metal and books instead of money." Charlie knelt down next to them with his medical bag. "That combined with the distance, we didn't figure the wound would be too bad. Figured I'd have time to shoot back and get to Cole before he bled too badly."

"And you called my plan stupid?"

There is a magic in that little word, home;
it is a mystic circle that surrounds
comforts and virtues never known
beyond its hallowed limits.
–Robert Southey

Oh, Michael, I dream of a life beyond this. For once it is not just nightmares. Now and then I see a future unlike one I used to imagine, a future I will never likely see, a future filled with love. Freedom. No more changing who I am, remaining in a life, one that is mine and mine alone. The sins of my past will forever plague me. Could such a freedom exist for a wretch like me? A love. A home. Family. Honesty. To live honestly again, as once I was, as once I did.

"Oh, my heavens, thank goodness. Jane, welcome home." Kat swept her into a hug tight enough to make her cringe. "I can't tell you how glad I am to see you again."

"Easy, Kathy. You're gonna break her." Cole's hand slipped along Jane's hip, pulling her close when Kat released her. "Between the horse and the train, she sure ain't recovered enough to be molested."

"She's alive. That's all that matters." Kat's tears shimmered at the edge of her cheeks. In a moment, they were covered with a bright laugh. "And in pants, to boot! Oh, how scandalously wonderful."

Jane tried to hide by moving closer against Cole. "We didn't have time to stop and buy a change of clothes."

"Don't let her fool you. She's enjoyed every minute of it." Tommy lugged the saddlebags on his shoulder. "Well, except for the pain and lingering degradation."

"Not helping," Jane muttered. She broached no argument when Cole squeezed her hip.

"Where is the clinic?" Charlie stepped up beside her, spotting Katherine. "Oh, good afternoon. Doctor Charlie Young."

"Good afternoon. Katherine Daugherty." Katherine held out her hand. "If you're looking for the clinic it's in the downstairs of the Silver Saddle. Mike still hasn't moved to the new place. Oh, that reminds me. Mike isn't here. Said he had business in Pueblo and took a train soon as he got back."

Jane paled, starting to protest, but a nudge from Cole stopped her. "Oh, I wanted to see him. I-I'm sorry, Katherine. I don't know if you've gotten proper introductions. This gentleman here is another of Clara's brothers, Tommy."

"I've seen you around town, haven't I?" Katherine laughed at his nod. "Wonderful. I'm glad you got to see that she's who we know, not who you knew."

Jane squeezed her friend's hand, pulling her into another hug despite the pain. "You always know what to say."

"Always is too strong a word." Kat cleared her throat. "Why don't I show you where Mike's place is? Clinic is small until the hotel moves out, but Daisy has been stocking up."

"I should put these away at the saloon." Tommy bounced the saddle bags for emphasis. "Then I should head out to make sure your boy is safe."

Jane protested. "I don't know how to—"

"Graham can show you where to put those." Cole pinched her hip again when she couldn't stop staring at him. "He forced David to tell him where the Injun was staying so we always know. He don't trust them redskins no more than you do."

Jane didn't flinch, digesting the clear lie. David would never reveal it, even under force. Somehow Graham knew for another reason, or maybe Tommy did and was just using Graham. With a nod, she forced forward a smile and nodded. "Tell him I love him."

Cole's hand tensed on her hip, pulling her closer. Before she could begin to ponder what that meant, Cole picked her up. "Don't care if you've been sleeping against me for days. You still need rest."

She pouted with a whimper. "I am not helpless."

"No, you ain't. Don't matter. I'm carrying you." His nose buried in her hair. "Where ya feel right."

Jane didn't stop the smile that flashed across her lips. After a moment she cleared her throat and nodded. "Lead on. Dr. Young, are you going to let me be when we get there? Or am I to be pestered again?"

"You already know the answer to that." Charlie's voice carried back over Katherine's laughter. "Why ask a question you already know the answer to?"

"Wishful thinking." Jane nestled into Cole's shoulder. "Promise me."

"What?" Cole's lips brushed her temple. "That I'll make you keep these pants?"

"No." Her chuckle rattled the tender rib.

"That I'll make sure you stop wearing a corset permanent?"

"Stop it."

"Then what?"

"No matter what." Her fingers latched onto his shirt. "Whatever is happening, whatever I don't know, promise me Jesse is safe."

"Measures are being taken."

"You sound like Charlie."

"He's safe." Cole's lips brushed across hers. "I promise."

One by one her fingers relaxed, her eyes closing. "I trust you."

"Good."

Jane only hummed in response. They'd arrived at the Silver Saddle, and not even the ensuing exchange of greetings disturbed her comfort until Cole set her down and she bothered to open her eyes again.

"Jane?" Daisy popped into her sight line. "I'm going to do a quick exam while Dr. Young makes himself at home. It seems like he has you all set, so it won't take long. I'll have Cole take you upstairs after."

"I want to go home." Jane squeezed Cole's hand tight. "Please."

"I'm afraid I can't let you do that just yet. When you go home, you have a tendency to ignore doctors' orders." Daisy grinned at Cole's agreement. "Dr. Young and I are going to monitor you."

"Doctors," Jane muttered, throwing away Cole's hand when he started laughing.

"Oh, stop being a ninny." Kat's laughter wasn't in the least bit hidden by the privacy curtain. "If it means getting healthy quicker, it means getting back to whatever you'd like to do in your room."

Jane wasn't able to stop her laughter. "Good point, Katherine."

"So then you'll behave?" Daisy smiled and squeezed Jane's arm. "I promise to be quick. Then you can get settled in."

After a deep breath and a brush of Cole's lips to her forehead, Jane closed her eyes again. She didn't fight the exam, only reacting when the worst of the wounds were examined.

The fact that Cole remained calm, whispering both sweet nothings and dirty thoughts in her ear, let her know he was behaving, too. If he'd watched the exam, she was certain that once again his temper would be flaring.

With her cooperation, the exam was over quickly and Daisy sent them upstairs to one of the rooms in the front of the hotel, one with a balcony with stairs for easy access. If nothing else, she knew Cole and his propensity for visiting at any hour.

"Need books?" Cole's fingers brushed along her cheek.

"Very much." Jane caught his hand and kissed the palm. "And take a bath."

"No fun without you."

"Too bad," Jane grinned. "Start getting that stain out of your hair. You look much better without it."

"I ain't the only one." A flash of red flipped into her vision before falling back.

"Soon as I can, I'm getting rid of this dreadful color. Katherine may be able to look beautiful with red hair. I look like a no-bit whore." Jane giggled when they both laughed. "Not even worth a nickel."

"Looks are deceiving." Cole leaned down, capturing her lips with a fire that left her breathless. His fingers laced into her hair and pulled her closer.

She didn't fight him one bit, reveling in the familiar planes of his mouth. She built on the passion he'd started with each tease of her tongue.

"Ahem." Katherine laughed. "Jane, Cole, stop it. Number one, I don't want to watch this display. Number two, Jane has orders to rest. Where you're headed is very far from resting."

Cole groaned, but pulled back. "Right. It's her fault. She mentioned a bath."

"Soon as I'm allowed, I'll help you with it." This time both Katherine and Cole groaned. Jane laughed out loud, wincing at the flash of pain. "Go. Hurry back."

Kat kept her arms folded across her chest when Cole dawdled all the way to the door. "Go, you brute. I'm here. Charlie is downstairs. She'll be fine while you wash off the stink."

Jane tugged on Katherine's pants. "You just can't be nice, can you?"

"He'd think I hit my head." Katherine giggled and plopped down to sit next to her on the bed. "I'm very glad that you're home, for many reasons. I would have had to kill you if he'd killed you, you know."

"Um, what?" Jane furrowed her brows, running the statement through her head. "Katherine, that made no sense. You are just being silly."

"Of course I am. What else would a bride-to-be be but silly? I'm supposed to be foolish, head over heels and—"

"Wait."

Kat pulled her lips between her teeth. Still bouncing on the bed next to Jane, her eyes sparkled with the uncontained joy.

"Bride to be?"

"Oh, I thought I was going to *burst*. Between that exam, then Cole's dawdling, I've been dying to tell you since you stepped off the train."

"You and Norman? He asked you?" Jane grabbed her hand. "Wait. Did you ask him instead?"

"After watching you and Cole before he left and you after he left, oh, the torment. It was just too much. I couldn't bear it." Kat wiped at her tears. "I'm the one that brought it up. We talked about it. Watching the two of you, he'd seen it too. Felt it too."

Jane grunted, trying to sit up. Gratefully, she accepted Kat's help. "Saw what? Felt what?"

"Oh, don't be so remarkably dense. No one missed the way you and Cole were. Everyone saw how much you love each other and how much it killed you to be apart. There might have been plenty of discussion about all the time you both wasted being such idiots." Katherine laughed. "We didn't want to waste any time. I was right. He did still have the ring. See?"

The ring flashed before her on a dancing hand, and Jane grabbed it, taking a deep breath, "Oh, I'm so happy for you."

Katherine clung to her when Jane wrapped her arms around her. "I never thought I'd get married. I never thought I'd want to. I bet you will one day, too."

"Doubtful."

"So what will you do?"

"Stay where I'm happy."

"With Cole?"

"Always."

Pride is the master sin of the devil,
and the devil is the father of lies.
—Edwin Hubbel Chapin

Four days had passed. Nothing.

Cole pulled his head an inch out of the cold tub, letting the soaked strands of his hair dangle into the water. As soon as he could, he'd had the long length cut off, but some of the stain still remained. He inhaled deeply to refill the breath he'd been holding long enough his lungs burned. After a few deep breaths, he dunked his head again.

Jane was beside herself in a panic. The delay killed her, leading her to all sorts of worry that the worst was happening where she could do nothing to stop it. Even worse was not knowing where Jesse was and if he was safe.

Certainly that's what Alan had in mind. He wanted her to suffer over and over again, but he wouldn't wait forever.

Free of her restriction to the room at the Silver Saddle, Jane had returned home to their bed and in his arms, although they were still warned by a surprisingly stern Daisy to forgo in their usual pleasures until Jane's rib healed more, hence his current cold water cleaning of his hair. Jane currently had no problems with the inhibitions placed on them. She was too worried.

He pulled out of the water again. Worried as he was about her, that didn't stop him from needing a cold water dunk once a day. Usually down to the waist. If that didn't work he got all the way in the tub. He used the excuse of wanting to get the rinse out of his hair to do it. Usually so observant, Jane didn't seem to notice the flimsy excuse.

Kat tried to help him out. To distract her with enough gossip and activities to bring Jane back to focus. She took Jane shopping for a new dress for a dance that was coming up. Then Kathy had had the gall to threaten him to ask Jane to go.

"If you don't take her, I will. Then she'll be dancing with every man in town but you. They will have their arms around her, making her laugh." Kat preened like a cat with a bird by its tail. "I'll pay them to dance with her and keep her too busy to come home to you."

"Like you could stop her if she'd wanted," he'd hedged. Didn't matter, she had him. Even the thought of Jane dancing with any other man was close to killing him. He'd caved.

Still Jane never settled on a dress, saying she'd wear one she'd worn previously. That was definitely not normal.

After one more deep breath, Cole went back into the cold water, this time to his shoulders. It was no good. Nothing could calm him down. Nothing short of calming her down would ever do the trick.

Cole straightened all the way. He immediately ran a towel over his hair to get out most of the water. Last he'd seen, she was at the library, trying to act like she wasn't as tense, which meant she'd returned to as normal a life as she could. He knew she spent hours by the window, watching and waiting. Before he could finish drying his hair, the sound of gunfire echoed through the walls at him, a lot of it.

He threw down his towel and shirt and stormed from the room toward the front of the saloon. Before he could make it to the doors Jane's scream raced through every nerve to twist his heart until it stopped.

"Jesse."

Cole rushed the bar and leaped right over it. Before his hand could make purchase on the shotgun, Graham took it off the shelf. Cole snarled. "Give it."

"No chance in hell. You aren't blowing that guy's head clean off with half the town watching." Graham didn't budge, even when Cole got in his face. "Your woman would kill you if you went and got yourself hanged."

Cole let out a roar of frustration before running from the bar. Around the corner he saw her in front of the library, on her knees with her arms tight around Jesse.

Up the street at the edge of town, came the group he was looking for. In front of it was David, who appeared to have no interest in what was going on behind him.

Three of the Young brothers each rode in silence. The pommel of each saddle had a rope tied to it that strung tightly back to Alan, who was walking like he hadn't a care, a cocky grin plastered across his sickening face. Hatred and bile rose in Cole's stomach.

Out of nowhere, Tommy's horse moved faster, yanking the maniac until he stumbled to the ground. After being dragged for a few feet, the whole group stopped just long enough to let him get to his feet.

Cole's breath came in short bursts as the pattern repeated, this time with Nick's horse. Once Alan was on his feet still grinning, they went through the pattern again. Every time a different brother knocked him down.

All action stopped right at the edge of town for the brothers. David kept riding slowly, ignoring the action behind him with tense lines drawn across his forehead. He slipped out of his saddle right in front of Cole.

"Next few minutes are about Jesse and Jane. I won't be seeing anything but them." David tugged the reins and led his horse across the street.

Cole didn't care a lick about his permission, but the ignorance was appreciated. He gave one last glance at Jane, who met his gaze over Jesse's head. When David whispered in her ear, there was a brief flicker where she looked away. Her jaw clenched, but from this distance he couldn't tell what she was thinking.

Graham grabbed his arm. "Don't be a fool."

"Leave him alone, Graham." Jane's voice was the clearest it had been in days. Her nod was small, imperceptible, but it was meant for him.

Cole took off like a shot, barreling toward Alan without another thought. A scream of protest from the crowd broke through for a moment, but then he only saw that grin. Alan still didn't get it.

With the first connection Cole's fist made, he heard a loud crack. It didn't stop him, didn't even slow him down. Every wound ever inflicted on Jane had to be avenged. Impact after impact shook through his arms, every ripple of flesh and crack of bone. Alan was pinned down, not going anywhere. Every tear she'd shed deserved a drop of blood. Every broken bone called for one in return. Every day of Clara's life that had been lost deserved the loss of one of his until his were all gone like hers had been for Clara and for Jane.

Cole pulled back, ready to land another when his arm was grabbed. "Let me the hell alone."

"Sheriff didn't say anything about not letting him suffer." Mike's statement was accentuated by Cole's fist making contact with Alan's jaw.

"'Cruelty is fed, not weakened by tears'. Syrus." Nick laughed, an odd sound from the stoic man.

"'Evil to some is always good to others'," Michael chuckled. "Austen, and I dare say this evil—"

Both men stopped their laughter as Cole landed another brutal punch, and Alan reacted with a pained groan.

"Well, it's good to quite a few of us."

"This guy still has to go to jail." Nick's hand hooked under Cole's arm. Despite Cole's fight, he didn't budge and even managed to pull him halfway to his feet.

Within seconds Mike's hand joined, and Cole found himself on his feet. "I wasn't done."

"Time's up." Nick kept a firm hand on Cole's shoulder. "It's not your kill to make."

"You really think a hanging—"

"Cole." Nick's voice cut through the protest without regret. "It's not your kill."

Cole shoved off his arm and stepped back, following Nick's gaze to Jane. His fists unclenched, and Cole studied the wounds across his knuckles. "I still wasn't done. Bastard deserves worse."

"Go to Jane. He's going to jail." Mike walked up next to him. When Alan moved, they both stayed silent as Nick kicked him. "Take care of Jane. Once he's settled, we'll stop by and talk about what's going to happen next."

"The marshal." Cole's jaw clenched. "Too good for him."

"We agree," Mike muttered. "Go take care of Jane."

Cole didn't move at first until Tommy was beside him, edging him away from the scene, toward the library where she was. With each step the adrenaline abated, leaving a throbbing in his hands and his head. Jane had seen the whole thing.

The mass of townsfolk moved forward to see the man at the root of it all, the one responsible for so much grief. The curious crowd moved around to watch the prisoner being taken to jail. Others lingered around the library, watching the small reunion or taking part. Daisy, Cora, and Kat were all close. Cindy and Cora's boys excitedly waited to see Jesse.

Jane wasn't letting go yet. David had joined her and the three stood huddled close together. Cole stopped, frozen by what he saw, like, for the briefest minute, it was Clara and her family—not Jane.

What if she remembered? It was the first time he'd wondered and worried it might happen. Would she give up the present if Clara ever returned? Give up him? He couldn't break up the scene before him. Maybe in this moment, he wasn't welcome.

Tommy stood next to him and muttered, "Coward."

"'Scuse me?" Cole didn't budge, despite the nudge from Tommy.

"No bigger coward than a man afraid to show his feelings. As it says in First John, chapter four, 'There is no fear in love; but perfect love casteth out fear'." Tommy grinned when Cole shoved him, shoving Cole right back.

"Your whole damn family's crazy, you know that?"

"So you and Jane fit right in." Tommy's laugh boomed out, drawing the attention of the group in front of the library.

Cole couldn't help but join in, feeling Jane's gaze on him. Without any further urging, Cole rushed toward her. With Jesse still wrapped tight around her neck she tried to stand, so he bent down and helped her up.

Over Jesse's head she tilted her lips up, and never had his kiss felt more welcomed than in that moment. He pulled her and Jesse close, finding David looking at him. He gave the man a nod, glad for the return of it before he pulled back to focus on Jane. "He all right?"

"He's all right. Thank God. He's all right." She leaned into his shoulder, sighing softly. "He's all right."

"Stop sayin' it, Ma." Jesse didn't sound near as grumpy as his comment.

"Why don't you go see your friends? They missed you, too." David reached over and helped Jesse down. "Your ma's not going anywhere."

"Mean it?" Jesse turned up his little face and pointed at her. "Promise?"

"I promise." Jane squeezed Cole's hand tight. "Never again."

Cole chuckled when Jesse took off to play with Isaac and Cindy, leaving Jane swallowed with hugs from Cora and Katherine. When David drew close, he tensed. "The marshal?"

"She won't leave town." David spun his hat in his fingers. "It would be my first suggestion. She won't do it."

"We'll figure something." If Cole had his way they'd just kill the bastard and forget the marshal. David wanted everything legal. Apparently he didn't care for the law of the land as much as Cole did.

"Sure we will." David stepped aside the moment Jane latched back onto Cole. "I should check everything at the jail."

"Cole needs Daisy or Charlie to fix up his hands. Jesse will be with Cindy and Kat." Jane poked Cole's side when he grumbled. "Your hands are a mess."

After a few quick goodbyes, Jane dragged him toward the Silver Saddle. "I thought you'd show less restraint."

"I wanted to blow his head off. Graham stopped me."

Jane stopped in the middle of the street. "Oh."

"He will die, Jane."

"Oh. I know."

"Good."

"Because I'm going to kill him."

Cole was the one that stopped this time. "Oh."

"Hands. Now."

"But…"

"I need these hands. They need to be clean and ready for use."

"You need my hands?"

"Yes." Jane winked, tugging him the last few feet toward the Silver Saddle. "I've been missing them."

"Didn't think you'd noticed."

"I always notice when we aren't enjoying our pleasures. However, even if I hadn't, watching you beat the hell out of him with your shirt off made me ache with missing your touch."

"Bully for me."
"No, bully for me."

Humanity is never so beautiful as when praying for forgiveness or else forgiving another.
-Jean Paul Richter

"Aren't you glad this whole thing is over?" David squeezed Jane's hand. A happy sigh filled the silence in place of Jane's answer. "He can't hurt you or Jesse anymore. He's in jail. I'm sure he'll hang."

Jane stared at their joined hands rather than answer. It would do no good to argue with him. Even after everything that had happened in the past year, he didn't understand how this truly needed to be handled, not like her family did. Or perhaps he did and just needed to turn a blind eye. Either way, all she could do was nod. "I am glad it's over. It is simply an unusual sensation to have it all over."

"You still have family to meet."

"With all I've been through that should be easy." Jane twisted in her seat. Over her shoulder she could see Nick sitting in the corner of Cora's restaurant. As had been the case since they'd met, his gaze looked through her, over her, anywhere but at her. "I suppose that might be asking a lot in some cases."

"If you can explain it to a husband you don't remember, telling your parents should be easy, especially after Mike got there ahead of you." The warmth of David's hand slipped away, drawing her attention back to the table where his hands clenched. "Then again, I guess that's a different comparison."

"No. It is not." She set her hand on his forearm. Her chair scraped the floor when she drew closer. "I handled things poorly with you. You were too nice to tell me any different or get angry. Your heart was too good to allow such anger."

"No, it wasn't."

"The only time you truly hated me was when you found out Clara had lied about Jesse." Jane smiled to soften the impact of the reminder. "At first it was shock, I'm sure. After that, you simply clung to the memory of what she was, what I once was. I do not know what kept you from fighting tooth and nail to bring her back."

"I'd mourned her. I lost her when she disappeared. I'd thought her dead and mourned and said my goodbyes." David readjusted his hat to cover his eyes. "Then there was the other matter of Cole."

"I know you're far from scared of him."

"I don't like him. Never did. Not scared of him, though."

"Well then what? Lee?"

"No, she was an incentive you pushed me toward, not that I mind one bit. It isn't why." The hat came off. In a moment he was nose to nose with her. "The way you looked at Cole is the same way Clara used to look at me. I knew I had no chance. I can't believe Al held on as long as he did."

The familiar tingle of embarrassed heat coursed across her cheeks. Her forehead pressed against his. "I'm sorry if I hurt you."

"Clara did most of it. You just made sure it stuck." He picked up her hand, playing with her fingers. "Just because we aren't the same people doesn't mean I don't still love you. You're always going to be family to me."

A tear slipped through her weak control to splash on the back of his hand. "I'm so sorry she wanted to forget."

"Only one thing you can do to make it up."

"There's nothing I can do."

"Don't ever wish it again."

"I won't. I don't. I haven't ever one day in my short life." Somehow Clara's past mingled into hers, turning one short year into a lifetime. "Even on the worst day, I have not wanted to forget a moment. I don't want to forget those bad days happened. Those nightmares still plague me. I want them all with a selfish greed."

"Good." He pulled her into a hug. In complete silence he held her, and he shook as he did so. His face remained hidden, so she ignored the reality of his tears, after all, she had a few of her own erupting.

"You deserved much more than Clara. I hope you've found it." Jane kissed his cheek. After clearing her throat and wiping another stray tear she pulled back and straightened. "As long as you trust yourself and your heart, you'll do fine. Clara was a fool, but she adored you. She failed to trust you. Don't do the same thing."

"Somehow I think you'll be there to remind me every day, every single time I argue with Lee until the day I die."

"I'm here to annoy you however I can until the day I die." She paused for dramatic effect. A hint of amusement rose to replace the somberness of the previous moments. "Again."

David snorted. "Third time's lucky?"

"So they say." She joined his laughter, relived he'd taken part in the amusement. "Well, Mr. Sheriff, I do need to return to work. Thank you for joining me for my midday meal. Cole has been busy making sure the supplies we ordered are put away."

"So in other words he'll be bored and pestering you at the library in short order? Is that the reason for your rush?"

Jane threw her napkin at him. "You are not very funny. Be nice."

"Don't have to. We aren't married, Miss Spencer."

"Oh, you." She smacked his arm and stormed off in as big a huff as she could manage in her laughter. At the door she stopped to wave, still laughing all the way into the street.

For the first time in a long time, she took her time walking down the street. Only half the carts were out that had been the previous year, most of the owners having store fronts in the growing town. Still, she stopped at each and every one, socializing without fear of attack—Indian or otherwise.

Along the way, she managed to acquire both products and gossip. All of it warmed her soul for the commonality and simplicity of it, even the questions as to whether she would be at the dance in celebration of Founders' Day the next night.

It was no secret she was thrilled to report she was going, even if she had been foolish and failed to acquire a new dress. Best of all she'd be going on Cole's arm, after he'd surprised her by asking at all.

Lost in her musing, she almost missed the library door. The figure on the porch startled her back from her own thoughts. "Oh. Nicholas, you startled me."

Nick didn't look up, staring at his own feet as he leaned against the porch railing. His nails dug into the wood, the slightest twitch of his fingers about all that moved.

A lump formed in her throat, pushing out the relaxation of her walk. Yesterday when all the Young boys, her, and Cole met at the saloon to discuss what to do about Alan, Nick hadn't said anything to her or even looked at her just like back at Cora's. Around her, through her, never once at her, it was unnerving.

"Would you like to come in? Talk?" Jane unlocked the door and held it open. "I can offer you whiskey or tea."

Nick pushed off the railing and went inside without a word.

Jane pursed her lips and blew out a long breath. Mike had told her that ever since Clara's disappearance Nick had refused to speak of her as if she wasn't dead, but simply didn't exist. He'd also said that the war took a heavy toll on Nick. He'd signed up with four of his childhood friends and ended up their superior after a time. In battle, he'd been the one that had eventually led them all into death.

Clearing her throat, Jane shut the door behind her. Whiskey seemed like the best bet for her nerves. She took a flask out of her hiding place in the bottom drawer. After another thought, she took out a second one and set it on the desk.

Nick wandered, scanning every book spine. If he wasn't going to say anything at all, this was going to get uncomfortable very fast, as if it wasn't already. She removed the top of the flask very quickly and tossed back a large swig.

A low rattle let her know the other flask was open. One more swig and she dove in. "What did she do to you?"

"You left."

"Clara left."

"No." His hands clenched on the desk, knuckles pressed into the wood. Each tendon and vein showed in sharp relief.

Jane sucked her lip between her teeth before it started trembling. This wasn't the time to argue, if she even could. At one time she'd been Clara, the very person Nick was angry with.

"You aren't gone. You can't be. You're right here. You work in a library for heaven's sake. You talk the same, walk the same, everything is the same."

It was the first true objection from someone this close to Clara. David had fought, but only for a while. Mike had always been close to Clara, but not even he'd grown up as close to her as Nick. Nick was less than a year older than Clara. They were only nine months apart.

"You did this. You lied to me." He pushed off the desk, studying the spines of the books again. Hands still clenched in fists, he moved restlessly around the room. "All the letters you sent, telling me to keep strong, that I wasn't to blame."

The feeling poured out of her body. Numb legs gave out beneath her. Thank God for her chair or she would have hit the floor. "Oh, God."

"First it was you took off without reason, and then Mike told me." Nick's arm pulled back, but before his fist made impact with the wall he stopped it. Gripping the shelves, he pressed into them. "I guess it wasn't everything, just that you'd been raped and blamed yourself. He said you were going to stay with him, but you didn't."

There was no argument. After telling Nick not to blame himself for the loss of his friends, Clara did the opposite, blaming herself for everything. "She was a hypocrite."

"You are a hypocrite." Nick's head dropped. "You lied to me. You cited Hugo, telling me to fight."

"'Those who live are those who fight'." How often she'd said it to herself in the past year.

"You didn't fight. You walked away. What in hell was I supposed to think? Tell me."

All of her words, thousands of words that had both frustrated and uplifted her, annoyed Cole, and kept her distracted during Alan's torment, all of them failed her. There wasn't anything she could say.

"Why didn't you fight?" he demanded.

"I don't know. I suppose it's easier to tell others what to do with their pain. When you're in it yourself, it's harder to deal with. She was wrong." No. That wasn't even close to what he needed.

"Stop saying that."

"I'm sorry. I don't know how to *not* separate us." Jane didn't move, staring at the desk like there were some answers there, any answers. "At the same time we'll never be separate. You're right. I am her. At the very least I was."

"It's that easy for you?" A short laugh escaped from his lips, a cold laugh. "Just say it was Clara and it leaves you with a clean slate."

"My slate is far from clean." Jane pushed to her feet. David and Mike had watched the transformation, seen the struggle. Nick hadn't seen any of it. It wasn't something that could be explained away. "It hasn't been easy."

Nick didn't move a muscle. The moment her hand touched his shoulder it twitched, but he didn't shove her away.

"Maybe it has. I'm the one that doesn't remember. I'm the one that hung for what she did. I answered for her legal crimes. I buried her." Her voice grew thick, the words getting more difficult. "I've tried to make things right for David and Jesse, but there is so much more to Clara, to me."

"You had no right to bury her."

"I guess I didn't." She stared at the floor, her hand slipping from his shoulder. "I may never be able to make it right. I want to be me, the one I know. I don't want to forget who Clara was, even when I don't really like her all the time."

"How would you know?" Nick glared over at her, "All you have is some letters. If you really don't remember, how could you know if she was so unlikable? Everything she did in the end, it was wrong, stupid, but Clara is my sister. She's not a bad person. She doesn't deserve your hatred."

"Does she deserve yours?" It slipped out before she could stop it. Damn her inability to censor herself. "Sorry."

"I have a right. I actually remember."

"What do you want me to do?" Jane met his gaze straight on. "Do you want me to apologize for something I don't remember? I will. Right now it hurts knowing that she…that I…that we once hurt you, lied to you, and became such a hypocrite when what you needed was the opposite."

"Does it really hurt?" Nick folded his arm across his chest. "Why bother? If it was her transgression, why bother worrying about it?"

"I just do. I can't explain the how's or why's. It hurts. I don't remember, but every wrong she did to those she loves hurts. I hate seeing David like this. I hate seeing you like this and the pain Mike tries to hide when I can't share in a joke he once shared with her. There are times I still wish I could remember. I can't. I have to live without searching for her. Yet every time I turn around I find her."

"Then she isn't truly dead."

"How can she be? She has six brothers and a son. She had a husband that is still a part of my life. Clara won't ever die. I may never remember, but I accept that she will always be a part of me." Jane fought the urge to run away from his intense scrutiny. "I have to. I can't ignore it. Her wrongs show me how to live right."

"Clara is more than the things she did wrong."

"Yes, she is. I hope the things I'm doing right show that."

"You're not perfect."

"Heavens no. I don't want to be." Exhaling slowly, Jane held out her hand to him. "I hope you can forgive me. Help me learn about the Clara you knew."

"To what end?"

"David helped me see some of her good. Mike has helped, too." Relief flooded her when he took the hand she offered, a small step in the right direction. "I want to know all of Clara to stop judging her. Plus, I would get to know you."

"You are Clara."

"I am Jane, but Clara is my constant companion."

"Is that supposed to be enough?"

"Sometimes it's too much."

Once a woman has given you her heart,
you can never get rid of the rest of her.
—Sir John Vanbrugh

"It's too much."

"No, it isn't." Charlie pushed the large box back toward Jane again. "Take it."

Jane braced her hands against it, pushing it back toward him once again. The box was large enough, no matter what it contained, it would be too much. "It's extravagant."

"No need to be worried. 'Avarice has ruined more souls than extravagance'." Charlie gave another good push to the box until she almost stumbled back. "Charles Caleb Colton."

"'Our love of what is beautiful does not lead to extravagance'." Nick's self-imposed silence broke with the surprise of a citation when by all accounts his memory wasn't as precise. She dared think he laughed under the goatee he hid behind. "'Our love of things of the mind does not make us soft'. Pericles."

"So many against one?" Jane didn't bother to hide her own grin. She turned toward the two that had yet to speak. "Et tu, Michael? Thomas?"

"Oh, we'll give you a chance to argue first." Mike laughed outright. "If you think you can win four against one."

"'Most of the luxuries, and many of the so-called comforts of life, are not only indispensable, but positive hindrances to the elevation of mankind'." Jane lifted her chin in defiance. Her exacting memory could beat the four of them easily. "Thoreau."

"'Stubborn and ardent clinging to one's opinion is the best proof of stupidity'." As if he hadn't just insulted her, Charlie's brow quirked and a grin broke across his features. "Montaigne."

Jane gasped and stepped toward him. Her humor was a poor defense over the desire to smack him for such a choice of words.

She didn't get far, for Tommy grabbed her arm. With a quick jerk he had her facing him instead of Charlie. His hands settled on her shoulders and he got in until they were face to face. "How about this? We're family."

"So?" Who cared if it meant stupidity? She would cling to it until she got a better argument, even if she was dying to see what was in the box.

Tommy's lips twitched against a smile, and she felt her own forming to match. He kept a stern dip to his brow. "We've been without our only sister for nearly eight years. We thought you had died—twice. We've missed seven birthdays, eight Christmases, and all those years of sibling torment."

Jane grinned and shrugged. "Can't you simply consider the mere fact of my absence as my gift to you and leave it at that?"

Mike snorted behind her.

Her attempt to convey an innocent, wide-eyed smile didn't appear to fool Tommy one bit. She folded her arms behind her back. With the corners of her lips tugging into a smile, she fluttered her eyelashes at him. "Isn't it a gift to be away from such torment?"

"We want to do this for you. Because we can, and because you are really here annoying the hell out of us." Tommy laughed and gave her shoulders a short shake. "Now take it and hush up about its extravagance."

"See? Was that so difficult? Goodness." Jane spun and grabbed the box. Rather than respond to the gape-mouthed shock of Charlie. "I cannot believe you ever thought calling me stupid was a way to get me to take a gift? I swear, I thought Clara's brothers would be smarter than that."

"That's it?" Charlie had found his voice, though it cracked. "You would have argued with me all day. You'd have fought tooth and nail against me. Thomas gives you a hard shake and you just go with it?"

"I'm rather enjoying the shade of red you turn when flustered." Jane pursed her lips to hide her giggle when he sputtered.

Tommy, on the other hand, had no issues busting a gut. His laughter bellowed through the room until it echoed off the walls.

Charlie stammered. The only coherent word he managed to form at first was, "But."

Jane ignored Charlie's stammering to open the box he'd given her. Gorgeous, plum color silk shimmered beneath the paper. Intricate details of a turquoise lined the bodice and wove into the underskirt. "Oh, my heavens."

"You would have kept it up."

"It's beautiful." The soft fabric slipped under her searching fingers, sleek and supple. She gathered it into her arms. Layers of skirts followed the dress out of the box. "I do hope it fits. I'll wear it tonight."

"All it took was being shook?"

Mike chuckled over Charlie's continued sputters of protest. "It had better fit right. Katherine snuck in here when you were gone and stole one of your dresses to use for the sizing. She did the tailoring herself. Charlie, are you done yet?"

"Apparently he prefers verbose and long-winded arguments. While I sympathize with his plight, today I have neither the time nor the inclination for such things." Jane shrugged, setting the bodice over the front of her dress to study the effect in the mirror. "One thing I've learned from Cole is that sometimes the direct approach is the best way to go."

"How many quotes did you have prepared for argument?" Nick spoke from his vantage point. Small steps were being taken toward repairing the relationship. He hadn't forgiven her, or Clara, but she could tell he was trying.

She draped the bodice over her arm and pursed her lips as she added in her head. "Oh, goodness. Probably at least fifteen ready. After that there are far too many variables. If Charlie had continued on calling me stupid, things could have gotten rather ugly."

"You want direct?" Charlie snatched the bodice off her arm, holding her at arm's length when she tried to grab it. "You're an infuriating woman and an even more infuriating sister, and I missed you."

The playful struggle drained out of her, leaving behind a slight tremble. "Oh, Charlie. Don't make me cry today. Please."

His arms wrapped around her, folding her into a tight hug. "Ma said they'd be out in July. Don't give them as much hassle as you did us."

"Don't tell me what to do." Silk brushed her fingers. She grabbed on and snatched the bodice back, shoving him away. "Brute."

"Loon."

"One more thing." Nick moved closer to the familial circle that had formed. "One thing we'd be remiss to leave un-discussed."

The busy work of laying out her dress hadn't left her immune to the seriousness of his tone. She smoothed her hand over the bodice before turning. The wall of Young brothers had united and stood shoulder to shoulder without any of their usual humor. "Oh, dear."

"Lou," Tommy started.

"Yes? You've all each had a chance to describe in detail just how many ways you will kill me if I ever pull what Clara did, not that I have any sort of intentions. So what could have you all so serious?"

Nick quirked a brow. "Cole."

"Oh." Her knees bent, ready to sink onto the bed, or should she stand? She had no idea at this point. If she sat she'd feel like a child being scolded. Yes, standing was the best way to face this. "What about him?"

"We know you don't remember us as your brothers. You probably don't care what we think." Charlie had his arms crossed like the rest of them, even Mike. How similar they looked despite their physical differences was eerie.

"You're wrong. Remembering you or not, I do care. You're family. I feel it here." Her heart twisted beneath her hand, every word was true. Somehow, she did feel it. "If I didn't still feel it, I wouldn't be standing here."

"Since you do care." Tommy was the first to break formation, scratching his beard. After a moment his arm dropped back down.

Impatience kicked in, and Jane sighed. "As if that would stop you from telling me anyway. Just spill it."

"As a man, he's a rake." Charlie started.

"Loose cannon," Mike added.

"A scoundrel and a brute." Nick seemed almost happy to add that in.

"I'm pretty sure he cheats at cards," Tommy finished.

"Thank you all for the information. I'm not an idiot." Jane decided she didn't really want an all-out battle. In a gesture of submission she perched on the end of the bed. "From the day I met him, I knew he was a scoundrel. At least he's a funny one."

"We weren't done." Nick let his arms drop.

"The guy's nuts about you, Lou." Tommy shook his head. "Damnedest thing is he likes what he hates about you, too."

Through the heat in her cheeks, her lips pulled into a smile. She chewed on her lower lip, "That's ridiculous, Tommy."

"You forget. We saw him in Sioux City before you got there and afterward when he saw what Alan had done." Charlie cleared his throat when his voice grew thick. "Even when he was cursing your inability to keep your mouth shut, he was poring over every word you wrote in that Whitman book."

"Then could you clarify the problem?" Jane had her hands folded in her lap, trying to swallow the depth of her enjoyment at the revelation. "You all looked ready to throttle me a few minutes ago."

"Are you happy?" came from Nick. "With him? This life? In a saloon? In charge of whores, drunks, and men that won't see you anything more than a private whore? With the knowledge he probably will never get married, no matter how possessive of you he is?"

"I am happy." It was the one thing she was sure of, without a doubt.

"You're certain you don't want more than this?" Charlie's hands dropped. The wall of brothers had all settled down, waiting on her answer. "You could have more if you wanted it."

"What more is there to want? I am happy; I have good friends, I have good family, and I have Cole."

"Who you love." Tommy broke formation to sit beside her. "Don't deny it."

"If I were to say anything of the sort, it wouldn't be to your ugly face." She forced an elbow into his ribs. With a grin, she shook her head. "Don't even try it."

"We had to make sure. We wouldn't be good brothers if we didn't."

"And you, Mike? Going along because you're one of them?" Jane giggled, "You didn't have much to say."

"I already knew how you felt, but we needed a united front. You can be rather stubborn." Mike pulled her off the bed into a hug. "They had to see what I do."

"Fine. You've all seen it. Now shoo. I need to clean my things out of this room." She sighed. "I hate doing this. It's just another lie."

"Do you want me to go calling in every favor I have to keep you from facing another trial?" Tommy stood up. "Would that be better for you?"

"I'm tired of the worry and fear," she admitted with a frown.

"Then it's just a few days. You'll be seeing plenty of Cole. We're not hiding you beyond taking your things out of this room." Tommy squeezed her hand. "Trust us this one last time. In a few days it will all be over."

"Fine. Then let me get the rest of my things packed. With the dress you gave me, it's going to take even longer to get ready for tonight's dance." Jane hugged Tommy tight. "Thank you all so much. You saved me. You saved Cole and Jesse. I can't thank you enough."

Tommy passed her off to Charlie. "Just don't forget us again. That's thanks enough."

After Charlie, Jane wrapped Mike in a tight hug. "Thank you for ignoring me and doing what you wanted anyway."

"It was my pleasure to ignore you." Mike chuckled. "I'll do it more often."

With a grunt, she shoved him away. Nick stood silent by, and when she held out her hand to him, he opened his arms. The clench of her heart released, and she rushed into them. "Thank you."

Nick peeled her off in a few moments, clearing his throat. "We'd best get going and let you finish. We'll see you at the dance."

"Except me." Tommy kissed her on the cheek. "I'm watching the prisoner tonight. I'll dance with you tomorrow. We'll find music."

Jane laughed and pushed them all toward the door. Once it closed, she leaned against it with a sigh. Somehow, the lot of them had convinced her that keeping out of sight of the marshal was best, rather than complicate Alan's arrest.

They swore she wouldn't have to hide again after that. Just this one time more would be to ensure there was no confusion as to Alan's guilt.

She hated it, though it was logical. Unfortunately, the logic had her loading her things back into a trunk that would be tucked away at Kat's. Jane would have to avoid the saloon for a few days and the library, her two regular sanctuaries. Still, she wouldn't disappear into the woods like the first suggestion.

After all, there was no way in hell she would seek solace with an Indian, no matter how much David vouched for him. After a shudder at the thought, she moved back into the room.

One by one, she pulled her dresses and petticoats from their hooks. Each one was dropped into the trunk without much care. She had to keep telling herself it was only for a couple of days.

Her perfume, brush, and hair pin got plucked off the dresser. Every one of them landed in the trunk with a soft thud. Shoes were gathered and stored, a notebook she'd been using for plans for the money and the saloon all got shoved into the trunk. All that was left was the books. Such a hassle to move them all. The closest shelf held a handful, and one by one she stacked them, moving along the shelves until she had a stack to her chin.

"What are you doing?" Cole shut the door. A book was yanked out from under her chin. "Don't do that."

"I have to pack. You all agreed, remember? I agreed to stop the arguing and get back to bed with you." For just a brief moment a smile flickered across his expression. What the hell was his problem? Why was he so grumpy?

Another few books were grabbed, "The books stay."

"The point is to remove the evidence of me from this room. In case the marshal gets wind of my un-demise. You can't have been harboring."

"The books *stay*."

"Cole, we agreed."

"I wouldn't get rid of the books. I *didn't* get rid of the books. They stay."

The first day back in the room, her trunk had been outside, but her books had still lined the shelves. The memory had stuck, but she hadn't thought to question then. She'd been too relieved to be home to wonder. Bit by bit the load in her arms lightened until every book had been shoved haphazardly back on the shelf. Why hadn't she seen? No, why hadn't she realized?

"They stay."

His kept his back to her, a fresh bottle of whiskey on the desk. Within minutes the bottle was half gone. Her freedom wasn't won, and she should push this aside. She couldn't with all of it right there in front of her. She couldn't leave him wound up like this. Her hand slipped along his back. "I'm sorry. I didn't realize."

"The clothes, the shoes, I don't care about that stuff. It all went." Another glass of whiskey gone. "Tossed it all out, but the books, they stayed."

"Cole." She leaned her forehead into his back. Books meant everything to her. The first thing she'd left in his room was a book. It was what she'd sent with him to think of her when they were apart.

"You know how much you annoy me with all that talking, all them words you pull out of those books." The glass clinked to the desk, and he stood still for a long minute. "But they're you. More than anything else, the books are you."

"Oh, Cole." She released his arm and moved around in front of him. He grabbed her hands when they drifted along his chest. Her heart fluttered when he kissed each palm. "Just a few more days. I won't be far. I'll still see you."

"Soon it'll be over."

"Over and done, and then I'll be free."

"No more hiding."

*Heaven would indeed be heaven
if lovers were permitted as much enjoyment
as they had experienced on earth.
—Giovanni Boccaccio*

"Damn." Cole's mouth went dry. While Jane had always prettied herself up, he'd never seen her as fancied up as she was right then. In the reflection, Jane's cheeks darkened to a pleasing shade of pink. He wanted to forgo the party and do whatever it took to make that blush go all the way down.

"Yes?" Her slim fingers smoothed over the rich purple fabric, down to her miniscule waist. She'd put a corset back on and he imagined plucking right off her trim form. Hell, he imagined slicing through the delicate fabric of the dress for expediencies sake.

"You just look…" He sucked air in through his teeth. It whistled out long and low, and the enticing pink on her cheeks deepened in response. "Damn."

"Thank you." With another tug at the bottom of the bodice, she turned to the side. She still paid him little mind, more intent on her own profile. He didn't mind because it gave him more time to take in every luscious inch of her.

Tommy had told him that her brothers had gotten her a dress. He'd failed to mention what a dress it was, high quality like the ball gowns he'd seen in the city. The top revealed just enough of her chest to make him want to run his hands along the soft flesh there.

Each line of the blue accent color highlighted her tiny waist. The layers of skirt flared out to help the effect. Everything about it was right.

He stepped forward to slip his hands around her waist and pulled her back against him. Instead of finding her delicate body flush against him under the many layers, all he felt was the firm cage of a bustle. A low growl escaped. "What's that for?"

"I needed the room, but mostly to keep you at a distance. I know better than to trust you to get me to this dance."

Her laughter resounded against his chest. Maybe he was supposed to join, but he couldn't bring himself to match her amusement. "Evil woman."

"Perhaps." Her hands laced with his, her back flush against his chest. "What if I promise I will make sure you are not sorry you waited?"

"Ya never do."

Again the pink filled her cheeks, and it was then that he noticed how it only filled the one. He spun her so he could brush his fingers along the cheek Alan had beaten continuously. The one that pained her so and was varying shades of purple as of that morning.

Despite her wince at his gentle touch, the skin was creamy, almost white. "What? How?"

"The girls had a large hand in this. A lot of their powders and creams and what-not went into making it appear to disappear." She slipped her hands along the buttons of his vest. "You look nice. Is this from the wardrobe of Mr. Hodgkins?"

"None of the bells and whistles I had to keep in Sioux City, but yeah." Cole shrugged. "I don't got anything nice of my own, so I wore the pants, vest, and shirt. You ain't gonna get me in no jacket."

"I wouldn't presume to, a jacket would not be befitting of the man I…" A smile tugged at her lips, then trembled and faded. He hung on for the words she'd yet to say, but she merely shook her head, and he knew why. She'd made it clear she wanted to be free before she said them.

"It ain't me," he supplied for her.

"Exactly. And with your haircut, Charles Hodgkins is nowhere to be seen. Thank you." She scratched her nails along the stubble on his chin. "I believe I may have to claim fatigue quite early in the evening."

"That so?"

"Yes."

With the finger he'd used to check her cheek, he ran a teasing line under her chin and down her throat. Inch by inch he drew close to the low neckline until he brushed along the swell of her breast.

Gooseflesh rose under his finger, a shuddering breath from her was his enjoyable response. At some point in his teasing her eyes had closed, a hint of her pink tongue disappearing behind freshly moist lips. *Forget the damn dance.* He captured her lips, not surprised to find her ready and waiting for him. Her tongue met his in a languid, heated dance, pulling him into her, open and eager.

Too soon the heat cooled. Somehow she knew how far to pull back to keep him from being frustrated, only enough to let them slow the path they were on. They had to. He knew it. He'd rather spend the night in the room—those activities were fare more enjoyable than what they'd planned in the coming hours, including the dance. It didn't matter. An appearance had to be made, even if they did leave early, very early.

"Yes. I do believe I am already growing weary."

It was like she could read his mind. Then again, considering her hand had a firm grip on him through his trousers, it probably wasn't his mind she was reading.

"Best get a cold drink of water to cool off your man at attention. It's nearly time to leave."

She was gone. Cool air filled his arms instead of her. *Damn it.* "You don't play fair."

"Says the man who started all the groping." She hadn't gone far, just a few feet away she stood at the desk. Or rather, not standing. Her bustles and layers pointed at him. A view he could enjoy all damn day long, for sure.

He groaned and poured himself a whiskey.

"I said cold water."

The bustle wiggled as she struggled with something in the drawer. He wasn't about to help her. Bent over and wiggling her bustle at him? No, she could stay like that.

"Cole Mitchell. Are you admiring my skirts?"

"Something like that."

"Boor."

"Damn straight."

With another grunt she stumbled back until she landed on her rump with a solid *oof.* "Oh for goodness sakes. Were you too busy watching?"

"Damn straight." He laughed and held out his hand to help her up.

"It was stuck." The box she clutched to her chest had been her final target, or rather what was inside it. He remembered putting the box in the drawer, it had barely fit so it was no surprise she'd struggled so.

"Should have warned you. Didn't fit in the drawer right."

She hummed and set it on the desk. "Is there anything else we need? I feel as though I am forgetting something."

"Just what's in the box."

"Obviously." Her hand ran along the smooth grain, and then her eyes darted around the room again. Shaking fingers danced along her neck. "I feel like I'm forgetting something else."

"We're going to be late." It was a stall tactic, but he had put a surprise for her in the box he knew she'd be getting out tonight. The stall tactic wouldn't work with him. "Let's get moving."

"Sorry." A gasp escaped moments later when the box opened. "Colton James Spencer."

"Hey now." Years had passed since he'd last heard his real name. It sounded good to hear it from her lips. There seemed no better time, no better person. It almost made him want to use it again.

"What did you do?"

"What does it look like?" He reached over her shoulder to pluck the necklace from where it lay on top of a Derringer. The gun was her matter; the jewelry was his. "You left me in Denver on business for four whole days. I wasn't about to keep busy the way I used to. I had to find something to keep me occupied."

"You bought me another necklace to keep occupied?" She took the gun from its case and the pleased smile she'd born on sight of the jewelry dissipated. She wrinkled her nose. "Stupid tiny weapon."

"Necessary weapon, your Remington is too large and heavy to be hidden."

She lifted her bodice and tugged at the back of her skirt. The tight fit of the gown and bustle didn't offer much room and her search for the pocket in her bustle became a battle. Her hands came dangerously close to ending their evening they were so close to him. She grunted and stomped a foot, shifting her skirts and bustle. "Damn it."

"Stop your fidgeting." The minute she did, he fastened the necklace. Once it was set, he shoved her hands away from her skirts. With a quick lift to the tail of her bodice he set everything straight, closed the pocket with the small gun inside, set it back in place, and re-hooked her skirts with some regret. "That should do it. Try jumping."

"You merely wish to see me jump."

"I want to be sure everything holds."

"Liar."

"And I want to see ya jump." He grinned when she rewarded his honesty with one delicious bounce. "Nice."

"Boor." Her snarl of protest didn't reach her lips, which still curved into a smile. The pleased flush he'd admired all evening spread along her neck, making her skin inviting and pink.

The moment he moved close, her hand flattened against his forehead and shoved him back. He stumbled a step and frowned. "Hey."

"It's time to go."

"I got better ideas."

"You always have ideas."

The minute she passed him he set his hand on her waist. If he couldn't do what he wanted, he had to at least touch her and have her close. The fact other men were going to want to dance with her bothered him a hell of a lot more than he cared to admit.

They made it around the balcony without incident, but halfway down the steps the usual din of the saloon quieted to silence. Nobody stirred except to further turn to see them better. Cole's tension rose at the blatant stares.

Someone yelled across the wide room. "Damn Cole. You look like a gentleman."

Jane giggled, the musical sound doused some of his tension. "It's possible for anyone to look like a gentleman, Hank. For Cole it's rather easy, but it would get boring if it happened every day wouldn't it?"

This time it was her possessive hand that slipped around his waist. Just as quick it disappeared to leave him cold again. If it hadn't been for the reason she'd left his side, he would have protested.

"Lady Jane." Gilbert Hamm bowed low before her. "I ain't ever seen a woman purty as you are tonight."

"Mr. Hamm, compliments will not get you free beer." Laughter rumbled through the saloon, returning some of the normal volume and conversation. Jane leaned in to give Hammy a kiss on the cheek. The man's ruddy cheeks darkened, as they always did when Jane paid him so much heed. She set her hand on his. "You are too kind to me."

"No, Janey. He's honest. You look real good. I might have to change my mind and head to the dance myself." Wills leaned back in his chair. "If I got to dance with you."

"Doubtful that would happen, Wills. My dance card is already quite full. Perhaps if you cleaned up and went you'd find someone you wouldn't have to pay to dance with you." Jane's foot snuck out from under her skirt, and Wills' chair toppled to the floor from her subtle kick.

Cole laughed along with the others. He wrapped his arm around Jane's waist again. "Get back to your beer and games. Jane and I ain't gonna be gone all night. She'll be back to make sure you stay in line soon enough."

"Cuddy, I was lying." Jane grabbed the doorframe on the verge of their escape. "Compliments do get Mr. Hamm free beer, the rest of the night."

"Giving away my beer?" Cole chuckled when her fingers pinched his side. They both stopped in the middle of the street.

Jane didn't seek out the distant sounds of revelry or the lamps moving toward it to add to the light filling the meadow. Instead, she turned the opposite direction. Down the street past the saloon toward the only building with the lamp lit— the jail

If someone wasn't at the dance, they were at the saloon. Between the two the town sat near deserted.

"I wish I'd had patience. He would already be dead instead of in jail where things could so easily get so much worse." Her thumb hooked into his waistband. "I wouldn't be worried about the fact you chose to go without your holster tonight, either."

"Hard to look fancy with that. Besides, no guns allowed at the party." Cole patted her bustle where the Derringer lay hidden. "No visible ones, anyhow."

"Except for the sheriff and his deputy, of course." Jane shook her head, and they started again toward the depot and the meadow beyond. "I suppose that should make me feel better."

"Not so sure about Davie-boy, but I know Mike ain't afraid to use his."

It wouldn't matter at the dance. Jane's tense shoulders relaxed. Out past the depot they could make out the events in the meadow more clearly. In the distance beyond the party the skeleton of the unfinished new schoolhouse stood silent beside the brand new church. Lamp upon lamp lit up the field where a dance floor had been constructed.

The music drifted toward them on the breeze while half the crowd moved in synch on the well-lit floor. The rest milled about while the children raced around through the adults playing their games. Their laughter and screams echoed above the instruments.

A small gasp erupted from Jane beside him and she stopped short.

Cole paused when she did. "What?"

"I never thought to ask. Will you and I actually be dancing?" She moved forward toward the dance at a slower pace than before. The question never had been breached, especially with her distraction in the days after he'd asked her. In the year they'd known each other the opportunity for dancing had never come along.

"Thought ya knew."

"Knew what?"

"I've got many talents."

"Oh, I am quite aware of that fact, Mr. Spencer." She used his real name again, low and quiet though they were alone. Just as before it gave him a little thrill when she did. Her hip bumped his, and her fingers laced into his where they sat on her waist. "I just do not know if you can dance."

"Can you?"

"Yes. It seems I can."

"How would you know that for certain?" Somehow they'd wandered into the fray. Greetings were exchanged along the way to the dance floor.

"Doesn't matter, just try me." Her hand slid into his the second he offered. The bright smile she offered was more genuine than he'd seen in what seemed like ages.

A gentle tug spun her onto the floor and right into his arms where she belonged. In the midst of the other dancers he fell into step. It had been years since he'd been to any sort of dance, but the memory stayed with him.

Once, maybe twice, Jane tripped up before her hesitation disappeared. For him it was the memory that carried him through the steps. She followed his lead effortlessly.

One step after the other, they danced like the crowd wasn't there. Nothing could separate them until the music stopped and friends and family began to take their turns.

Revenge is an act of passion,
vengeance of justice.
Injuries are revenged,
crimes are avenged.
-Samuel Johnson

They believed they had won. Locked him in a cage. A cage he could easily escape from. They left him alone enough.

Clara's brothers were proving to be as arrogant as she was. Believing they'd actually captured him. Like he was so stupid. It had been his intention to get captured all along. After all, this way he could learn about the rest of her family first hand.

Once the marshal came it would be so easy to escape. The marshal would watch him with even less diligence than these inept ruffians. Then Clara would see her end. Then his life could return to normal.

Too long his focus had remained on her.

On Constance. She had always been his weakness.

The vile plink of tobacco into the pot pulled Alan's focus away from his inner thoughts.

Tommy.

He'd been the one. The one that had missed Alan's careful scrutiny. It was like he didn't exist. In a way that Alan had always succeeded in not existing. It made no sense.

Tommy was vulgar. Crude. Chawing tobacco. Laughing at every stupid little joke. Like a donkey braying. Firing his weapon off for no other reason than to get attention. How did someone like that disappear? He drew attention to himself wherever he went.

Alan wrinkled his nose and closed his eyes again.

They hadn't even bothered to shackle him to the bed. Left him to roam the small cell freely. Often he'd been left alone in the jail. Every time a Young brother was on watch duty he found himself alone. It was too convenient. But he was learning that they weren't vigilant even when watching him.

Little mistakes.

The biggest mistake was in the way they ignored him. Acted like he didn't exist. By doing that, he'd managed to swipe a pair of scissors from the medical bag of Charles. So far there had been no need for it, but it would be helpful eventually.

Every time there was more than one Young in the room they fought. Small arguments. Large arguments. Distractions upon distractions. They were undisciplined. Uncouth. Incapable.

He ought to escape just to prove how incapable they were.

Cocksure bastards.

They wouldn't let Clara come see him. Several arguments had been over her desire to do just that.

He had to admit he was curious as to why she would try. Another ploy, perhaps? Or maybe just to admit how right he'd been. It was just another scheme on her part. That she had something major in mind for the town.

That was unlikely.

Just like she'd been with David, she was enamored with Cole. No. She wanted to flaunt. Like her brothers. That he was behind these bars. While she wasn't. While she had tricked death. He would trick it, too. Like he always did. Did she truly believe he'd never been caught? Once she'd been left alone for a full week while he was trapped behind bars.

He'd escaped then, too. And just like the obedient, naïve fool she'd been, Clara had waited for him.

These days she thought herself better than him. Soon she would know better. For the moment, he had to put up with the continued ignorance. The lazy, non-existent beast currently *guarding* him. Leaning back in his chair, chawing and wiping down his rifle. Singing *Molly Malone* horribly off-key.

Alan got to his feet, Tommy ignored him. The small cell didn't afford much walking room, but it was enough. Enough to keep the blood flowing and his brain working around the possibilities.

Even when he got close, Tommy didn't move or pay him any mind. If the man tilted back any farther, he'd fall right over. The chair cracked under his weight. He just didn't care.

Alan ignored him right back. Difficult as it was with the horribly off-tune song ringing in his ears. It wouldn't do him any good to allow small annoyances to distract him. He was smarter than them. Their distractions wouldn't blur his thoughts. Every option was before him. This time when he got to Clara, there would be no rescue for her. This time.

Shouts echoed down the street. Bouncing off the empty buildings into the open door of the jail. Alan listened as the shouts carried words of cheating, cards, lies, and money. The shouts faded, only to grow again.

Tommy didn't budge. Lazy. Then a shot rang out. A scream. More shouts, growing louder.

Tommy flew to his feet, the unbalanced chair clattering to the floor. Without another glance at Alan, he dashed out the door. His shout was closer, but got lost among the continuing sounds of battle.

Alan resumed his pacing, until a glance at the desk revealed the keys. Just out of his reach. It wasn't possible. It was too easy.

More gunshots echoed through the town. More screams, shouts. The unmistakable sounds of an intense and large scuffle. The battle was too intense, not a soul paid any attention to the jail. In quick succession his mind ran over the possibilities. Even if it was a trap, he could escape into the night before they had a chance to catch him. That he was certain of.

Waiting another day for the marshal seemed pointless. The keys were well out of reach. The chair that had fallen to the floor was not. Through the bars he grabbed the chair leg with both hands, grunting at the effort to lift it from the awkward angle. Within a minute the back of the chair clattered onto the desk top.

Alan dragged it toward him, catching the keys and a bag of tobacco Tommy had left on the desk. Inch by inch he tugged until they both dropped to the floor. The chair followed behind, cracking under the impact. His mouth pinched in effort, but with a little more maneuvering the keys were in front of him. He paused, listening.

Gunfire still rang out. In between the fighting someone cheered, laughed, sang. Drunk tunes punctuated with gunfire. Alan chuckled, releasing himself from the cell. From there it was easy. Slipping into the shadows of the building. Waiting long enough to make sure no one was watching. For the minute he was still. He watched the fight that had spilled into the street. The growing crowd of curious onlookers from the dance. Every time one fight quelled a little, another broke out.

Alan slipped around the jail, keeping in the shadows as he ran toward the edge of town. Into the tree line. From there it would be easy. Easier if he had a horse.

After just a few seconds of contemplation he headed toward the unfinished hotel of the youngest Young. While the hotel remained unfinished, the private home of Mike stood complete. The stable had several horses to choose from. It was only two miles outside of town. No one would be the wiser until morning. Then he'd be long gone.

The sounds of the bar fight faded into the night. Sounding more like whispers until only the occasional echo of gunfire reached his ears. Alan grinned. Now he would win. They would never win. They just weren't smart enough.

He slid open the door of the barn, the quiet huffing of horses the only sound within. The smell of hay, feed, manure. The shuffle of a hoof. In the dark he moved along the stalls, his eyes adjusted enough to see the shadows of the horses.

A long scratch. A match? A flicker of light, growing brighter.

"Alan."

She wasn't that smart. It couldn't be.

"Did you really think I would let you go with the marshal?"

"Clara."

"You want to know the funny thing?"

He turned around, seeing her helped him believe this wasn't his imagination. "How did you know I'd come here?"

"You had four days before they caught you. I figured you checked out the entire area. Once we all talked about it, we agreed this was the most likely place you'd choose to make your escape. Plenty of horses and hiding places, and no one around to hear or see you leave."

"Liar."

"Plus, we had someone set to follow you when you did leave. It's your fault for believing the Young's are as inept as you believe everyone is."

Clara didn't move. The lantern she'd lit cast eerie shadows across her features. She looked like a ghost. A demon.

"I really didn't remember, you know."

"I think you've just proven you do remember."

"I really don't. If you hadn't ever had coffee with me that day, I would have taken no notice of you. My amnesia isn't a game, Alan."

Still she insisted on continuing the ruse. On the ongoing lies. "Lies. I taught you how to lie. You can't fool me."

"No, you taught Clara." She disappeared into the shadows, reappearing a moment later. No. It couldn't be. Constance was gone. What did she do?

"Constance." A burning pain ripped through his stomach a moment before he heard the small pop of a gun.

"You will not die easily, Alan, but you will die for the pain you caused me. You wanted me to love you. You wanted me to join you."

"Constance. You did." It wasn't Constance. It couldn't be.

"Belly wounds are nasty things. Your insides rip open, leaking the poison of your own flesh back into you. It will hurt. You will suffer like we did."

It was Clara again, or was it Constance?

"You couldn't leave well enough alone. Because you decided to destroy me, you suffer now."

"You have no idea who I am. Why I did this."

"I know all too well the depths of your insanity, your depravity. I've seen the real reports from Dr. Abrams. I know what you did, Alan. Clara figured it all out, too. She chose to stand up to you. You tried to destroy her, and then you tried to destroy me. You counted on me being weak like Clara. You didn't count on my amnesia being real or my love for these people being stronger than your pull."

"It's not real. You're weak." Alan retched, and blood filled his mouth so fast he choked on it. The wound made him weak. This wasn't happening. She wasn't strong enough to kill. "Weak."

"Clara was." With a rustle of petticoats, she drew close to the lantern. "The minute I realized someone tried to kill me, I stopped being weak. I learned to trust others and let them help me. The scars Clara had were long forgotten. They didn't make me susceptible to you."

"You have no idea." His knees wouldn't listen to him. Wobbling, bending when he should be tall. She wouldn't win like this. She couldn't kill. Never could.

"Oh, but I do know. You taught Clara well. All those years while you kept her through manipulation and force, she wrote letters to her brother and mailed them when you were stupid enough to leave her alone. She found a way to trick you. She was going to destroy you."

"She failed. I won." He had won, by pushing Constance's husband in front of the train. Clara had lost her mind. "With one push."

"You did kill him then. It wasn't Clara." A low chuckle reached his ears. "Well. That's good you admit it, one more reason for your death."

Blood soaked his hands and dripped to the floor. He had to keep fighting. "Bitch."

"Alan. Such vulgarity."

A scarf over her head. It was Constance again. "Constance." It was her. Just as she had been, when it had been her throat coated with blood.

"Think of me Alan. I want my face to be the last you see. This face, filled with the disgust and hatred you've instilled in me. You made this of your own doing, and I want you to know how much you failed. I don't love you. I revile you. You sicken me. After tonight I will not think of you again."

"Constance." A whisper of breath reached his ears as the lamp flickered before going out. A small whinny and a clip of hooves later and she was gone. In the dark again. The welcome dark. She won. Constance. Clara.

The murdered do haunt their murderers,
I believe. I know that ghosts have
wandered on earth.
—Emily Brontë

Tommy tapped his fingers against the keys on his hip at a rapid pace. The marshal had arrived on today's train, and everything relied on the next ten minutes, minutes that could mean having to pull more strings than ever before to keep his sister's neck out of another noose. "Train's been here five minutes already. Isn't he dead yet?"

Charlie didn't bother to lift his head at Tommy's complaint. He continued to examine the man that lay near death on the cot beside him. "Your impatience for the death of another human being is touching."

Nick sat behind the desk, the only sign of tension in his tightly clasped hands. Poised to take the fall, it would be easier for him, too, if the guy didn't talk.

"Calling him a human being is a stretch." Tommy stayed in the doorway of the jail, one eye on the street for the approach of Marshal Lewis and David. It could get confusing and pretty damn ugly if the bastard was still alive and talking by the time David got done relaying the story as he knew it.

"Don't even think of asking me to speed this up." Charlie had a knack for knowing the ugly thoughts running in Tommy's head. Tommy suspected Charlie thought a fair amount of them himself. He was just better at hiding them. "It won't be long before he's dead. I just won't force him into your timetable. That isn't what I do."

"You're far from innocent. You've killed plenty."

"We all have." Charlie rose from the cot before shifting to a nearby chair. The cell door was wide open with no reason to lock it. Soon enough Alan would be dead. Of course, that didn't stop them from shackling him to the cot. "War tends to do that to men, you know. It turns them into killers."

"Or saviors. St. Chucky."

"I'm no saint."

"Of course not." Already Tommy could see David and the marshal heading their way. They'd passed the saloon and were yards away. "You just act like one. Don't fool me, though. I do know all of your secrets. I know exactly what you were doing down South and your reasons for going."

"You know, I've been wondering something, Tommy. For a guy that knows so much, that uses his connections to get dirt to use on his brothers, how is it you never knew where Clara was all these years?" Charlie kept his calm and stoic appearance, but Tommy knew better. Underneath that calm was pure fire.

A chair screeched across the floor, and Nick was on his feet. Fists clenched beside him, the pure white heat of fury flashed behind his steel-blue eyes. "Tommy?"

"You didn't wonder too, Nick? I'm surprised. You're pure suspicion these days. Of course, since you decided it was best to disavow your blood rather than search for her, I shouldn't be shocked." Charlie picked at a loose thread on his pants. The tense lines of his features were the only true disclosure of his anger.

Tommy wasn't in the least bit fazed. Secrets were something he was more than used to. "Sit your ass down, Nick. Chuck's just mad that I'm calling him out on being a spy. He'd prefer to be remembered for the supposedly noble reasons he defected to the South."

"We're family." Nick was more of a crapshoot. Ever since the war he was much harder to read. He might just kill for this. "If you knew all this time and didn't tell us anything, then maybe you aren't family."

"Watch yourself, Nick. You can't disown everyone that upsets you. Family is family. Period. Sometimes that means you have to accept things you don't like Sometimes it means you have to let secrets lie where they fall. Life isn't meant to be easy. Neither is being a family. Blood is thick."

"He's right in here, Marshal Lewis." David's voice filtered into the cramped jail just in time. Any longer and there might have been a scuffle. "Dr. Young has been keeping watch over the prisoner."

Tommy stepped aside for the marshal, keeping a strong eye on Nick rather than the situation at hand. It wasn't until Nick sat back down that Tommy felt he could return his attention to the newcomers in the room.

"Clara Young's brothers are here to keep an eye on the prisoner?" Marshal Lewis was just finishing what was probably the latest in the litany of repetitive questioning. The man seemed the kind to question everything until he was sure he had the truth.

Problem being, the truth was a tricky tightrope they were all walking.

"Mike and I are deputies. Who else was he going to ask?" Tommy didn't balk at the marshal's attention being on him. It was expected in this situation. "Mike has been his deputy for as long as he's been sheriff. I was a deputy in New York before I headed out here and took this job."

"How did he get beat up?" Marshal Lewis straightened.

"Resisted coming in." Charlie spoke this time. "After shooting Cole, he made a run for it. Didn't get too far, but he wasn't too interested in being put in jail."

"Sheriff Shaffer had some interesting accusations to make against the prisoner. Back in December, Mr. Bingham murdered twelve people and stabbed Mrs. Daugherty. Then there is the matter of this man being guilty of the very murder Miss Young was accused of and hanged for." The marshal looked between the three brothers. "I guess I don't have to ask what you think."

"It's not an opinion. He admitted it." Nick stayed in the seat behind the desk. His face remained the same unreadable mask it always was, but Tommy knew he wasn't lying. Nick had been right there when Alan had been shot. He'd heard everything.

Tommy would say that Nick sound almost proud of the way Clara handled herself that night, although there hadn't been any elaboration to the story. Nick wasn't telling what exactly had gone down, only the admittance of the murder. "Marshal, this is Nick."

"You're the one that shot him?" Marshal Lewis stopped when Alan grunted. "Can he talk? Verify any of this?"

"Your guess is as good as mine." Charlie didn't move at the grunt, the tension of their previous argument gone. Like Tommy, he didn't worry one bit about the line of questioning. David looked more worried than them, and he didn't know anything. They'd kept it that way on purpose.

"Aren't you the doctor?"

"I am. Quite frankly, I'm surprised he isn't deceased already. The wound tore through his intestines. By the time they got him to me, it was too late." Charlie still didn't move. Good man. "I have only been making sure he wasn't in excruciating pain. The poison of his own filth has infected him too far to be saved."

"Clara." A weak cry came from the cot. Damn that maniac. He was going to stir the marshal's curiosity. "Clara…"

"Mr. Bingham?" Lewis gestured for the chair, pulling it closer when Charlie vacated it. "Can you hear me?"

"His fever is through the roof. He's delusional," Charlie supplied. It wasn't far from the truth. Actually, it was the truth. The man was close to death. Anyone could see the sweat pouring off of him. "Make it fast. I don't think he'll be able to answer anything much longer."

"It was…Clara." Alan's voice was barely a whisper. Everyone in the jailhouse held their breath. Listening to what he'd admit. "Constance…was there…They…did this."

Tommy had to give David credit. For the ten levels of shock and horror that crossed his features, he kept perfectly silent. Then, like the rest of them, his features settled into calm acceptance. Tommy hoped that meant he knew it had been necessary.

"So a ghost killed you? I thought it was Nick." Marshal Lewis stood, moving aside to give Charlie room. "I guess he is delusional, then?"

"As any man can be, and as near as I can tell, always has been." For that Tommy got a sharp elbow in the side from David.

"Mr. Young." Lewis turned his attention to the silent form sitting behind the desk. "What happened?"

"I had no cause to go to the party. I am not a deputy, and I don't hang around in saloons. I went to Mike's house and turned in for the night." Nick's honesty would make Jane happy. "Around ten I heard a noise in the stables. I discovered Alan. He'd obviously escaped, as last I'd seen him he was behind bars. I brought him back."

"With a belly wound."

"It would appear so." Still telling the truth, Nick never said he'd shot the man. Only under intense pressure would he admit to it, as a last resort. That had been the agreement. "I got him back to town soon as I could. It was too late."

"You say he shot Mr. Mitchell?" Lewis left the cell, stopping in front of Tommy. "What reason would he have for that?"

"He wanted everyone that knew about Clara's past gone. Cole was the one stupid enough to try to go after him first and got shot for his efforts." Still true, Cole had been the one dumb enough to agree to Jane's plan.

"Just how did so many of Clara's family end up here? Right at this time?"

"Mike told us about her hanging. We came out as soon as was possible for each of us. With the weather and family obligations it took us a while." Tommy's jaw clenched. "Is there something wrong with coming to see our sister's grave?"

"Not at all. The timing is just fortuitous."

Marshal Lewis wasn't stupid, but he wasn't pushing the matter too hard. Maybe there was hope that this would all be over sooner rather than later.

"If fortune had been in our favor sooner, Clara wouldn't have swung." Tommy couldn't stop it, the anger over the fact he hadn't been allowed to help boiled. "She didn't deserve that."

"Tommy." David spoke up in a quiet tone. "Not now."

"Right." Oh, but he wanted to. He wanted to get in Lewis' face and rant at him, whether it was his fault or not.

"I should go see how Mr. Mitchell is doing then, after his injury." The marshal's suspicions were not well hidden. They definitely didn't have Lewis fooled.

Whether they liked it or not, Tommy was going with them. Soon as he stepped outside Jane ducked behind a cart across the street. Curiosity would get that girl hanged again if she wasn't careful.

The conversation ahead of him didn't sink in. If he let it, he might end up fighting off the urge to lay into the marshal again. It wasn't until they were in the saloon and the group of drinkers fell silent that he paid any attention.

"Mr. Mitchell." Lewis took note of the chaos left behind from the bar fight. Cole hadn't bothered to clean anything up. Nice touch and even better when you took into account his bedraggled appearance. "Mind if I ask you a few questions?"

"What about?" Cole threw back a whiskey. "I really don't feel much like dealing with you. You're the one that did it."

Still pure honesty. Cole had made it clear he hadn't wanted to see one hair on the marshal's head, even if Jane still walked around alive. "Maybe this isn't the best time, Marshal. Cole's got his hands full with the saloon destroyed again."

"Just had a few questions about last night. The injury you sustained from Mr. Bingham and about Miss Young."

Cole leaped over the bar in a heartbeat. He snarled in the marshal's face. "You don't get to talk about her. It ain't your right."

David stepped back in surprise at Cole's attack. "Cole, it will only take a minute. I promise."

"Would you mind if I saw your room?" Lewis caught them all off guard with that. Even if they had planned for it, they hadn't actually expected it to happen.

"I would. What do ya gotta see that for?" Cole's grip on the whiskey bottle he'd managed to keep hold of tightened. "No one goes in there."

"Mr. Bingham seems to think Miss Young is the one that shot him, that she's still alive and kicking." The marshal took his turn to stretch the truth, trying to catch Cole in a lie. "I'm told it's delusions of an injured and dying man. I'd like to believe it, but seeing proof of her being gone would help."

Tommy had to wonder if Lewis had seen Jane as well, before she'd hidden out of sight. If so, he might have to do a little recovery work, making sure nothing got farther. For now, keeping Cole from killing the marshal had to be the focus. "Cole, what's it going to hurt? Just let him see so he'll stop bothering you."

Cole's nostril's flared. "Schaffer ain't welcome."

With a sigh of relief, Tommy clapped David on the shoulder and followed Cole and Lewis upstairs. It would be over in just a few more minutes. After that everything would be simple procedure with nothing out of the ordinary after investigating a ghost.

"I'm sure you understand." Patronizing wasn't the right route for Lewis to take, unless he wanted to poke the bear. "I just have to verify every aspect."

It was getting more likely that Lewis had seen Jane. Tommy was prepared for that, even if he didn't like it. "Verifying that there is no such thing as a ghost seems like an extraneous detail."

"Of course, but as long as I'm here asking about Mr. Mitchell's injury, I should check every avenue." Lewis stepped into the room when Cole held open the door.

Tommy hung back by the door. Even though Cole had let Jane in, he still didn't like anyone else in his room. "Verified now?"

Lewis lifted the curtain where the clothes were hung. "An awful lot of books you have, Mr. Mitchell."

"What? I read." Cole folded his arms across his chest.

Tommy couldn't stop the snort that escaped if he tried, not that he did. Clearing his throat, he held up his hands when Cole glared at him. "Sorry, funny how no one believes is all."

"You read Faust?"

Lewis wasn't letting it go. Stubborn ass.

"It was hers." Cole drew up taller, his fists clenched tight.

"Didn't picture you as the sentimental type."

There was Lewis' mistake. Before it got ugly, Tommy bolted into the room. He forced himself between the men, holding Cole back. "Just what in hell is provoking him going to do, Marshal?"

"She hanged." Cole wasn't faking this anger. It had been festering for far too long, and Tommy wasn't sure he could hold it all back. "You said yourself she was dead. Why dig her up? Let her be."

"Cole?" David became lifesaver in that moment, ignoring the order to stay away. "What's going on?"

"The marshal thinks it's a good idea to provoke Cole." Tommy grunted. Cole wasn't letting up. "Cole kept her books."

"So? I kept them too." David stayed in the doorway. "And I didn't know how to read. I kept them for a year. I still have one."

Cole's fight faded a little. "Get out. All of you."

"I think that's a good idea." Tommy was glad the worst of the fight was over. "Let's just get out of Cole's hair and let you see Clara's letters."

"He don't got a right to them." Cole's voice was tense.

"It's not your call. They are Mike's letters." David waved at Lewis. "We should go. The letters are at my homestead."

"We have yet to discuss what happened here last night, Mr. Mitchell, or the wounds you supposedly suffered at the hands of Mr. Bingham?" Still being persistent, Lewis couldn't take a hint. This was something Tommy was definitely going to have to handle.

"You mean this?" With a rip of fabric Cole exposed the healing wound. The jagged line in his shoulder was more pronounced with the black thread Charlie had used to stitch it up. "I got shot by that bastard. I'm glad he's gonna die."

"Any other questions?" Tommy moved closer to Lewis, edging him toward the door. "If they're about the fight last night, about anyone in this town can handle them. Most of us saw it. Graham can help answer for Cole, too. He's part owner. It might be best if we let Cole be."

"Of course. Thank you for your time, Mr. Mitchell."

Was that amusement? What was this guy's game?

"Get out." Cole slammed the door in their face, a smash of glass echoing out a minute later.

"What the hell was that about?" Tommy folded his arms across his chest. "He's not exactly a suspect here. Everyone saw him cleaning up the mess."

"Just making sure. It's what I do, Mr. Young."

"One of these days, remind me to tell you what exactly it is that I do, Marshal."

There are people who think that honesty is always the best policy. This is a superstition; there are times when the appearance of it is worth six of it.
-Mark Twain

Tommy had asked his question almost five minutes before. Still, Jane had yet to respond. Her mouth opened a few times, but she said nothing.

The question would be a complex one for most people, for Jane it was probably more so. Of course, the endless flow of words trapped in her odd brain should have helped. It shouldn't be so hard for her to cite a line that represented herself. He'd asked as a lark, after all.

Moments before he would have asked again, she sighed. "Honestly? It would be, 'a dark unfathomed tide of interminable pride, a mystery, and a dream should my early life seem'."

"Those are the words you choose to represent yourself?" Tommy tugged on the line of his fishing pole when he picked up the gentle flicker of a nibble to his bait. To keep Jane out of as much trouble as possible with the marshal still in town, Tommy had demanded she join him on his fishing excursion.

She'd obliged, but showed up in a simple cotton gown. Instead of being well behaved and sedate, she'd insisted on swimming. Afterward she seemed to have calmed and now lay on the bank next to him, soaking in the patch of sun that filtered through the leaves above. Her dress had already dried, but she left her feet bare and had them set in the cool water to ease the heat of the day.

His challenge to use the millions of memorized words in her head to describe herself hadn't been meant to trouble either of them. He'd anticipated an indecent rendering of Ovid or Goethe, perhaps even Whitman. One thing he hadn't expected was Poe's *Imitation*.

Despite the question lingering between them, Jane remained silent. She'd taken the extra step of closing her eyes to avoid both the silent question and answering it. Tommy wasn't about to let her win. If he had patience to fish, which he hated, he had the patience to wait her out. It didn't take long.

Much sooner than he'd anticipated she caved with a whisper so soft he hardly heard it over the trickle of the creek. "At this moment, yes."

"Why?" In truth, he couldn't blame her. Unlike those that had burst into her life before him, he'd been able to observe Jane in secret without foisting himself on her.

She didn't know who he was, that much had been clear from the start, so he'd been able to do what he did best. Observe and learn. Without meaning to, David and Mike both placed expectations and hopes on her. Never verbalized, but clearly felt by her. Having three other brothers around was undoubtedly suffocating.

While he waited she didn't move a muscle. Her hands folded over her stomach, she hardly breathed. He was inches from shuddering when he realized she'd probably looked much the same as she lay in that coffin after her hanging.

Before he could yell at her to move, the slightest of movements came from her lips. "I am not having this discussion again."

"Get used to it. Ma and Pa will be here in a few weeks and you'll be having it again." Tommy rubbed his hand over his face. "So it's my fault you feel like an imitation? What about around Cole?"

"No, never around Cole."

"That's why you love him?"

"No."

"So you do love him?"

Never had he seen her move that fast or turn quite that shade of red. She was on her feet and turned away from him before he could start laughing. "I didn't say that. If you'd let me finish."

"Of course." There was no curbing his laughter over her violent reaction, so he didn't bother trying. Even when she smacked him upside his head, pretty hard, it didn't stop. "Just go ahead and finish already."

"Never around anyone that didn't know Clara, is what I meant." An annoyed grunt reached his ears. Seconds later she tumbled out from behind him in a heavy fight to get her boot on. "I think it's time to head back."

"I'm not done fishing. Sit your annoying ass down and talk to me."

"Talking keeps the fish away. They don't like noise."

"That isn't the type of fishing I'm doing."

"Jump in the creek and drown for me, would you?"

Tommy swiped the untouched boot from the ground. When she tried to grab it away he threw it into the water. "Jane."

"You're a bastard. Did you know that?" She waded back into the creek. Once she was up to her knees she bent over to fish the boot off the bottom. "There are ways to convince me to see your way of thinking that don't involve such inane behavior. I'm not saying they would have been more successful, but you could have tried."

"This is more fun." Tommy waited until she'd stomped back up onto shore, cursing enough to make a cowboy blush. "Would you stop fussing at me and making this so difficult if I told you I'm not of the same mind as Nick."

"Probably not. I'm tired of discussing it. In a few weeks I'll have to face the parents I don't remember and attest to my part in George's death. I'll have to face James and do the same about my part in his near-death. I really just want to—"

"I'm not them, Lou."

"You can't even stop calling me Lou. So don't even tell me you aren't."

"You are more like a Lou than Clara ever was, I stopped calling her that years ago. Clara was weak."

That got her attention. With a thump she dropped to the ground. "All I ever hear is how much like her I am. I look like her. The reading, my memory…"

"I think you're very different in a few pretty noticeable ways. I know what they've been saying." He scratched his beard, taking a moment to let her quiet down. As her breathing slowed, he leaned forward on his knees, the fishing pole set aside. "I get that. I mean, Davey didn't let go of the belief you were faking it until you stepped into that noose."

"What?" Ashen and slack-jawed, it was clear she'd been blind to that fact. Or perhaps it was wishful thinking on her part that he'd truly accepted it.

"He spent all those months thinking maybe you were still hurt, angry, and if he just kept reminding you by his simple presence that he was the man you loved, you'd get over it." He shrugged and grabbed his canteen to take a long drink.

"That's why he was so eager to share the good over the bad."

"Guess it was the fact that even faced with death you didn't change your story that did him in. That's when he started to accept it." Tommy handed her the canteen. "Whiskey, not water."

She snatched the canteen away. A few drops dribbled along her chin in her rush to down as much as she could. "You aren't helping."

"Mike was the worst, probably because he doesn't see things the way I do." Tommy snorted. "You were older than him, bigger than him, and mean as a little devil to him. Of course he saw you as tough, strong. Clara beat him up—a lot. Probably to make up for the hell we put her through all the time."

"You saw it different?"

"Clara was weak and weak-willed. Around us she put up a good front and acted tough as nails, but she was so easily used and abused by us. George, James and I were always using her to play tricks on Charlie and Nick. She had a razor wit, but common sense and a true strong will? Not so much."

She pulled her knees to her chest and rested her chin on them. "She didn't think she was."

"No, she thought she could handle anything. That's why she went as far as Attica to find her teaching job. She wanted to be on her own. In some ways she was all she claimed to be. Strong, capable, able to handle a class and a household on her own and she excelled at teaching."

"You're contradicting yourself."

"I said she was weak-willed. It wasn't so bad when she was home, but it got worse when she moved away." Tommy stood, rubbing the back of his neck. He didn't like to talk about this. He'd been sworn to secrecy. "Even worse during her second year of teaching. I tried to get her to come back home after…"

For a long time silence filled the space between them. It was likely she didn't want to know any more than he wanted to admit it. Either curiosity or a sick need to return the pain into herself spurred her on. "After what? Tommy, just tell me."

"Clara was sixteen and had only had her teaching license for just over a year. One of her students was the same age as she. A few were fifteen, and then she had three little ones." Tommy's eyes narrowed at a nearby tree. He wondered how bad it would hurt to vent the reemerging pain against the bark of the tree with his fist.

"You're stalling."

"The big kid's name was Fred. He saw fit to teach Clara a few things she didn't want to learn. A lesson she would later take and turn into a healthy appetite for sex just to hide how often it was against her will." He leaned against the tree rather than hurt himself punching it. "I only found out because I went to visit a few days after it all started. Clara hadn't figured out how to hide it from me yet."

"Wait." Jane appeared around the other side of the tree. He hadn't even heard her move, but there she stood. Like the ghost of Clara, pale as could be, whispers of tears at the edge of her eyes, a weak tremble to her lips. "The Indian was not the first to rape her?"

"Not by a long shot."

"There were more?"

"I don't know how many, and couldn't begin to guess with the way she became so open in later years. This first time, though, I threatened to make the Fred kid stop. She told me she would handle it, that school would be out of session soon anyway." Tommy ran his hand through his hair, knocking his hat to the ground.

The ghost disappeared on a wave of fury. Cheeks flushed, her eyes flashed. The question stood, who was she mad at? "She refused? What did she do? Let it keep happening? Run away?"

Her gasp let him know she'd figured out the answer to her own question. He nodded. "Utah was good and far away. She somehow convinced ma and pa to let her move, and found a job far enough away that I couldn't keep checking up on her every week like I'd started to. Ma moved her a few months later and helped her settle in."

"And when you did check on her there?"

"Once the war started, I couldn't get out to Utah all that much. Mike did, but he was blind to Clara's weakness, and knew nothing of why she'd left New York. I heard plenty about the number of suitors she kept. When I was able to confront her, I got the impression, from her careful wording, that not all of her suitors were by her choice."

"So she became good at hiding it."

"Would seem so. After a couple of years she was able to tell me straight to my face that the company she kept was all by choice and to stay out of her business. She was an adult, and I would do well to let her be one." Tommy pursed his lips against the lingering annoyance and hurt at how she'd shoved him out. "Without any proof or any idea whom it was, I couldn't do anything to stop it."

Jane leaned back against the tree. With her back to him, he couldn't get any read on the thoughts in her head, only what she said. "That's what she meant. She thought that being with David would protect her, instead of being strong on her own or confiding in her husband and finding strength there. The fool."

Tommy couldn't think of anything to add. It had been foolish to start down this path, but maybe it was better that she knew.

"What else?"

"That's all I know. I mean I visited her a few times after, but by then she was good at hiding it. Even catching her by surprise, I got nothing."

"No, you idiot. You were telling me what was different about me."

That was it? She didn't want more on that story? Then again, he couldn't blame her. The subject was immensely distasteful.

"I can't talk about it any longer. I need to think about it for a while. Try to make sense of it, if there is such a thing." When she turned to face him, her eyes were rimmed red, but she looked strong. "Go on. You said I was different."

"Unlike David and Mike, both so shocked at seeing you they inserted themselves in your life right away I got to stand back." He picked up the canteen again, taking another large swig. Once it was snatched from his hand, he went on. "I was able to watch you and see how you acted and lived. Like I said, you're strong."

"Don't feel it."

"You went into the lion's den, and the only thing that made you afraid was the fact you might never see Cole or Jesse again."

She was still drinking the whiskey, shoving the canteen at him when she stopped to take a breath. "It had to be done."

"Exactly."

"All right. You've made your point. She was weak. I'm strong."

"You hate kids."

With a snort, she grabbed her boots again. "Several people would argue that point. They would point to Jesse, Arthur, Isaac, and Cindy."

"A few isolated children with a distinct exception. Any other child comes near you, and you shy away. I've seen it. Felt bad for a few kids that got in your way." He grinned, nudging her with his elbow. "You have only been with one man since you got here. I've heard rumors to the contrary, but Cole says different."

A boot hit him square in the stomach. Her slap hit his right cheek. "Nosy."

He caught her wrist, holding it tight. "And then there's this."

"What?" Jane tugged at her hand, grumbling when he kept hold.

"You're left-handed."

"Of course, I am."

"My sister did everything with her right hand."

Jane stopped her struggling, staring at the hand he had clasped tight. Then her right hand rose, pulling her eyes toward it. "No, my penmanship is the same."

"It's damn close to perfect. When Clara was little she broke her right wrist and was forced to use her left. Months of practice didn't make her any good. It's the strangest thing I've ever seen. You write, hit, shoot, all with your left hand."

"I could have learned. Alan might have made me learn."

"I saw no mention of it in Clara's letters." Tommy released her wrist, folding his arms across his chest. "Considering Clara took the time to detail everything down to what knots she'd learned, dishes to cook, and even how she made the dye for her hair, I would think she'd mention something like that."

"She didn't mention it." Jane shook her head, "How does that happen?"

"I have no idea. I'm not a neurologist. I'm just your nosy bastard brother."

"If I'm so different, are you my brother? That's just biology."

"It's more than biology. You know that." Tommy pulled her close and hugged her. "It's just more fun if I have a reason to pick on you. Being my sister gives me a hundred times more cause to do that."

Her hands beat on his back, her laughter loud enough to scare up some nearby birds. "Bastard."

"I know." He joined in her laughter, pushing her back a bit and holding up his hands in fists. "Think you can take me now that you're all strong and tough?"

"I'd just go for your weak point, your mistress there."

"My what?" An *oof* escaped when she punched him in the stomach. "What the hell was that?"

"I think she's grumpy, Tommy. When's the last time you fed her?"

"Oh, that reminds me, I'm hungry." Tommy dropped his hands and grinned. "Let's go eat."

"That's it?"

"It's much more fun when I'm not fighting on an empty stomach."

"You have more fun when you're eating." Jane shoved him, laughing all the way back to their horses. The rest of the way back to town the seriousness of the discussion was gone, at least on the surface.

He knew eventually she'd want more information, but for the time being she was more relaxed than she'd been in days. That's why he didn't tell her why he was going to follow her in after a few minutes.

Despite her teasing, he pushed her up the stairs toward Cora's. He let her joke about ordering him one of everything and waved her off. Once she'd disappeared inside, he turned toward the coming confrontation.

Marshal Lewis didn't make it past him. Tommy grabbed his arm, stopping him from going up the steps. "Leave it be, Marshal."

"I believe that's my decision, Mr. Young." Lewis moved to peel Tommy's fingers from his arm, but couldn't quite manage it. Tommy's grip was too strong. "I can have you arrested."

"No, you can't, and you won't."

"Excuse me?"

"Do you really want to push this? You were there when Clara was hanged. You helped proclaim her dead. You saw her nailed in a coffin." Tommy stepped closer. Every bit of laughter he'd felt earlier was gone. His eyes narrowed, and he got in Lewis' face. "All things that never would have happened if I'd known about this."

"She was found guilty. You couldn't have stopped it."

"You sure?" Tommy chuckled without humor. "You have no idea the connections I have. One doesn't protect the president without forming a few very key associates. I can have your badge revoked before you can have me arrested."

"I don't like threats."

"If it was a threat, you'd know it. This is just something to keep in mind. Bingham was the true criminal here. He manipulated and conned my sister, the sister you had hanged. The man is dead after trying to escape. Let's just leave it at that. Certainly no one can complain about how things are."

"She's a criminal, too."

"She was hanged. No one is complaining, Marshal. Let's not make this uglier than it needs to be. An evil man is dead. Justice has been served."

Lewis stared him down. "This isn't over."

"It is for now. I'll see you at the depot tomorrow. Make sure you get off safe."

"I'll be back."

"I'll be here."

Oh that it were possible,
After long grief and pain,
To find the arms of my true love,
Around me once again.
-Lord Alfred Tennyson

"Jane." A sharp kick cut through the layers of petticoats to hit her shin. Kat laughed. "Where was your head? Oh, wait—how silly of me. It's down the street in the saloon."

"Hush. It's not. I was listening for the train." Jane fiddled with the pages of the book in front of her. Just to be safe she hadn't stepped foot in the saloon for the three days Marshal Lewis had been in town.

"So that you could go to the saloon."

It wasn't untrue. The closest she'd been to Cole had been two days before. Tommy had brought him by while David had the marshal at the homestead reading Clara's letters. For thirty minutes they'd done little more than hold each other.

"Jane." Once again the sharp toe of a boot breeched her petticoats. "You are pitiful. I mean really. What is that you're reading?" Kat gasped, snatching the book from her, "Marriage Morning by Tennyson? Really? Is there something I should know?"

"Oh please, Katherine." Jane pulled the book back toward her. "The last thing we're going to do is get married."

"Of course. I forgot. No one who ever says they aren't interested in marriage changes their mind."

"I'm not you." Jane looked back down at the book and a brief passage she couldn't let go of, a verse that ran over constantly in her head.

> *Light, so low in the vale*
> *Heart, are you great enough*
> *For a love that never tires?*
> *O' heart, are you great enough for love?*

"I'm just waiting for the train to leave." She repeated in a heavy monotone. With great effort, she fought off her sigh as she closed the book. "That is, if Marshal Lewis does actually leave on it like Tommy said he would."

"If you continue to mope about, I'm going to make you wear pantaloons for my wedding. I promise you that." Kat squeezed her hand. "The train will leave when it's scheduled, and you'll get right back into your life."

"I'm not moping. I'm waiting," Jane corrected. Despite her efforts to stop it, her leg bounced in a rapid pace. Her heel tapped into the floor, drawing attention until Katherine's hand clamped onto her knee. "Sorry."

"This seems to go beyond simply wanting to see Cole for your usual unseemly acts, or because you missed him. What's going on?"

"Nothing." Jane knew she'd said it too quick. Kat was too smart to miss it, but maybe kind enough to let it go or maybe not.

"Liar."

"I don't lie."

"Liar." This time Katherine let it out in a sing-song voice. "There is something else. Tell me. I might die if you don't."

"You will not die." Jane smacked her hand. "Behave yourself. I just…I'm looking forward to this being over. Done."

"I have a question."

"Be nice."

"I will be." Katherine scooted closer. "I promise. I just want to know." The train whistle interrupted the question, and Jane flew to her feet. "That was the first call. It's going to be five minutes. Sit back down."

Jane kept her eyes on the door, no longer into the conversation like she had been. The waiting was almost over. She would be free.

"You haven't heard a word I've said, have you?" Katherine wrapped her arm through Jane's and pulled her to her feet. "Of course, you haven't. Let's just wait outside. You can watch the smoke get further away."

"I'm sorry, Kat."

"No, you're not. It's fine. I'll just ask my questions later."

"Thank you." Jane could hardly breathe. It was taking far too long for the train to actually pull out. Another whistle echoed across the town, warning of the train's imminent departure, soon, very soon.

Where was Tommy to let her know Lewis had gotten on the train, that she was free to go home to Cole?

"You're telling him, aren't you?"

The question broke through her impatient thoughts. It cut under the whistle of the departing train, right through to stick into her heart and twist it around the sharp edges of the question. "I don't know."

"Yes, you do."

"Yes, I do."

"Jane."

"If the marshal has left, if this is over, if I'm free." It was like the air was just gone. There was nothing left to breathe. The squeeze on her arm brought the air back briefly, and Jane breathed in deep. "Then yes."

"It's about damn time." Katherine's laughter filtered in to soothe the tension that had ripped through her body. Slowly, the laughter tickled until Jane laughed along with her. "I've been telling you for months."

"I wasn't free."

"And you are now?"

"In every way that counts. The past is no longer a secret. Clara is gone, but always with me. She doesn't imprison me." Jane gripped the railing, staring at the departing trail of smoke. "Alan is dead. The threat is gone. The only threats that remain are what everyone expects in life."

"Then what are you afraid of?"

"That saying it will change things, that he'll run."

"That man isn't going anywhere. He took a bullet to help rid you of Alan." Katherine squeezed her around the waist. "I don't think three words will change that."

Jane had to believe that was true. After all he'd wanted her to say it. He'd told her to say it. She was the one who'd frozen and been unable to speak the words.

A whoop nearby shocked the thoughts away. The horse Tommy rode on blasted through the street, rearing up at the base of the steps. "Jane."

The grin he wore said everything she needed. She didn't bother to wait for the rest. She tore down the stairs and into the street. Straight toward the saloon she ran, darting around any person or animal that crossed her path.

Just two buildings from her destination she caught sight of him and froze. In the middle of the street Cole waited, watching her every move. Her heart froze for two solid seconds before fluttering up into her throat.

The stony serious lines of his features folded into a bright smile, his laugh reached her ears over the crowd. "Get your ass over here, Jane."

With a laugh she raced toward him, lifting her skirts higher with each step. Just a few feet away from him she jumped. He caught her with one step back at the impact, his lips meeting hers with searing heat.

She locked her legs around his waist, burying her fingers in his hair. All that mattered right then was the heat of his lips and the grip of his fingers. His presence filled her soul, burning away the last few whispers of doubt that clung to her.

Breathless he pulled back from the kiss, the firm grip of his hands holding her legs right where they were. His forehead pressed to hers. "He's gone."

"It's over." There was no way to stop the tears, the impact of the end of the past year's turmoil hitting her too hard. "It's really over. Alan's dead."

"And then some." Cole moved out of the middle of the street. In moments he pressed her against the post outside the saloon. "Burial was too good. We fed him to the pigs."

Maybe it should have caused a reaction, but she couldn't bring herself to care. There were many more important things. She clasped her hands on his cheeks, searching every familiar plane of his features. "It's really over."

"Yeah."

"I'm free."

"Yeah." He cleared his throat against the gruffness in his voice.

"Cole."

His lips were soft against hers, his hands running along her body, his breath shaky. Tenderness, urgency, relief, desire, all wrapped into every moment. "Jane."

"I love you."

The searing heat of his kiss erased any fear that he'd run. His hand buried in her hair, his tongue massaging hers until she couldn't stop a small moan from escaping.

With a low chuckle she pulled back, her fingers running through his hair. "You are much better with actions than words."

Tommy grinned down at them from his saddle. "Damn, Lou. You two always like this when you're all healthy and happy? I mean, you got a show going on here. You're getting a pretty big audience."

"Shut up, Tommy." Jane didn't spare him more than a moment's glance.

"Damn, Lou, we can see your garters. I shouldn't see that."

"Shut up," Cole's voice didn't quite carry the anger it might have been meant to.

Jane grinned when the pressure of wood left her back. Cole was on the move. When the saloon doors swung open, she leaned in and nibbled at his neck. The low groan that rumbled through him brought another laugh out of her.

"Everyone out." Cole ignored the protest from the patrons, setting her on a table before leaning in for another searing kiss. When he pulled back, his Colt was free of its holster. He fired it into the ceiling. "I said get the hell out."

Jane bit her lip, tugging him closer and undoing the buttons of his shirt. The screeching of chairs and crash of glass didn't stop her slow progress. By the time the saloon was clear, she was done with the last button. "I just have one question."

He set down the Colt and leaned into her. "What?"

"Will you get bored with me now?" She unbuckled his holster and set it aside before letting her hands slip along his bared chest. Someone slammed the doors shut. She didn't care who, but she was grateful.

One finger hooked under her chin, tugging her lips closer to his. "Why would you think I'd get bored with you?"

"Oh, I don't know. The mystery is over. My past is no longer a secret. You know as much about me as I do. It's just me."

His fingers danced along her shoulder and around to tease the nape of her neck.

"Just me," she said and sighed. "And a son, an ex-husband, annoying broth—"

Shutting her up with another kiss, his lips teased hers before leaving them to kiss along her jaw line.

"Is that a no?"

The only response she got was a sudden release of pressure when her bodice popped open.

Carpe diem.
Rejoice while you are alive; enjoy the day;
live life to the fullest;
make the most of what you have.
It is later than you think.
—Horace

Never before had waking up brought such a sense of peace. No fear, panic, or hint of worry nagged at her.

Jane was at peace. She didn't move a muscle, lying still on her side, the warmth of Cole's arm draped across her waist. His warm, even breaths brushed along the back of her neck. Perfection. A smile ghosted across her lips, but she still didn't open her eyes. If it lasted all day she would revel in the peace. Too soon the peace was disturbed.

Then again, if it was going to be disturbed she could think of no better way for it to happen.

With a tickling soft touch to her shoulder, Cole's lips slipped along her flesh. It took every effort to stay still, let him think he was the cause for her waking. With every passing moment she knew he'd get more insistent. He didn't disappoint.

The arm laid across her shifted, his hand brushed along her stomach. One short tug pulled her toward him, rolling her onto her back. "I know you're awake."

She tried to stick out her lip to form a pout, but the rising giggle won out. "What gave me away?"

"You always wiggle your ass at me when you wake up. Why do you think I'm so awake?" He caught her lip and suckled on it before closing his mouth over hers.

A soft sigh escaped when he released her. "Sorry."

"Don't be. No better way to wake up than at attention."

"You mean than at attention with someone willing to salute."

"True."

"I imagine waking up at attention without anyone to salute is the most miserable way to wake up." Jane had to bite her lip. The conversation was too funny. If she laughed too hard it could just ruin the mood or bring them unwanted attention.

"Glad I never have to find out."

"Never, hum?"

"Plenty of women around."

"Oh, really?" At his nod, she quirked an eyebrow. Her fingers twitched, tempted to cause him pain for the statement. No, she'd give him one more chance to keep in her good humor. "Well, if you really want to be saluted by one of them, you'd best get at it. Just don't expect me to scrape and bow upon your return."

"Or salute?"

"Or anything."

"Can't have that."

"No?"

"Ain't no one can make me stand at attention like you can." The corners of his eyes crinkled up in her favorite playful smile. The spark in his eyes was less familiar, but set her heart pounding.

She let the playfulness slip away, her fingers dancing up to trace along the edge of his chin. A small gasp slipped out when he grabbed her hand and pulled her fingers to his lips. Anticipation pulled her lips between her teeth, but he never finished his task. A pounding on the door startled both of them out of the moment.

"Get your lazy asses out of bed," Tommy bellowed through the door. "We got things to do today."

"Nothing lazy about what we're doing," Jane called back with a laugh.

"Just get your asses out of bed."

"No." Cole's grin caught up to hers, and he ran his fingers along her spine. "We're busy. Gonna be all day, too."

Tommy ignored them and shoved open the door with enough force to bang it into the wall. "You promised you'd be there today. Cora made enough food to feed the whole town. It's a damn party to celebrate your freedom, and you're going."

With a sigh, Jane propped herself on her elbow and stuck her lip out at Tommy. "You are ruining a perfectly good lazy day."

"I'm sure you'll have many more lazy days. For now you're going. Cole, don't you have a surprise for Jane?" Tommy's brow quirked up along with the corner of his mouth. "Would hate to miss out on seeing her face for this one."

Cole's smile let her know Tommy wasn't just kidding around. Something was up. If she wanted to be, she could be solidly stubborn on it. Unfortunately her curiosity was too great. "What surprise?"

Tommy grinned. "Won't find out unless you get your ass out of that bed."

"I could tell her," Cole supplied, his fingers dancing along her back. The man was as antsy as she was to get back to what they were doing. God love him.

Despite her glee at the idea, Tommy continued to derail her train of thought and her libido. "I'm not moving from this spot until you both are ready to go. The minute you start pawing each other, I'll dump a bucket of cold water on you."

Bastard. She knew him well enough he wasn't bluffing. The exasperated sigh that came from Cole confirmed that he agreed. "He's not gonna budge, Jane."

"Fine." Without shame, Jane threw back the covers and stood. Tommy diverted his eyes immediately, as well he should. Though shyness had never plagued her, she'd meant to get him out of the room. "Then I'll get ready. This had better be a good surprise."

"It is."

Both men had responded at the same time, and Jane snorted softly. "Glad you're both in agreement. I don't think I like you two getting along this well."

"You'll come to appreciate it." The laughter in Tommy's voice didn't help her disposition.

Cole's hand slipped along her side and pulled her close, his lips pressing to her neck before he grabbed her corset ties. "I think he's right. You will, once you see the surprise."

"You're doing this on purpose. Both of you are trying to drive me crazy." She swatted away his hands and tightened the strings herself. "What is going on? What secret plan have you two formed? Am I really going to like it?"

"Finish getting dressed and find out," Tommy smirked, no longer looking away now that she was half decent. "The longer you dawdle with questions and accusations, the longer you have to wait."

Cole only winked at her in the mirror, leaving her stymied as he turned away with a chuckle of his own.

Huffing with every movement, she finished dressing as quick as she could. "There. You happy? Can we go so you two can stop tormenting me?"

"But it's so much fun." Cole chuckled, his hand slipping around her waist. "It's not often I manage to keep a secret from you."

The sounds of the busy day in the bar kept her smart retort hidden. Instead she held silent all the way outside until they stopped and turned her around toward the saloon again. The grins they wore grated on her last nerve. "What?"

"Look up, Janey." Cole winked and pointed above the porch.

Jane pulled her brows together. "Hammy? What in hell are you doing on the porch roof? You haven't been spying, have you?"

Tommy's braying laughter covered whatever reply Hammy tried to make. Jane kicked him in the rump, knocking him to the ground. "Be nice."

"Lady Jane, I would never spy on you." Hammy grinned. "I was s'posed to show your present."

"What present?"

"Go on, Hammy, before she kills us all." Cole's rich laughter wove through her aggravation, soothing it down to a minimum. "You haven't noticed yet, have you? What he's standing by?"

"The sign. Why is it covered?" Jane exhaled sharply when Cole kept laughing. "Oh, just show me."

At a gesture from Cole, Hammy pulled aside the cloth covering the sign. Where it had once said simply 'saloon' it proclaimed in bold letters 'The Hangman's Inn'.

Amusement tugged at her lips, even as she tried to force herself to maintain a calm mask. She allowed her brow to rise. "Is this supposed to be funny?"

"Not a lick," Cole said. The warmth of his voice didn't indicate any amusement, just pure truth. She could live with that if he'd offer an explanation. "I thought maybe some of your nagging wasn't so wrong."

"Nagging?" He was toeing the line again. Jane set her hands on her hips, still eying the sign. "What nagging are you talking about?"

"That I could make more money, maybe if I listened to your ideas. While we were in Sioux City we had time to talk." Cole kept his hand at the small of her back. "Tommy and I did, I mean, and Charlie some, too. Thought maybe I'd make it a real hotel. Maybe let in some entertainment, like ya said."

"Name was my idea." Tommy was still laughing, but it was more subdued. "Thought it was appropriate, after everything, of course."

"So what do you think?"

Jane thought about delaying her answer, making him suffer. Truth was she loved it and found the name almost as amusing as Tommy apparently did. Instead of answering, she turned and started down the street toward Cora's.

They'd made her suffer. She'd do the same. When they called after her, she gathered up her skirts and took off down the street. By the time they caught up, she was halfway up the steps and refused to look at either of them.

The excited greeting from Jesse interrupted their attempts to get her reaction out of her, and she took full advantage of it. Within minutes she'd eased into the party crowd, making her way to Katherine's side.

"There's something I'm curious about." Katherine didn't bother with a greeting.

"I do hate to keep your curiosity hanging out there. You know what they say it does to cats." Jane let her laughter free, glad for the quick excuse to use it. Somewhere nearby Cole was watching her. She had no doubt about that.

"The money." Katherine handed her a cup of coffee, pursing her lips. "What are you going to do with it? That was an awful lot of money that really was ill-gotten gains."

Cora gasped softly and joined them. "Katherine, I don't think we should be asking."

"You were wondering, too, and you know it." Kat's lips curved into a smirk. "I'm just not afraid to ask Jane anything."

"It's all right, Cora. I don't mind. Kat's right. The funds are ill-gotten, and I know the curiosity is running rampant through this gossipy town." Jane set down her coffee cup. "My first priority is Jesse, his future and needs. I hope to put aside a third of it for him. I do think I'm going to keep a little of it for myself for a rainy day as well."

"Or until a gorgeous dress comes along or you feel the need to fill up another full library." The wicked giddiness in Kat's tone wasn't missed. "But anyhow."

Jane kept talking even as her laughter joined Katherine's. "The rest will go to the town."

"What?" Cora gasped. "Jane."

Jane grinned. "What? This town has done more for me than I can ever make up for. It is my home, and I can't think of anything better to do than to give it to the town. The Town Council can decide how best to use it, whether it be paving the roads, or implementing plumbing, or both."

Katherine squeezed her hand. "You're far too generous."

"If I could give it back to those that he brought harm to, I would. However, despite everything I couldn't possibly find them all, and he caused plenty of harm to those in this town."

"And to you." Katherine smiled. "It's good that you decided what to do with it."

"I'll have to go to that council meeting." Cora's soft giggled burst between them. "It'll be a blood bath."

"To say the least." Jane shook her head. "That's why I'm leaving it up to them. I'll have no part of that. Let the politicians decide what's best."

Strong hands circled her waist and pulled her away. Soft lips brushed her neck, and Cole turned her away from the crowd.

Despite the giggle she couldn't fight, Jane smacked Cole's arm. "That wasn't very nice. I need to be sociable. I should go see Martha since she's here."

"You hate Martha." His hot breath brushed along her ear. "And you don't want to see an Injun baby."

"She's leaving in two days for the Indian Territory. I should be polite. She did let me live in her boarding house for free for months."

His teeth caught her earlobe, sending a shiver right to her toes. "You aren't being polite to me. Didn't even say thank you for the present."

"Reminding me daily of my hanging is supposed to be a present?" Damn him, he knew just how to get to her. Her voice was far more breathy than it should be. "Don't see where I should express gratitude with the reminder, or you calling me a nag, or—"

He spun her fast and closed his lips over hers, pushing her back against a counter. When he pulled back, the smirk he wore did not piss her off like she wanted it to. "You aren't good at lying."

"Guess I wouldn't be."

"Not to me."

"Not to you." Since she'd never really been mad, she'd let him win this time. "I'm very proud of you."

"Huh?"

"You didn't ever have to listen to what I said. You're plenty successful without my nagging."

"You're smarter than me."

"No." This time she yanked him into the kiss, holding him there until she was sure his protest was gone. "I love it. You happy?"

"Are ya?"

"Interminably."

"That a yes?"

"Yes."

"Then so am I."

*Marriage is neither heaven nor hell,
it is simply purgatory.
—Abraham Lincoln*

Jane didn't listen to a word of the ceremony. Cole, dressed in his finest for the wedding and standing across the aisle from her in the new church, drew far too much attention for her to pay any mind to Reverend Greene.

If Kat was paying any attention to anyone other than Norman, Jane might have been in trouble. Lucky for her, the two being wed were as wrapped up in each other as she was in Cole.

At the end of the ceremony his lips curved into a wicked smirk, and the touch of his hand to her arm as they followed the newlyweds down the aisle and out to the meadow sent shivers down her spine. "You're giving me ideas looking at me that way."

"You always have ideas." Jane laughed at his grunt of agreement. "Today will be an exercise in patience then. I have brothers to dance with, a friend to send off on her honeymoon, and a son to tend to."

"You gonna be able to squeeze in some tending for me?"

"Hours and hours, but only if you're patient."

"Can you two cease for an hour?" Kat laughed and wrapped her arms around Jane in a tight hug. "This is supposed to be my time, and you two can hardly keep your hands off each other."

"I was just telling him he had to be patient." Jane pulled back with a sigh and squeezed Kat's hands. "Congratulations. For a woman bound and determined to never marry, you've done a fine job of it."

"Are you certain you're going to live a life unmarried? My glowing joy won't change your mind?"

Jane nodded to where Cole had wandered off to chat with Norman. "I'm quite content. We don't need all this fanfare. I think we made our point rather clear about where we belong."

"If you ever change your mind, you'd best be telling me." Kat nudged her. "Now go on. It looks like Jesse's planning on sneaking a cake off the table, and I've got things to do."

Jane kissed her on the cheek. "Congratulations." After another tight hug, she darted toward the dessert table Cora had set up, kneeling next to Jesse.

"Look at the cookies, Ma." Jesse's gaze never left the spread of food. "So many and the cakes, and there's some candies, too."

"Miss Cora certainly went all out." She wasn't about to say no to him, not with the pleading expression on his face. Instead she grabbed one of the cookies and slipped it to him. "Just don't tell your pa I gave that to you."

"Teaching our son to lie?" David nudged her back with his knee.

"David." Jane swatted his leg. "Don't sneak up on me like that."

Jesse hugged her tight and whispered a thank you before scarfing down the cookie. He grinned up at David before he ran toward Cindy and dragged her into a game of tag.

A small sigh escaped on her way back to her feet. Jesse's peals of laughter brought the tug of a smile to her lips. "He's going to be all right, isn't he? After all of this, somehow he's going to be all right."

"He sure is." David's hand rested on her shoulder, filling her with the added warmth that they would be too. "How about you?"

"I'm going to be better than all right. I'm going to be happy."

"I can tell." His low chuckle broke the brief quiet. "Do I finally get to meet your parents? Never did when we were actually married."

"They'll be here in July, along with James. He's shown remarkable improvement. The doctors just don't understand how."

"Of course not." After a squeeze his hand slipped from her shoulder. "You didn't want to go out there?"

Despite her attempts to block it, a shudder ran through her. "Last time I was there wasn't pleasant. Besides, after the past few months, I don't want to leave home for a long time."

"Home."

"Yes, the people I love most in the world are right here. That makes it home." She let another sigh escape, releasing the last of the melancholy. "I think I'm ready to live a simple, boring life right here."

"You? Live a boring life?"

"Well, as boring as my life ever gets."

His laugh was short but heart felt. "Even as Clara you were never boring."

On impulse she kissed him on the cheek. "Boring is not fun."

"So you say."

The first strains of music filtered across the meadow, and her reply was cut short into a yelp. The world spun as she did until she landed secure with Cole's strong arms around her.

"Didn't think I'd let that ninny get the first dance, did you?" Cole's blue eyes sparkled in response to her laughter. The dance of his fingers up her spine made promises of the night ahead.

"He'll take his first dance with Lee, you brute. You had no need for concern. You wouldn't be claiming me as property again, would you, Mr. Mitchell?"

"No man ever could."

"You could." Damn if he couldn't still make her breathless. The surprised grin and tighter grip he took on her made the fire the simple admission had sparked grow stronger.

Without another word he spun her away, turning her until he stopped some distance from the crowd. "That so?"

Pinned against a wagon she didn't try to struggle. Heat flooded her cheeks and rushed through her body. "I don't lie."

"Think you might want to get married again after this?"

"No, I still can't see it. Why? Do you?" She detected none of the usual tension in him at the mere suggestion. His only response at first was a shake of his head. While she found it interesting, it still didn't change her mind.

"You don't want to get married again, and neither do I."

"Seems that way."

"Wanna stay not married…together?"

*The End
For Now...*

*Coming Soon
Book 4 of the
Dominion Falls Series
Green Eye*

Other Books in
The Dominion Falls Series

Independent Brake
Changing Tracks
Derailed
Green Eye
Runaway Train
Home Signal
Red Zone

Upcoming Books in
The Dominion Falls Series

Dust Raiser
Blizzard Lights
Dead Man's Switch
Birdcage
A Highball Arrangement
Ball of Fire

Books by Sarah Cass

The Tribe Series
The Tribe
The Wolf
The Chief
The Raven
The Lake Point Series
Santa, Maybe
Deep-Fried Sweethearts
Stalled Independence
Witch Way
A Thorough Thanksgiving
Eve's New Year
Heartstrings & Hockey Pucks
Luck of the Cowgirl
Stars, Stripes & Motorbikes
Free Falling
Love for Hire
Haunted Hearts
Stand Alone Novels
Masked Hearts
Leap

About the Author

Sarah Cass, author of over twenty novels in 4 series, is devoted to giving her readers well-crafted, emotional stories, with depth to even her secondary characters—to give readers a full world to explore. Stories that explore not only the labyrinths of the heart, but the nightmares of the soul. A RONE finalist, she is also owner and creator of Redefining Perfect. By day, she's a nurse, a mother, wife and cat-mom to 4 mischievous beasts. By night she crafts stories that take her across centuries. From the old west of Dominion Falls, to the small town of Lake Point for the holidays, and even into the paranormal land of Shifters and Magic in The Tribe. She loves hearing from her readers. Visit her at www.authorsarahcass.com

Divine Roses Ink
DivineRosesInk.com